# ATHENA'S
# FORUM

## A Historical Novel

D1522791

# OTHER BOOKS OF INTEREST FROM MARQUETTE BOOKS

Melvin DeFleur, *A Return to Innocence: A Novel* (2006). ISBN: 0-922993-50-5

Dan Robison, *Death Chant: Kimo Battles the Shamanic Forces* (2006). ISBN: 0-922993-52-1

Dan Robison, *Kimo's Escape: The Story of a Hawaiian Boy Who Learns to Believe in Himself* (2005). ISBN: 0-922993-28-9

Dan Robison, *Wind Seer: The Story of One Native American Boy's Contribution to the Anasazi Culture* (2005). ISBN: 0-922993-27-0

Ray Edwards, *Justice Never Sleeps: A Novel of Murder and Revenge in Spokane* (2005). ISBN: 0-922993-26-2

John M. Burke, *From Prairie to Palace: The Lost Biography of Buffalo Bill* (2005). ISBN: 0-922993-21-1

Tonya Holmes Shook, *The Drifters: A Christian Historical Novel about the Melungeon Shantyboat People* (2005). ISBN: 0-922993-19-X

C. W. Burbank, *Beyond Zenke's Gate* (2004). ISBN: 0-922993-14-9

David Demers, *China Girl: One Man's Adoption Story* (2004). ISBN: 0-922993-08-4

Larry Whitesitt, *Higher than Eagles: Spokane's World War II Pilots* (2006). ISBN: 0-922993-31-9

Larry Whitesitt, *Northern Flight of Dreams: Flying Adventures in British Columbia, Yukon, Northwest Territories and Alaska* (2004). ISBN: 0-922993-09-2

# ATHENA'S FORUM
### A Historical Novel

## PHIL TICHENOR

MARQUETTE BOOKS
SPOKANE, WASHINGTON

This book is a work of fiction. Names, characters, places, and incidents
either are products of the author's imagination or are used fictitiously.
Any resemblance to actual events or locales or persons,
living or dead, is entirely coincidental.

Printed in the United States of America

**Library of Congress Cataloging-in-Publication Data**

Tichenor, Phillip J.
    Athena's forum : a historical novel / Phil Tichenor.
        p. cm.
    ISBN-13: 978-0-922993-51-2 (pbk. : alk. paper)
    ISBN-10: 0-922993-51-3 (pbk. : alk. paper)
    1. Journalists--Fiction. 2. Investigative reporting--Fiction.
3. Lynching--Fiction. 4. World War, 1914-1918--Minnesota--Fiction.
5. Minnesota--Fiction. I. Title.
    PS3620.I26A95 2006
    813'.6--dc22

                                    2005033915

Marquette Books
3107 E. 62nd Avenue
Spokane, WA 99223
509-443-7057
books@marquettebooks.org
www.MarquetteBooks.org

# DEDICATION

$A$thena's Forum is dedicated, first, to the memory of Eileen Tichenor, my spouse of 47 years until her death in 2003 after a prolonged struggle with Parkinson's Disease and Chronic Leukemia.

She read, with enthusiasm, the first draft of the work and encouraged its development throughout the period when she was being overtaken by the ravages of her multiple ailments. She was a supportive partner in this project, just as she was a caring and dedicated wife, mother and grandmother, and volunteer mitten maker for hundreds of immigrant children in the St. Paul school district, many with backgrounds not dissimilar to that of the poverty-stricken children in the novel.

This book is dedicated, secondly, to the numerous graduate students in mass communication and rural sociology at the University of Minnesota, who were—and in many cases still are—immersed in the study of the performance and history of the community press in America.

Phil Tichenor
Winter 2006

# TABLE OF CONTENTS

# AUTHOR'S NOTE

 The main characters of this novel, including all in the Lindfors' lineage, are fictitious. There are no such places as Graskoping, Sweden, or Belleville and Athena County, Minnesota. Certain events and political figures of the times are portrayed in varying detail.

The warship Vasa did in fact sink in Stockholm harbor in 1628 and King Gustavus Adolphus was indeed a military genius of the Thirty Years' War. There was a Minnesota Commission of Public Safety during World War I and Judge John McGee was a prominent member of that body. A. C. Townley and Senator Robert M. LaFollette are described according to the record, with two exceptions. Townley's speech at the Athena County picnic is wholly an invention, although it is crafted to reflect his persona and oratorical style. Judge McGee did not write a letter to the Athena County farmers refusing to debate Senator LaFollette. McGee did, however, express, to a U.S. Senate committee in Washington, D.C., various views contained in that fictitious letter.

Given the scope of the novel, the circumstances in Sweden at the turn of the century, and a time of near-upheaval in the rural Midwest during World War I, a rather vast literature was consulted and the help of several individuals must be acknowledged.

The first acknowledgment is to Hazel Dicken-Garcia, a colleague who read and thoroughly critiqued the first draft. Also reading and offering important suggestions were LeAnn Tichenor, Trish Marx, David Chidester and Paul Lindholdt, an English professor at Eastern Washington University. Pat Berg provided translations of technical materials on Swedish printing.

In Sweden, Karl-Erik Rosengren and Charlotte Bengtsson at the department of Media and Communication Studies at Lund University located critical but not-easily-found materials on the Swedish press, the Baltic coast of Sweden and printing history there. The House of Emigrants at Vaxjoe, Sweden, was a vital source of information on the massive immigrations of the time period. The Vasa Museum in Stockholm contains the actual—and restored—remains of the famous ship that sank at the start of its maiden voyage in 1628.

In Minnesota, the vast collections of the University of Minnesota Wilson library and its Rare Books collection were invaluable, as was the UM's Diehl Hall medical library. A number of critical materials were found through the help of numerous individuals at the Minnesota History Center.

Among the various bibliographic materials consulted, certain ones stand out as rich and readable references for those who might wish to delve into certain periods or themes of the novel. They include:

## THE THIRTY YEARS WAR AND PROPAGANDA OF THE TIME

Beller, E. A. *Propaganda in Germany during the Thirty Years War.* Princeton N.J.: H. Milford, Oxford University Press, 1940.

Coupe, W. A., *The German illustrated broadsheet in the seventeenth century; historical and ichnographical studies.* Baden-Baden, Germany: Heitz, 1966-67.

Edwards, M. U., *Printing, propaganda and Martin Luther.* Berkeley: University of California Press, 1994.

MacMunn, G. F., *Gustavus Adolphus: the northern hurricane.* London: Hodder and Stoughton Ltd., 1930.

## SWEDISH CULTURE, POLITICS AND TRADITION

Backlund, J. O., *A century of the Swedish-American Press.* Chicago: Swedish American Newspaper Co., 1952.

Hoppe, Goran, and John Langton, *Peasantry to capitalism: Western Ostergotland in the nineteenth century.* Cambridge, UK: Cambridge University Press, 1994.

Laslett, P., K. Oosterveen, and R. M. Smith, *Bastardy and its comparative history: Studies in the history of illegitimacy and marital nonconformism in Britain, France, Germany, Sweden, North America, Jamaica and Japan.* Cambridge, MA: Harvard University Press, 1980.

Litell, D., *Swedish music past and present.* Stockholm: Muxikrevy, 1967. (Translation)

Midgeld, K., K. Molin, and K. Amark, *Creating social democracy: A century of the SDL Party in Sweden.* (Translation) University Park, PA: Pennsylvania State University Press, 1992.

Nyberg, Janet, *The Swedish immigrant press in Minnesota.* Minneapolis: Unpublished M.A. paper, University of Minnesota, 1975.

Toler, John, *Per Jonson Rosio: "The agrarian prophet."* Stockholm: Almqvist & Wiksell International, 1992.

## THE NONPARTISAN LEAGUE IN MINNESOTA AND NORTH DAKOTA

Chrislock, Carl H., *The progressive era in Minnesota, 1899-1918.* St. Paul, Minnesota Historical Society, 1971.

Langer, William. *The nonpartisan league, its birth, activities and leaders.* Bismark ND: Morton county Farmers press, 1920.

Morlan, R. L., *Political prairie fire: The Nonpartisan League, 1915-1922.* St. Paul: Minnesota Historical Society Press, 1985 (reprint from Univ. of Minnesota Press, 1955).

Russell, C. E., *The story of the Nonpartisan League: a chapter in American evolution.* New York: Harper & Bros., 1920.

## WORLD WAR I AND MINNESOTA

Bullock, Edna D., *Mothers' pensions, selected articles.* White Plains, NY: H. W. Wilson Co., 1915.

Chrislock, C. H., *Watchdog of loyalty: the Minnesota Commission of Public Safety during World War I*. St. Paul: Minnesota Historical Society Press, 1991.

Folwell, William W., *A history of Minnesota, Vol. III*. St. Paul: Minnesota Historical Society, 1969. Originally published 1926.

Jessup, Dwight W., *Joseph Gilbert and the Minnesota sedition law: A case study in American constitutional history*. Minneapolis: Unpublished M. A. thesis, University of Minnesota, August, 1965.

Murphy, Paul L., *World War I and the origin of civil liberties in the United States*. New York: W. W. Norton & Co., 1979.

Neuzil, Mark R., *Muckraking and the progressive movement: The interaction of journalism and society, 1902-1911*. Minneapolis: University of Minnesota unpublished Ph.D. dissertation, November 1993.

Peterson, H. C. and G. C. Fite, *Opponents of war, 1917-1918*. Seattle, University of Washington Press, 1968. Originally University of Wisconsin Press, 1957.

Raff, Willis H., *Civil liberties in Minnesota: World War One Period*. Minneapolis: Unpublished M.A. thesis, University of Minnesota, July 1950.

Raff, Willis H., *Coercion and freedom in a war situation: A critical analysis of Minnesota culture during World War One*. Minneapolis: Unpublished Ph.D. dissertation, University of Minnesota, October 1967.

Smith, Victoria M., *Newspapers and freedom of expression: Minnesota press reaction to suppression during the World War I era: 1912-1920*. Unpublished M. A. thesis, University of Minnesota, January 1986.

Torelle, Ellen, *The political philosophy of Robert M. LaFollette as revealed in his speech and writing*. Madison WI: R. M. LaFollette Co., 1920.

## TEST TUBE BABIES, HISTORICALLY

M. Schellen, A. M., and S. J. Kleegman, *Artificial insemination in the human*. Amsterdam: Elsevier, 1957.

# I. CONVICTION AND SHAME

Ivar Lindfors gazed wistfully across Stockholm Harbor that autumn day in 1908, wondering how he would fare in America as a would-be crusading editor in disgrace. Dare he hope that his shame in Sweden would be unknown in Minnesota, except by one of the two immediate victims of his folly?

These two victims were beside him, along the gunwales of this rusty and aging steamship. His wife, Inez, cradled his infant daughter, Charlotte, in her arms and slowly rocked her—the infant cooing to her more as a nanny than as a mother, which Inez was not. Together, the threesome would ride this rude vessel around Sweden's southern tip and up to Gothenburg, where they would board a large passenger ship for the Western Hemisphere. They would leave their troubled past behind them and hope that Ivar could finally realize his unfulfilled crusading dreams.

Ivar's mind roiled with the ironies of the fix he was in. He believed with indignant, self-righteous conviction that he had devoted the best of his 28 years to the most noble of causes, becoming a journalistic champion of the poverty-stricken masses, especially the multitudes of woebegone children sired by men who disappeared or simply avoided acting as fathers. Yet, here he was, kicked out of his family business and ancestral land, accused of being one of those same wayward, errant men.

Nothing short of such humiliation would have torn him away from the secure and promising career he anticipated a short few months earlier. He had fully expected to extend an illustrious Lindfors family tradition in Swedish publishing, and thereby contribute mightily to the churning but progressive changes that would lift downtrodden Swedes out of abject poverty and elevate them to more comfortable, satisfying, and noble livelihoods.

He marveled at his one consolation: Innocent as Inez was, she had chosen to stand by him even though this meant sharing his disgrace. For such a blessing, one could hardly be thankful enough.

* * *

Stockholm harbor was where Ivar's great family publishing tradition had begun nearly three centuries earlier. It was a legend that Ivar knew by heart. On an August day in 1628, a very famous progenitor, Anders Lindfors, apprentice printer-turned-seaman, perched high on the masts of the splendid new Vasa, a warship about to be launched on its maiden voyage with the triumphant fleet of a brilliant young King Gustavus Adolphus.

That proud new ship, garishly resplendent in her plump hull of green, blue, gold, and red, slipped away from the wharf before a multitude of cheering Swedish patriots, noble and common, on its way to take command of the Baltic Sea. But in one of those monumental blunders of maritime history, the Vasa was so badly designed that it capsized when the first winds caught its sails, only a few meters from the dock.

This much was well known Swedish history. Less known to the nation, but dear to the Lindfors family, was the legend of Ivar's revered ancestor Anders Lindfors, who was a seaman on the Vasa that fateful day. Ivar knew the tale by heart, and looking out over the harbor he could hear it being told by old-time family members:

*Yes, Anders Lindfors was clever enough to not drown, as did most of the 150 crewmen. How did he do it? He caught a broken boom and floated to shore. Did he help save others? It was too late. He was so angry at the stupid people who had caused this that he went to the print shop where he worked before joining the navy.*

*Why did he do that? Because he wanted everyone to know who was at fault. He picked through his clutter of wood and metal type and put together a pamphlet and printed a hundred numbers. Did he make a woodcut? No, he didn't have time. He did it fast, just with words. He then dropped it around town.*

*Do we still have that pamphlet? One copy, in the museum. It said the ship was badly designed and the officers had heads like oxen. They couldn't keep the world's best warship afloat for 10 minutes. Those criminals should pay for their misdeeds.*

*What did the Navy people say when they saw the pamphlet?*

*Well, as you would expect—they were angry and defensive.*

*They said the ship was designed by King Gustavus Adolphus himself, and who was this common sailor—this Anders Lindfors—to say these treasonous things? He is the one who should be brought to trial. Where is he now? He must be arrested. That's what the Navy people said.*

*Anders saved his neck by escaping Stockholm as a stowaway on a fishing trawler, landing on the Pomeranian coast. He hired out to a Stettin printer, publishing pamphlets and broadsheets.*

*Yes, in Pomerania, Anders Lindfors was Martin Luther's best printer. His pamphlets told how Roman Catholic priests have no better connection to God than a man laying bricks. And when our great King Gustavus Adolphus brought his army to Pomerania, Anders printed things that aided the holy war against the Catholic armies. Go to the museum and see his first broadsheet. There is the King, astride his magnificent horse, leading the cavalry charge against the Army of the Holy Roman Empire. Lion of the North, that's what the broadsheet called our famous king.*

In their fascination with family lore, Ivar's aging relatives even seemed to know—or insist they knew—what people said 280 years earlier on the streets and in the inns of Stockholm, when this broadsheet arrived.

*Yes, everybody said, see how our King is winning great and glorious victories. Sweden is the greatest power in Europe. The Papacy is doomed, for sure. How wonderful it is to see a picture of how our Swedish soldiers deal with those Imperial soldiers of the Pope. Oh, yes, they are great pikemen. See how they shove their long lances through those barbarian Catholics.*

As the story continued, however, it seemed to Ivar that Anders Lindfors must have seen the aftermath of the carnage and oppression of war. Anders had left a letter about his personal life that was long lost, but the Lindfors family oral tradition kept it alive.

*Anders caught a German peasant stealing potatoes from an Army food wagon. When he yanked the potatoes away from her, she told him how Imperial soldiers had run a sword through her husband and children and spilled their guts over the floor of the family hut. Soldiers took her cows, killed and ate her pigs, and burned the buildings. She thought soldiers were all brutes.*

The rest of the Anders Lindfors story was less clear and certain, and Ivar remembered how the family discussions often became contentious.

*Well, we all know that the Imperial Army was full of brutes. Well, maybe some of the Protestant soldiers were brutish, but not the Swedes. Our King wouldn't have allowed that. Oh, are you sure of that? Weren't there atrocities on both sides? And what happened after our King was killed at Lutsen? Didn't Swedish soldiers run in disarray from the field of battle? Well, they lost some battles, but Sweden still kept Pomerania—don't forget that.*

Everyone agreed that Anders Lindfors and his German wife left Germany shortly after the King's death and returned to the town of Graskoping on Sweden's Baltic coast, where they established the Lindfors Publishing Company.

Then they worked out this Treaty of Westphalia in 1648. That was the end of the gruesome Thirty Years' War. To show what a great day that was, Anders did another broadsheet. This one showed the human tragedy of war. The title was "The Great War in Germany gave tragic witness to man's inhumanity to man."

Ivar knew this 260-year-old woodcut well. It was now stored in Ivar's meager collection of publishing materials, in a trunk below deck that would accompany him to America.

In the coarse but solid lines and bold Gothic letters that Anders had cut into the wood printing block, the broadsheet portrayed soldiers running lances through a peasant man and woman, while four small children nearby covered their eyes in horror and an older one sought to flee another soldier wielding a cavalier's sword.

This 17ᵗʰ century broadsheet touched a raw nerve in the Lindfors family, and Ivar remembered well the disputes about its meaning.

*We all know it shows Saxony soldiers killing Protestant civilians. Oh, do we? How is that clear? The soldiers didn't have uniforms, so they looked the same on both sides. Ah, but this was in northern Germany, where we know the peasants hated the Pope. Oh, maybe so, but that doesn't guarantee that our soldiers were nice and gentle people, does it? Well, what do you expect soldiers to be?*

In any case, the "Man's Inhumanity to Man" broadsheet from 17ᵗʰ century Sweden had ensured the lasting, if somewhat dubious, fame of its creator. There was one other copy of the broadsheet in existence, displayed in the same museum, along with a citation that bestowed on Anders Lindfors the status of mythic hero.

It was a family treasure, revered by nearly every person named Lindfors—with one exception. The one skeptic was Klas Lindfors—Ivar's tall, austere father.

\* \* \*

Brooding on ship deck, Ivar remembered when, as a much younger man, he had stood one day in the typesetting room, at the ancestral family printing business in Graskoping. He was gazing at and enthralled by that famous "inhumanity" broadsheet that he had pulled one more time from a flat storage drawer. Klas Lindfors, known to his family as "Papa," appeared behind him, bemused if not mildly annoyed at his son's fascination with this old family artifact.

"Yes, Anders was a great Swedish patriot, in our family tradition," Klas said, putting his preferred definition on the aging, musty print.

Patriotism was not exactly what Ivar was thinking. He rubbed some ink off his scruffy leather printer's apron, searching for a way of telling his father what he thought.

"It seems to me, Papa, he was telling about all the killing."

"My son, war IS about killing. That broadsheet shows how the inhuman Catholic armies put helpless Protestants to the sword. What else did you think the broadsheet meant?"

Ivar was too troubled to respond. He had told a history teacher at his Gymnasium School about the broadsheet, and that teacher said the Thirty Years War was the worst catastrophe in all of Europe's history. This teacher had added some dark details about Swedish soldiers slaughtering civilians not only in Germany but earlier in Poland.

"I thought," Ivar said, haltingly to his stern, heavily breathing father, "that printed things like broadsheets and newspapers should help end wars."

Klas thundered: "Newspapers tell about wars, why enemies are cruel, and help their nations be victorious. Newspapers must be patriotic, for their nations and their cities."

Ivar wanted desperately to be a good printer, publisher, and newspaper writer. He expected to take over the family business, since his older brother Sten left several years earlier to go into the shipbuilding business in Stockholm. Yet

Ivar wasn't seeing things the same way as his formidable—and financially quite successful—father and veteran publisher.

"The big daily papers are telling about the problems of our poor people, the starvation, the diseases. Shouldn't we do more of that?" Ivar almost choked on the word "more," since the Lindfors newspaper had so far done no reporting of that kind at all.

Klas Lindfors was blunt. "Those newspapers in Stockholm spill too much ink on what is wrong in Sweden. They want us to weep and fuss and spend our public money on the poor people. That is not for us. Moreover, you waste too much time on this.

"Put that old, crumbling, broadsheet away. And let us get back to finishing the pamphlets the shipping company needs. That is what makes us profitable."

With that, Ivar's irritated father turned and stomped from the room.

Ivar felt frustrated and unsettled. He knew that while the winds of reform were blowing strongly in Sweden, the family business that he would one day inherit was deliberately lagging behind. At least, it would so as long as the company was owned, managed and controlled by his stubborn, archaic, and domineering father. And while he knew his father wouldn't live forever, he also knew the prominent men in Graskoping—a regional town of modest size—shared Klas Lindfors' views of what a newspaper should be.

But now, in 1908, even more annoying to Ivar were the circumstances of the disgrace that had forced him to emigrate.

* * *

Ivar had been a rather odd child who never got into much trouble. He was tall and lanky, yet soft-muscled and sometimes called a weakling. Even during his later years in

Gymnasium, he had preferred the duties of a printer's devil to the rough and tumble of soccer, rugby, skiing and sailing that so captivated his elder brother Sten. He was a good enough student to avoid severe reprimands from teachers. He befriended less fortunate youths, so his sensitive side was well known if not always appreciated.

A troubling yet salutary experience in his early youth was the gain and loss of a companion—the audacious, belligerent and bellicose Olof Moller. Olof never knew his father; he was known as a bastard child.

Olof and Ivar would walk and talk, run along the moat edges at the old castle, play board games, and spend hours ruminating on the world as they saw it. They were an odd but complementary pair. Where Ivar was physically weak, Olof was strong. Where Olof was aggressive but socially awkward around adults, Ivar was on the shy side, but courteous and correct. Where Olof was trouble-prone, Ivar was restrained enough to keep both of them out of serious difficulty. Ivar would talk about his interests in music and the printing trade, while Olof would boast about his exploits on the game field. Ivar would marvel at famous paintings of tall-masted sailing ships, and Olof would wax ecstatic over prize-fighting. Neither of these youngsters had the knack for striking up conversations with girls, although the bluff Olof was a bit more successful this way, especially among those from the poor streets.

Olof wore ragged clothes and he smelled bad. Once when Ivar took him into the Lindfors kitchen for sweetbreads, Ivar's mother Ulrina asked Olof if he would like a bath, an offer that absolutely terrified the otherwise pugnacious lad. He ran from the house and never went near the Lindfors place again—a fact that brought no protests from Ivar's family.

A short time later Olof said that his mother was acting queerly. "Stares out the window, for hours. Never hears anything I say. Forgets mealtime. Starts sobbing for no reason and weeps and cries all afternoon." Olof's father was no help. He was a ne'er-do-well who was often caught stealing food and liquor, spent time in jail and met an early death in a brawl on a seaside wharf at Kalmar.

The distraught woman was committed to a mental institution, and a social service agency sent Olof to an orphanage at Stockholm. He and Ivar exchanged a few brief notes by post, and after a time Olof failed to answer Ivar's letters.

* * *

With his best friend gone, an adolescent Ivar became absorbed in his family's printing business. He learned to set type, clean the cases, ink the galleys, run proofs and spot typographical errors as quickly as the seasoned proofreaders. He had the smell of printer's ink up his nose early, some said.

In the year 1900, Klas Lindfors decided to send Ivar to the University in Lund—a picturesque town on the southwestern coast. Ivar did reasonably well as a serious, chaste student during his first two years. His contacts with female students—who were few in number—were limited.

As his third year began, he hankered for something more than English language study, physics, mathematics, and classics.

He had attended some student Social Democrat meetings on the cobblestone streets in Lund's central square. Speakers railed about poverty, underpaid workers, and social misery. All these things interested Ivar, yet he didn't find the meetings fully satisfying. The arm and fist-waving speakers told of needs for new laws to aid poor people, but somehow they never seemed to really touch the problems of people like his young, one-time friend Olof.

Ivar's philosophy finally came together when he registered in 1903 for the Social Philosophy lectures of Professor Elverna Eklinden. She was well-known among the young reformers, he learned, and he was the first in her lecture hall when the term began.

So fixated was he on the upcoming lecture that he barely

noticed the husky, raw-featured young woman who eased into the chair beside him. "I am Birgitta Gejvall," she announced. "I know Professor Eklinden well. She is unlike the men who teach here. You will learn from her much of what is wrong with our country."

Now Ivar was truly excited. This brash young woman—not gorgeous but full of vitality—had sought him out. He had seen her at some of the political meetings, but they had not actually met.

His reserved nature left him searching for a response to this vivacious student. He was saved when Professor Eklinden walked into the room and began a discourse that reached into Ivar's mind in a way no teacher before had succeeded. Her soft but deeply vibrant voice resonated as a poignant peasant ballad over the lecture hall. Deceptively so, since her spoken truths materialized not from rote memorization, but from deep conviction and shrewd calculation forced upon her evidence and her rapt listeners. She neither thundered nor gestured nor manipulated her vocal cadence to take the measure of flagging attentiveness. Her mildly cleft chin jutting just slightly forward, she spoke directly and with an intelligent warmth that seemed so common and natural.

She began by weaving social philosophy into the fabric of Scandinavian history. She explained how an old warrior culture could adopt Lutheranism and accept a remarkable theological doctrine called predestination, taken from the thoughts of Protestant reformer John Calvin.

"Everyone," she said, pausing to let the idea sink in, "was predestined, but without knowing for what. If you were predestined, would you go to heaven or to purgatory? All one knew in seventeenth century Sweden was that those to be saved showed outer grace. The problem was that having grace was not guaranteed, and you could do nothing to change it. Imagine what these beliefs did for the Swedish view of life and the world."

Ivar was astounded. A Swedish teacher talking this

way? Ivar could only imagine how his father would react to such heresy.

It wasn't the formidable woman Professor alone who was arousing Ivar. He sensed the responsiveness of the emotionally and intellectually charged Birgitta sitting next to him in this musty old lecture room, her breathing changing almost in rhythm with the tempo of the engaging lecture.

"You see," continued the Professor in her soft and mellow, yet overpowering voice, swaying easily from side to side to accentuate her words, "you're in quite a mess if you never know whether you are saved or damned. It gets even worse when you realize that if you worry about it, you may just prove that you really don't have grace. It might be said," she smiled, now with her hands on her ample hips, "that the stone faced stoicism of the Swedish man covers up his confusion about whether he's headed for heaven or hell."

*My stoic father confused about his salvation?* Ivar was astonished that such might be possible.

At this point, a mischievous Birgitta shoved Ivar a note asking if he was a stone-faced stoic. Now shocked—and yet tantalized—by such brash behavior, Ivar turned to find her looking straight ahead, stone-faced herself as if nothing had happened. Never had Ivar encountered such impishness among students. The few female students in Swedish universities were usually models of decorum, never speaking in class and deferring to the males. Reform of all kinds was alive in Sweden, but he hadn't seen young women act this way before.

When the Professor softly concluded the lecture, she left Ivar exactly where she intended: hungry for more and eager to delve in. Later that day, on an impulse, he found Professor Eklinden's office in a remote and dark hallway, and knocked on the door. The rich voice of this full-bodied woman quickly and warmly invited him in.

Ivar entered, snapping to attention in almost a military way, quite out of place given her easy, open manner and the very unmilitary surroundings in her cluttered and musty office. Among the piles of ragged edged books, papers, scattered pencils and dip pens sat this amiable woman with the cleft but rounded chin. Her modest woolen garments, including a heavy dark sweater, in color and tone seemed a natural extension of her simple wooden desk with the chipped corners.

Her soft gaze overwhelmed her unexpected visitor in a way that was both scholarly and, oddly, motherly—although not in the manner of his own mother Ulrina.

"I am Ivar Lindfors," he said. "I am in your lecture."

"Yes," she replied. "I remember you. I hope you can tolerate all of my bunkum. But tell me, what interests you about social philosophy?"

Again, Ivar was nonplussed. She could refer to her profound lectures as "bunkum?"

He had hoped to impress her with his zest for improving the human condition through creation of uplifting words. In his romantic fantasy, he was atop the mainmast of a gallant ship of human progress, spreading words to the winds, to shower out upon a receptive multitude, there to take root and blossom into an energized curiosity that would cry out for still more words to be scattered again.

Yet, with all his excitement about words, Ivar struggled for any to say, and his life-long reticence took over. Her self-effacing modesty would make his thoughts—as they rested in his mind—seem pompous, if not ridiculous. He bowed his head and blushed.

Could he tell this tall, amiable woman scholar about his father Klas? How the man was a strict and haughty publisher of the middle aristocracy who actually disdained reformist newspapers? Should he let her in on his embarrassment and disgust with the mediocre Klas newspaper, the *Veckoblad*? How cheap it looked in comparison with the proud and imposing *Dagens Nyheter* and *Aftonbladet* from Stockholm. Should he look into the Professor's eyes and tell her how proud he was of ancestor

Anders Lindfors—a patriot and publishing wizard who knew also how to turn a profit?

"I want to write about people, for newspapers."

She nodded.

"What kinds of things? About what kinds of people?"

Could he now pour out his concern about his coarse and smelly friend Olof, and people like him? The poor kids on back streets of Graskoping who talked openly and brazenly about drunken and missing fathers and frantic mothers who died from overwork in their thirties? And sisters hardly past puberty who found themselves pregnant, sometimes by brothers, fathers, and uncles?

No, he couldn't put these things in words to this kindly but overpowering teacher.

"There are too many poor people in Sweden," was all he could say.

Professor Eklinden nodded again, never shifting her mild yet penetrating and unblinking gaze from this agitated young man.

"Yes, that is so true. And you wish to be a journalist who helps make these things right?"

A relieved Ivar shook his head rapidly in agreement.

"That is a good wish. I hope you find the lectures helpful. Meanwhile, you might like to read this."

She handed him a worn magazine, with the name *McClure's* across the front. "It is American. One of the writers is a woman named Ida Tarbell. You read English well? Fine. She has written many times about a big oil company and how it has failed to do the good for common people that one might expect.

"I heard this writer speak at a university in Paris, where she studied and worked many years ago. She is one of the world's best journalists. See how she writes."

Ivar took the magazine, thanked the Professor, and left.

In the hallway, he found Birgitta waiting. For him? His pulse quickened.

"Were you surprised I saw how 'stoic' you are?" Birgitta

asked. "And that it all comes from this ridiculous belief about predestination?"

Ivar grinned, happy to have this uninvited friendship and common interest. He was pleased that Birgitta said "stoic" when she could have said "shy." Searching for something to say, he fell back on the recent lecture about predestination.

"I'm not sure about this," he offered. "I thought Christians believed, as my family does, that whether you go to Heaven or Hell depends on how good a person you were."

"You've never heard someone call a child a damned brat?" Birgitta responded. "Damned from their first moment on earth? Did it ever occur to you that people act badly because they think they are already damned and just give up?"

*No,* he hadn't thought about it that way but wondered whether that was part of Olof's problem.

Birgitta changed the subject. "I've seen you at the meeting of the student Social Democrats. We meet again Thursday evening. Will you come along?"

He certainly couldn't refuse. They met on the outer fringes of the gathering in a dingy meeting room just off the cobble-stoned town square.

The meeting fulfilled two purposes. It meant more time with this intriguing, if combative, Birgitta. At the same time, the raucous speeches and heated exchanges seemed like a laboratory for the inspired lectures by their mutually esteemed Professor Eklinden.

Ivar found Birgitta even more infused than he with political passions—suffrage, alleviation of poverty, and orphaned children. Besides, being around her and among the reformers loosened Ivar's tongue, much the way aquavit did for his uncles and older cousins. So, after the session, he and Birgitta chattered incessantly, arms waving, as they skipped past the medieval-era buildings of the Lund campus. They paused in full debate on the spiral stairway of the musty old King's House tower—first Birgitta above and Ivar below, then with positions reversed. They continued this animated exchange through the shadow of the ancient Domkyrkan, a cathedral rarely used any more for Christian worship.

"I like these talks," he told Birgitta. She looked at him askance, eyes turned more toward him than her head.

"They have possibilities," she said.

*Was this suspicion, honesty, or flirtation?* Ivar hoped for the latter.

They met again at the next lecture, when Professor Eklinden talked about the "social contract" idea of such writers as the Frenchman Jean Jacques Rousseau. This impressed Ivar. The idea of a striking a deal—a social contract—between governors and those who are governed appealed to him, as it had to millions before.

The Professor folded the thoughts of various Swedish philosophers and Rousseau into that of the American Thomas Jefferson.

"If the social contract fails, or the governing group is oppressive and does not respect it, the people have the right and the obligation to change it—by force, if necessary. That was, essentially, what the American Revolution was all about.

"This notion that the contract can be changed was, of course, anathema to the religious order, the monarchy and most western philosophers for millennia. At the same time, it stimulated the minds of revolutionists in both France and America."

To Ivar's delight, Professor Eklinden next turned to newspapers. She noted Jefferson's statement that newspapers are essential to democratic government. "What was impressive about Jefferson is that given a choice, he would prefer newspapers without government to the reverse condition."

*Was she responding to my brief conversation with her? Or was it simply part of her lecture plan?*

Either way, Ivar thought, these are fine words. *Why can't we think that way in the Klas business, in Graskoping?*

He stopped at the Professor's office again, and her intellectual warmth once more overtook him. This time, she handed him a copy of Alexis de Tocqueville's *Democracy in America*, written in 1838.

"Read especially the chapters on newspapers and how they advanced American life," she said. "Tocqueville wrote that in a democracy, people get control over their lives and government only if they stick together. The glue is the newspapers that report what the associations do and think."

*The glue of society! What a great way to think of newspapers.*

Ivar wished that Anders Lindfors had expressed the richness of his "inhumanity" broadsheet in a book, because he was certain his legendary ancestor would have anticipated Tocqueville.

Professor Eklinden, who was aware of the Ivar-Birgitta friendship, added, "You two might do a joint study project on a better life for the masses, especially through aiding the poor, the feeble-minded, unwed mothers, and bastard children. It comes down to rules set and enforced by men. This is not dogma. What we have is a logical outcome of everything that went before."

Ivar later told Birgitta about Tocqueville and the American writers he had learned about from the Professor. Birgitta wasn't as impressed as he expected.

"Elverna told me about all those writings last term," she said. "Why don't you just read Charles Dickens. His novels swarm with children who came into the world without their asking. They were born to unmarried and destitute women or to couples too poor to feed them or school them."

Ivar was stunned. She had called the Professor by her first name. Were they personal friends?

"My family always taught me that causing childbirth outside of marriage is the most unpardonable of sins." He told Birgitta about Olof, his hapless, but bastard, friend from younger days.

"This poor fellow was born because his mother, a

seamstress, had slept with many men. He had no father, so he used his mother's surname. She was so poor she even resorted to prostitution. She and Olof were scorned by polite company. On the street, people would say 'how's the little bastard,' and then spit in his mother's face. Finally, she went mad and they put her into an asylum."

Birgitta shrugged.

"So you are saying that Olof's mother committed the most unpardonable sin?"

Ivar hadn't thought out that part of it.

"Well, not what a proper woman would—"

She leaned forward, roughing his shoulder with her strong hand. "Ivar, Olof's mother was the victim of men who were all sex and no responsibility. And then, she tried to live in Bourgeois society, or what you call 'polite company.'"

"Now see where that left her? You see, if she's going to practice free love, she should be either a noblewoman in a castle or a stitching woman in the countryside."

Birgitta's eyes flashed. "Both places, bastards are accepted. They get the worst treatment of all among people like you, Ivar. Maybe you don't know it, but you and your kind are totally infected by Victorian morality."

"What do you mean, Victorian morality?"

Birgitta, exasperated, glared at him.

"Your education has a long way to go, Ivar."

She paused to underscore the gravity of his obtuseness.

"In Queen Victoria's time, the English middle class became so puritanical that nobody could even talk about how babies are made or what men and women do to get them. They designed women's clothing to cover the entire body, the way it does now.

"Look at the dresses today. They make women look as if they have no legs, because legs are sinful."

Ivar stole a glance at the calf-length flared skirt Birgitta was wearing.

"Go ahead, Ivar, have a good look. All you can see is an ankle covered by a dark stocking. And what of it? Does that do anything to your imagination?"

She didn't wait for a response.

"Don't you see, Ivar? Hiding the female body leaves men in charge, so they can have a nicely perfect family at home and then go to bawdy houses for their extra entertainment. Brothels flourish in that kind of society.

"So the proper woman becomes a creature of divine mystery and procreation never gets discussed. Tell me, how many discussions about sex and procreation did you have as a child?"

Ivar, rattled, answered self-righteously. "Nobody in our family would talk about such things."

He wasn't telling the whole truth, because, from her seventh until her eleventh year, his younger sister Gretchen had discretely peppered him with questions about human origin. As a most proper lad whose parents had put the fear of Lucifer in him about such matters, Ivar would rarely attempt a substantive answer to Gretchen's questions. He did remember that she had piqued his own interest in the ultimate adolescent puzzle.

"Ivar," Birgitta asked, "if your family never talked about it, how were you supposed to learn?"

"That comes later, with adulthood."

"You're an adult now. How much do you know?"

Ivar's face turned red. "Know?"

"For example, what do you know about the process of ovulation?"

This, he thought, was easy, because his biology class had covered it. He gave a brief textbook description.

"That's a good answer for mice, but tell me: When in the human menstrual cycle is human conception most likely?"

The texts hadn't covered that point and Ivar was perplexed.

"Yes, I have a lot to learn, but doesn't a pastor tell young couples these things just before they are married?"

Birgitta rolled her eyes upward.

"Ivar, what pastor will tell you anything biological,

except perhaps how to keep the wife from becoming pregnant when she doesn't want to? Or when the man doesn't want kids?"

"But are pastors supposed to be biologists?"

"Well, Ivar, that's the point. They aren't, and they don't tell you the most elemental things. What do you know about the pleasure spots on the female body? Or do you think women are supposed to just enjoy the man's ecstasy? So the man just climbs on, has his thrill, and climbs off?"

Ivar reddened again, then came up with a response he thought appropriate.

"Wouldn't education about that kind of thing make young people more anxious to sleep together before marriage? And then have more fatherless children."

Birgitta threw up her hands.

"Isn't sleeping together what young people—especially men—have on their minds all the time?"

Ivar couldn't dispute that. It was exactly what he had in mind at the moment.

Birgitta was relentless, but shifted direction.

"You're hopeless, Ivar, because your middle class doesn't want everyone to do as well as you do. Your kind doesn't want village people to have your income or your life—or to go to the well-behaved childhood dances you did, because then your life wouldn't seem so high and virtuous. If poor country people did those things, you would stop doing them because they would seem cheapened."

Ivar recalled the dancing school where he and a dozen other eight-year-olds paired up around a flower circle. Boys wore white and blue sailor suits while giggling girls skipped delicately in frilly white pleated dresses with large light blue ribbons in their smoothly combed hair. Ivar's mother Ulrina often said how fortunate he was to attend such wholesome and enjoyable events instead of cavorting with the boisterous, naughty children, like Olof, on the back streets. He often wondered, with some shame, whether this boisterous and naughty side of poverty was what attracted him to it.

Was it the voluptuous charm of the back street kids that attracted him to Birgitta? What was her background?

As if reading his mind, Birgitta told him about her family. Her father was a dock worker in Stockholm and her mother worked in a grocery.

"Did we envy richer kids, like you? You bet we did. We wanted your wealth and ability to have nice houses and clothes, but not your way of life.

"Did my parents tell me not to sleep with boys? What they said was, 'don't get pregnant and have a bastard child. Because that's what men will do to you, if you give them a chance. Especially rich boys.' Like you."

But she softened these remarks with a smile, leaving Ivar aroused but confused.

* * *

Ivar was walking across the village square near the Lund campus, when he was jostled by a rough hand on his shoulder and a bellowing laugh from a husky, tousle-headed and broad-shouldered fellow slightly shorter than himself. It was Olof Moller, now several years older, better dressed but still carrying a strong smell. After warm handshakes, Olof said an older couple in Stockholm, whom he laughingly called his "uncle and aunt," adopted him after he left Graskoping. He spoke almost derisively of these people, as if their sending him to the University was somehow a cute trick he had played on them.

"I fooled them into thinking I would eventually wear suits and fancy overcoats," he grinned. "I talked to them like I thought you would."

The camaraderie of more youthful years could not be recaptured fully. Ivar had become more inward, Olof more brash and crude. Ivar nevertheless convinced his old friend to attend Professor Eklinden's lectures, but Olof's assessment after a single lecture was swift and blunt. "So much manure" he called it, an earthy observation that Ivar patiently dismissed as unfortunate ignorance.

Olof was outspoken, irascible, and unpredictable. He would skip lectures for weeks and yet do reasonably well on exams. He needled Ivar about his relationship with Birgitta.

"You won't get a good roll in the hay with that one," he laughed. "That is, unless you first wrap her in the socialist flag. And promise that any brat you produce will be raised a Marxist."

Ivar decided to spend less time around Olof, in favor of seeing more of Birgitta.

Ivar now felt strong passion for Birgitta, although with mixed feelings. He was unsure about what to do with an opportunity—should one occur—and how he should follow through. He burned with realization that Birgitta saw through his naïve beliefs about youth, love, and poverty.

Then, opportunity arrived.

It was a Saturday afternoon, after one more discussion of the Eklinden lectures, when Birgitta made the offer.

"I have a paying job shelving books in the old storehouse. Why don't you come help me, and we can continue to talk." She turned to face him directly as she said "talk," implying that it would be more than that.

She led him to a musty back room of the storehouse, an ancient building for storing books out of date and badly worn, but still too precious for a money-strapped university to throw away.

At the end of a darkened hallway, Birgitta put an experienced hand on Ivar's smoothly combed blond head, ruffled his hair and kissed him. He tried to conceal his arousal.

"Ah yes, Ivar, you are indeed a stoic. But can't a stoic also be passionate?"

Ivar, green and clumsy, botched the moment. He didn't understand her garments and he feared disrobing. So he awkwardly asked whether it would work if he simply unbuttoned.

She responded by almost brutally yanking his trousers

down, breaking buttons in the process.

"You don't know how to undress yourself, much less a woman," she scolded.

She then undid her own clothes and grabbed him, knocking a row of books off the shelf behind them.

Ivar feverishly achieved the male high point, then withdrew and quickly redressed.

An angry and unsatisfied Birgitta berated him.

"Just as I feared, Ivar. You are like a wild stud horse. Shoot your wad and then ignore your partner. And I thought that with your concern about people, you would somehow be different."

She dressed, shook her hair, and refused to look at him.

This inept and unsatisfying sexual experience left Ivar with pangs of humiliation, shame and guilt. Had he exploited Birgitta in exactly the way they both abhorred, or was she merely toying with him? Either way, she was obviously badly disappointed with the result.

He assumed that with all she knew about ovulation, she wouldn't get pregnant.

Ivar remembered that the headman at the dormitory had an old violin that needed repairing. This was an escape he relished, making new pegs and fixing the bridge of the old instrument. It was one of the skills he had mastered, along with the craft of printing.

While Ivar was rated well in Professor Eklinden's course, the joint-study paper she had suggested was never written.

* * *

His friendship with Birgitta now eroded, Ivar put more energy than ever into his human mission. Since he found it hard to go alone to meetings of the Social Democratic Labor Party, he sought out Olof and took him to one of the gatherings. Once there, Ivar again listened raptly to the renunciations of violence, advocacy of universal suffrage, and calls for a wide range of societal reforms. His complicated friend, though, was hostile to the socialist view.

"Yeah, I hate the king as much as these people do. The king is a whoremonger and the members of parliament are a bunch of bloodsuckers. But would the socialists be a political improvement? Frankly, Ivar, they are a bunch of vermin, too. They just want to cringe and grovel to the king and get his blessing. I say down with the king and all the other leeching bastards. Maybe the Bolsheviks are right."

That was the last time Ivar saw Olof at the university. It was said that Olof tired of school and returned to Stockholm.

* * *

Ivar finished at Lund in 1904 and returned to Graskoping, where the family print shop was making good money publishing pamphlets for the emigration business. Steamship companies glorified the myth of an American Utopia, through billboards and pamphlets that offered an exotic way out. Sail to America to opportunities of one's dreams, for a wondrous future, the companies urged. Their messages were posted in gristmills, way stations, railroad depots, market squares—wherever gathered those souls without hope or means except enough hoarded cash or borrowed funds or saleable possessions to pay for a one-way steamship ticket to the New World. These billboards and pamphlets were read with longing by those having little to lose and, or so they hoped, much to gain in the New World.

While his firm printed these glorifications of emigration, Klas Lindfors thought the Myth of America was rubbish. He agreed with the higher circles of Graskoping that America was little more than a dumping ground for lost souls, the depraved, and the delinquent. But if promoting that myth was a way to rid Sweden of its 'problem' population, so much the better.

Klas was pleasantly satisfied with his lot. His wife

Ulrina had borne him five children, three of whom had survived past age ten—Sten, Ivar, and Gretchen, in that order. Sten, unfortunately, had eschewed printing and publishing and was working for a shipbuilding company in Stockholm. Gretchen had married early—and satisfactorily—to an accountant who was well positioned in Gothenburg.

Sten's leaving Graskoping left Ivar destined to take over the family business, and he initially received much encouragement from his stern father. Klas enjoyed watching Ivar slide the type from the cases onto the composing stick and drop the assembled lines deftly into the galleys. Ivar understood steam engines and presses, and what it took to keep those wide, flat belts from whirling off pulleys on line shafts. In the print shop, he could anticipate and deal with such problems as uneven inking, maladjusted pressure levers, and static electricity in paper.

But then, Ivar went to the University, and, when he returned four years later, Klas was worried. He was annoyed by the young man's obsession with the problems of poor people. "Leave that to the churches and the Poor Relief Board," Klas tried to counsel Ivar. "Not our worry."

About two years after returning to Graskoping from Lund, Ivar noticed a bakery worker named Fredrika Grinnhaal. The handsome young woman had arrived, destitute but vivacious, from the birch woods and rolling grasslands of rural Smaland. Fredrika, with a tall and strong frame, ample bosom, and almost muscular shoulders, was a semiliterate fugitive from a fearsome past. She was the eldest of nine children, six surviving, born to Axel Grinnhaal and his successive wives on a small farm in the poverty-wracked countryside. In 1903 Axel deserted his most recent wife, Ana, so this woman forced Fredrika to care for a houseful of irritable younger children. On the day of her 18th birthday, Fredrika left abruptly for Graskoping and took a job in the bakery near the Lindfors printing firm.

Ivar knew the bakery well. It was in the sharp end of a V-shaped building, where three streets crossed and thus assured that no structure using all its space could be square. The warm aroma of yeast, moist flour and sugar frosting wafting from the pointed front of the bakery offered a pleasant contrast to the oil-and-ink smell of the print shop. He would stop there in the morning and, oftentimes, on the way home in the evening.

Ivar's first encounter with Fredrika was a pleasant if mildly embarrassing collision. Standing at the end of the bakery shop's high counter, she caught his eye while handing him his pack of coarse-grained brot and havrckaka. Gazing back to her moist, dark pupils under brunette eyelashes, Ivar fumbled the package. It dropped and both he and Fredrika stooped immediately to retrieve it. His nose brushed her dark, auburn hair and he absorbed her alluring scent. Her breast touched his arm.

He excused himself profusely and reddened a bit. She slowly straightened, smiled softly, but showed no embarrassment at all. Instead, her manner radiated warm invitation. All he could do at the moment was thank her, turn and leave. He returned for more bread the following week. No miscues this time. Their eyes connected briefly, without overdone expression but nonetheless with silent electric energy.

Ivar thought it was time to think ahead. He saw a young doctor, whom he had known as a medical student at Lund, who loaned him a book about human reproductive anatomy. He thus gained some technical knowledge as a response, he admitted to himself, to what Birgitta accurately called his ignorance. This would be useful should he see this alluring bakery worker again.

It was June, when Graskoping's young people chattered excitedly about the coming Midsummer's Eve, a traditional romp of gaiety that promised raucous fiddle music, dancing and much beer and aquavit. Ivar and two male friends decided to be part of this most uproarious, rollicking, and potentially erotic, adventure of the year. The frolic was in a large barn at the outer edge of Graskoping, with fiddle and folk music quite different from the piano and violin concertos through which Ivar had struggled under his mother's strict tutelage. There would be shanties of the sea, melancholy herdsman's ballads from the summer "fabods" in the mountains, plaintive love tunes from the villages, and rousing beer-drinking songs.

Scores of young men were already drunk when Ivar entered the barn, and at least one fight had broken out. His friends went in separate directions, toward one group of young females or another. A rough hand grabbed at his shoulder and the slurred male voice behind it challenged him. He shrugged off the dare and eased himself to the other side where Fredrika stood in anticipation. Like most young women there, she wore a full dark skirt held up by shoulder straps over a blowzy white shirtwaist. Unlike the others, she wore no white scarf with points fore and aft. Her reddish-brown hair curled openly and daringly down her shoulders, one lock reaching almost under her smooth, country-tanned chin.

"So you do come to these things," she said and without hesitation led him into the panting, stomping, and shouting that passed for dancing. His blood rushed as she grasped his hand and shoulder. Her energized body leapt and swung in sensuous rhythm, with sometimes jerky, sometimes smooth motions, but always with vigorous vitality. As they were swept up in the lustful gaiety, Ivar was transported back to pre-adolescence and the vibrant wrestling with the appealingly aggressive girls, some a year or two ahead in age and eons ahead of him in back alley wisdom. Yes, he acknowledged, those in poverty have their own delightful magnetism.

Ivar felt a tugging at his back, from the same oaf who had jostled him earlier, but now with an equally thuggish companion. They weren't after him so much as Fredrika. She spat an insult at them with a verbal ferocity that nearly stunned them from their drunken stupor. She grabbed Ivar's hand, pressed it tight against her warm thigh, and led him quickly out of the barn and away from the beery merrymaking. They headed straight for the woods, where Fredrika found an isolated glade and pulled Ivar down to her. She opened his shirt and his trousers, a maneuver reminding him of his vexatious escapade with Birgitta at Lund.

This quickly became very different. Instead of yanking at his garments with the impatient disgust of Birgitta, Fredrika deliberately and methodically folded them back and free, much as one peels away a fruit rind in delicious anticipation of satisfying an overpowering hunger.

She ran her fingers through his blond hair, and asked him if he liked that. He murmured a yes. She then guided Ivar's hands to help with her own disrobing, so expertly he thought he was doing it all himself. She was, in this way, a much more accomplished teacher than Birgitta. And he was a better love partner because of Birgitta's assessment and his recent study of the medical text.

Fredrika made love to Ivar, giving him—and her—an ecstatic thrill that had been missing in his tryst with Birgitta.

Thus began a two-month affair of lust with Fredrika that completely contradicted Ivar's own ideals. Not that it was unusual. In fact, it was almost commonplace among other single professional men in their late twenties. It was primal passion, exploding sexual paroxysm without commitment. The ecstatic energy transmitted by Fredrika's nubile body and feminine scent captivated him, much as his newly found male strength and self-assurance seemed to attract her. They continued to meet clandestinely, retreating to a wooded park, a stable barn, or her cramped room for untamed, often acrobatic love, during late summer of 1907.

All sense of admonitions from his earlier days left him, replaced by what he frankly accepted as the unbridled passion of the dispossessed. He allowed to himself that Birgitta would have denounced him for taking advantage of a troubled woman. What would the idolized Professor Eklinden say? Well, he couldn't allow himself to even imagine that.

One night after making love with Fredrika in her cramped third-floor room, he asked her about life in the crude village of her childhood. She told him matter-of-factly that young women were often impregnated early, by men both young and older, often relatives.

"They watched bulls ram their rods into heifers, and acted like bulls with any woman they could get their hands on."

Ivar asked, "Do these women ever find husbands?"

She shrugged.

"Sometimes they do, more often they don't. Take Katreena, whom I called my sister. She was Ana's kid—had her long before marrying Axel. They signed her away to work at first the Soderruds, then at the Svennebring farm and I don't know where after that. She was pushed over by so many men, no one knew who fathered her brat. Nobody would marry her."

Ivar eventually ended his trysts with Fredrika, deciding that it was the proper thing to do. Given his righteous distress over poverty and illegitimacy, hadn't this really been a mature study experience? As for Fredrika, she was a knowing, capable adult quite unlike her hapless stepsister Katreena, *wasn't she? So, it was a mutually agreeable arrangement.* For diversion, he now spent more time mending his sister Gretchen's old violin, the one that always needed bridge repair.

\* \* \*

Since returning from Lund, Ivar had continued to read socialist literature—but privately, without talking with his father about it. He refined his printer skills and gradually worked into management of the Lindfors family enterprise. For the next two years, he worked on the technical side as well as the business.

His first real experiment with newspaper crusading

followed the brief affair with Fredrika, and he regarded his writing as an uplifting inspiration from his Lund days rather than escape from his own moral transgressions. He set in type three articles, intended for subsequent editions of the *Veckoblad*. The first was CHILDREN WITHOUT FAMILIES, which was about fatherless children, their numbers in a particular local parish, and the Poor Relief Agency's work with them. When he saw this piece in print, Klas was aghast.

"It makes Graskoping look bad," he thundered

He concluded, ruefully, that giving his immature son so much editorial latitude had been a major error. Then as he feared, he was reproached in strong terms at lunch with town notables two days later for putting such bunkum in print.

Klas again confronted his son. "Printing such things is like breaking the law."

"But Papa, that doesn't break any law at all. Sweden has had a law giving freedom to the press since the 18th century."

"You don't know the whole history," Klas shot back. "But I do. That law was passed by a new party in power, so that they could turn up some secret papers that showed how corrupt the old party was. It was a revenge law, pure and simple."

"But it is still the law, and shouldn't we observe it?"

"Not in the way you have in mind. We don't mistake the intent of the law. We have to respect the wishes of the community, what is good for it."

Later, to Klas' further chagrin, Ivar wrote another piece, about a charismatic country reformer named Per Jonson Rosio who spoke at a gathering in Vaxjoe, calling for reform of laws that—in the opinion of many—would eventually be harmful to rural people.

Ivar's headline was: IS PER JONSON ROSIO AN ACCURATE PROPHET? Klas saw this one in galley form, before publication, and was again displeased. As a businessman, he mistrusted Rosio as a man opposed to development of Swedish industry. This time Klas put his foot down, and decided to personally review all of Ivar's writing before it appeared in the *Veckoblad*.

This included another item that Ivar had set in type, WORKERS WITH STARVING FAMILIES. Klas dumped the galleys of type into a bin. Ivar's crusading career would be on hold until he took full control of the family business from his domineering father.

\* \* \*

Meanwhile, Ivar saw more and more of Inez Zetterlund, a worker at the Lindfors publishing firm. Like Fredrika, Inez had grown up in a rural home, but the similarities ended there. Inez was raised on the island of Oland, just a few kilometers off the eastern coast from Graskoping. She and her two younger brothers were all born to the same parents— a Swedish father who operated one of the ancient wind-driven flour and gristmills that dotted the long, flat island, and an immigrant daughter of a Portuguese sailor. Having a modest but dependable income, her father Larss managed to keep his children in school

Inez, who grew to be an attractive and amiable blonde, had darker eyes than usual for a light-haired person and an almost perpetual, ingratiating smile. Neighbors said she had her father's hair and her mother's eyes and lovely smile. So congenial was her personality that as a child she was commonly known in school and neighborhood as "Jovialisk Inez." Her disarming demeanor coupled with a low toleration of nonsense enabled her to neutralize annoyance and wrath among those around her. When she was 10, a young male ruffian slightly superior to her in physical size foolishly yanked her pigtails. She caught this rascal and pummeled him to the ground, without losing her smile. The boy was never so foolhardy again.

She was not given to long sentences. She spoke generally in short, blunt statements—a characteristic learned from her immigrant mother that would greatly affect her manner of speaking when she shifted to a second language, English.

As an able singer, Inez fantasized becoming another Kristina Nilsson, a daughter of a lowly tenant farmer who rose to fame with her balcony arias in Stockholm opera houses. Yet, Inez was not a born or coached advocate of suffrage or other female privilege and was quite accepting of the ways of the world as she knew them. Like most women of her generation, Inez contemplated motherhood and a family. She was educated enough to secure a lowly paid office clerical job at the Lindfors Printing Company when she was nineteen.

She and Ivar became acquainted as a matter of course and occasionally had conversations, which were brief at first and grew longer over time. Inez Zetterlund enjoyed her work, which consisted mostly of menial tasks in the production of books, magazines, calling cards, social announcements, and pamphlets. She quickly acquired a sense of design and artistic symmetry in printed work—a talent highly valued in a small publishing firm like the Lindfors. She gained confidence in her growing expertise and modestly offered her advice whenever it seemed needed and appropriate.

Thus Inez and Ivar's first contacts were more or less technical. She showed some curiosity about the printing cases and the new letters the firm had acquired.

"Mr. Lindfors."

"Please, Inez, call me Ivar."

"Yes, of course, Ivar. What are these new cases of type—the ones delivered this week?"

"That," Ivar said, "is actually an eighteenth century Italian type, called Bodoni, named for the man who designed it."

"Bodoni. With letters thick on one side? And thin on the other?"

"Yes. It is an old type but not used much before by us. Some even think of it as modern. We are considering it for the headlines in the *Veckoblad*."

Inez smiled her approval, knowing that the *Veckoblad*

looked like pages torn from an ancient Bible. But she said little because it was not her place to be too opinionated, or to presume to sanction decisions large or small at the firm. Instead, she pointed to the large glass-covered picture of an ancient engraved printing in the hallway just outside the pressroom.

"Ivar, what is the type called, just above the picture of a king on horseback?" This question allowed Ivar to ease into his favorite family legend—the story of the heroic 17th century publisher Anders Lindfors. Ivar said little about military gallantry portrayed in this broadsheet and instead led Inez to a display cabinet in another room, where he pulled out a carefully preserved copy of the yellowed and crumbling broadsheet with the violently grotesque village scene—the one over the words "man's inhumanity to man."

"Anders Lindfors saw the horror of war. How military campaigns destroy whole villages, murder people, leave thousands of children as starving orphans in rags."

"How terribly awful. I had been taught the Swedish army was kind. Even to people in conquered lands."

Ivar and Inez shared this moment of common compassion for unfortunate peoples, and from that time on saw each other more frequently. They lunched together, in spite of Klas Lindfors' known intolerance of fraternization with lowly hired personnel.

All of this became moot when, in December of 1907, Ivar asked Inez to marry him.

"Of course, Ivar," she responded.

Their formal courtship lasted three more months. It included a train trip—with his uncle Karl-Henrik and aunt Inger—to the charming Royal Opera house in Stockholm for a performance of *The Queen of Golconda* by Swedish composer Franz Berwald. More enjoyable for Inez was a shorter trip to Malmo, where she was entranced by the wistful strains of Beethoven's Seventh Symphony, played by a Swedish-German orchestra.

They were chaperoned to such formal affairs, but

sometimes met privately for job duties around the print shop. One day they managed to stay late in the afternoon after others had left, ostensibly to inventory the paper stock. They moved together. Their bodies touched, then their eyes. She curled her hands around his neck and said, quietly, "I'm deeply in love with you, Ivar."

"And I'm deeply in love with you, Inez."

Ivar Lindfors and Inez Zetterlund were married March 7, 1908, in a ceremony marked by dignified festivity. On their wedding night, Ivar tenderly practiced all the biological and emotional aspects of lovemaking that he had learned. He hoped Inez would never discover where these talents had been acquired.

*   *   *

Klas Lindfors never quite got over his pique about Ivar's interest in reform-minded journalism. He accosted Ivar at the type galleys one day, and this time Ivar argued with him.

"If Swedish newspapers were responsible, Papa, they would tell us what is really wrong in Graskoping. The hovels around Graskoping are crammed with people lacking food and warm clothing, living in filth, their children always sick—"

"They moved in from the farming country, where they failed," fumed Klas. "Why should we bother our readers with those failures? Are we responsible for them?"

"We should let the facts be known—let people know what the conditions of the poor are, and what the authorities are doing about it. That's what an independent paper should do."

Klas shook his head and stated with vehemence that "a good newspaper tells people what their neighbors are doing, what their clubs are doing, and not the private troubles of people."

"Papa, the hospital people say one child in four here eats poorly and wears rags."

"I know hardly a single case," Klas responded. "Except, of course, for the child of Fredrika Grinnhaal—that poor thing who used to work at the bakery. Her baby has no father and no future, but the Poor Relief people will take care of her. No doubt the child will be one more for the orphanage."

Ivar paused and said slowly: "That's the thing. If we talk about the women on poor relief—like this Fredrika you mention—nearly half of their babies nowadays are illegitimate."

Father and son had reached another impasse and ended their conversation, lest it degenerate into acrimony. Besides, Ivar was eager to terminate this particular debate.

Fredrika Grinnhaal had told a social worker that her baby Charlotte was Ivar's daughter. A week earlier, Elmira Lidstrom, an agent with the Poor Relief programme, had called Ivar into her office and had given him the shattering news.

A stunned Ivar wondered why Fredrika hadn't known how to avoid pregnancy.

"She—has a child?" he stammered. "But when? I did not know."

"The child is named Charlotte and was born June 12. You did not know because Fredrika knew of your recent marriage and at first did not wish to embarrass you."

"Too many men," she added, eyeing Ivar narrowly, "sleep with women and then leave them, as if they were simply promiscuous prostitutes. New laws are putting a stop to that, and Fredrika has been apprised of her rights and your obligations. Elmira added that Fredrika had seen several men, but that she knew "as only a woman could" that Ivar was Charlotte's father.

Ivar was humiliated by this woman, who scolded him as Birgitta might have.

"So what am I compelled to do?"

"Whatever the judge decides when Fredrika presses her statement about your fatherhood."

"And Fredrika? What will she do?"

"It depends on her holding a paying job. Her bakery work hardly kept her fed and clothed, let alone pay for rent or care for a baby. Furthermore, her despondency is such that she may be committed to the pavilion for the mentally ill."

Ivar wanted to escape to the family workshop and work on Gretchen's old violin some more, or maybe one of his father's fowling guns. Now, though, no escape seemed possible.

Ivar had to act. *But how?* He took a train to Stockholm, to consult his brother Sten. The elder brother had blunt advice: either pay her off or take the child to America.

Ivar next went to Gothenburg to talk with his sister Gretchen. She showed little sympathy for him but much for Fredrika. "Ivar, the only way you can keep your head high is to support Fredrika and the child until Fredrika is able to do it alone, either through occupation or suitable marriage. Adoption leaves a sad mother without a child and quite alone, perhaps to repeat the same tragedy."

Ivar decided it was time for the difficult confession to Inez, but he was too late. When he returned from Gothenburg and approached their home, Inez did not greet him at the door. She sat in an inner room, staring at the floor in stony silence.

Her vacant posture obviated his question.

"Inez, you have heard?"

"Yes," she screamed, shaking. "Yes. I have heard. All about the fine man I married. And you know who told me? I heard," she quavered, "from a woman you made love to. So much love she bore you a child!"

"Inez, I didn't think—"

"You didn't think what? That she wasn't with child? Or just that she wouldn't worry you about it when it arrived?"

She turned away, then back toward Ivar.

"Ivar Lindfors, what was I to think when this woman comes to my door, arms folded? 'Are you Mrs. Ivar Lindfors,' she asks. 'I am she,' I answer and 'what may I do for you?' And then this woman, calm as a morning sea, tells me she is

Fredrika Grinnhaal, who has 'just dropped off' your brat, as she put it."

"And then you know what?" Inez was screaming even louder now. "She asked me if I was satisfying you in bed. Because if I wasn't, she could give me some useful advice! And with the most horrible smirk on her face, she walked away from the door. But still staring back with that terrible, vicious look, like a wild person.

"Ivar, do you know how that makes me feel? Dirty. Betrayed. With a husband I cannot trust!"

Ivar didn't know what to say. He left the room.

Two days later, the word around Graskoping was that Fredrika had committed suicide. This news further deepened the crisis between Ivar and Inez. For days, the recently wedded couple engaged in clumsy, stumbling conversation, punctuated by more than a few heated outbursts of indignation, accusation and contrition. Inez alternated between outrage over Ivar's secrecy and worry that her own righteous appall at Fredrika's visit may have somehow caused that woman to take her own life.

Ivar struggled for a statement. He acknowledged that he had taken advantage of Fredrika, but pointed out that he had stopped seeing Fredrika long before asking Inez to marry him. He then promised Inez that he would never be unfaithful as a husband.

Inez was in doubt. She left for her home in Oland, but found her parents far from sharing her sense of indignation.

*This was the result of a fling before marriage? But this is rather common. You have married well. Overlook what is past.*

*There is a darker side. If you leave Ivar, you will be shunned by other men of his level of education and class. You might have to marry a carpenter or even a wagon driver, a man who always smells like the back end of a horse.*

While Inez was gone, Ivar retreated in his consternation to the print shop, seeking a craftwork escape from his dilemma. He offered to do a signature etching on his father's double-muzzle bird gun. He smeared some engraving wax on the shotgun's metal breech and blackened it with candle smoke. He then traced his father's own signature on the wax with a thin stylus.

It didn't look right. The signature had to be enhanced, and Ivar's craftsmanship failed him at this crucial point. His cursive sweeps were not smooth and bold; his flourishes looked like limp spirals. He smeared the wax again but still failed to make the right twirl. In frustration, he put the project aside.

When Inez returned to Craskoping, she refused Ivar's advances. But she accepted his child. "Ivar, we must speak to the Poor Relief agency. They must allow us to adopt Charlotte. We will raise her as our own child. I believe that is the best course."

Ivar was so gratified by this offer that he didn't know what to say. Then he recalled Inez' talent for design and adept use of marking crayons.

"Inez, I need your help." He told her that he was unable to create the stylistic strokes on the shotgun he was trying to etch. Would she give it a try?

Bemused, she agreed. She looked first at Klas' original signature, replicated it at least a dozen times, and embellished it. She suggested that the personal signature with the big K would not work well. "Let's just make it, 'Lindfors,' she said, and Ivar acquiesced quickly.

"Now let's do it on the gun," she said. Inez then created an elegant calligraphic script version of the Lindfors signature, with sweeping curlicues at the beginning of the capital "L" and after the final "s." Ivar did the rest. He brushed the exposed metal with hydrochloric acid, enough to bite the traced lines into the metal in neat, sharp grooves. The result was an exquisite work of gunsmith art. Inez and Ivar were again working together, joining their talents with splendid results.

By early October, the adoption was arranged and Ivar and Inez took Charlotte home.

ACADEMIC/TRADE BOOK PUBLISHER
Dr. David Demers, Publisher
Editing / Design
Marketing / Promotion   3707 East 62nd Avenue
Custom Publishing   Spokane Washington 99223
Binding / T-shirts   509-443-7057 (voice)
Lamination / Printing   509-448-2191 (fax)
books@marquettebooks.com
marquettebooks.com

Ivar's mother Ulrina was more silent about this arrangement than he wished, and his father was truculent. *Why not simply provide a sum for the child's support, now that the poor wretch Fredrika had taken her own life? Let the child be adopted by another family, one not previously connected with the child's background in any way?*

These questions Ivar put aside. What he could not put aside were his parents' apprehensions about what was being said around town. Klas was hearing untidy talk about the bastard child. Worse, people were noting that Fredrika had hanged herself less than two days after calling on Inez. No one was making accusations directly, but there was talk.

Ivar noticed during the next few weeks that he and his father met less frequently. Then one day his father approached him.

"Ivar," Klas said, "it is no longer possible for you to take over the family printing business. Too many things are being said around town, for reasons I'm sure you understand.

"They are even saying, incorrectly, I am sure, that your unfortunate piece about children in the *Veckoblad* was nothing more than attempted atonement for what you knew you had already done. Some even call it hypocrisy. You will be compensated fully, I assure you, at least to the extent that is possible, since business has not been quite as good as it was four or five years ago."

The news stunned Ivar. He asked what arrangements would be made for the future of the firm. His father said there would be different management, but it would take some time to work this out.

A week later, Ivar found out about the "different management." His brother Sten gave up his shipbuilding career and moved back from Stockholm to take over Ivar's position within the family firm. Ivar was given a modest sum and kicked out—replaced by a brother who had once deserted the family.

When the disgraced trio packed to leave Sweden forever, Klas Lindfors brought the beautifully etched fowling gun to

Ivar.

"Take this with you to America," he said flatly. "I won't be needing it. I'm giving up bird shooting."

Within a month, Ivar, Inez, and adopted daughter Charlotte booked passage to the United States of America. Their only major possession was a large trunk, which contained the gun, the famous and deteriorating "inhumanity" broadsheet from Anders Lidfors, and a few personal possessions.

Ivar, standing at the ship's rail, looked again across Stockholm harbor and sighed.

# II. MINNESOTA

During the twenty-one-day trip across the North Atlantic, amidst the usual seasickness, strained conversations and constant caring for an infant child, Inez told Ivar that she had a miscarriage. After talking with the one doctor aboard, Inez had doubts whether she would ever have a normal pregnancy again.

"Charlotte might well be an only child," Inez confided to another woman on board.

"If the Lord wants you to have a child, you will," the woman answered.

"Yes, if the Lord wishes," Inez mumbled to herself.

Holding a heavily-wrapped Charlotte on the open deck, facing a stiff wind from the rough sea, Inez was at least satisfied to have accommodations that were a modest step above steerage. This relative good fortune prompted her to ask Ivar: "The Lord has treated us as He sees fit. We should be thankful. Will we be close to the Church when we reach America?"

"I suppose so. Both our families went to services regularly."

"You suppose so. Isn't it important for your—our—daughter to grow up in a Christian home?"

Ivar hesitated. He knew of people leaving Sweden because they were Catholics—rare in Sweden—who felt persecuted and sought the religious freedom of the New World. America was the land of freedom of religion. He knew others who were seeking freedom from religion.

He thought of himself as a printer and publisher—as

well as a Christian.

"Inez, we will somehow and somewhere be with a big newspaper. There are many Swedish language newspapers in America. They will speak strongly in support of the Lutheran Church and against Godlessness."

Inez frowned. "So we are Christians because it is good for the newspaper business?"

Ivar squirmed, then forged ahead with his point.

"Inez, I have given this much thought. I hear that many Swedes in America are trying to convince more pastors to go there. They are needed to keep the faith alive. In fact, the *Dagens Nyheter*, the big newspaper in Stockholm, carried an advertisement a while ago.

"I remember that advertisement well. It said: 'Pastors who are dedicated to Jesus, you are needed in America. All sense of grace, salvation, and prayerfulness that had been part of Swedish upbringing seems lost to hordes of our people. Without inspired Christian leaders, America may become a Godless and satanic nation.'

"You see, Inez, people in Sweden aren't going to church as much as when our fathers were young. So our church may actually do better over there than back in Graskoping. And I'm told that the Swedish language newspapers are the flame that keeps the faith alive."

Inez looked over Charlotte's bundled head at her husband. *Was this conviction talking, or business-like calculation?*

Ivar tried to bolster his ideas about promoting religion with his life-long convictions about reporting on the problems of poverty and orphan children.

"Just think, Inez. We might start a newspaper that helps the church cure the problems of poverty and orphan children. Our journal will spell out a social contract for immigrants like us in America."

"A social contract?" Inez asked. "For what? For a job to build houses? To work in a factory?"

Ivar had never told her much about his heady days at

Lund. "Not that specific, and not for each person," Ivar answered, now parroting the words of Professor Eklinden. "A social contract is for everybody, like a good constitution, between the people and the government. It tells how laws will be made, what the government can do and not do. What rights people have."

"So the contract is good for all time?" Inez asked.

"Not exactly," Ivar said. "Maybe the main idea lasts forever, but the details change. We were seeing many changes in Sweden. Hjalmer Branting and the Social Democrats are changing the social contract there. Sweden needs more changes, to make life better for children, for mothers, for farm people. We would expect changes in America. We don't expect it to be perfect, maybe far from it.

"There will be much thinking about change in America, we can be sure of that. The job of our newspaper will be to explain different ideas for changing the contract. Then, people can choose the best."

This would be a newspaper with vision, Ivar thought, encompassing the full sweep of human life, enthusiasm, and inspired venture. He assumed that the Church and immigrants generally would provide him with a ready-made and eager audience, receptive to his eager notions—though not developed well—about how things should be done.

Was his idea feasible? That was the big question.

While Ivar's words were racing ahead in this newspaper dream, Inez' thoughts took a different turn.

"Perhaps, Ivar, we should have a contract."

"You mean a newspaper contract?"

"No. A contract between you and me. About Charlotte. And whose responsibility she is. Yes?"

To underscore her point, she handed Charlotte to Ivar, and led him inside their modest and cramped cabin, away from the driving ocean wind.

"Inez, of course, we have an understanding. We treat her as our real daughter, do we not?" He patted Charlotte, awkwardly but affectionately. The infant squirmed slightly.

Inez squinted at him—whether with mocking mischief or absolute certitude, he was uncertain.

"An understanding," she suggested, "is a contract, is it not? So let us say we have a perfect understanding? That we go, let us say, half and half? She is half yours and half mine?"

\* \* \*

Ivar had heard about a well-known Swedish language newspaper, edited by a famous Swede in Minneapolis named Swan Turnblad. Ivar had also learned that the reputation of Turnblad did not extend to Minneapolis' city government, which had become known as one of numerous cases of wholesale urban corruption in America. Syndicates, corruption, crime, prostitution, gambling, and other vices were rampant. A mayor had been exposed, indicted on criminal charges, and convicted. Lincoln Steffens, a muckraking journalist, had published a magazine story under the sensational title, "The Shame of Minneapolis: The Rescue and Redemption of a City That Was Sold Out."

As a young printer in Graskoping, Sweden, with few reliable ways of checking up, Ivar in the years before emigration had found the Minneapolis story both stimulating and depressing. It was stimulating because it romanticized an energetic newspaper and magazine industry that Ivar wished to join. It was depressing because of the logical conclusion that burgeoning Scandinavian immigration had not yet made this city the idyllic place of his dreams.

\* \* \*

The Lindfors trio followed a route familiar to immigrants: to Ellis Island, by train through Pennsylvania, Ohio, and Indiana to Chicago, and then through Wisconsin to St. Paul and Minneapolis, where they arrived in early December of 1908.

The hard bench seats of the railroad cars, along with the

clicking and clacking on every rail connection, kept all but the most hardened travelers from relaxing. Children fidgeted. Babies cried, some incessantly. Inez was proud that she knew how to keep Charlotte cooing contentedly, even though they had no Pullman car. While they had enjoyed modest cabins at sea, their funds were now stretched to where first-class train travel was unaffordable.

For Ivar, English was no great problem, since he read English well and had tolerable speaking skills. His schooled accent was different from the typical Smaland immigrant, more clipped and without a sing-song cadence. Inez knew the language less well, but with Ivar's tutorial help, was a willing and able student. On the ship, they had gone entire days conversing in English alone. It was a fresh and exhilarating experience, although Inez was privately relieved after the end of each "English" day to revert to her native tongue. Her way of speaking in short sentences was accentuated when she adopted the new language.

Not suffering the privations of most of their predecessors, the Lindfors family was nevertheless a rumpled and tired lot when they stepped off the streetcar on Minneapolis' Cedar Avenue and sought the lodging house run by an earlier Swedish immigrant. It stood among shabbier hovels in an area heavily populated by Scandinavian Americans and would eventually be known jocularly as "Snoose Boulevard."

* * *.

Ivar had one distant relative in Minneapolis, a man who worked on Swan Turnblad's Swedish-language newspaper, the *Posten*. With his aid, Ivar was employed immediately by that newspaper as an apprentice printer. It was a start, a place where he could get his feet wet in American publishing and support his family while looking for a better opportunity.

As a skilled worker at the *Posten*, Ivar did no writing or creative work. He worked entirely with printing equipment.

He soon became a foreman in a composing room, working eight to 10 hours daily but with few evening demands.

Ivar—in his long black printer's apron, hands continually smeared with ink, wrist skin cracking from exposure to desiccating paper and cleansing agents, nostrils invaded by redolent fumes from cleaning solvents—honed his expertise in the gadgetry of American publishing.

From the newspaper proofs that he read routinely, he became impressed with the commercial side of the Turnblad paper. Its advertisements extolled the virtues of such products as "Pillsbury's Best Flour" and "Cassarets candy cathartic." The paper promoted tickets for cultural events throughout the region, including Ibsen's plays and opera productions in Chicago.

Ivar, though, found he was learning little about the newspaper world, apart from the printing technology. He needed to learn American politics. Inez had similar interests. As the wife of a crusading newspaper man, she wanted to know more about the English language, and about Minnesota and its history.

The two worked out an agreement.

As part of their "contract," Inez said they would each spend two evenings a week at the Minneapolis public library, while the other cared for Charlotte. Most husbands in those days would have objected, but given the circumstances, Ivar hardly found that wise. The contract between him and Inez was firm and there would be no violating it.

An energized Inez immersed herself in books and old newspaper reports about Minnesota history and politics. She was struck by an 1885 law that created a large public orphanage in southern Minnesota, organized as an agency for placing children in homes through adoption or other arrangements. She read with admiration about John Lind, a popular politician who from 1899 to 1901 served as Minnesota's governor.

"This Governor Lind," she said to Ivar in her characteristic short sentences, "he wanted a state law for insane asylums. It was a law he copied from Wisconsin. Each county, eighty-seven in Minnesota, would have its own asylum. The insane people—half of them work on the farm. They are near family who see them often. It works good in Wisconsin. Each county gets state money to keep the people. But the political people here didn't want that. They voted instead for two big asylums."

"One at Anoka, one at Hastings," she said, stressing the vowels in these strange names.

Ivar thought a moment. "That's odd. You mean each county had a chance to get something from the state if they followed the Wisconsin plan, but turned it down? Why would they do that?"

Inez shrugged. "Well, these politicians—legislators, they call them—from those two towns said they hadn't got treated good from the state. Other places had different things they wanted. University in Minneapolis. State prison at Stillwater. Orphanage at Owatonna. These towns wanted their share.

"There was another thing. Many people worried about their neighbors. Didn't want crazy people scattered around every town. Put them in one or two big places. Get them out of the way."

Ivar nodded. If they had their own newspaper, he was sure they would have written strong words backing up the ideas of this former Governor Lind. A countryman like that could use strong editorial support.

Inez told Ivar about Minnesota's governor at that time—John Albert Johnson, a second-generation Swede, whose alcoholic father had died in a poorhouse.

"This man," Inez said, "went to work at a store at age 13. Then for the railroads, to support his mother who washed clothes for a living. All this while teaching himself about literature. He joined debating clubs. He was a big man in St. Peter and was editor of a Democratic newspaper there."

Inez was amused by an incident that helped Johnson win the 1904 election for governor.

"It was political mischief that—how do they say here—backfired."

She told Ivar how some hostile public official, in a moment of dubious inspiration, put out a campaign pamphlet that told what a miserable, sotted wretch John Albert Johnson's father had been.

"During the election," Ivar said. "What did Johnson say about that?"

"Well, he just said it was all true. And then you know what? Many people think a lot of people were pretty unhappy with that pamphlet. They said it made Mr. Johnson look good. He worked his way up from a poor family. So they elected him."

"Like Abraham Lincoln, yes?"

* * *

As months went by, Ivar and Inez wondered whether they would ever be able to publish, write and edit their own paper in a place that would be their town, as Graskoping had been—where they would put down roots and become immersed in local life; where their newspaper would be a guiding light if not a propelling engine.

These lofty aspirations, Ivar reflected, were remarkably similar to the ideals of Klas Lindfors. What Ivar had rebelled against a year ago now seemed increasingly like his own convictions. One day he took out the faded, crumbling, and ancient 'inhumanity of man to man' broadsheet of Anders Lindfors and wondered whether he would ever publish anything with so much impact.

Ivar and Inez were not penniless, but paying several thousand dollars for a small town newspaper and its print shop was far beyond their means. Ivar talked of these ideals and constraints with Inez and his new acquaintances, who included Pastor Ernest Bjornholm—a clergyman who would eventually help them achieve their goal.

* * *

In autumn and winter of 1910, the Reverend Ernest Bjornholm was named pastor at a Lutheran church in Minneapolis, not far from where Inez and Ivar lived.

Pastor Bjornholm was a short, slightly rotund and balding man in his mid-forties, with sweeping eyes and a quick, reactive manner that lacked the smoothness of most people accustomed to speaking before crowds and congregations. Not an immigrant himself—his parents had come to the United States from Vaxjoe in 1862—he had grown up in a bilingual household dominated by a deeply religious mother who was determined to keep the Swedish heritage alive. After graduating from Gustavus Adolphus College in St. Peter, he developed the manner of the devout and pious clergyman. His verve for upgrading the religious convictions of Swedish-Americans matched those of the letter writer to the Stockholm Nyheter that Ivar had seen shortly before coming to America.

Ivar and Inez first met Pastor Bjornholm in a most unplanned and accidental way, through a horse-and-buggy incident on an Autumn Sunday. Like most ministers, Ernest Bjornholm did not enjoy automobile ownership. His deacons provided him with a well-worn carriage and an equally worn sorrel mare whose usual calm demeanor was sorely tested that day by a backfiring delivery truck near the church.

The mare bolted toward the sidewalk path where Ivar and Inez walked with two-year-old Charlotte in a folding perambulator contraption known as a Go-Cart—so-called because it could be packed up and hauled in wagon, train, streetcar, or automobile. A startled Ivar reacted by instinct, grabbed the horse's bridle, and kept it from prancing over the Go-Cart.

All the while, the pastor was shouting to the horse, while bracing his feet and pulling back on the reins with his arms behind his head and back. A professional horseman he was not; he had been driving with a loop in the reins, allowing himself no holdback room.

A humiliated Pastor Bjornholm was effusive in his gratitude. "Ah, you saved me for certain, my friend. You are? Oh, yes, Ivar and Inez Lindfors. And this is your delightful daughter Charlotte? May the Good Lord bless you all. And perhaps one day I can take lessons in horsemanship from you."

The pastor's lack of humiliation turned into acute embarrassment for Ivar and Inez. In his sermon, the clergyman introduced the Lindfors family by publicly and profusely thanking Ivar with a highly embellished account of the incident. An uninformed listener might reasonably have gathered that Ivar had leaped heroically from his chariot to throttle the runaway stallion of King Agamemnon in the battle for Troy.

The two new members of the church prayed less for salvation than for baby Charlotte, hoping she would not fuss and draw even more unwanted attention to them.

At the end of the service the pastor repeated his gratitude to Ivar personally, with even greater enthusiasm. He said he would call on the Lindfors soon.

"Wednesday evening? Very well, we shall see you then, and may the Saviour bless you all."

Inez was not particularly pleased with the prospect of this ministerial visit. She said with obligatory pleasure: "Yes, we'd love to have you come by."

Ivar thought this would be fine, given the notion that his dream newspaper would certainly involve working with clergymen.

Although Inez displayed more genuine religiosity than Ivar, a new church presented problems she found hard to face or even discuss with Ivar.

She told herself that she was a good mother, as devoted as any natural mother could be. But for obvious reasons, she had never been able to nurse the child. She thought they should tell people the truth.

Their story onboard the ship, usually glossed over

rapidly, was that she had married Ivar as a widower, soon after his first wife died giving birth to Charlotte. This lie was not necessarily believed by all. It was rarely questioned, either, since for many immigrants, entanglements from the Old Country were happily left in a state of benign mystery for the good of everyone. They may have been gossiped about frequently, but the targets of gossip were rarely confronted. Except possibly by a professionally inquisitive clergyman.

Ivar and Inez Lindfors had an edgy discussion about the matter.

"Ivar, the pastor—he will ask about Charlotte's baptism. What do we say to him?"

"What we have been saying. That Charlotte's mother died two years ago."

"And her mother was your wife?"

"Well, not unless he asks."

"And if he does?"

"He won't. He'll assume we were married."

"Ivar, that's dishonesty. To let him believe that. That you and Fredrika Grinnhaal were man and wife."

"Well, we have been letting others assume it."

"Yes. And we are tangled in a sticky web."

"Inez, you call it dishonesty. Can't we just treat it as our own business, and none of theirs? I mean, isn't this the land where people can have their own private lives, to themselves? Something we came here to find? You know, we don't need to even tell people that Charlotte's mother is anyone other than you."

"But is that what we will say? Will you tell the pastor that all of this is our private business? And none of his? Charlotte's birth and baptism? If that's what we do, why even go to the church?"

Ivar paused at this, because he had asked the same question of himself. But he found it hard to make this point now to his wife, for a most practical reason. As he had already admitted to her, his future in publishing might well be tied to the Church. Affronting or perplexing Pastor

Bjornholm might jeopardize that future.

Inez said it instead. "Ivar, we talk often of a newspaper in Swedish. And that means close work with the church. Doesn't it?"

Ivar sighed, "Yes, it does."

"So, Ivar, there's one way out. We tell the pastor the truth."

"If he asks?"

"Yes, if he asks. That you and Charlotte's mother were never married."

"And if he doesn't ask?"

"Then we act like Americans. We mind our own business. And everyone else minds theirs."

She chewed the inside of her lip a moment, then added: "And make sure you mind Charlotte as much as I do."

\* \* \*

As the Lindforses expected, Pastor Bjornholm Wednesday evening asked immediately to see their daughter. He picked up the child in a grandfatherly way, said a blessing, and then to Ivar and Inez: "A lovely name, Charlotte. It is a family name?"

Without hesitation, Ivar answered: "Actually, Reverend Bjornholm, Charlotte was the name of our pastor's wife in Graskoping."

"Indeed. How beautiful."

Inez fired a bewildered glance at Ivar, in both reproof and admiration for a response that put to rest the whole matter of christening. Ivar's statement was technically correct, even though the fact was simple coincidence. He had no idea why Fredrika had chosen her daughter's name.

The deception was intact. After the pastor left, Inez stood with arms folded and her mouth set in a straight line. Acknowledging her silent question, Ivar asked, "I've been wondering, Inez, what do we tell Charlotte when she is old enough to understand?"

"Her first word was 'Mama.' Remember?"

* * *

Pastor Bjornholm had a concern far more pressing than Charlotte.

One Sunday he asked Ivar and Inez to see him in his cramped little office in back of the sanctuary, after the sermon. The office—little more than a broom closet—had a single chair, other than the pastor's. He graciously offered it to Inez, holding a momentarily quiet Charlotte.

The Pastor took Charlotte from Inez, chucked the two-year-old under the chin and said again, "What a beautiful child." In terror, Inez wondered whether the baptism question would come up after all.

It didn't. The clergyman eased Charlotte to the floor and watched her scamper to the next room. Then he went to what was on his mind.

"My good friends, Ivar and Inez. While we have known each other for such a short time as members of Christ's Fellowship, I must share with you an urgent matter. It will be in the letter I am sending to the congregation tomorrow. The Bishop, after prayerful consideration, is sending me to fill a vacancy in a small town northwest of Minneapolis.

"It is Belleville, in Athena County. You wouldn't gather it from either name, but Belleville has a large number of Scandinavians, and primarily Swedish at that. The town has slightly more than two thousand residents, yet two Lutheran churches. Many of the members are farm people, from around the county."

In a more modest tone, he added, "I shall become the pastor of the Trinity Lutheran Church there, which I am told has the largest membership of all churches in Belleville."

After humbly accepting congratulations from Ivar and Inez, Pastor Bjornholm proceeded strategically and tactfully to his next point.

"I should say, Ivar and Inez, that I fear my reputation as

a clergyman is outdistanced by yours as members of the publishing professions. In the few months you have been here, your names have been mentioned frequently as those of citizens with much to contribute to our Swedish-American heritage.

"There is a small Swedish-language newspaper in Belleville that has, unfortunately, languished in inspiration, quality, and ultimately in circulation. The current publisher, an unfortunate soul, has decided to offer the newspaper for sale. We in the Luthcran ministry hope to attract Ivar and Inez Lindfors to take it over."

Ivar in his short time at the Turnblad enterprises had seen the pile of other Scandinavian language papers delivered there, including the Belleville *Veckomonitoren*, meaning *Weekly Monitor*. He had noted its thinness, a mere four pages. It was a mixture of news items, various letters, weekly contributions from the pastors, a few advertisements, and "boiler plate" from a variety of other religious and Scandinavian-American organizations. It was a most unimpressive publication, badly edited, and saturated with grammatical and typographical errors.

Ivar also remembered the name of its editor, a recollection he had mentioned to no one, not even Inez. It was Olof Moller, his troubled old chum from Graskoping and Lund University.

Ivar had no doubt that this sloppy mess of paper reflected the character and marginal competence of its editor. Olof was sharp with words but inept in editing. This in itself was not unusual, since the publishing of small papers did not require language expertise. Most of Moller's readers were semi-literate in Swedish, at best, and rarely noticed the shoddy editing. Many actually read Swedish for the first time after reaching America.

Ivar learned from Pastor Bjornholm that Olof continued to drink, as he had as a Lund University student, frequently and heavily. His French wife had packed up and taken their two children to Quebec a year and a half ago. Moller had been escorted home often by police.

"This editor has a mischievous side," Pastor Bjornholm noted. "Quite on his own, it seems, he wrote a piece on the sorry differences between the Missouri and Ohio Synods. This was the predestination controversy.

"This idea that certain persons are elected—that is, predestined to be saved and possess grace because of that predestination—has been at the root of much debate. It is an unfortunate position, in my view, since it leaves a person powerless to do anything to achieve salvation."

Ivar recalled Professor Eklinden's lectures on predestination in earlier Swedish culture, and how it led to Birgitta's needling him about his stoicism.

"Do any Lutherans here accept that notion?" he asked.

Choosing his words carefully, the pastor replied, "Pastor Ray Kurtz, my predecessor, has shown sympathy for some aspects of predestination. However, he and I heartily agree that it is a matter for the clergy and not public discussion, since it invariably leads to strife and confusion. Putting all this in print for popular reading, as Mr. Moller did, was unfortunate."

Ivar asked about the price. The pastor replied that so far as he knew, the entire publishing company, including press equipment, name and circulation, could be purchased for about three thousand dollars. Ivar expressed interest in buying the newspaper, but would need to look into the matter further. This meant visiting the print shop and Olof Moller.

# III. The New *Veckomonitoren*

Ivar and Inez now took Charlotte for her second long train ride since leaving Ellis Island, which, of course, the child did not remember. Now, she stood on the edge of Inez' seat, peering out the coach window as the train, hissing and screeching and belching clouds of vaporized steam, pulled into the Belleville station. Just before the stop she pointed and said "Hat. Hat."

A puzzled Ivar wondered what headwear she saw, but Inez knew what she meant. A gleaming new water tower, with "Belleville" freshly painted over it, stood gracefully on a frame tower some 50 feet above the streets of this small town on the edge of the prairie. To a child, its tapered peak made it look like a tin can with a pointed hat on top. In fact, the water tower was a pleasing sight, especially to Inez.

"They have city water here. Good. We can have water from a faucet, and hot water for the bath. And a toilet you flush."

Ivar nodded but wondered if all houses in town were yet so equipped. More importantly, he thought, would be electric wire poles, which he didn't see yet. No electricity, no electric motor power for the presses. Or press. How would the newspaper print shop be equipped?

\* \* \*

On the way to the small and drab *Veckomonitoren* building, Ivar told Inez for the first time that this Olof Moller was someone he knew at Lund University and, earlier, as a child in Graskoping. Inez was both startled and annoyed.

"So he will know all about us and Charlotte?"

Ivar shook his head.

"Not likely. I never saw him after my third year at Lund. I heard that he left Sweden several years ago." Ivar then laughed. "Disguised as a woman, that's how he left. Probably running from the police."

Then a loose plank board, arching upward against a weakened spike in the weather-beaten oak sidewalk, caught Ivar's leather heel. It caused him to stumble awkwardly into the front door under the faded sign reading "*Veckomonitoren*—Scandinavian Print Shop."

A familiar odor reached Ivar's nostrils—a smell carried by paper soaking up printer's ink and percolating its aroma into the atmosphere much as a lamp wick takes oil up to a level where it vaporizes for a flame. Nearly overpowering the odor of printer's ink were the biting fumes of solvents that imperfectly dissolved the old ink on the type cases and presses. Evidence of that imperfection was readily available, in the fuzzy edges of headline type visible in last week's edition that cluttered the floor and tables. Dirty type means a dirty page, Inez scowled to herself.

Olof Moller recognized Ivar immediately.

"Welcome, old comrade," Moller boomed in Swedish, from behind Franklin spectacles astride a vein-streaked bulbous nose. His rugged visage had not been threatened by a razor for at least three days.

"What mischief brought you to America, Ivar? And this is your wife? What is your name? Inez? I hope you can keep this rogue tied down." He roared at his own crude humor.

Ivar thought: *Such obvious exaggeration won't fool Inez. I haven't told her much about Lund, but she knows as well as Moller that I was a quiet fellow, and he knew next to nothing about my brief affair with Birgitta, not to mention Fredrika.*

While Ivar stood quietly in his reflections, Inez squirmed uncomfortably and turned away, her face betraying wonderment about just what sort of rogue her husband was.

After some brief exchanges about old times, in Swedish, Ivar said "Olof, we hear you have the paper up for sale."

The Ben Franklin glasses on Moller's nose returned to stare at the galley of type their wearer was setting slowly and deliberately. "Call me Ollie," he answered in English. "That's how they know me here in Belleville. Yah, it's for sale to anyone dumb enough to buy it," he added as he slid the type from the stick into the galley and locked it in.

He sat back on the rickety wooden stool, raised one foot from under his ancient printer's apron encrusted with years of ink and rested his heel on a paper bale, stacked next to the type cases for lack of a better storage place. He was liberal with sarcasm and bent on sharing his misfortune with his successor.

"So you're gonna do wonders with this paper?" he sneered. "Just like you were gonna reform Sweden when you were at Lund?"

Without waiting for a reply, he continued.

"And, maybe you think you're going to write the word of the Lord? If you believe that in this town, then you got to believe the Lord works for the railroads."

Ivar answered rather stiffly that he thought the ministers were sturdy contributors to the paper. Moller raised his eyebrows and twisted his head in partial agreement.

"Ah, yeah," he mused. "You're right. This paper couldn't make it without the preachers telling their members to subscribe, and putting their sermons in it. It's always been that way. And then I print it. Now ain't that a laugh? A sinner like me doing the Lord's work?"

He scowled. "Except I wasn't so good at it. Nothing worked. One time I talked to the pastor at the German Lutheran Church about this predestination thing. I'd never thought much about it, but that German preacher was all fired up about it. He was wondering how to tell his flock that whether you go to heaven or hell is all set the minute you are born.

"Well, when it came out, a few readers who understood it were mad as wet hens. Said it sounded like an old fight they wanted to forget. That got the preachers upset, too.

"So you can't get preachers too riled up. In fact, you really need them. I have to admit, the day they quit pluggin' the paper, that's the day you shut it down and make a living printing birthday cards and auction bills, or start a paper in English. Or get out, go raise tobacco or pickles, or maybe sell oysters." He chuckled without humor.

Inez settled down in a hardwood swivel chair and asked about the town and its big people.

"Big people?" Moller said. "Everyone knows banker Higgins was in on the railroad land grab, right in there with Marty Johnston's old man. Hebermann got his share too, or did you think all the money he's going to lend you is what he earned with his two hands?

Inez asked:

"Do you ever get complaints about things in the paper?"

Olof chuckled again, this time with a touch of humor.

"Well, you can get away with a certain amount o' stuff, printing a Scandinavian newspaper. That's just because these big hootey-hoots on Wells Street can't read it. But don't forget, if it's too hot a story, someone reads it to 'em and then you better tie everything down, 'cause there'll be one hell of a dustup.

"Don't get the idea," this soon-to-depart editor added, "that you can get into any of this muckraking stuff. Not like those high-falutin' writers like Sinclair and, what was her name, Tarbell? That doesn't go in this town, not in any language. Or any town like it."

Moller hesitated a thoughtful moment, then with twist of his face, said:

"'Course, in a way, you do get in the muck here. You don't rake it like the big time newspapers and magazines. You edit this paper and you'll be shoveling the dung they give you—shoveling it out for people to see and breathe."

"Do you write editorials?" Ivar asked.

"Editorials? Oh, now and then. I thought Teddy Roosevelt ought to get another shot at the White House and Johnson made one damned good governor. Except I never wrote that hogwash about his being great in spite of his old man's dyin' drunk and in the poor house. Fact is, the old guy was probably a good-hearted father until the tightwads in St. Peter drove him to drink."

This, Inez recalled from her Minneapolis library reading, was a reference to John Albert Johnson, state governor from 1905 to 1909.

"Sure, you can scribble all the editorials you want about outlawing saloons," Moller continued. "Don't think you can speak up on women's right to vote, though. And, oh, yeah, you'll never write an editorial about the scalawags in town. They'd cut off your ads, run you out. Are they running me out? Hell, they don't care if I breathe or fall off a bridge.

"Your case is different, though. You, Ivar, you look like the white shirt and tie crowd here in Belleville, just like you did at Lund. Those patent leather shoes of yours will look good around those fat toads. Come to think of it, how can you afford those duds if you're going to run a paper like this?"

Moller didn't wait for an answer.

"Yeah, they call me a drunk. Just wait—you'll look to ol' John Barleycorn yourself after you've been at this place for a while."

Ivar asked Moller if he ever wrote about orphanages.

"Orphanages? For children born out of wedlock, or dumped on a doorstoop? Or the old man goes off and leaves them, so neither the wife nor judge can find him? You want to write editorials about that? Get into that, even in Swedish, and you're gonna be in hot water even sooner than I thought."

Inez was somewhat relieved by this last exchange. Ivar had actually asked about children like Charlotte, and Ollie Moller hadn't made any connection at all. *So maybe it was true that he hadn't seen this man since Lund. But that crack about Ivar being a rogue. Just harmless mockery?* Inez sighed with lingering doubt.

* * *

Ollie Moller had his own haphazard way of preserving the Old Country culture. "The oil that keeps the lamp of the Swedish culture burning," his newspaper said under the logo. Some immigrant newspapers called themselves Apostles of the Faith, but that would have been too much for Moller.

Ivar thought the paper should be a billboard for the thoughts and traumas of a people struggling to cope with a new and forbidding culture. It would be, under his guidance, a counseling center for those who wrote to the editor, inquiring on everything from "how to measure flour you are buying" to "how to understand grades of potatoes you are selling." Or "how to build corn cribs or raise beets or tobacco as cash crops."

He looked forward to advertisements that would introduce his countrymen to the new culture, but in a familiar language. He would tell them about automobiles, clothing, food products, medicines, fashionable hats, corsets, patent medicines, pump jack apparatuses, windmill rigs, Model T modification—things that promise a healthier, easier, more satisfying, and fulfilling life.

He talked about these ideas in the print shop, while Ollie Moller was shuffling through his unpaid circulation bills. The rough-hewn and blunt-spoken editor snorted.

"Hell, Ivar, a paper for immigrants won't get far with new-fangled social and political ideas. Like I said, you can say everything about Jesus Christ and Valhalla that the pastors can dream up. And you'll get piles of scribbled stuff from the women who write up Mrs. Steenberg's tea party, Elmer Gulbardson's operation on his big toe, or the Bergtold kid's wonderful grades at the University.

"Yeah, Ivar, you hear about foreign language newspapers saying things that would get the editors burned at the stake in the old country. But being what you call a beacon of social reform? Forget it."

Ollie Moller in many ways was more typical of immigrant newspaper publishers than Ivar or Inez. In spite of what he had told Ivar at Lund, he had little experience in publishing before leaving Sweden, and his inept use of the language now embarrassed his more literate readers. Some of his strongest critics were the very pastors who had encouraged him at the start but now felt betrayed by such uncultivated coarseness in print.

There would be few reminders about Olof in coming months, except for his name being seen on old documents around the print shop. He left town shortly after the Lindfors couple took over his newspaper, and no one seemed to know, at the time, where he went.

* * *

Inez wondered one day whether a newspaper in the "Old Country" language could last.

"Aren't people learning English? And talking it? Like us?"

"Yes," Ivar answered, "but they still want to hear things in the native tongue. Just think. There are more than a thousand newspapers in the country now that are printed in some Old Country language."

"But their readers' kids. They will learn English and not the old language?"

"We don't know that for sure, Inez. Yes, Charlotte will go to an American school. But some places in Minnesota have Scandinavian schools. The language will last a long time"

"I don't know, Ivar. My English is not good like yours. But we already speak English to Charlotte. We are now Americans. She will go to the regular school. So when she grows, she won't know much Swedish talk."

"But Inez, that's the point of the Swedish language newspaper. We will read it to Charlotte, just as other parents will in their homes."

"So then we keep using both languages, yes?"

\* \* \*

The Lindfors couple, notwithstanding the obvious problems, concluded that the Belleville *Veckomonitoren* on the corner of Oak and Wells streets was probably the chance they were waiting for. Ivar had his philosophic reasons; Inez saw it as a way to stay connected to a homeland she had left so abruptly.

More capital would obviously be needed. Even for 1910, the equipment left by Ollie Moller was outdated. The ancient and badly worn Washington hand press was inefficient and the hand-fed Chandler and Price press was barely usable. The belt-driven platen press would be adequate for job work for the time being but would eventually need replacement. The ideal would be a Brantjen-Kluge model that could be set up and then left to run a job while the person in charge did something else.

The old Fairbanks-Morse gasoline engine was sufficient for operating the Chandler and Price. It was not powerful enough to run a full-sized flatbed press that would be needed very soon, above all other capital expenditures. Next would be a Linotype machine and, by that time, Ivar hoped the town would have electricity and it would be powered by a motor rather than a noisy, smelly, gasoline engine. Or steam, as in Sweden and for older presses in America.

Then there were peculiarities that left English-language type inadequate for Scandinavian words. Letters unique to the Swedish language, such as the "a" with a circle over it, were in short supply. Moller had handled that problem by often spelling Swedish with English letters, much to the chagrin of literate Swedes. This would not do.

In addition, the type cabinets, or "cases," were undersupplied with the letter "k," which in Swedish regularly occurs in place of the "c" or "ch" of English. Church is "kyrka," chicken is "kyckling," chaste is "kysk," crash is "kvadda." A composing machine adapted to Swedish, such as the Linotype, casts letters into a line slug from molten lead. *This would solve the problem.*

A 1906 Underwriter typewriter with a wide carriage, cast off by a wealthy subscriber, was the most modern and workable piece of equipment in the entire shop. Its good condition owed much to its underuse. Publisher Moller had poor typing skills and often composed his type galleys by working directly from hand-written items. Such was the nature of the *Veckomonitoren* at the time.

Belleville had one English-language newspaper at the time, the weekly *Gazette*. It was on the verge of suspension, with the local bank threatening foreclosure. With its own antiquated equipment and underpaid editor, it did third-rate job printing and was not popular among advertisers. Between Moller's *Veckomonitoren* and the *Gazette*, printing services in Belleville were shoddy.

On the pastor's advice, Ivar went to furniture dealer Ernst Hebermann as a local influential who might finance improvements in the *Veckomonitoren*. Hebermann proposed a plan to be worked out with Martin Johnston, who needed a good paper to advertise his clothing store, and with the Belleville Independent Bank, J. B. Higgins, President. So the bank was the next stop, with the Lindfors couple introduced by Hebermann.

Higgins, dressed in an expensive three-piece tweed suit and patent leather shoes partially covered by white spats, bustled from his oak-paneled office and brusquely—too brusquely for Inez' tastes—greeted his visitors.

"Ernst, old fellow, how are things at the funeral home? People dying to get in? Heh, heh. Ah, so this is Ivar Lindfors. Good to meet you, Ivar. And you, too, Mrs. Lindfors—charmed I am to make your acquaintance. We've heard a great deal about you. Understand you've had a good job with the Turnblad newspaper. People say you did splendid work."

Ivar wondered how a printer constantly in ink up to his

neck could get a reputation for splendid work. *Well, meaningless flattery might be harmless.*

Higgins was prepared not to discuss financing options, but to state the arrangements with smooth finality. "You say you have how much capital of your own to invest? About seven hundred dollars? That's, let's see, around 14 percent—

"Well, everyone agrees we need a good Scandinavian-language paper in this town, people are asking for it. Ernest here and Martin Johnston will each supply a fourth of the investment cost, and will be major stockholders. The bank will provide half, less your own seven hundred."

Ivar read the fine print slowly, and found that he and Inez would in effect be employees of a newspaper they technically owned. The entire assets of the paper were collateral, most of which in case of early bankruptcy would go to the bank. Hebermann and Johnston would get less and Ivar and Inez would lose everything, including their personal possessions and their home, if they owned one. But the Swedish immigrant publishers had their start.

Of course, most men going into business in Minnesota in 1911 would have signed the deal and then told their wives about it later. Ivar mused over this, knowing that his father, Klas, had never been known to consult with Ivar's mother, Ulrina, on any business matter.

Perhaps it was his reading about the suffragists in Sweden, Ivar thought, or his familiarity with the Social Democratic Movement that made him see things differently. Or was it deference to his strong-willed sister Gretchen, whose flaming stare at him over his fatherhood of Charlotte tormented him still? Or could it be his sense of guilt toward Inez? And yes, he had caught her irritation over suddenly meeting Moller as an old acquaintance. *Better not annoy her further.*

Inez now stood in his consciousness as a grove of mighty and sturdy oaks stands against the summer breeze: magnificent in appearance and not to be dodged or blown over. She would not rant or rage or throw a tantrum. She would simply confront him with that unblinking look of serene confidence. She had the poise that occurs only in those of strong character, with whom no person related or unrelated thinks of trifling.

Inez would necessarily be a working partner in publishing the *Veckomonitoren*. There would be virtually no budget, at first, to hire assistants. Inez had needed skills. While her command of English was limited, her flair for page makeup and layout design—to the extent that creativity was possible on a four-page paper—exceeded that of Ivar.

Inez did express some doubts about the business arrangement. "So we both work at the press shop. And how do we take care of—our daughter?"

Ivar ignored the hesitation. "We hire somebody, a helper, until Charlotte is old enough to go to school."

"And we can afford that?"

"Perhaps we can get someone willing to live with us for room and board."

"Which means some poor immigrant girl? A girl without a choice? I thought Social Democrats called that wrong." Inez now, except for her abbreviated sentences, sounded uncomfortably like sister Gretchen. Her point was plain. In Sweden, the Social Democrats had waged inspired war on the commonplace practice of taking in teenagers from poverty-wracked rural families and treating them as bonded servants. In America, it now seemed much the same, getting them either from the farm or just off the boat.

A minute passed before either spoke.

"Ivar, I know this is the chance—we—want—what we were waiting for. Maybe it is not hopeless. But so much of what we earn will go to the bank. And to these other people. How do we get ahead?" She still pronounced "these" much as Ivar did, with the "th" sounding as if the tongue was too far back.

Ivar had done some calculations. If they could get the circulation up to fifteen hundred from the current thousand, they could set a good advertising rate, maybe a full twenty-five cents per inch of column space. And the prospect, however dim, of a future merger with a rejuvenated Belleville *Gazette* provided some possibility of survival of the business should the *Veckomonitoren* fail. It would still be a chancy venture.

\* \* \*

The most pressing problem, however, was finding a place to live. The funds Klas Lindors had given to them were almost gone. But this problem was solved by Ernst Hebermann, who recognized that his investment in the newspaper required a comfortable editor.

"Ivar, my brother Karl last month moved to Fargo, and still owns his house here. You can rent it, maybe buy it later on. Nice place. Easy walk to the newspaper printing shop."

The house was a modest but comfortable bungalow on Belleville's Canada Street, named for the origin of the town's founders. It was about 15 years old, the first structure on this lot, constructed without disturbing two older trees, a white oak shading the back and a smaller maple in front. It had carbide gas lights and a hand pump over the kitchen sink.

"See, Ivar, Belleville is up and coming. We have a new electricity plant on the river, right at the edge of town. So in a year or two, they'll be bringing the line through. Might cost some for wiring, but it'll be worth it."

They took in Andressa Dahlgren, then a fourteen-year-old from a poor family of immigrants, as a helper and caretaker for Charlotte, who now was nearly three years old. Andressa would receive, in addition to her meals and tiny room in the back of the house—over a stone floor, not above the cellar, which was limited to the main part of the house—three dollars per week.

Ivar wondered how he would describe this arrangement in his obligatory monthly letter to his sister Gretchen, who would scold him soundly for exploiting a poor girl. Inez would read Gretchen's scathing words and nod in silent agreement.

Well, he hoped it would be silent.

Ivar mused about the old adage that behind any journalistic inspiration lies a need for money. Whatever the moral purpose of the paper, a brisk job printing business would be essential to keep the weekly afloat. The newspaper would need advertising from local merchants, enough to pay its way and bring some return over and above debt retirement. Given its dismal existing reputation, that would take some doing. Ivar wondered whether his ancestor Anders had similar financing problems for his famous broadsheets about war and its horrors.

Ivar worked 14 hours daily for three weeks getting the newspaper started. Inez was at the "shop" as she called it, every day until nightfall. Clara Ferguson offered to continue on as a correspondent for the *Veckomonitoren*. She had written for both this paper and the *Gazette* and had learned enough Swedish from her immigrant parents to get by. The agreement was that she could submit items, for which she would be paid 1 cent per column inch, or about a nickel for a page of typewritten reports. She and Inez became instant friends.

Ivar's first use of the Chandler and Price was the printing of a poster in forty-two-point type, in both English and Swedish. He tacked it to a wall where it could be seen by all who entered the building. It was the First Amendment to the U. S. Constitution:

Congress Shall Make No Law Respecting an Establishment of Religion, or Prohibiting the Free Exercise Thereof; or Abridging the Freedom of Speech, or of the Press; or of the Right of the People Peaceably to Assemble, and to Petition the Government for a Redress of Grievances.

"There," he said with satisfaction, "we publish in Swedish, but we do it in America where no one can tell us what to say or not to say."

The first edition of the *Veckomonitoren* under "Ivar and

Inez Lindfors, Publishers" appeared on the second Thursday of January, 1912. On the front page, in perfectly edited Swedish, was the publishers' note:

> As the new publishers of the *Veckomonitoren,* we look forward to serving the Scandinavian-American community of Athena County. We will strive to fuel the flame of Swedish culture in America. Look to our pages weekly for news about Scandinavia, news, and inspiring messages from the church, useful ideas for farm and home and for leisure time.
>
> We will be a publication of news, of revelation and of entertainment. We shall welcome letters from our readers on all subjects, and especially from those who have things to share about our mother countries. We will be neutral on questions of religion while willing to express our own opinions as well as those of readers on matters of politics and morality.
>
> We hope to become known as a forum, or perhaps we should say a bulletin board, of news bits, ideas, and views. The philosophy of newspapering that we will pursue was stated a century ago by Thomas Jefferson: that a press must be free, subject only to liability for personal injury; that spreading information brings all abuses to the bar of public reason; that the press is the best instrument for improving man as a rational, moral and social being; that a free press is the triumph of humanity over oppression.
>
> As a great European scholar and diplomat, Alexis de Tocqueville from France, said, "only a newspaper can drop the same thought into a thousand minds at the same moment." we shall endeavor to make it our goal each week: to reach a thousand minds.
>
> —*Ivar and Inez Lindfors*

Innocent as this salutation might have seemed, it unsettled Pastor Bjornholm, who was at the *Veckomonitoren* office the next morning, wearing a perplexed frown.

He leaned his arm, in the sleeve of his stained sack suit, over the counter just inside the printing shop door.

"Ivar, we agreed this will be a newspaper of the Lord, yet the Church and Christ's work were hardly mentioned. Worse, if Thomas Jefferson really said the things you quote, he was blasphemous about where the truth may be found."

Ivar noted the pastor's column on the second page, but Bjornholm shook his head.

"Not the same, my friend. The Church was not to be one of an odd lot of columnists. It was to be the centerpiece of the newspaper. That was indeed our agreement, was it not?"

Pastor Bjornholm was no longer the effusive but bumbling buggy driver thankful for Ivar's restraining a startled horse. His bluntness left no doubt that he felt betrayed.

Ivar's life-long loss for words in tense conversation returned to stifle him. Tapping his fingers on the publisher's statement, the pastor said he feared the local reaction to the *Veckomonitoren* getting into "matters of politics and morality."

"This sounds as if you intend, Ivar, to open the pages to propaganda of all sorts. We have far too many opinions being bandied about these days, and not enough words of loyalty to God, Community, and Nation.

"We are Scandinavians, Swedish first of all, in a new nation that will be as godly as we make it. You are proposing to mix religion and politics, perhaps the way those scandalous Swedish newspapers out of Chicago are doing. Please don't forget that it was our distaste for those troublesome sheets that led us to your editorship at the start."

As the distressed pastor spoke, Ivar relaxed some, realizing that he was not taking this pastor or his concern seriously. Yet that lack of concern was itself troubling, since the clergyman had indeed paved the way for this enterprise.

Ivar repeated his well-memorized speech about the newspaper being the life of the whole community, of sharing ideas. He made a big point of how people seize, and thrive on, words in print about what they already know from experience, and that printed news gives events reality, makes them part of life. He sounded, Ivar noted to himself, like Klas Lindfors in Graskoping. He also agreed to give more prominent attention to Church news and religion in future editions. He sought to placate the clergyman to the extent possible.

Later, when he told Inez about the Pastor's visit, she paused and then said:

"We WILL be the voice of the Church, yes?"

Ivar simply shrugged, as if in agreement but without conviction.

\* \* \*

The "Readers Ask" section was easily the most popular part of the newspaper, running just ahead of the personal items supplied by Clara Ferguson. A mother of six asked about the best remedies for whooping cough. A farm wife wanted to know how to feed chickens to get a stronger eggshell. A farmer wanted to know how big a cistern a windmill could keep full. A herdsman sought a way of getting grubs out of the hide of cattle without causing infection. A young woman of German ancestry wanted to know the name of a good book for learning to read Swedish since she was marrying an immigrant. A seamstress asked about repairing bobbins on a Davis sewing machine, and "was it the same as with a Singer?"

The "Readers Ask" section included an invitation for anyone who had relevant information to write a brief reply to last week's questions. One or two such responses would be included in each edition. Ivar and Inez prided themselves on this section, since it "got people to talking" and writing each other about useful things. The editors did not pay any of their "experts" who responded to these queries. That would have required an expense far beyond their means. It was a volunteer, community activity, and the experts seemed happy to oblige.

So successful was the "Readers Ask" feature that Ivar thought of ways to expand it and maybe get into more politics.

* * *

"Politics?" Inez asked.

"Yes—what people think about the new laws they are talking about down in St. Paul," Ivar answered. This was 1912, and the "new law" in his mind was a so-called "Mother's Pension" bill that would pay money to a widow with small children.

This proposed legislation touched on an old, troubling concern of Ivar's that had been with him from his days in Professor Eklinden's lectures sitting alongside the combative and sensuous Birgitta Gejvall—and exacerbated by the later tryst with Fredrika Grinnhall, which of course led to the birth of his daughter and her mother's tragic death. The thought of children born to misery tormented Ivar. It was agony kept alive by primeval romanticism about an ancestor who had carved the poignant woodcut about the horror of brutalized women and children.

Inez continued to allow all to assume she was Charlotte's biological mother. Not that she was entirely at ease with this arrangement. She simply couldn't imagine how public knowledge of all the details would help anything. She remained unsure of when, or whether, Charlotte should learn these details of her parenthood. After all, the woman whose womb bore this child was dead in a now-distant land, and reviving the lamentable tale would do that woman's memory no benefit.

*Better to put all this behind us*, was the way Inez sized it up. She had read with approval, at the Minneapolis Library, about the orphanage at Owatonna. *Nice to know we had those things, but why get into it in the Veckomonitoren?*

When Ivar continued to ruminate about the Mother's Pension law, Inez asked:

"Ivar, do you feel guilty?"

"About what?"

"About how Charlotte got born," she answered, her mild unease betrayed by ruptured grammar. "Maybe writing about it is—forsoning—gottgorelse—what is the English word?"

"Atonement. That what you mean?"

It wasn't easy having a wife who could cut through his shell so easily, Ivar thought. And with such abrupt bluntness. He considered mentioning the legendary Anders Lindfors and his published distaste for war's aftermath, then thought better of it. Last time he did that, Inez was unimpressed.

"Maybe it is atonement and maybe not. Professor Eklinden years ago impressed me a great deal with her lectures about the misfortune of orphan children."

*Yes,* Inez thought, *so impressed you went about creating one of those misfortunes.* But her directness had ventured far enough, even in a marriage where most things were in the open. For Ivar, the whole matter of the orphan or neglected child was an obsession that would somehow find its way into print. Publication would be his catharsis, if not his atonement.

It occurred to him that the same might have been true of the mythic Anders Lindfors. His "inhumanity" woodcut may have been an ambiguous confessional. After all, no one really knew much about the peasant German widow he had married.

An agreement was reached. Alongside the "Readers Ask" section would be a new column, called "Forum." It was a good, simple word, which happens to be the same in Swedish as in English. The editors got it started with an invitation for letters on "matters of public interest" in one edition and immediately they had a letter on farm prices for the next.

None of the letters mentioned the Mother's Pension bill. If Ivar wanted that to be an issue, he would have to stir it up, somehow.

Meanwhile, he was happy that Charlotte, now approaching her third birthday, was much like any first and only child: alternately happy, noisy, curious, fussy about food, and occasionally cantankerous. Thanks to Inez and Andressa, the child's tantrums rarely seemed out of control.

Among Charlotte's toys were a set of colorful wooden

blocks, each with a raised letter in a different color. One early evening, Ivar watched the child clumsily stack the blocks and let them fall. As they scattered on the floor, three blocks—quite by accident—fell into perfect order, spelling "GOD" in three colors. When he remembered that ancient printing started with wood letters rather than metal, he was reminded again of Anders Lindfors and his woodcut engravings extolling the Reformation. Charlotte's accidental spelling pleased him.

\* \* \*

Succeeding in publishing meant that for at least 15 hours each week, Ivar would pull the lever on the old Washington hand press, with Inez or Clara placing sheets of paper on the platen, first one side, then the other. For the four-page *Veckomonitoren*, the printing and hand-folding took about twelve hours. If it was a week of heavy (and profitable) advertising, there would be a second sheet to expand the size to eight pages. This doubled the time at the press.

Yet, for the new editors, the first crisis was neither printing nor substance. It was delivery. Unless a newspaper reaches readers, it does not exist. In the case of the *Veckomonitoren*, all copies went out by mail, with the bulk sent out into the countryside. Hiring carrier boys for such delivery would have been both impractical and too costly.

Inez had just returned from pushing the high-wheeled cart loaded with 1,043 copies of the first edition of the new *Veckomonitoren* to the Post Office. The cart, however, still bore a substantial pile of those papers.

"What's this?" Ivar asked.

"Mr. Grumman at the Post Office. He says these are undeliverables."

"Undeliverables?"

"People dead, moved away."

"Maybe their addresses are wrong? Can't we forward them?"

"I asked him that. He says these are people who don't live here anymore."

Ivar picked through the jumble of papers, many with smudges of a stamp saying NOT AT THIS ADDRESS. Several were out-of-town addresses, from subscribers in other counties or even other states who had once wanted a newspaper in the tongue of the motherland.

Ivar and Inez counted the returned papers. They came to a total of 163, meaning the actual circulation was well under a thousand. Worse, the problem didn't stop there. Among the circulation renewals, 96 were still unpaid. They had fewer than 800 paid subscribers.

Inez was incredulous. "But your old friend Moller insisted he was printing 1,075 copies, and the bundles show that he was."

Ivar recognized, too late, a nefarious old scheme of disreputable publishers—the "advertiser's press run."

"Advertiser's press run?" asked Inez.

"You see, we charge for advertising according to circulation. How do advertisers know what that circulation is? They don't. They have to take the publisher's word for it. If they get suspicious, they may come by on press day and see how many copies are printed.

"A dishonest publisher prints as many copies as he says he is selling and then discards or burns or hides what he doesn't sell. Reputable publishers would never do that."

"So we are charging too much from advertisers?"

"Exactly."

"Why didn't we find that out when we were buying the paper?"

It was not a question Ivar could answer well. Moller had told them that "maybe a couple dozen subscribers were overdue" in paying for their renewals, and Ivar and Inez had taken this statement at face value.

The *Veckomonitoren* was off to a shaky start.

\* \* \*

One editorial problem was the negative news of crime and malfeasance. Many readers expected and even demanded news that the Nelson ruffians had been caught stealing kerosene from Axelson's farm, or that Albert Stowberg, a perpetual souse, had been jailed over the weekend for public drunkenness.

Far more problematic was Sheriff Alfred Mayberry's arrest of Peter Edberg for stealing three links of bologna from Vernon Graham's Meat and Sausage Shop. Graham had pressed charges. Peter's father Helmer was a respected local plumber who subscribed to the *Veckomonitoren*. How could Ivar or Inez face Helmer Edberg the next day after the news came out in print?

Ivar knew the court listings would worry him less in the case of the socially marginal Nelsons and Stowbergs than in the Edberg story. This knowledge was of no comfort to an editor who was trying to retain his Social Democrat convictions. Such convictions, reinforced by his immigrant ardor for American equality, deprived him of any satisfaction from reporting misdeeds of lowly citizens.

Ivar and Inez worked out a crime reporting practice that seemed more or less satisfactory. Unless it was a heinous crime of a type that hardly ever occurred in Belleville, the simple fact of arrest alone would not be reported. The only mention would be of sentences passed down by the local courts and even then with utmost brevity. For a bit of a light touch, the crime and justice column was headed GOOD MORNING, JUDGE. A typical entry was:

> Emil Vilenius, 28, pleaded guilty to loitering in downtown Belleville; sentenced to 21 days in the county jail, with work time to be spent working in the Belleville City Park.

This seemed democratic, since the entire court docket would now be printed in this capsule form. The question of unequal treatment was thus shifted to the judicial system itself, where it was well known that social rank of the culprit had strong bearing on who was formally sentenced and who was sent home by the judge with an admonishment. GOOD MORNING, JUDGE did not mention cases heard and dismissed.

* * *

These publishers concluded that to get both subscribers and advertisers, up-to-date equipment was essential. They had another conference with banker Higgins and their other financiers. All were convinced that the paper needed a flatbed press and a Linotype, and a larger engine to power them. Press and Linotype could probably be acquired secondhand, judging from advertisements in a publisher's "supply monthly."

This equipment, a Babcock "drum-flatbed" press and a Mergenthaler Linotype, arrived three weeks later at the rail station. They required only minor repairs that Ivar capably undertook himself.

Ivar learned that Cletus Hoffmann had a workable 6-horsepower De Laval gas engine for sale at his local machine shop. This would be adequate to run the presses and a folding machine, all at the same time, each one belted from a different pulley on the overhead line shaft. Ivar and Inez bought this engine and, with these capital additions, the enterprise was open for expansion in job work, newspaper size, and numbers of copies.

The engine was housed in an attached, shed-like room in the back of the shop, with the exhaust piped outside where it announced in the intermittent chugs and pops that the shop was running along. Popping along in its hit-and-miss ignition sequence, the DeLaval gave the print shop the kind of sound and oil-gasoline-smoke aroma characteristic of many a thriving business in that era. It would be some time before the Lindfors presses would run by electrical power.

Carrying one of her hard-bodied dolls dressed in lace and ribbons, Charlotte would scamper through the print shop shouting "Pup-apup-apup-POP!" in childish imitation of the happy engine. Then Andressa or Inez would steer the toddler away from the machinery and back home, because it didn't look right if a child had too much free run of a family business. Charlotte would often fuss when taken away, because she enjoyed the noisy hubbub of the print shop, and all the paper readily available for scribbling and scrawling.

Inez and Ivar were deeper in debt than ever, but they now had a credible business. For the next three years, they gradually worked the circulation up over the 1,000 mark—unusually high for a small-town immigrant paper—and took in a substantial amount of job work on the old Chandler and Price job press, including wedding invitations, greeting cards, auction and sale bills, church flyers, mailing pieces for various merchants, and the occasional circus or Chatauqua bills. The couple became respected as competent local business people serving other businesses as well as individuals. Their success eventually made possible the purchase of a good, used, self-fed Brantjen-Kluge platen press to replace the klunky old Chandler and Price. The operation became increasingly efficient.

Formal readership surveys were unheard of in 1912. Ivar and Inez knew from what readers told them that the personal items and the "ads" commanded substantial time among those who spent their hour or so each week with the *Veckomonitoren*. Inez, with her native talent and useful experience from the Graskoping business, relished designing advertisements, especially for clothing stores. She was known as a "decent dresser" herself and saw the advertisements as a way of holding that reputation and making a profit.

* * *

As time went by, Inez thought it right to return some social favors that she and Ivar had received their first years in Belleville. The last week of April 1912, she invited nineteen persons to a "Svenska" dinner in their bungalow.

There were no guests with Scandinavian names, although at least one was changed from Danish. Most of these prominent Belleville citizens had last names sounding Anglo-Saxon or Gaelic. One—Hebermann—was German. This festive occasion required turning the kitchen and small living room of the bungalow into one continuous dining room. Such procedure was common even in the more substantial homes of the time.

Inez' smorgasbord featured some standard old country fare, including royal beef Slottstek prepared with brandy, molasses, fat, port, and anchovies. As an added attraction, Inez served gravadlax; that is, marinated salmon alongside a kabeljo pudding of salt dried cod. She served the slottstek expertly cut and surrounded by brussels sprouts, carrots cooked in molasses and brown sugar, cabbage, and assorted vegetables. J. B. Higgins, the banker, offered his compliments for her dessert of rice porridge with cinnamon.

The dinner was a success. Inez, dressed in a strikingly handsome frock with full skirt, restrained lace work, and practical short sleeves, demonstrated her talents with food and fashion as well as with typefaces, calligraphy, and graphic design. She thoughtfully decided against serving lutefisk. Four-year-old Charlotte didn't like it.

Among the guests were Martin Johnston, owner of the clothing store, and his attractive and formidable wife Irma. When the other wives privately praised Inez' dress ("so fancy when you have dinner to fix, but it doesn't seem to bother you a bit"), Irma beamed and simply agreed. The women guests all assumed, correctly, that Inez had bought the outfit at Johnston's Clothiers, at Irma's suggestion. And at a nice discount from a store that depended heavily on *Veckomonitoren* advertising.

# IV. INSIDE THE PAGES

Irma Johnston, when she wasn't seeking Inez' help writing ads for Johnston's Clothiers, saw herself with some accuracy as an influential educator in fashions. Her study materials were the advertisements—this week for skirts in broadcloth, poplin or serge in double-twist or warped fabric. Another week, the ads would offer waists or blouses of cotton charmeuse, embroidered voil, flannel, or silk. Or made with nun's veiling, albatross, and cashmere. At least once a month, an ad would display women's suits, often in wool broadcloth and in colors ranging from blue to green and brown, with fur trimming for those who could afford it.

Then there were the full furs, such as the black Baltic seal cluster scarf, with a round muff to match; cluster scarf of brown Belgian coney (rabbit), mufflers of gray squirrel, eastern mink, or blended water mink.

Waists and blouses were advertised frequently. Entire fronts might be embroidered in open work design, with plaits and tucks from shoulders, plaits in back from shoulders to waist, buttons in back of black, navy, or red. These were favorite show window items.

Men's suits might be in another section of the same ad or—when the newspaper grew larger—in a second and different ad. These would feature a variety of wool fabrics. As the Great War approached, men's suits took on a highly streamlined appearance, with cutaway coats and semi-straight or peg trousers. So slim were these trousers that farmers joked: "Gotta grease your legs to git 'em on." Ads for these garments boasted permanent creases that wouldn't bag at the knees. Fabrics were preshrunk with "coat fronts and pockets that never sag."

Irma followed the catalogs regularly, and advertised carefully those items that were both in high demand and priced to compete well with Sears, Roebuck, and Co.

As important as clothing was to self-satisfaction of citizens, Inez knew that "fancy duds" should not be the only advertising in the "VM," as the paper became known.

"Ivar," she pronounced one day, "we must advertise groceries, and household goods. Why aren't these grocery men coming to us? That would be big ad pages, and many more ad dollars for us."

Ivar scratched his jaw and suspected he knew the problem.

"Maybe, Inez, it's because our VM goes to only 40 percent of the homes. I hate to say it, but the grocers maybe don't trust us. The need to sell stuff in a hurry. Things like cabbage, celery, rutabagas, oranges, bananas and fresh meat. So they just put up chalk boards, or something like that, in front of their doors."

"So why don't you convince them to advertise?"

Ivar frowned.

"Well, once in a while they ask us to print a pamphlet, or flier, and it would be like nagging if I asked them to buy advertisements, too."

Inez thought about this and worked out a strategy. She simply asked other women whether they would like to see ads in the VM. These women thought it was a good idea and a good number of them acted on Inez' gentle suggestion that they speak to their grocers:

"Wish I'd known you were gittin' cannin' cherries in your store this veek. When will you have fresh oysters? Will you announce them in the Swedish paper?" "Oh, the way we have to watch our pennies, it'd be nice to see your prices in print." "Marie Haugsrud, she said she got some fresh strawberries last week. Wish I knew you were getting some, so I'd know when to come to town."

Soon after, grocery ads were standard fare in the *Veckomonitoren*.

* * *

By mid-1913, circulation growth of the *Veckomonitoren* stagnated at around thirteen hundred, and Ivar and Inez saw signs that it might even drop. Immigration was slowing, children were going to "regular" schools, and immigrants were speaking English at home. The Swedish language was slowly fading from use.

Ivar and Inez tried to promote their newspaper among Swedes who had never subscribed and those who had stopped paying. They wrote down some thirty names from the "unpaid" address cards and started with those residing in Belleville itself. They had no automobile yet and horse-and-buggy rental was too costly. So they walked, to places inside the city limits.

In addition to its retail shops and the Johnston rock and gravel operation, Belleville had a small foundry, a sawmill, a slaughterhouse, and a pickle-canning factory. Most of these businesses were owned and managed by men with English, Scottish, Irish, and a few German names. These managerial people did not read the *Veckomonitoren*, but many of their Scandinavian workers did, or had in the past. One of these was Einart Dahlgren, a meat plant hand who had for some reason stopped paying for his subscription to the Swedish newspaper.

On a dreary March day, Inez decided to visit the Dahlgrens, who were the parents of Andressa Dahlgren, the live-in caretaker of Charlotte Lindfors. This call, Inez reasoned, would have a dual purpose. She could get a feel for what these people thought about the paper and, at the same time, meet Andressa's parents.

Inez walked south of the railroad tracks past the slaughterhouse and foundry, along a narrow, rutted street. She found the Dahlgren home, an aging and unpainted clapboard house, shrouded in its gray patina. Its second story made the building seem too high for its small, almost square, foundation.

A decrepit buggy, one wheel broken and badly mended with wire and nails that split the hard wood, sat in obvious nonuse in front of the house. The buggy only partially obscured a privy in the backyard that yielded a dirty-faced child of six or seven, trying vainly but unsuccessfully to close a door sagging from hinges perilously close to wresting the mounting screws from a rotted doorframe. The gaping doorway exposed an older child still inside the structure and perched on the familiar but foul bench that offered two openings of different sizes.

Gingerly, Inez mounted the small step to the house's single door facing the street, under the outline of an overhang that had long since fallen off, leaving a pyramid of slightly darker wood marked by jagged ends of four rusty nails and two wooden pegs, all broken off in unsuccessful attempts to yank them out. The door, opening slowly, released rank stench begotten from accumulated fried grease, burned pastry, slop pails, and unbathed human bodies. Inez learned that six human beings lived in this cramped and crumbling abode.

The tall, spare and raw-boned frame of a 33-year-old woman in a tattered cotton dress and a soiled apron emerged with the reeking odor. Whether the fetor was of her person or the room was hard for Inez to tell.

"Yah, you'll yust have to excyo-o-se my mess," Vera Dahlgren mumbled uncomfortably. Inez introduced herself as a co-editor of the *Veckomonitoren* and as Andressa's "employer." This was a first meeting. Inez and Ivar had worked out Andressa's arrangement through Pastor Ernest Bjornholm without seeing the parents.

Vera motioned Inez to a hastily wiped and heavily scarred table in the one crowded room that served as kitchen, dining room, and family activity center. "Vell, you see, I don't read Svedish so good," she offered. "Einart, he reads it, or, he use' to. Ven he hass time. He vorks so many hours at the butchering place, don't you know, and he gets paid so little, maybe feefteen or seexteen dollars a veek."

In a mixture of rural Skane Swedish and fractured English, Vera related her tale. Her husband, after five years of schooling in Ystad, left the hopelessness of Sweden and brought Vera and their two children to America. Now, after eleven years in the United States and three more surviving children, he was losing touch with the old country.

Einart Dahlgren worked at the small slaughterhouse with men of different backgrounds, many of whom mocked his singsong speech. Trying to feed and clothe a family of five underclothed and underfed children on such meager income, Einart decided the one-dollar per year subscription to a paper that his fellow workers derided was a needless expense.

And needless to an illiterate Vera. "Vee need more money, don't you see. But how can I go to vork, ven vee keep hafing all dese kids? Maybe I put a board down the bed middle?" Inez did not smile. This was bitterness, not a try at humor.

Vera leaned her jaw on the heel of her upturned left hand, stared idly out a smudged window and added slowly: "Take Bertha, she is four now, vouldn't she like it to go live in a nice place? Like Andressa, who hass it so nice vit you now? Then I could get a yob, and make some money, and then Bertha, she comes back home and vee haf better things for her."

Inez thought that in another ten or eleven years, Bertha would at best be working as a housekeeper and child caretaker, following Andressa's footsteps—that is, if she didn't die from a combination of malnutrition and measles or some other disease. The Dahlgrens' marginal existence differed little from life in the old country.

Inez left the Dahlgren house without making any effort to get the subscription paid. She would keep it on the books; Ivar couldn't possibly object.

Having Vera and Einart Dahlgren's oldest daughter

living in the Lindfors house in what amounted to bondage troubled Inez. Oh, Inez could tell herself that this put Andressa in a warm, clean home where she could eat and dress well. But education? Andressa had not gone to school since she was 11 and did not speak or write English particularly well. She wanted to go to dances and parties, but strict supervision by Ivar and Inez limited those ventures drastically. So what did the future hold, for her, Bertha, and all the other Andressas and Berthas?

First thing, Inez told herself, was to get Andressa into school. Ivar first wondered why, but Inez shot back with unusual vehemence that as things stood, Andressa was a slave to them.

Ivar was incredulous. Did Inez see Andressa as another Fredrika Grinnhaal? He hadn't thought of it that way. Yes, the good of children in poverty was a great cause. This was his credo. But no, the things that occurred in his own family had seemed somehow apart and unconnected with his cause. That's how it had been with Fredrika; that's how it was happening now. That is, until Inez, in her passion, made him see all these things as thoroughly wound together.

\* \* \*

The weekly editions of the *Veckomonitoren* in these years before the Great War featured such headlines as:

700 NEW IMMIGRANTS FROM SWEDEN
ARRIVE IN RECENT MONTHS

———————

LUTHERAN CHURCHES IN MINNESOTA
GAIN IN NUMBERS OF MEMBERS

———————

MRS. GUSTAV NYBORG TELLS
OF RECENT VISIT TO SWEDEN
Spent 6 Months in Stockholm

SCANDINAVIAN LANGUAGES BEING TAUGHT
AT BELLEVILLE'S HIGH SCHOOL
Adds to German in Language Instruction
for Energetic and Culture-minded Pupils

SWEDISH GOVERNMENT RELAXES REQUIREMENT
FOR COMPULSORY MILITARY SERVICE
Readers Ask and Experts Reply

Keeping the flame of Swedish culture alive called for more than current news from the old country. At least two short items each week, depending on scarce space, reminded readers of some favorite old tale, legend, or monarch from Sweden's colorful history. One item told of a runestone in Soedermanland, with an inscription that explains how Sigurd decapitated a dragon and roasted its heart while listening to birds sing. It explained how runic writing often follows from the head of a snake to its tail and must be read in that order.

Another item reminded readers that Sofia of Nassau was queen of both Sweden and Norway from 1872 until Norway went independent, and that the current queen Victoria did not enjoy good health. Still another noted that much of Pomerania was once controlled by the Swedish government, during the "Great Power" era of the nation.

Ivar considered but resisted the idea of doing a story on his Great Ancestor, Anders Lindfors, the printing hero of the Thirty Years War. That might raise questions about more recent ancestors in Graskoping—questions he didn't wish to confront.

There were numerous items about the present, the times and turmoil of the readers and their neighbors. Some would have ordinarily gone under the "Good Morning Judge" heading, but were either innocuous enough, or humorous enough, to run separately:

## Dead Cow Comes Back to Life?

There is one butcher shop manager in Belleville who is sighing with relief these days. It seems he was accused of stealing a prize cow that had been missing for a week from the Sanderberg place. Someone suggested to Mr. Sanderberg to look in the butcher shop one day, and there was a familiar black and white cow's head, except it had been severed from the body and was quite dead.

Mr. Sanderberg said, for sure, that is my cow, and the butcher shop manager was hauled off to the police station and charged with cattle thievery. On the way, someone told him that in the West, this would be called rustling and being guilty would mean being hanged from the nearest oak tree.

Things looked very bad for this manager when he was brought in to court. The jury heard from Mr. Sanderberg, and then found the manager guilty of cow stealing. Would there be a hanging? Just as the verdict was read, a shout was heard at the back of the courtroom. Someone led in a very healthy black and white animal. Mr. Sanderberg leapt up, pointed to it, and said, "My god, that's my cow, alive." A very relieved butcher shop manager decided right then and there to keep a sales slip handy for every animal he slaughters in the future.

The unnamed butcher and slaughterhouse operator was not particularly upset with such publicity, since he was vindicated in court and Sanderberg was the one who looked foolish. Sanderberg didn't say much, since he had spread the story widely—and loudly—and had brought it to the *Veckomonitoren* in the first place.

Another story, however, left a machinery seller angry:

## Farmer Doesn't Have to Pay for Binder

Arthur Strundlin doesn't believe in paying for something that doesn't work. He purchased a new grain binder a year ago, one that seemed to have a very good twine tying mechanism. As any farmer knows, getting bundles tied nice and tight is all-important when harvesting of oats, wheat, barley, or rye.

Unfortunately, this machine never tied bundles well at all, but would scatter grain stalks all over the field. Mr. Strundlin complained to the seller, who tried but failed to get the manufacturer to fix the machine. Mr. Strundlin had to ask his neighbors to help him get his grain ready for threshing.

This past fall the seller demanded the rest of the payment for the binder, which Mr. Strundlin refused to remit. The case ended up in court much to the machinery seller's dismay, since farmer after farmer came in to testify on Mr. Strundlin's behalf that the machine didn't work. "A sorry piece of junk," one witness called it. Mr. Strundlin won his case, without even hiring a lawyer, and the chastised seller was heard to grumble that this was one binder company whose implements he would never sell again. Whether the seller will get his investment back from the company is not known at this time.

The "seller" of the machine that Strundlin bought was a pair of men, Manfred Walster and Geoffrey Blankston, who jointly owned a farm implement business. Neither read the *Veckomonitoren*, and neither was told about the story until a week later. Upset as they were about it, Walster and Blankston wouldn't stop advertising this time—they were going to start selling Buicks in the near future and would want to advertise them in the "Swedish paper." But they told Ivar to never drag them through the papers on this kind of thing again.

* * *

There were some light moments in the life of the *Veckomonitoren*. Every so often some jokester would bring in a rumor, like the one about Erna Hettegren's chickens eating all the seed corn in neighbor Alvord Swenssen's freshly-planted field. Or the one about Oskar Iverson getting so inebriated that his friends dumped him in his buggy on a warm June evening and expected his faithful mare Queenie to take him home. Queenie's homing instinct was said to get so mixed up that Oskar woke up the next morning not at home but in front of his mistress' house.

Ivar or Inez stopped most such stories, but not all.

Then there were the printing shop pranks. One time a part-time helper actually printed up a bogus front page with the headline SIX IMPORTANT BELLEVILLE CITIZENS ARRESTED IN BAUDY HOUSE RAID, and left a folded copy on Ivar's roll-top desk as if it had been printed and sent to the post office. Among the six "accused" were J. B. Higgins, Martin Johnston and Pastor Ray Kurtz. Ivar destroyed it, hoped there were no more copies around, and dismissed the helper.

One ancient prank that Ivar himself practiced on novice workers was the Type Lice Gag. First day on the job, the initiate would be told to watch out for type lice lurking in the storage cases and galleys. "Don't let them get in your hair," the amateur would be told; these infinitesimally small creatures live on lead dust and can be seen only when washed from the lead type with water.

To demonstrate this biological improbability, the printer would tell the neophyte to watch closely as water was poured between two separated galleys, of wide column type. "Get down close, where you can see them," the printer would shout. "See, there they are. Get closer." And when the beginner had his nose about two inches from the galley, the printer would slam the two bodies of lead type together. Water then gushed upward with tremendous force, full in the face of the bamboozled helper. His victim now dripping wet from hair to chest, the printer would guffaw: "Shucks, too bad you missed them. Better luck next time."

* * *

Seeing Vera Dahlgren's plight first hand led Inez to reassess her aversion to discussing the Mother's Pension law being proposed for the Minnesota legislature. It wasn't easy. In her home, the father without any question had looked after his children after her mother died. And, of course, Inez had more or less taken over a mother's role in that household, hadn't she? Kept her siblings fed, clothed, ready for school even when she had to get herself ready? All the while feeling rather scornful toward those women who had children and couldn't keep the fathers of these children at home. So she had grown up as a champion of family self-sufficiency.

Her initial distaste for the Pension law had another, darker basis. Pregnant but unmarried women reminded her uncomfortably of Fredrika Grinnhaal, Ivar's pre-marriage lover. Never could Inez forget that look of hateful derision when Fredrika revealed Charlotte's birth and Ivar's fatherhood. That cackling laughter had humiliated and demeaned a young woman who up to that moment had been a happy bride.

Listening to the wrenching words of Vera Dahlgren, though, put the whole question in a new light for Inez. She had once thought that giving Andressa a job, education, and a home was ample curative for the Dahlgren poverty; she now saw that was not enough. If the unstable Einart were to leave, Vera would be destitute. So a mothers' pension law might be the answer.

Now that she had switched her view, Inez thought about how to recruit others. Yes, she might get one or two persons to write a letter, a practice familiar to editors. "You have to cultivate the garden of public opinion if you are to get any bloomin' ideas," she had heard editors say.

She took her idea to Irma Johnston. Besides knowing fashions, Irma was one of the few Belleville women past 30 with education beyond high school—a year at a normal school in preparation for a teaching career that never materialized. Irma had organized a few Chatauquas and had started a short-lived literary club.

Inez told Irma about her visit to Vera Dahlgren, and what she had read about unfortunate children—without any reference to what she and Ivar called the "Graskoping business." Would Irma arrange a public debate that would explore the Mother's Pension idea, and whether it would be better than orphanages and charity? This was the kind of thing Irma could handle capably if she took a mind to it, given her reputation as an organizer. Neglected children were a concern that clergymen mentioned often. On the other hand, there was some strong feeling, which Irma's husband Martin was known to share, that private charity was a better way to pay for orphanages.

Irma decided this debate would give her an unusual opportunity to go on public display. Exquisitely attired in an expensive dark-brown wool broadcloth suit, tastefully trimmed with genuine beaver fur, she would stand before a panel of government, business, and philanthropic leaders and an audience of notable citizens. Johnston's Clothiers would come out ahead.

So it was settled. Inez told Ivar what she and Irma had lined up. Privately, Ivar admired the idea, but he showed surprise. Wasn't the whole thing—getting behind the Pension Law—his doing?

Inez bristled. "You think you, Ivar, are the only one worried about poor mothers? Please. It is everyone's worry. You wanted it in the paper. Now we get it in the paper. So?"

Exactly 26 persons attended the debate, mostly spouses of the Belleville Commercial Club. Others included a librarian, two social service workers, a civics teacher, and the panel members. Panelists on the "pro" side were the state senator, Alfonse Burkeman, who was talking of sponsoring the Mother's Pension Bill and a social service worker, a woman from Minneapolis, who favored the legislation. On the "anti" side was a well-dressed older man who was executive secretary of a philanthropic Institute that sought contributions from wealthy individuals for private orphanages. There was also a college teacher from Northfield who opposed any and all laws that intruded on the purely private sphere of human life.

Using a tactic she had picked up from a school debate coach years ago, Irma Johnston announced that the proposition to be debated was: "Resolved, that the Mothers' Pension Law would be good for modern society." Each panel member spoke to the issue, either pro or con, and had a chance to rebut other speakers. In the subsequent question session, a doubtful Marilyn Code raised a sour note:

"Isn't this 'pension law' just a cute way for some hussie to collect for kids who are really living with Aunt Hilda?"

Irma handled this deftly and sweetly.

"Oh, you have that delightful way of getting right to the point, Marilyn. What does the law say about that, Senator Burkeman?" And the Senator gave his well-rehearsed view that the law requires full investigation of all claims, that every situation is different and that good judges would make sure the law works.

A local stenographer made a complete transcript of the debate, from which Inez and Ivar extracted a "question and answer" exchange that quoted no person by name but distilled the essence of the discussion. This account appeared in the *Veckomonitoren* with this introduction:

### PROS, CONS OF MOTHERS' PENSIONS
### DEBATED AT BELLEVILLE FORUM

In an unusually inspiring and enlightening debate, four eminently qualified authorities met with a group of Belleville's leading citizens last Friday to discuss the virtues and shortcomings of the proposal to pass a Mothers' Pension law in Minnesota. This law would allow widows and wives with disabled husbands to remain home to rear their offspring instead of being forced to work and leave the children without adult supervision.

This was followed by a series of questions and answers, about how the law works, how judges allot the funds and thereby assure fairness, why charity does not solve the problem alone, and why this pension is not to be a hand-out that makes mothers more dependent and lazy, but instead gives them a measure of self-respect and makes for a better community.

* * *

Since the *Veckomonitoren* report was in Swedish, Ivar thoughtfully printed an English language version and sent it to every boxholder in town. This report elicited a few letters, mostly favoring the law that he published in subsequent editions. Those written in English, he published in English, a decision vociferously protested by Pastor Bjornholm and two other staunch members of the Swedish-American community. Regardless of these objections, the report brought favorable reaction to Ivar when he attended next week's gathering of the Belleville Commercial Club, made up of mostly non-Scandinavian men.

"Good stuff on the mothering law, Ivar," Manfred Walster said. "Course, can't say I favor all this gov'mint help."

"Nice job, Ivar," Ernest Heberamnn added. "Got to keep an eye on some of those people though. You know they'll grab every nickel they can."

Martin Johnston couldn't attend the meeting, but he told Ivar he talked about it with his wife. "Interestin' debate, Ivar. Sorry I couldn't make it, but Irma got all fired up organizing it with Inez. People there said it was most educational. Guess we could trust Judge Branson to hand out pensions fairly, but yuh gotta wonder." Ivar wondered whether Martin and Irma had really discussed the topic at all.

Reggie Code, hardware store owner and husband of Marilyn who had shown some doubts at the debate, was skeptical. "You know, Ivar, you kinda made it look like every question got a good answer. Way I heard it, some tough questions came up that nobody settled. You gonna write up those problems some time?" Ivar thanked Reggie for his interest.

Notwithstanding the mild doubts it raised on Wells Street, the debate accomplished something far more pragmatic. It established the newspaper as credible and responsible according to the prevailing ethos in Belleville. It was promotion of something useful without getting anyone riled up. Ivar felt exhilaration, as might a general who had just won his first battle. He was blind to the fact it was really no contest—that all danger of serious repercussions had evaporated when Inez enlisted the influential Irma Johnston to preside.

Less than a year later, the 1913 Minnesota Legislature passed a Mothers' Pension law, becoming one of the first among a group of states to do so. It was the beginning of what in future decades would become known as laws for Aid to Dependent Children.

Inez read about the law's passage in a Minneapolis newspaper while combing five-year-old Charlotte's hair. She wondered how this law might have affected this child if she had not been married to Ivar when she learned he had a daughter. The thought raised again the nagging old feeling that she was a woman of convenience for Ivar, and she tried hard to push it out of her mind.

* * *

People said Charlotte had her father's blond hair, fully evident at five years of age, and self-confidence that was invariably attributed to Inez. "Even has her mother's dimples and smile," people would say to Inez. Even if she heard them, the frolicking child had no reason to object. Inez was her Mama and that was that.

Inez often mused about the fact that Charlotte was blond, and not brunette like her birth mother, Fredrika. Inez was blond, too, though not quite the same light shade as Ivar, so a dark-haired child would have been quickly labeled as adopted. How convenient, Inez thought. But suppose Charlotte did have dark hair? Things would surely have been different, but Inez quickly put that thought aside.

Charlotte had begun mimicking her Mama as early as age three. By the time she was five, she was using the new Crayolas to color black and white pictures in advertisements—especially pictures of attractive, slender young women sporting the latest fashions.

Inez saw all of this with a mixture of marvel and consternation. She saw in Charlotte many of her own childhood actions—similarities obviously not based on biological linkage. Could it be simple learning of character without Inez realizing what she was transmitting? Should she flatter herself so? Or was it all happenstance? Was Charlotte acting as an infant as Fredrika Grinnhaal would have in comparable situations?

Such thoughts kept Inez in a state of wrenching wonder. She convinced herself that she had accommodated herself well to adoptive motherhood. She even allowed the possibility that her own inability to bear children increased her devotion to this child. Inez could sustain these self-congratulatory thoughts for only so long, after which she would suffer the same old visceral gnawing. Charlotte was, after all, her husband's daughter. She had been entrapped, much as she suppressed the thought, and that entrapment was the acid source of private gnawing that always recurred when her thoughts dwelt on her adopted daughter.

* * *

Shortly after Charlotte's 5th birthday, in 1913, an incident briefly rattled Inez' doubts about her husband's sense of fidelity. It was an evening gathering of the "Wells Street Happy Timers," as the town's elite social group called themselves, at the home of Martin and Irma Johnston. The guests included the social register of Belleville: J. B. Higgins and his wife Carol, who made a rare appearance, sporting an expensive silver fox fur recently acquired in Minneapolis; Dr. Irving Blake and wife Amanda, and four other couples owning Wells street businesses, including Ernst and Maria Hebermann.

Maria, a small and vivacious brunette, was an aggressive flirt. Inez was aware of guarded talk about Maria's alleged but unverified liaisons. Maria had emigrated from Trier in the Mosel Valley at age 15, and retained a slight, and lilting, accent that gave her voice a provocative edge. She was about 12 years younger than Ernst, and had publicly chided him more than once for his "fuddy-duddy" ways.

This evening, she obviously had her eye on Ivar, well dressed as usual and deceivingly athletic in his erect posture and reasonably decent musculature. "Publishing must be so-o-o fascinating." Inez heard Maria breathe to Ivar from disgustingly close range over a tray of cheese, crackers, pickled herring and sliced summer sausage.

Ivar answered in a studied monotone, but then Inez heard how Maria would just lo-o-o-ve to get to know a print shop better. Inez would have listened more, but her friend Irma Johnston at that moment whirled her away to "talk a little business, you know." Carol Higgins' fur piece had given Irma an idea for promoting some arctic fox (really muskrat) fur coats that just might sell to a few well-off people in Belleville, and what did Inez think?

Inez had almost forgotten the incident around the tidbit tray until the following week when Maria appeared at the print shop in a dashing spring outfit. She asked to see Ivar about a possible advertisement for the funeral home business. After learning that Inez usually did the ads, Maria suddenly remembered she had forgotten the slip with the ad's wording.

Maria returned the next day before Inez arrived and gushingly approached Ivar, again, with her intense interest in printing. Not quite an hour later, Inez, on her way to work, met Maria striding ferociously along Oak Street, away from the print shop. Her usually well-done face was wiped clean of powder, rouge, and lipstick, but was oddly lined and on fire with outrage. When she saw Inez, Maria glared and spluttered, "Fine manners that husband of yours has. I never." And she lifted her chin and marched on without another word.

Puzzled, Inez went into the shop and asked Ivar what had happened. Ivar shrugged, saying Maria had a lot of questions about printing and type and so forth. He had explained, he said, how different presses work, how engraving is done, how printing wedding invitations differs from printing newspapers, how one paper stock is different from another. Then, he recalled, Maria had one more question.

"Someone had told her about type lice," he said, "and she wanted to see them. So I showed her." An amused—and relieved—Inez smiled, "Ivar, you are a real printer's devil."

* * *

Bjorn Nygren, or "Bo," as people called him wasn't a bad farmer, just an irritable one.

He was slightly above average in height, stoutly built, and a bit overweight. He had coarse but potentially attractive features, except that his mouth tended to turn down at the corners and accentuate the cynicism that often oozed from his cranky talk. He had smoked, but quit. He had tried Snus, but quit that, too. "Why waste good money on that junk?" he would snort when anyone offered him tobacco to roll or a plug to chew.

His irritation was cultivated since boyhood. As the second born in a large family of Swedish immigrants, by age 14 he was larger than his brother who was a year and a half older and was far more capable around the farm or on the baseball field. Yet his father, he thought, had never appreciated him and was always too busy with the five younger children. Bo's self-sufficiency had distanced him from the family, and he had contempt for them all except his mother—a patient and kindly but overworked woman who never berated him as did his father.

He never got along especially well with other men his own age. He was malcontent, suspicious, and querulous. Yet, somehow, he often had a convincing way of sizing up the politics of Washington and St. Paul in a way that made people listen.

Now, his childless wife Eva, who did little around the farm, irritated him. He compared her unfavorably to his own mother, who could raise children and do hours of farm work besides. And now Eva was nagging him about an embarrassing cattle deal with Albert Theide.

At a cattle auction, Bo had talked Albert out of bidding on some Guernsey heifers, so that Bo could get them for a cheaper price. In return, Bo would sell Albert the calves from these animals later for five dollars apiece—a very good price. Albert hadn't said specifically whether he would go along; he just stayed silent without bidding, and Bo did get the heifers for a bargain.

Trouble began at the Equity stockyards a month later, when Albert asked Bo for the calves and Bo said only two had lived. "Vell, den," Albert said in his carefully preserved accent, " you can yoost show me your other calves and I'll pick the ones I like the best."

Bo had thundered that it was all a joke—that Albert had never really agreed, and a loud argument ensued that almost led to blows. Someone called Sheriff Mayberry to quiet them down. Bo later delivered six calves and Albert paid thirty dollars for them. Bo figured that was the end of it, except that Albert told members of the Equity Co-op a month or so later that three of the calves hadn't been healthy at all. "Why, dey had scours awful bad," Albert said, adding that two died.

A witness to the dispute told his wife, who mentioned it to Eva Nygren, who said it looked for all the world like she had married a fool. She later called Bo a fool right to his face.

Bo later had a problem that would hit his pocketbook harder than the sorry business with the calves. It was the price for wheat—the crop that accounted for more than half his income.

It had been a good growing year; the wheat kernels filled well and the field had few weeds. Bo figured most of it would grade out as Number One. But the buyer at the Belleville elevator had frowned when he reached deep in the wagon box of Nygren wheat, pulling a handful out and letting it spill slowly back into the wagon. "Lotta dead kernels in there, Bo," the elevator man had said with a rueful shake of his head. "Ragweed and other stuff too. If it's all like this, I'd have to grade it down. Number Three, mostly, maybe some of it number Two."

Bo told this individual to kiss his behind, and drove his team and wagon full of wheat to an elevator in Little Falls, an overnight trip. To his dismay, things were even worse here than in Belleville. This elevator operator suggested grading Bo's wheat as low as Number Four.

Now Bo found himself in quite a pickle, because going back to Belleville with the wheat remaining in his wagon would mean more humiliation as well as financial disaster. So he made one more try, at a third elevator near St. Cloud, where he sold all but a few sackfuls of his wheat as Number Three. He barely broke even on the whole-wheat crop, after paying for the seed.

When he took his payment, Bo said to the elevator buyer, partly as accusation and partly as a test, "Hnn-n-yah, you'll probably send this wheat to Minneapolis as Number One and Two, won't yuh?" And the elevator buyer shrugged and said he would ship it straight to his company's terminal elevator at Minneapolis. And, yes, they would put it through a huge fanning meal and get rid of all the dead kernels and weed seeds and, sure, that's an improvement that would upgrade the wheat. "You gotta remember, too," the buyer added, "after they blow out the weeds and dirt, there ain't as much left as I'm paying you for."

Bo saw the potential for corruption in this system but refrained from giving this buyer a real earful. He didn't want to anger the buyer enough to sink the sale in hand, but the whole thing rankled him. On his way home through Belleville, he stopped at the *Veckomonitoren* and asked if Ivar had heard other farmers complain about the way wheat was graded. Ivar said he had heard some talk about this. "Would you write a letter on wheat pricing, for the paper?"

This was exactly the question Bo wanted. He modestly said he didn't write well in Swedish, though he could read it, so Ivar offered to do a translation. The next edition of the *Veckomonitoren* ran the letter, in Swedish:

> If Athena County farmers think they have a beautiful crop that will sell for Number One Durum price, they're in for a real waking up. Take the wheat to any elevator in this county, or maybe go to another county, and you'll get the same business at every one.
>
> You will meet a buyer who shuffles a handful of your nice wheat through his hands and then thinks up a reason—one he's sure you can't argue with—for why it's really only number two or maybe number three or even four. So will the elevator companies sell it for that? Not on your life. They sell it to the flour mills for a higher grade and better price, and this way they pocket a nice profit.
>
> Now think about the prices you pay for things you buy and the prices you get for what you sell. You need flour for baking bread and you ask the grocer what his price is today. Then that's what you pay, or you go without bread.
>
> So what happens when you have the wheat to sell to the elevators and flour mills—the wheat they need to make flour to distribute to grocery stores? Do those elevator folks come to you and ask what you are charging for wheat today? No. Do they ask what you are paying today for groceries? No. The elevators and mills have this crooked business all worked out with the railroads, and it goes against the farmer every time.
>
> You don't need to take just my word for this. Some professors up at North Dakota College in Fargo wrote about it a while ago. The grain buyers are stealing from us in broad daylight.
>
> We've got to do something about this, so farmers can get a fair shake. But first, my friends, we have to wake up to what

is going on. We can't be suckers any longer.
　　—Bjorn Nygren

This time, Bo calculated right. Publicly raising a popular issue did wonders for recovery of his respectability. The letter brought nearly two dozen more in response and Bo knew when he walked around the Equity feed store the next week that this one had hit home. The way wheat prices were set seemed to be the sorest of sore points in the rural townships.

Ivar and Inez Lindfors found that the question of prices for grain and other farm produce was a festering old sore. Prices farmers paid, and prices they received, aroused passions like no other subject, even the weather. This was no parlor-room debate over a Mothers' Pension Law. Here were the seeds of real political war, and therefore lively newspaper writing.

* * *

Eager to ensconce himself on Wells Street, Editor Ivar Lindfors thought he might do some stories on the history of Belleville and Athena County.

He learned quickly that Belleville was largely a railroad creation. Named for a group of French-Canadian immigrants in the 1840s, the town was populated initially by descendants of English families from Pennsylvania and Ohio, along with a few Germans from Chicago and Milwaukee. Belleville languished with a few hundred inhabitants as a lumbering town until 1873, when Martin Johnston's father Henry convinced the railroads to put a line through Belleville and make it a major water and fuel stop. Local timberlands, not yet depleted, and a Mississippi tributary easily bridged, made Belleville a fairly logical choice.

There was more to the deal. Henry Johnston used his influence with a Congressman to get substantial acreage of land granted to the railroad companies. He was also first in line to buy some of that property at a reduced price three years later after its timber was cut off. The land he bought had extensive limestone and granite deposits, making it feasible for Johnston to establish a quarry and rock-crushing operation.

Henry Johnston was careful to arrange railroad benefits for Belleville. The same month of his own purchase (at $10 per acre), the railroad sold a parcel in downtown Belleville to Athena County for the sum of one dollar. On that site in 1892 workers completed the Athena County Courthouse, a magnificent Romanesque Revival structure of rust and sandy-colored limestone and pressed brick—all purchased from the Johnston quarries.

A famous St. Paul architect designed the edifice to have three corner towers—two as turrets and the other square—framing sets of quadruple Roman arches over the south and west entrances facing Wells and Taylor streets, respectively. Through these stately arches would tramp legions of citizens registering their land deeds, paying their property taxes, or facing judges presiding over trials for their alleged crimes or civil entanglements.

Henry Johnston died in 1908. His son Martin inherited the growing store with its expansion partly financed by quarry profits. Martin's brother Maynard took over the quarry business and expanded it through loans from a group of local merchants. Maynard Johnston's crushed rock business was bolstered substantially around 1905 by a contract to sell gravel to both the railroads and to the newly-created Athena County highway department. The Commissioners, without consideration of any other bids and without dissent, approved the contract.

Ivar thought about the Johnston story—and then about Inez' friendship with Irma, Martin Johnston's wife, and all the advertising business from Johnston clothiers.

Ivar abandoned his idea for the Belleville history stories.

# V.  A Rising Prairie Storm

In 1915, after a year of war in Europe, no gathering of sweaty, dust-caked wheat farmers around the Belleville grain elevator and no confab around the watering tanks where sweaty, smelly horses slobbered away their thirst was complete without a chorus of rural voices cursing the price of wheat. And on the heels of that cursing were vows to reform the railroads, Big Biz in Minneapolis and Chicago, and the Crooks in Washington who were blamed for the worsening prices paid to farmers.

When Bo Nygren wrote his letter about the price of wheat, he was speaking to an anger that war could only amplify.

As a newspaperman, Ivar Lindfors knew well of this moral outrage. Not only did he hear the talk around town, he saw it in print—in newspapers that came by train from Minneapolis and other cities. On a warm spring evening, he read one of these papers as he strolled slowly back to the Lindfors bungalow on Canada Street. After his (too brief, in Inez' opinion) play with Charlotte while Andressa helped with the evening meal, he showed Inez the paper.

On the front page was an incisive and biting cartoon. It portrayed "Big Biz" as an overfed, cigar-puffing, fifty-ish man in cutaway coat, black bow tie, striped pants, shiny shoes with white spats, silk top hat, and gold watch chain hanging from a vest over an ample middle. A tag hanging from the vest stated, "Railroad Owner."

"Inez, the same railroad that brings us our bales of paper, the *Minneapolis Tribune*, and everything else—do you know how much farmers around here hate it?"

"Of course I know. How not to know? I walk with Andressa and Charlotte past bunches of farmers. I hear grumbles and bad words between some farmer and the man who runs the elevator. Very bad swear words, about how the railroads and the grain buyers cheat farmers.

"Just listen around church, Ivar. The men, and women too, cuss and cuss the railroads, and what they call 'shysters' in Minneapolis and Chicago. So, yes, you bet I hear."

She then studied the cartoon and chuckled lightly.

"Looks like a fat greedy man. What is called a tycoon."

Then, impishly:

"Ivar, who does he look like?"

Ivar hadn't allowed himself to think that way.

Inez' chuckle diminished to a giggle. She was still smiling about the cartoon when she went to the kitchen, brought back a steaming bowl of gravy-covered roast pork and potatoes, and placed it in front of Ivar. As she motioned seven-year-old Charlotte to the table, she showed the child the cartoon, and asked her who the cartoon figure looked like.

The child looked dully at the picture, then her eyes popped and sparkled with recognition.

"Oh, Mama, someone drew a picture of Mr. Higgins at the bank! "

Inez laughed out loud, and a curious Andressa looked over the child's shoulder to see what the mirth was all about.

Charlotte added, "Papa, are you going to put this picture in our paper?"

Ivar saw this getting out of hand. Remembering his near-adoration of the Swedish reformers, he sympathized with the plight of the farmers. But as a publisher of a modestly successful local newspaper, he had other concerns: His advertisers and his creditors.

"No Charlotte, this is from a Chicago newspaper. It's a cartoon, what they call a symbol. It's a dig at a few business people who aren't honest. Many people think they cheat farmers. Now, none of this goes outside this house. About this picture looking like anyone in town, I mean."

Andressa saw the resemblance, too. She smiled lightly but said nothing. Sensing some rare tension in the Lindfors household, she tried to usher Charlotte out of the room. The child had one more question. "Papa, is it okay if I take that picture to school? Our room just got new Crayolas, and I want to color it for Mrs. Everson. She says I color good."

Ivar's answer was quick but soft. "You mean you color well—well is the correct word. But no, Charlotte, I need that paper to show to some other people at the paper." In truth, he wanted to get it out of sight.

Andressa then, more firmly, walked the child out to the back yard.

Inez was still chuckling but didn't argue. She knew that no matter how rambunctious the editorials against the railroads in other newspapers, the *Veckomonitoren* had not betrayed a word of such complaint—at least up to now. Never had a local newspaper written about the deals of local businessmen to get the railroads or the cheap land given the railroads by Congress. Such talk about the largesse that produced the magnificent Athena County courthouse would have been virtually sacrilegious.

Charlotte, now 7, soon forgot about coloring a picture that looked like the Banker Man. She had heard puzzling talk around school that she wondered about. One afternoon she interrupted Andressa who was helping her with McGuffey's Reader.

"Andressa, where do babies come from?"

Andressa paused. "Aunt" Inez had not told her how to handle this question.

"Have you asked your Mama?"

"No, but I will. Beverly said 'they come from the Mama's 'tumach.' But Angeline, she said 'no, you go to the hospital to buy them.' Do you know?"

"Well, you ask your Mama. Oh, look at this cute little kitten."

"Know what I think, Andressa? I think Beverly was

right. But how does the baby get there?"

"Oh, Charlotte, you really are the berries, aren't you? You'll find out soon enough. Now finish coloring that ribbon on the kitten's neck. No, not green, blue."

Andressa smiled ruefully to herself. In her case, the source of babies became known well before her seventh birthday, because everything the parents did in the Dahlgren household was an open secret. She wished she had been as unsure at that age as Charlotte was now.

*　*　*

Charlotte did exactly what Andressa suggested. When Inez was tucking her in one evening the child asked her question. Not that she was totally naïve—she was clever enough to start with the part she was quite sure was untrue.

"Mama, do people buy babies at the hospital?"

A long pause. *Here it is*, Inez thought, *the big question.*

"No, Charlotte. But go to sleep now. We'll talk about it later. When you are bigger."

"Beverly says they come from the Mama's 'tumach. Mama, did I come from your belly?"

*Oh, my heavens the child doesn't realize that she is asking two questions.* As often as Inez had worried over dealing with the ultimate life puzzle for Charlotte, she had no good, quick answer.

A long pause.

"You see, Charlotte, Beverly was right. Babies do come from the Mama's belly. But let's not talk about that now. Hush, now. Go to sleep. We talk more later."

Charlotte could sense those times when her Mama was tense enough to drop some of her words. Ordinarily, Inez would have said "We will talk more later."

In their own bedroom later, Inez told Ivar about this conversation. Ivar had one question:

"So did you say she came from your belly?"

"Not exactly that way. But that's what she think. Yes,

Ivar, this gets me so worked up I don't talk right."

But Inez, almost a stoic herself, regained her composure and said it bluntly: "Yes, Ivar. I lied to her. Not by what I said. By what I did not say. We are both lying to her. We are letting her think she came from my belly. But some day we will tell her the truth. Ivar, when will that day be?"

* * *

Around Belleville, one heard and read endless uses of a wide range of weather metaphors to explain political things.

"Well, how are the political winds blowing this spring?" "Yah, that caucus thing with the Republicans, some say that was a straw in the wind." "Oh, the storm clouds are rolling over the State House in St. Paul." "War clouds in Europe, you know." "Too bad Teddy Roosevelt's Bullmoose party didn't have enough thunder to win the voters back in 1912." "Yah, that President Taft, he wasn't worth a fart in a whirlwind." "Wilson, he breezed in after Taft and Roosevelt got into that dustup."

Then, on the eve of the Great War, a full-fledged political storm roared across the Northern Prairie with a vehemence threatening to blow away the entire framework of state government. It was many years brewing, hitting the prairie with a thunderclap in 1915. Its surging energy was from the Nonpartisan League of North Dakota, a political organization that in its home state aroused human passions to a fervor not seen in this region since the Civil War.

It either aroused or frightened both the native-born and immigrant. Its target was the entire marketing machine that controlled the way wheat was sold by farmers, bought by elevators and priced as bread, as well as governmental agencies behind the machine. While wheat was the epicenter of the tempest initially, it eventually engulfed other farm markets, including cows, pigs and milk.

* * *

The key figure in the Nonpartisan League was a gifted and charismatic individual born the same year as Ivar and imbued with rather similar political ideals but markedly different notions about how to arouse humans to act in their own interests. His name was Arthur C. Townley, who on a February day in 1915 was going from farm to farm in McHenry County, north of Bismarck, North Dakota. He was launching an organizational drive that would emblazon the Townley name and the Nonpartisan League across the Upper Midwest. It enrolled hundreds of thousands of farm families and upset the politics of several states, including Minnesota, to the east across the Red River. Dubbed the NPL, this League became the target of one of the most remarkable governmental counterattacks on collective action in rural American history.

Townley grew up on a Minnesota farm less than two hours by train from Belleville. He grew tall and lanky, had a prominent nose, dark hair, and had a deep and resonant voice that never quite lost its country timbre. A high school debate coach noted his oratorical talents, how he would look out upon his audience through soft, brown and confident eyes with a manner that bespoke utter sincerity, whether his debate topic was sanitation in meat factories or the ideal credit system for farmers like his parents in Brown's valley.

Shortly after high school graduation, Arthur met three local businessmen—a tailor with socialist leanings, a jeweler enthusiastic about the materialistic philosophy of Herbert Spencer, and a carpenter taken with writings of Ralph Waldo Emerson. Young Arthur Townley met regularly with these three local sages who served as his de facto college faculty.

Arthur taught in a local school for two years but abandoned that career in favor of finding ways to put collective action to work for farmers. He knew that farmers had tried often to organize but had little to show for it, even from the grandest rural insurgency of all time, the National Farmer's Alliance. During the 1870s and 1880s, this aggregation had become part of a populist movement seeking to elect sympathetic members of Congress and a supportive President.

A maturing Arthur Townley dimly recalled the hoopla of 1892, the 12th year of his life, when the Populist Party tried to elect James B. Weaver as U.S. President. This party had pulled in the wheat-belt farmers of the Alliance, the Rocky Mountain groups calling for "free coinage" of silver. The southern wing of the Alliance was as concerned with upholding white supremacy as it was with shoring up market prices.

The Populists excoriated the railroads, telegraph and telephone companies, and wealthy industrialists in general. They called for government ownership of the first three and a graduated income tax on the fourth, along with free coinage of silver. Yet organized as they were, the Populists still lost the 1894 election. They threw in with the Democratic Party and William Jennings Bryan in 1896 and lost again.

When he was 24, in 1904, Arthur and a brother found their way to the gently rolling open prairie of Golden Valley County, next to the Montana border in western North Dakota. They tried wheat farming, but in a modern way. They replaced the horse and mule teams with two mammoth steam-powered tractors that could pull plows big enough to turn 10 or 12 furrows at once. But how could they pay for this equipment?

Collective organization was the answer. Arthur convinced a number of men to form a farming syndicate that would buy the tractors and equipment on credit and do the planting and harvesting in stages. The syndicate members would work as a crew, planting on first one farm, then the next. Harvesting would follow the same schedule.

This scheme worked well the first year. During the second, inevitable problems of group cooperation arose. Who would pay for repairs of a binder that broke down after falling into a rutted ravine on one particular farm? The owner of that field? Or would all repairs be shared equally, regardless of how or where they became necessary? And how would "equal" sharing of costs and work be determined? On a farm, or on an acreage basis? How is a syndicate member compensated if he has less acreage to plant and harvest than on a neighboring farm where he must work as well? What if the weather does more damage on one farm than another—do the rest share the loss? The syndicate fractured over such questions.

Arthur decided to pull out of the syndicate, taking a temporary job plastering homes and office buildings. Those remaining in the syndicate, however, did well the next year. The weather improved, the crop was good, and even though he was now reduced to menial labor, Arthur Townley could tell himself that his first experiment in farmer organization had been a success.

In 1907, he heard of a scientific break-through that would lead to his next and most momentous farming venture. A plant breeder at North Dakota State Agricultural College in Fargo had developed a strain of flax resistant to the wilt fungus that had decimated the crop in previous years. Given the worldwide demand for good linen, flax was an inviting crop if it could be depended upon to grow to maturity. It also had unusual aesthetic appeal; the soft blue color of flax blossoms over a 100-acre field was a sight to behold.

He became so disenchanted with the group approach that Arthur Townley decided to go it alone and make a big plunge. He returned to Golden Valley County, where bankers recalled him favorably for starting the syndicate that had nicely retired its machinery and production debts several years earlier. He bought more steam tractors, plows and harvesting machines on borrowed money and hired a crew to operate them. His first years were so good that people called him the "flax king." Fliers published by the railroad companies exploited the Townley success story to encourage further agricultural development and thus more rail business in this part of the nation.

It was the crop year of 1912 that abruptly dethroned the recently-crowned flax king. Emboldened by his recent successes, Arthur had bought or rented 8,000 acres of land and bought still more machinery on credit, to be paid for out of the earnings from his fall harvest.

Disaster struck from two sources, the first being the vagaries of the weather. Rain was sparse in early summer and snow came early in the fall, frustrating the harvesting crews. The yield was roughly half of what he had expected. Still, at going prices, Arthur figured he would break even and try again next year.

He didn't break even. Instead of prices for flax going up, as growers had good reason to expect in a short crop year, they collapsed. Speculators in the Chicago market, trying to capitalize on the shortage, dealt wildly in flax futures. In the process, they drove the worldwide price down sharply. After getting only a third of the price he had banked on, and for only half a crop, Arthur Townley was $80,000 in debt and bankrupt. A few months earlier, he had been a regional hero. Now he was scorned as a fool, a patsy and a crook.

"Knew all along ol' Townley would go bust. Just a matter of time, before his ways would catch up with him." "Yup, never can trust a man who gets his fingers in so much of other people's money. They say he's going into politics. Ain't surprising. Many a' them politicians is fellows who couldn't make it at honest work."

\* \* \*

The way Arthur Townley saw it, responsibility for his financial disaster rested squarely at the feet of an evil marketing system. He ruminated on his early dialogues with the three elder sages of Alexandria, his readings on Socialistic philosophy, and the woeful history of Populist insurgency. Regardless of the efforts of the late Ignatius Donnelly of Minnesota, or Governor Robert LaFollette of Wisconsin, both of whom had fought politically for tighter government control of the railroads, Townley believed little had changed. The railroad owners, the big city banks, the grain elevators and Minneapolis flour mills, and the commercial system in general were still in charge. As Townley saw it, most farmers were getting crumbs as usual.

This embittered man met with officers of the Socialist Party, which had gained some prominence in North Dakota by working for farmer's causes against the existing system. The party supported state-owned flour mills and elevators and other reforms. It had succeeded in a few local election contests, but its name scared most farmers away.

Arthur worked briefly for the Socialists as an organizer, but left when they realized that he was working for farmers who owned land. To a dyed-in-the-wool socialist, interests of landowners and interests of laborers were simply incompatible. Arthur then moved to the state capitol in Bismarck and, with other discontented farmers, put together his plan for a Nonpartisan League. It was a creative synthesis of older ideas rather than a new vision. At its core was nonpartisan endorsement of sympathetic political candidates regardless of party affiliation.

* * *

Thus, it was that A. C. Townley, as he became known, went from farm to farm in McHenry County, signing up the first members of the Farmer's Nonpartisan Political League of North Dakota. His operational scheme was both simple and effective. An organizer—Townley on this first day, others he trained in later days—would go to a farm with a neighbor who had already joined up. After introductions, the organizer would take over the recruiting job, while the neighbor stood back or even took over the plowing so the farmer could stay and listen.

To join, a farmer would pay $6 a year or, eventually, $16 for two years because the state had a biennial legislature. No cash? Then give the organizer a post-dated check, payable when the farmer's wheat is sold in the fall. With such checks as collateral, the young League bought 10 Ford runabouts, costing just under $400 apiece, to speed up the organizational work across the vast state in time for the upcoming primaries.

Under a dictum of grass-roots politics, the League would recruit only those candidates having no political ambition other than to serve their constituents. This policy had dramatic consequences for a naive but aspiring candidate for office who wrote to the League in its early months asking for endorsement. Rejection he may have anticipated, but he was horrified by what actually happened. His letter was published in a League newspaper under a banner labeling it as a splendid example of just exactly the kind of candidate the League would oppose.

This incident destroyed that man's political career, demonstrated the power of the League, and drew the rabid ire of the existing political and commercial leadership. It earned the League a reputation as both powerful and vindictive, neither of which bothered Arthur Townley or his NPL lieutenants. To them, vindictiveness was an old political tradition that in the past had always gone against the farmer. To turn such a weapon to his advantage was simply overdue as democratic justice.

Thousands of farmers revered the Nonpartisan League as the savior of American agriculture and "little people." Others reviled the League as an unabashed contrivance of Satan and the Bolsheviks that would lead to nothing short of anarchy and destruction of the American Way. Especially for its detractors, the NPL was referred to not with the weather metaphor, which implied natural causes, but as a "Red Flame," meaning Bolshevistic combustion ignited through mischievous human design.

Apart from what he had read in the Minneapolis Journal and occasionally in the *Literary Digest*, Ivar Lindfors had little first-hand knowledge of the Nonpartisan League in its formative months of 1915. Sitting between Minneapolis and the North Dakota border, Belleville was surrounded by mixed farming, as ripe for the League as in the wheat country of North Dakota and northwestern Minnesota. Nevertheless, Athena County would listen carefully to A. C. Townley and his hefty vocabulary of crude rural sayings that swelled the NPL membership.

* * *

As maple and oak trees flaunted their coloration on a September day of 1915, a worried Ivar sat at his cramped roll-top desk inside his shop. A stale odor of Bull Durham tobacco hung over the printing shop. Ivar didn't smoke, but it never occurred to him to prevent his subscribers and advertisers from having their puff when they came to see him. The last visitor had been Helmer Knutson, who thoughtfully rolled his own cigarettes with small papers, licked the edges, twisted each end to keep the short-cut tobacco from falling out, and then licked the whole cigarette before putting one end in this mouth. Helmer had a way of making this personalized cigarette hang tight to his lip while he chattered away. He was still talking this way, cigarette bobbing up and down, as he left.

Ivar blew his nose, because the four cigarettes Helmer had smoked during the past half hour stirred up his allergies. Helmer had spent all that time explaining why he couldn't pay his subscription for another three months, adding to Ivar's tight financial circumstances. Ivar, now back at his roll-top desk, pondered his bills and his slow-to-pay advertisers and 113 overdue subscriptions while Inez checked out the advertisements for the next VM. Seven-year-old Charlotte sat on a high printer's stool near the type galleys, drawing a picture of a bird made of two circles, one for the body and one for the head.

Charlotte was well past the stage of drawing tail feathers, beak, legs, and claws as all straight lines. She had watched with fascination as Inez would write out advertisement copy in a flowery cursive script that was even more delicate than the printed version. She worked with determination on mimicking her "Mama," using pencil and crayon. It was still a child's work, but visitors who watched her were impressed.

"Just you wait, that girl is going to be a good secretary, some day." "Yes, she'll learn dictation well." "Oh, she'll go far, that one." "Well, wait till she gets boys on her mind." "Oh, shush, much too early to think about that. She's just a little squirt." "Yes, but an awful cute one."

"There's someone here," Charlotte announced.

The farmer at the doorway was in his mid-fifties, average in height, adequately muscled, and lightly tanned in a face that was probably protected in the fields by a brim far wider than the short visor of the go-to-town Scotch cap he wore today. The cap hardly covered the heavy clump of prematurely white, but handsome and well-combed hair that flowed almost over his ears and shrouded the top of his broad forehead. His blue cotton shirt was tightly buttoned, not open at the neck as some younger farmers favored. When he opened his dark wool dress coat—unusual for a farmer on a feed haul to town—he revealed a serge suit coat pulled over freshly washed and starched overalls. This mixed attire marked him as a well-to-do country elder.

"Howdydoo," he said. "I'm Leonard Huisby. I farm over in the northeast corner of the county, up towards Bridgeford. I thought I'd drop in and talk some about the Nonpartisan League. You've heard of it?" he asked. He eased his strong frame into the one chair near Ivar's desk, moving his eyes from Ivar to Inez and back to Ivar.

"Oh, we've heard of it," Inez said. "And I'm curious about it. You're a member?"

Leonard studied her briefly and noted her accented but generally correct English, absent the inflections he associated with Scandinavians. She didn't sound at all like Albert Theide, who spoke with a heavy, singsong accent even after living in America for more than two decades.

Inez found Leonard instantly likable. He was direct, he showed common courtesy without fawning, and his hazel eyes under that magnificent crop of whitening hair were capable of dignity, compassion, and spirit. She was pleased to see that unlike Helmer before him, Leonard had no cigarette or cigar in hand and made no motions suggesting that he smoked at all. He did not cast his eyes about looking for a spittoon and his cheeks showed none of the telltale brown streaks, signs of using Snus.

Leonard said "yes," he was a member—officer in fact. He gave Ivar and Inez a brief account of his life story—raised in North Dakota, grew wheat in McHenry County, came to Minnesota to take over his father-in-law's 240-acre farm, and found he liked dairy and hog farming better than wheat.

"What I mean to say," he said, "is that farmers really have a tough time everywhere. There's a war in Europe, big business men are getting rich shipping food over there and what are we getting out of it? Very little, if you ask me.

"The farmer today is the most abused man in America, and up to now he's had no choice. A man in Minneapolis buys a loaf of bread for 11 cents and how much of that goes to the farmer?" He looked questioningly to Inez, then Ivar, neither of whom had any idea.

"Seven or eight cents?" Ivar shrugged.

Leonard's eyes glared, then softened. "Don't I wish he did. Fact is, the farmer gets hardly a cent for that loaf. So who gets the other ten cents? The railroads, the grain elevators, the flour millers in Minneapolis, the bakers. Big Biz, all of them. And why don't we get our fair share? Because farmers have never organized, that's why.

"Now, take the business crowd, they know what organization is. They stick together, well enough to keep the farmer where they want him. They give the farmer no choice but to sell his milk and wheat and eggs and pork for whatever somebody gives him and still pay what they ask for butter and bread and pork chops that they got from other farmers in the first place."

"So what will the Nonpartisan League do about it?" Ivar asked.

Leonard Huisby was emphatic. "This will be the first outfit to really put the farmer in the driver's seat, I tell you. Arthur Townley has this idea—"

"So what about this Townley?" Ivar interrupted. "Isn't he just another politician looking for a good job in Bismarck, or maybe Washington?"

"No," Leonard continued, "Townley promises to never run for any office himself. He is a leader we can trust, and he really knows how to organize. Why, they started organizing last February and we already have thousands of members. Any day now, we are going to have our own daily newspaper published at Fargo.

"I don't mean you people, now, but, well, most newspapers are in the pockets of the bankers and the merchants and the private elevator operators," Leonard said, with hard looks at the two editors. "Some have come over to our side," he added, pulling from his shirt pocket a ragged clipping and handing it to Inez. The clipping, from a weekly northeast of Minot, said:

NONPARTISAN LEAGUE BEING ORGANIZED TO AID
FARMS IN FIGHT AGAINST UNFAIR WHEAT PRICES
Hundreds of Local Farmers Sign up

Finally, the farmers of North Dakota have an organization that will give them the power they have long looked for but never attained in their fight against the unfair grain prices they receive every year. A Nonpartisan Political League for Farmers is being organized by a group of well-known and very reputable local farmers, to present a force with which the grain trust in Minneapolis will have to reckon.

It costs just $6 a year to join, and the organizers will accept a post-dated check from those without cash on hand. Those dues go to an organization that will help us for the first time elect members of the legislature and state government who will finally put the grain market in the hands where it has belonged all the while, the good farm people who give America its wheat.

Big Biz people, watch out. The rural people of North Dakota are finally taking over their government. You have handpicked the governor and the legislature in the past, but you're fired from that job now. We're taking over. We are finally going to have what one of our great Presidents said we deserved. A government of, by and FOR the people.

If you were missed by the organizers and want to join up, ask a neighbor member who has a League flyer. Join us and help make Democracy work in favor of the farmer.

—Albert Clark, Farmer and NPL member

"Like I said, some papers aren't on our side. Here's an example of what these kept papers are saying." Leonard produced a different clipping, this from a paper on the fringe of the Red River Valley of eastern North Dakota. This item viewed the League with alarm:

FARMERS WARNED TO BEWARE
OF HUCKSTER ORGANIZERS
Purported "League" Said to Be
a Scheme to Fleece the Unwary,
Local Authorities Say

In recent weeks, various reports have filtered in to our office about teams of "organizers" visiting farms around the county, asking for a $6 membership for some type of "protective league" that is claimed to be the savior of American farmers. We are told that these money-seekers are making all sorts of wild promises about an organization that will build a state flour mill and elevators, establish a rural credit bank &etc.

It seems to us that these promises are much like the ones that quack medicine and gimmick peddlers use all the time, and we are confident that astute local people will not be taken in.

Our attempts to talk with these organizers have been fruitless, and we take this reticence to be a bad sign of unsavory individuals with devious intentions. No one in a position of authority or leadership in our county has been contacted by these roaming money-grabbers, but all responsible officials advise against giving 1 cent to such a nefarious scheme.

Anyone so contacted is invited to contact the sheriff first and then our offices, so that we may have more details and may continue to warn our readers and fellow-citizens to fend off one more attempt to bilk them of their hard-earned cash.

We have heard all these blue-sky promises before, about state mills and elevators and banks. Knowledgeable leaders assure us that all such notions are hopeless. Don't be a sucker. Show these meddlers your driveway gate and maybe even point to your NO TRESPASSING sign and whistle for your faithful farm dog. A sharp nip in the britches will tell these shysters that the good people of our county don't need any more socialistic bunkum.

"Well, you can see what we're up against with these papers," Leonard said as he folded the clippings back into his shirt pocket. "We've signed up some prominent farmers here in Athena County. People like Jerrold Pflueger, Albert Theide, Arnold Hedlund, and Bjorn Nygren, which brings me right up to my reason for being here. A lot of folks read that letter in your paper last fall from Mister Nygren—the one about how wheat gets graded—and there's a lot of agreement with what he said.

"We want more people to hear about us and see what's going on. You print a paper in Swedish. A lot of our members, and people who ought to be members, are Swedes. So we'd like to get you on our side."

As Ivar and Inez showed some discomfort, Leonard added, "At least, we'd like to get our side printed in your paper."

Ivar was first to answer. "It's our policy to print all sides of these things. Maybe you've seen our 'Readers Ask' section? We invite and print letters, and replies to earlier letters, on everything from tablecloths to turkeys."

"So you will print more letters from our League members?" Leonard asked.

"Certainly," Inez replied, "but if we get a dozen at one time we might not have space for all. Then we pick ones that show different ideas."

Leonard shrugged agreeably. "How about if someone writes a nasty letter about the League?"

"We'll print that, too," Ivar said. "Of course, it's got to be decent and all. But that goes for what we say on both sides."

With a half smile, Leonard asked, "What do you call 'decent?' We've been called shysters, crooks, peddlers, socialists."

"What are you calling the opposition?" Ivar returned.

Leonard grinned. "Oh, greedy tycoons, plutocrats, the grain trust, parasites, market gamblers."

"Not very nice things at all," Inez smiled.

Leonard grinned.

"Any way, sounds like your Swedish newspaper will give us a fair shake. But we need something more. Lots of fliers, posters to put up, pamphlets and things to hand out, all printed in the Swedish language. Would you print them for us?"

Now this was a business proposition, an opening for new work and new income. "Why not?" Ivar said. "Those are things we do well. Pleased to be of service."

So it was agreed. Ivar and Inez could expect letters in Swedish promoting the League, and within weeks, they would receive a sizable order for Scandinavian-language materials. This new business, Ivar reasoned, might justify hiring a youth part-time to operate the creaky Brantjen-Kluge platen press. Well, this was the way a business grew.

After Leonard Huisby left the printing shop, Inez reflected on what had just transpired. The deal, she concluded, was simple journalistic corruption. After Leonard was assured that his followers could see their words in print in the *Veckomonitoren*, he had offered them some printing business. Both editors had happily agreed, and this made her anxious.

"Ivar, did we just sell our souls? I mean, yes, the

Nonpartisan League is a wonderful thing. And we might say so in an editorial. But Leonard Huisby, nice as he is, got his way with us. Then he gave us the printing business. Do Social Democrats do things this way?"

Her bluntness made Ivar wonder whether they had mimicked Anders Lindfors worst impulses of 300 years ago when he sold his propaganda printing services to the highest bidder. Ivar suppressed that troubling trait of his renowned ancestor and turned Inez' question around.

"Social Democrats in Sweden, Inez, would admire Thomas Jefferson. You see, these League people are putting Jefferson's ideas to work. Jefferson feared the big cities and the manufacturing businesses within them. He preferred farming to city commerce. Don't you think that when Leonard Huisby curses 'Big Biz,' he's talking like a true American?"

"So, then, Ivar, we are going to become the voice of the League? We will now be a League paper? Is that what we do now?"

"No Inez. We run an independent newspaper. Leonard Huisby asked if we would print their letters, and we said the same thing to him we would say to anyone—the Belleville Commercial Club, a Church, the Kiwanis."

"We would say that to anyone? How about the Anarchists? Or someone who speaks nice about Bolshevism? Or maybe someone writes a letter about a patent medicine? A medicine that will end a pregnancy?"

"A letter about abortion? Inez, you can't be serious."

She wasn't joking, and Ivar knew it, so he said more slowly, "All right, we don't print just anything. Libel is only part of it. Yes, we both know there are some things that are right to say, and some things that aren't. We can't offend the town."

There was too much in this assertion for Inez to take on with her husband and business partner at this juncture. She wanted to yell that it maybe isn't "the town" they were worried about, but the Hebermanns and the Johnstons and the Higginses. It was the Wells street crowd whose sensibilities governed what was printable or not.

A week after Leonard Huisby visited the newspaper, its front page carried a Swedish translation of the clipping from the North Dakota weekly. The headline appeared under a larger one across the top right three columns of the page, which said, "The Farmer Finally Has a Voice." The North Dakota paper was credited at the end.

* * *

It was later, in spring of 1916, when 8-year-old Charlotte learned that the flag with the white stars and blue background and red and white stripes was apparently not meant for everyone. Ordinarily exuberant, she came home from school one day in a dejected sulk. "Papa," she asked at the supper table, "why are we empty ellers?"

A nonplussed Ivar asked her to repeat the question. Inez listened intently.

"You know. Empty ellers. The kind of people who the flag isn't for. Ones like me who shouldn't look at the flag?"

"Who told you this?"

"Kids at school. Especially Beverly Bridges. And Calvin Brooks—he says the same thing. He pulled my hair, he bent and broke my bandeau."

Still perplexed, Ivar continued: "Why do they say you shouldn't look at the flag?"

"'Cause empty ellers aren't patriotic. They like the Kaiser. Papa, do we love and kiss the Kaiser? Isn't he the king of Germany?"

And then Ivar understood. Wherever the expression originated, "empty eller" was a child's way of saying NPL'er. It was the latest of history's epithets generated by one group of people to brand others who don't conform in the way they look, think, talk—or all three. What they might call Charlotte, if they knew the circumstances of her birth, Ivar feared to imagine.

Inez answered Charlotte's question.

"Charlotte, the letters NPL stand for Nonpartisan League. It's a group of farmers who want better prices for things they sell."

"So we would have to pay more for our milk and carrots? Say, if carrots cost too much, maybe we wouldn't have to buy them."

Instead of arguing economic justice, Inez decided to be playful with her surrogate daughter.

"Oh, if they get too costly, we'll raise them in our garden in the back yard. Next to the peas." To this, the child frowned and tossed her "Mama" a mild pout.

Ivar wondered something else. "Charlotte, what did you do when Calvin pulled your hair?"

Charlotte shrugged. "I socked—I mean I pushed him away and he fell down. I got the better of him and stuck my tongue out at him. It made Beverly giggle."

*Just as I would have done as a child on the island of Oland,* thought Inez. She smiled to herself and then admonished Charlotte to stay away from Beverly and Calvin for a while.

# VI. NEWS, OPINIONS AND YOUNG LOVE

Fall and winter of 1915-16 were, all things considered, a decent time for the Lindfors Publishing Co. at Oak and Wells Streets in Belleville, Minnesota. This was true even if the *Veckomonitoren* was hardly holding its own, at just under a thousand in circulation. Those who watched local business closely—and this accounted for most of the Wells Street merchants—saw increasing quantities of paper and ink jugs either at the depot or being hauled to the printing shop. They also saw farmers picking up bundles of Scandinavian-language pamphlets and fliers.

Mostly, the printed materials were handouts to potential recruits on the farms of Athena County and elsewhere in the region. During these first months of the "NPL contract," as Inez liked to call it, printed output went largely out of town, with few copies left in Belleville. Given their family backgrounds, very few of the Wells Street business people could have read the pamphlets even if they had been readily available. Eventually, they did find out what the Lindfors Publishing Co. was producing, and they weren't particularly happy about it.

Leonard Huisby, the prosperous farmer and NPL organizer who had worked out the deal with Ivar and Inez, left one of the League's Swedish-language pamphlets in the office of Dr. Irving Blake after being treated for a bad gash on his wrist, suffered when he accidentally poked a short ladder through the glass panel in a door. The glass shattered and fell on Leonard's arm, slashing it so badly he feared he might bleed to death before getting to Dr. Blake's office. While the doctor patched him up well, Leonard was so shaken by the experience that he forgot about the pamphlet that fell from his denim jacket.

Dr. Blake didn't know a word of Swedish, but he showed the pamphlet to Myrtle Hedgren, who did the Blake's house cleaning. Myrtle could read just enough of the pamphlet to tell Irving that it was "how the farmers are mad at the business people who don't pay right for grain." And she said there was something about "how farmers were going to set up their own banks and businesses and set their own prices."

When J. B. Higgins came by Dr. Blake's office to see about his ulcer, it occurred to the doctor that this banker could probably read Swedish, and no doubt with more facility than could Myrtle. The name "Higgins" was actually an Ellis Island replacement for "Hansen." The banker was 8 years old when his parents emigrated. Higgins could read the pamphlet all too well, and it enraged him, especially the sentence that said "the bankers and the grain trust and the railroads are in cahoots against the farmer." The bank president had written a loan—and on good terms, too, he assured himself—for a paper spewing out garbage for, of all things, the Townley organization. In 1907, a banker friend of Higgins in North Dakota had been fired for having recommended a loan to Townley. Higgins would not forget that.

Higgins had seen many a newspaper editorial over the past 10 or 15 years that excoriated the "steel trust" or the "railroad trust." Those things never bothered him much, since they were critical of big business in the East, centers of economic power that took advantage of small towns farther west. But when the criticism was of "bankers" in general, that included him.

J.B.'s experiences had also taught him an important lesson about how to work as the number one influential in a place like Belleville: Contain your rage and never use profanity. The "harrumph." may have been a cartoon cliché, but it was a sound to be mastered as the most extreme expression of annoyance. He hoped his color didn't rise too much as he read the pamphlet, because Dr. Irving Blake, while one of the more affable and mild-mannered of the downtown crowd, was very perceptive, and an immoderate outburst here wouldn't do.

So Higgins simply read aloud a translation of some phrases in the pamphlet, enough to give the curious doctor an adequate comprehension. Then he looked up at Irving, harrumphed gruffly, and asked, "Well, what do you think of that?"

"Seems rather strong," the medical man answered, satisfying J.B. that he had handled the translation properly. There would be plenty others on Wells Street who would agree with Dr. Blake's view but in far more vehement terms.

Indeed, Martin Johnston dropped his jaw in shock when told of the pamphlet's contents. "I'm advertising in a newspaper put out by a man who prints this stuff?" Martin told Ethan Kendall and then Reggie Code, who came straight to the bank to see the pamphlet and hear the translation himself. Careful to avoid badmouthing a business person, Higgins said, "Yes, it does seem to have some strong words. But, as you know, I'm Danish and the languages are not exactly the same, so you might want to show it to someone perfectly fluent in Swedish like, say, Pastor Ernest Bjornholm."

Pastor Bjornholm shook his head in dismay. He had already seen the pamphlet, brought to him by a rural parishioner the Sunday before. "Most unfortunate that this sort of thing is being stirred up, and to think that our local publisher who is entrusted with spreading the Lord's word among our Scandinavian brethren is publishing it. It would be so much better if parishioners would bring up their problems in a prayerful way and in concert with responsible leaders."

Wells Street seethed with furious denunciations of the Nonpartisan League, of the pamphlet and, especially, of the traitorous publishers who were either Socialists or dupes who would do anything for a dollar. Most observations from the Wells Street merchants were far more blunt than the views of Pastor Bjornholm.

"Can't have someone getting the farmers all worked up against the business people. Not at all. First thing you know, they'll be coming after us, right here on Wells Street. It's one thing to snipe at the trusts in the East, but this is getting close to home." "Well now, say, just who the blazes is this Ivar? A Red? Doesn't he know what side his bread is buttered on? First we get this Olof Moller who drinks like a fish, then we get this polished Swede who goes way off into socialism." "Beats all how a businessman could turn against his own kind. Where would farmers be without businessmen serving them, in towns like Belleville?"

\* \* \*

One of the noticeable side effects of the Nonpartisan League's rise in 1915 was its popularizing of the automobile. It was a godsend for League organizing, for selling, for hauling, and for human freedom and excitement.

Only a decade earlier, the place to buy flour, barbed wire, tea, and gingham was the place a farmer could reach and return from in a day, by an amiable mare pulling a buggy or a patient team pulling a wooden-wheeled wagon. The automobile stretched the distance and capacity of the haul. With a full gas tank and radiator, the automobile required no watering stop, no rest.

Automotive sales people spiced up their pitches for automobiles: "Motorcars promise you adventure, an expansion of the spirit, a taste of the future, total exhilaration. The muffled explosions from the combustion chambers and the surging response to the throttle enhances your physical and psychic being. Farmers: it brings the town closer to you. Young men: it tells the world what a dashing, masculine person you are; for young lovers, it gives you privacy. Ladies: you can learn to drive and, some day, have your own motorized carriages. Yes, the motorcar gives you a heady feeling of independence and a romantic way of travel."

Auto manufacturers advised their dealers to put boiler plate ads in papers such as the *Veckomonitoren*—ads that recognized these feminine attractions of the automobile. Inez was impressed by the well-sketched pictures of women in flowing hair and blowing scarves, roaring in rakish roadsters around uphill curves and through the bucolic countryside. Few women actually purchased these low-slung roadsters, settling instead for the cheaper and more reliable Ford with higher clearance and better chance of getting through the inevitable mud and ruts that besot virtually all Athena County roads in spring and rainy weather. While the roadster ads attracted some to the showroom, the jalopy was the utility vehicle for most *Veckomonitoren* readers who could afford motor vehicles at all.

As soon as they could, Ivar and Inez bought a Ford—a used 1914 runabout costing $175. Paying $1,200 or more for a Hudson, Buick, Studebaker, or Paige would have to wait.

In those years, Ivar and Inez wrote, when they could find time, essays about the visible world about them—automobiles, train riding, movies, Chatauquas, grain threshing, cyclones, and once even (with great input from Irma Johnston) on women's fashions. These essays were not exactly original, but adapted, or simply lifted, from boilerplate promotional pieces. Many were about the wonders of motorcars.

During a muddy spring, Inez thought it "might be fun" to remember that old-timers believe it is contrary to human nature and God's will to abandon horses for gas buggies.

Having recently acquired a second-hand but serviceable Kodak camera, Inez decided on Easter Sunday of 1915 that a mired Buick and a platoon of young Belleville citizens pushing it out would make a good photo. The vehicle had bogged down near Trinity Lutheran Church.

When Inez reached the mud-bound Buick, Elmer

Gustafson had already hitched up to it with his team of magnificent Percherons. Inez snapped a photo of the straining equines and 10 or 12 cheering young men pushing from the rear. The driver of the car was waving with hearty amusement. It was Bert Allcott, who didn't own the car but had simply leaped behind the wheel when he saw Inez with the camera.

Half-tone printing was an effort. The photograph needed to be sent by train to an engraver in St. Cloud, who returned the engraving just in time for next week's paper. The pleased editors put the picture on the front page, under the headline, in Swedish:

GET A HORSE, SAY MUD-WEARY
CITIZENS TO CAR OWNER

The essay followed in a double column format alongside the picture. The picture was a hit with readers. Dozens wrote or spoke words of amusement, cajolery, or advice on how to deal with such mishaps, often based on their own experiences getting stuck in mud. The reactions produced a number of colorful letters.

A few readers were displeased, however. They included businessmen Roy G. Evans, a lumber dealer, and Manfred Walster and Geoffrey Blankston, who had recently added the Buick automobile dealership to the farm implement business that they jointly owned. Evans was sore because, in the first place, he had loaned the car to a brother-in-law who had driven down the muddy street against Evans' advice.

Furthermore, they all wondered aloud, why should stalwart members of the community, and advertisers in the *Veckomonitoren* be held up to ridicule this way? Walster and Blankston said they couldn't see advertising in a newspaper that was undercutting their product. They'd let it go this time, but don't expect them to be so forgiving in the future.

* * *

Located on Oak Street, perpendicular to Wells, the Veckomonitoren Publishing and Printing Co. did not enjoy pavement, but it did share with other establishments a dilapidated wooden sidewalk that led to Wells Street. That allowed Ivar or Inez to push or pull their four-wheel cart to the Post Office, or to bring paper supplies from the train depot, even when their own street turned into mud after a heavy rain or spring thaw.

This weary boardwalk had another marginal benefit: It was more effective for announcing visitors than the tinkling bells on the entry door of the print shop. Only the stealthiest could maneuver these rickety slats without giving fair warning to Ivar and Inez that they were approaching. So on a day muddier than usual, the clomping of Amos Ferguson announced his arrival for one of his provocative but, usually, welcome discourses with the editors of the *Veckomonitoren.*

Amos was about the same age as Ivar, but quite different in appearance. Short, stocky, with near pugilistic features, sandy-reddish hair that was never combed, he was a respected and feisty history teacher at Belleville High School's "Normal" program for future teachers. He would never pass up a chance to debate with anyone in the newspaper or magazine professions.

Like Ivar and Inez, Amos was fairly new to the area. Unlike them, he was no immigrant. His father was an Illinois cabinet-maker of Scottish ancestry; his mother, Elma, was an 1870 immigrant from Stuttgart and had a brother who had been shot by police in the infamous Haymarket riots of Chicago in 1886.

While he was studying history at the University of Chicago, Amos wrote a paper on those Haymarket riots, including the trial that sent four men to the gallows while others were pardoned by Illinois governor John Altgeld. To Amos, Altgeld was a hero, and the McCormick reaper factory, the *Chicago Tribune* (owned by a relative of the reaper factory owner), and the entire Chicago police force and judicial system were tyrants exploiting underpaid workers.

The autumn after his graduation, Amos married Clopping Nederstrom, daughter of Swedish immigrants in southern Wisconsin. She had by that time changed her name to Clara and studied for two years at a small college there.

The Ferguson's came to Belleville the following year, and Clara's facility with Swedish made her valuable as a correspondent for Ollie, who paid her a miserly wage for helping with the editing. With his grammatical lapses in both languages, he needed the help. She stayed at the paper when Ivar and Inez took over, and the Fergusons became the closest friends that Inez and Ivar would have in Belleville.

Tossing off his Mackinaw jacket and crumpled felt hat, Amos slouched comfortably in the chair Ivar and Inez kept for visitors.

"Read the VM the other day. Saw the thing about farmers finally having a voice."

Ivar nodded. "Seems people are interested."

"It wasn't the kind of thing we usually find in these small town papers. Unless there's more than one paper and they're trying to see who can print the biggest shocker," Amos added.

He paused, then asked, "Have you heard from the Wells street crowd about that piece on farmers having a voice? What are they saying about it?"

Ivar scratched his chin. "Haven't heard much. In fact, hardly any of them read Swedish."

"But they advertise?"

"Yes, they tell us what they want to say, we put it in Swedish words. Clara helps Inez with some of that."

"One of these days, they will find out what you said, and be mad as hell."

Ivar shrugged. "Maybe, maybe not." But he knew better, especially when he recalled J. B. Higgins' vicious hatred for A. C. Townley and the Nonpartisan League.

"What do you say to an advertiser who starts chafing in his underwear over something you had in the paper?" Amos said. "Assuming he knows what it was?"

Ivar shrugged. "Depends on how he asks. Generally, we offer them a chance to have their say, if they wish. Write us a letter, and we'll print it."

A stock answer, as Amos knew.

"Don't you ever tell them it's a free country with a free press, and you'll print whatever you like? That it's all in the U.S. Constitution?"

"I haven't up to now, and, frankly, I'm not sure how far I'd get," Ivar responded. "I'm not sure these people really care all that much about their Constitution, which they should have known about all their lives, more than immigrants like us. We're just trying to get people to see all sides, to think about what's going on."

"Those are good, noble words," Amos said, clapping. "Are you sure you believe what you just said?"

"Why wouldn't I believe it?"

"Because I can't imagine any editor not being for some things and against others."

"If we're for something, we say so in an editorial. But that doesn't keep us from letting people on the other side have their say. Isn't that the way it should be? Get all ideas out on the table? So when people vote, they've heard it all and then make up their minds which name gets the X?"

"Hurrah. You sound like a high school civics teacher."

Ivar was uncomfortable with such cynicism from a friend.

"Ivar, are you trying to be a muckraker, chasing the great American phantom?"

"Phantom? You ask, am I chasing a ghost?"

"Yes—ghost, illusion, call it what you will. Walter Lippmann, a young political scientist out east, wrote a book on American politics. He says, and he may be right, that the muckrakers had their day, and that's past. That the idea of the perfectly pure politician and perfectly honest politician is not very appealing to most Americans."

Warming up somewhat to the debate, Ivar responded, "You say idea. The word needs an 'L' on the end. It's an ideal that we try to reach. Isn't it? If that's your ideal, you'll never reach it. That's why Lippmann is not very encouraging about muckraking. No, the American system works by different sides struggling for advantage. You've heard one side from the NPL and another from Wells Street. Let's say in coming months you air every notion they get, cockeyed or not. Do you really think for a moment that either one of these outfits wants the people to listen carefully to all sides and then make their minds up rationally?"

"Hell, no!" Amos exclaimed. "Each group wants to win, and they go at it by promising more than they can deliver and castigating the other side and anyone who disagrees. Logical argument is never enough. They attack the character of the people on the other side. Now you call that getting all rational arguments heard?"

"You're maybe right about those two groups. But not everyone belongs to one or the other. That's exactly why we need newspapers. So do the people in the middle. They can see what both sides have to say. Then make up their own minds. We drop the ideas in a thousand minds. Yes, we do. But what the thousand minds do, comes out in a thousand ways."

Amos shook his head. "You talk as if the VM is a meeting hall, where a different debate happens each week. That's a fine notion, if the public owns the meeting hall. But, rats, Ivar and Inez, you're no public meeting hall. You're more like a lodge hall, and if I know this town, the Belleville Commercial Club owns the lodge."

"We serve all our readers, not just a few," Ivar said, retreating to his platitudes.

Amos laughed. "Who do you think you're fooling, Ivar? If those people had all been able to read your piece about farmers having their voice, you'd have one hell of a time saying anything more about the NPL."

\* \* \*

Ivar recalled what happened a few months earlier when

he published a letter from Niel Gulbrandson, complaining about the prices of funerals and caskets. Ernst Hebermann, an early investor in the *Veckomonitoren*, had the only funeral parlor in town and was thus the obvious target of the letter, even though he wasn't named.

It didn't take Ernst long to be told about the letter. He stormed into the printing shop and interrupted Ivar who was readying paper for another printing run. He didn't even wait for Ivar to put the paper down or greet him.

"That was a damnable letter you printed from Niel Gulbrandson," Ernst thundered. "Know somethin'? Niel still owes me for his wife's funeral after that car wreck. Seventy-five bucks, no less. And that was a tough job to prepare that body, all busted up from that car accident that killed her. And then her sisters wanted a fancy casket made in Chicago, my reg'lar ones wouldn't do. So I even made a long-distance telephone call. I went to great lengths, I must tell you, Ivar, to do what a family wanted, grieving and all as they were. Niel isn't the only one behind, either. Last year I arranged 81 funerals, and I'm still owed for 25. Ivar, how do you dun a family in mourning? Tell me that, before you print another letter bitching about casket prices."

A chastened Ivar had not apologized for running the letter, but he had made a note to himself to be more careful the next time he got a written gripe about the state of local services.

* * *

Ivar told Amos of the funeral-prices incident, including his own incapacity in responding to Ernst Hebermann.

Hearing this, Amos softened his voice, shifting from challenge to moderate counsel.

"Next time, Ivar, ask him just how much those 25 owe him. All the cost? Or are they paying a certain amount each month? Hell, it may not be unusual for 20 percent to fall behind, especially for a funeral they don't plan on having. So if he says they still owe him, that's not the same as really losing money. Just don't let the Ernst Hebermanns get the best of you."

Ivar agreed with Amos' advice, but then, he had found himself in frank agreement with Ernst's bitter reproach as well. He wondered whether he was, after all, really up to newspaper work. Maybe it would be better if Inez handled such complaints. She had more tact, more poise in spite of her clipped sentences, and, he was loathe to admit, more strength of character.

* * *

By the time Andressa Dahlgren reached her 17th birthday, life had improved greatly over what she recalled from her "baby days." She was startled when her "aunt and uncle," as she called Ivar and Inez, insisted she go to school. She hadn't liked school and had left after the 5th grade. Going back to a 6th grade classroom at age 14 was humiliating, although two or three other students were as old as she was, and from similar home circumstances.

She did improve her reading ability and her grammar. At the end of the first year, she had done well enough to be "moved ahead" to the 8th grade and, in 1914, she began high school in Belleville. She was now, in 1916, a 17-year-old high school freshman, older than most of the silly adolescents in the rooms and absolutely intimidating to the males there. As a result, her contact with people her own age was limited.

Andressa was smaller than average, physically strong, and even athletic in build, although sporting events didn't really interest her. People complimented her often on her soft blond hair. She could almost pass as Charlotte's older sister—or very young mother.

Andressa took pride in her appearance and enjoyed the fact that nowadays she dressed respectably. Gone were the tattered cotton dresses and dirty, ragged sweaters from the Dahlgren home. Irma Johnston had fitted her out with an assortment of ankle-length straight and pleated skirts, a middy blouse with a sailor-type back collar flap, and adult-style waists of cotton, flannel, or wool. She even had a "dress up" blouse of taffeta silk.

Andressa walked proudly in her dark brown winter coat and plaid tam-o-shanter over the blond hair that cascaded from under the cap and over the coat's heavy collar. People would smile when they saw her, and privately comment on "how nice that Dahlgren girl is turning out, living with those editors."

Not all Belleville citizens were so favorable. Einart Dahlgren, Andressa's father, confronted Ivar more than once about why he was keeping "my daughter from seeing or writing to me." Ivar expressed surprise and concern, but Einart growled on.

"What you doing, Ivar, gittin' back at me for not buying your goddam Swede paper? Keepin' that girl away from her family? By rights her wages should go to me, you know that?"

Ivar of course knew that in old Sweden that was precisely the custom: rent the child out, more or less like a workhorse.

"That wasn't the arrangement, Einart," Ivar answered. "Remember what we said? We would see to her clothing, her room and board. And now, she is going to school, which she couldn't do if she had a full-time job somewhere.

"But we are sorry if she isn't writing to her parents," Ivar had added. "Inez and I will speak to her about that."

"Ah-h-h, you won't do nothin'," Einart had answered combatively. "You've got so fired up with that goddam Nonpartisan League, you ain't worried about poor folks right here in town. You think farmers is poor? Horse manure. They's doin' well, better'n poor devils like me who have to stand there in the blood and guts of their damned cows, day after day."

Ivar noticed that Einart's accent was less that of the immigrant Scandinavian and more that of the poor American whose family went back for generations, to Ohio or

Pennsylvania or New York or Massachusetts. Ivar saw more here than hostility to a family who took in a man's destitute daughter. The Einarts of Belleville had taken on the views of their employers and were, therefore, rabidly hostile to the Nonpartisan League.

\* \* \*

Andressa's social life being unexciting, she looked forward to the weekly youth group classes at the Trinity Lutheran Church. She sang in the youth choir and enjoyed it; she had a decent alto voice and could handle harmony well. She did meet more girls her own age here, even a few males, although they were outnumbered in the choir by females, at least two to one.

Her "Aunt" and "Uncle" watched over her as surrogate parents and urged her to be more punctual in writing to her parents. Nonetheless, she slacked off to one letter a month, then one every two or three months and now she hardly wrote at all. One day, walking downtown with Charlotte, she saw her father at some distance entering Graham's meat shop. She quietly steered Charlotte in a different direction.

\* \* \*

During the winter of 1915-16, Ivar and Inez printed an assortment of Nonpartisan League pamphlets, fliers, and signs for posting, whatever Leonard Huisby, or Albert Theide brought in. As winter turned to spring, Albert began insisting the editors come to meetings to "hear the farmers" first hand. "Den you can yoost say in your own vords, from vot you heard vit your own eers and saw vit your own eyss vot t'is means to t' farmers."

Thus it was that Ivar and Inez took Charlotte and Andressa to a meeting of the Nonpartisan League at the Jefferson Township hall, eight miles southeast of Belleville. It was a Saturday afternoon under a warm spring sky, with the familiar oak and elm and cottonwood trees in full leaf. The Lindfors Ford chugged through a winding road decorated along the ditches and banks with white trilliums, cowslips, and the early shoots of a multitude of grasses and weeds.

Only the adults went inside to the meeting, where an NPL organizer from St. Paul thumped his fist on law books.

"Here, my friends, is the legal basis for bringing a stop to the crooked grain buying at elevators. Laws don't work by themselves. Farmers have got to organize. And get their neighbors to join in. Look up and down your neighborhood. You see someone who hasn't joined up, get him in. Twist his arm."

After this exhortation, Ivar Lindfors took the floor and asked what NPL members thought about their news in the *Veckomonitoren*. Eva Nygren slowly stood up, her hands finding their comfortable, familiar spots on her hips. It was a stance that "meant business." As blunt as her husband, she spoke loudly and clearly.

"Ivar and Inez, quit wasting print and paper on recipes. We know all we want about apple puddings and casseroles and devils food cakes. The farm magazines are full of that. Tell us how the farm wife can get her share. This ain't just an outfit for men, you know."

Murmurs followed. Some were aghast, even though plain talk was nothing new for Eva. Leonard Huisby didn't move a muscle. Bo Nygren, Eva's husband, nodded imperceptibly. Marie Pflueger silently but distinctly nodded agreement. Jerrold Pflueger simply stared at the floor. Inez stood and said the *Veckomonitoren* editors would give that suggestion some real thought.

The meeting turned to other matters.

On the playground swings behind the town hall and within odor range of the privies, Andressa met Rudolph Pflueger, a farm lad about her own age and well-browned even in mid-spring. Unlike older men, Rudy rolled his sleeves up to expose his entire arms. The conversation was tentative and restrained.

"Bet you don't know me."

"Betcha I do. You're Andressa Dahlgren—work for the editors of the Swedish paper."

"They call me Andy," Andressa said, a statement technically correct although "they" meant two or three other girls she knew.

"Andy, now that's a boy's name."

"Isn't really. It's a nickname. You can call me Andy," she said.

He said nothing. He didn't like calling a girl Andy any more than he liked his own name of Rudy. Rudolph either, for that matter.

"Why aren't you in the meeting?" she asked.

"Pa's in there. He can have it," Rudy answered. He wasn't impressed with the Nonpartisan League. His respected uncle over in the next county talked against it. Besides, he was trying to get close to Marjorie Kiefer, whose parents lived in Belleville and said disparaging things about the League. He feared his parents' choice of farm clubs might hurt his social life."

Andressa looked him over. "Bet I know something about you."

Eight-year-old Charlotte was on the next swing, not missing a word.

Rudy feigned a look of dismay. "Aw, you don't know anything about me."

"Bet I do."

"Betchoo don't."

"I saw you talking to Marjorie Kiefer last week."

"You di'n't neither."

"Oh, yes, I did. On the steps of the church."

"How could you uv seen that? You don't go to our church."

"You go to the German Lutheran Church. I was walking past, with my aunt and uncle, to the Swedish Lutheran Church." This was the local designation; the official names of First Lutheran and Trinity Lutheran, respectively, were rarely used.

"Aw, come on, you didn't really see anything."

"Oh, yes, I did, and it looked like you two were awfully good friends."

That was just exactly the impression Rudy had wanted people to gather, except Marjorie wasn't doing as much as he hoped she would to make that impression credible.

"Oh, sure, I see her some times—at church, mostly," Rudy said with as much nonchalance as he could muster. "She's going to go to Normal school," he said. "She's not a working girl."

Andressa regarded him steadily, wondering how to respond to the obvious slight.

"Do you go to high school?" she asked.

"Not any more. Took too much time; too hard to get there. Rode with the cream truck a few times, but never got there in time," Rudy explained.

"Hard to get home, then, 'cause the cream truck only goes on the route once a day. Too far to walk and no place to keep a horse." He added that he hoped to go down to the University of Minnesota next winter and stay in a dormitory and go to a special winter school for farm boys.

Andressa wondered how all this would help him snare Marjorie, who was known as a "town girl," through and through.

"You want to be a farmer?" Andressa asked.

"Maybe, Pa and Ma want me to take over the farm. Not a bad place, neither."

Andressa twisted slowly in the swing, her left hand grasping the chain above her blond hair and its wide white ribbon, her right hand on the swing board, against her skirted thigh. The point of her button shoe traced lazily in the dirt.

"Not sure I'd want to be a farmer," she said slowly, looking away.

"Town girls usually don't," Rudy answered. "Then, I ain't sure I want to, neither. It can be fun though. Outside a lot, ride horses, play horseshoes, go hunting, fish in the creek."

"You have any brothers or sisters?" she asked.

"Just a sister. Sarah, she's 11," Rudy answered.

Charlotte suddenly announced she "had to ask Mama something" and ran into the Town Hall. Andressa watched her go, then looked back at Rudy and asked: "I bet you and Marjorie kiss a lot, don't you?"

Rudy went red from the sudden and direct question. He took it with delight as assuming the answer, not realizing Andressa suspected the truth. He hadn't gotten that far with Marjorie.

"What you wanna know that for?"

Andressa felt mischievous. "Does she kiss good?"

"Now wouldn't you just like to know that?" Rudy didn't mind the way this was going, now.

Andressa turned and saw Charlotte running back toward the swing.

"Mama says you lovebirds gotta break up now, because we have to go," Charlotte announced authoritatively.

To Rudy, Andressa seemed a more promising companion at the moment than did Marjorie Kiefer. Andressa didn't seem as much of a town girl as Marjorie. Dressed smart, all right, but more down to earth, he thought. Marjorie wouldn't have talked that way. Kept her chin more in the air, Marjorie did. Rudy couldn't get over Marjorie's chin, the full lips above them and the dark eyes.

Rudy made some effort to see Andressa more in the next few weeks, when he wasn't working on his preferred relationship with Marjorie. He even danced a one-step with Andressa at the Starlight Pavilion one night. Her "aunt" and "uncle" were there, but this time he had his first genuine touch with a young female, a touch so far denied by Marjorie. Thighs brushed briefly but warmly and firmly as Rudy and Andressa danced. He held her hand during a half-hour conversation under a portico of the dance hall and they shared a kiss that promised more.

Now feeling increasingly familiar, Rudy complimented

Andressa on her soft blond hair.

"You like it this way?" she asked, touching a strand under her left ear. "It didn't used to be this long. Pa always wanted it cut short, like this. Square across, too." She demonstrated by pulling the strand with her left hand and making a scissors with the index and forefinger of her right. That length would have almost fully exposed her ears.

"Why would your Pa want that?" Rudy thought of how both his parents admired his younger sister's long hair.

"Oh, I suppose to keep me from boys. Or maybe he wanted me to look like one." She shrugged, then looked at Rudy.

"You see Marjorie Kiefer this week?"

Rudy resisted the temptation to make it another guessing game. "Not really; she wasn't at Church for choir practice."

"You sing in the choir?"

"Sometimes." And only because it gets me near Marjorie, he thought to himself.

Andressa startled him. "Rudy, you and Marjorie, you ever done it?"

Rudy noted again how his real or imagined association with Marjorie was paying dividends with Andressa.

"Done what?"

"Oh, you know. Like married people."

"I ain't tellin'."

Andressa looked at him, then turned, and continued the slow stroll.

"How about you," an emboldened Rudy asked. "You done it?"

"Not with any boy. I—I mean, not with anyone, really."

She lost all traces of coquetry and her face was serious.

"Not that I don't know what it's about. I grew up in a small house. Ma and Pa walk around naked a lot. Yes, they do, you might not believe it. You can hear everything that goes on there. Even see a lot of it.

"One time my Pa came in to the upstairs bedroom when

my sister wasn't there. Ma was sick downstairs with the flu. He sat on the bed for no good reason, put a hand on me where he shouldn't. Oh, nothing happened. I yelled to Ma, pretending to answer her calling for me. She wasn't really, but it got me out of there. I hated that house."

Rudy was dumfounded. Such things in his own household he could not imagine.

She continued. "You don't know how glad I was when the minister came by, said I had a chance to go live with the new editors. I'll never go back home. Not as long as Pa's there."

Charlotte saw the couple walking into the clearing and ran toward them. This conversation was over.

* * *

On a Sunday in late May, Rudy and Andressa both appeared, again with their families, at an NPL picnic in the county park in Wilshire Township. This time, the two managed to slip away without Charlotte for a long walk deep through the woods on the park's eastern side. They crossed a boundary fence into the large woodlot of an adjacent farm. They kissed, and sank to the soft grass under an umbrella of sumacs that shaded them in total seclusion.

Rudy remembered being badgered by lascivious men, including an older one who had seen him dance with Andressa. "Thing to do, Rudy," the older lecher said, "is get your hand right up under those bloomers." Rudy was uncertain whether that was advice or mischief; his one attempt to become physically familiar with a girl, back in grade school, had earned him a slap across the face.

Andressa seemed genuinely impassioned and eager, a reaction that aroused in Rudy a feeling of mild scorn. If she were going to be that easy, he would oblige, but not because of any particular fondness for her. Marjorie, he thought, maybe I can learn something here. He made a clumsy attempt at Andressa's billowy cotton dress, uncertain how to proceed, when she said calmly, "Here, I'll help you" and removed her undergarments.

Now completely bold, Rudy ran his husky hands over the softness of a young woman's body in ways he had only before imagined. His entrance required help from both partners. They were equally inexperienced.

This intimacy under the sumacs was the first for both, physically conclusive for Rudy and both painful and disappointing for Andressa. She had heard older girls say, "Once you done it, there ain't nothin' to it," and that's exactly how she felt about it. One girl had told Andressa that "a real lady's man" could "give a girl a great thrill," but it was obvious that Rudy wasn't that kind of man.

Worse, Andressa hadn't thought about what Aunt Inez had told her about biological cycles, and she wondered now whether she was pregnant.

Meanwhile, a terrified Inez, deep in chatter with others at the picnic, realized too late that Andressa hadn't been around for an hour.

"Charlotte, have you seen Andressa?" Inez asked, worriedly.

"Well, Mama, see them now, walking back from the woods? Mama, they really are a pair of lovebirds, aren't they?"

* * *

Rudy Pflueger couldn't resist the temptation to brag about his first conquest. He first let it be known to a youth he hardly knew, and then told his closer friend Will Hoffmann—slightly older and more experienced than Rudy. Will was direct, on the crucial question.

"So did you put it all right in her? Get her pregnant?"

"Yeah, I did, but there's nothin' to worry about, way I see it. It was her first time, and women don't get pregnant until they've done it more."

Will was dumfounded.

"Where the hell did you hear that? She's been menstr'ating, ain't she? Once she is, she can get pregnant anytime."

Rudy felt the color drain from his head. It wasn't the first time he had acted on misinformation. The older lecher who had advised him on getting his way hadn't warned him about this. But then, Rudy challenged Will.

"You've been with many women, and you ain't married. Any of them ever get pregnant?"

Will's answer was quick and crass.

"Nope, never. You see, Rudy, I've got the perfect way. When we get too feverish, I leap out of the old Ford, crank it up, and take the girl home."

\* \* \*

Rudy's loose talk about his conquest filtered back within a few days to Andressa herself. She was furious. She thought they had tried to have a tender moment, and now she finds he was just using her. *What a lout. He hadn't even called her Andy, the way she asked.*

The male grapevine was even quicker, taking less than 48 hours to reach Bert Allcott, the handsome but truculent son of a prominent clothing store merchant in Belleville. The gossip amused Bert, because it signaled opportunity. He couldn't pass up a chance to move in on the romantic ties of other fellows less capable than he around women.

Medium in height, broad and well-muscled, Bert had been a promising fullback on the Belleville High School football team. He might have been a statewide star, except for his proclivity for finding beer and girlfriends on weekday evenings, though not necessarily in that order, and missing practice.

Andressa went to the dance hall with Ivar and Inez less than a week later, and this time Charlotte chose to stay close to Inez. Rudy was not there, to Andressa's relief. One who did appear was Bert Allcott, who asked Andressa to dance. They made arrangements to meet the next day and did, for an afternoon stroll, while Charlotte was at a friend's house and both Ivar and Inez were at the printing shop.

The stroll ended in a livery station hay shed just off Wells Street. This time, intimacy was much more satisfying for Andressa, partly because it was silent vengeance against Rudy's crassness and partly because of Bert's expertise. For Bert himself, it was a way to add luster to his Don Juan image and to humiliate Rudy, who learned as quickly about this liaison as Bert had learned about the first.

Andressa later found herself pregnant. She cornered Bert with this fact late one afternoon near the city park. He grinned and more or less called her a whore.

"You've been sleeping around. Could be anyone, like Rudy Pflueger, for instance, couldn't it?" While the first was untrue, Andressa couldn't deny the second possibility. She had no interest in Rudy, now convinced that his attraction to her was merely physical. She chose to persist with Bert.

"That's a mean way to talk. You did it with me like you really liked me."

"Say, look, you little bibbaloo. You just wanted a good roll in the hay, and I gave you one. So you hadn't thought about getting caught. That's a worry for you, I'd say."

"No, it's your worry, too. I've got your baby in here." She pointed to her middle and paused, biting a lower lip. "I'm gonna talk to your pa. That'd be a nice mess, wouldn't it, big storeowner in Belleville, has a son gets a girl pregnant. I'll tell him I'm taking you to court. That his wonderful son got a girl in trouble and he's going to get sent down the road."

Bert laughed. "You go right ahead and tell my Pa. And you know something? You wouldn't be the first filly I been with, who went crying to him about getting knocked up. And you know what he'll do? Soon's you mention court, he'll just ask me if I can find five or six other guys on the football team willing to tell a judge they got up inside your bloomers. And I'll say, sure, that's easy. I got lots of good friends." He laughed insolently again.

A devastated Andressa turned and left. It had started out to be an exhilarating summer of new, first, experiences. Now, in late June of 1916. she was pregnant after her first two intimacies, each with a different young man. As she started back toward the Lindfors bungalow, she saw Rudy Pflueger's father, Jerrold, walking to the Lindfors printing shop. With relief, she saw he was alone. Rudy was the last person she wanted to see.

# VII. A Barn Burns

$J$errold Pflueger was pleased to pay in advance his year's subscription to the *Veckomonitoren*. "I don't read Swedish so good," he admitted to Ivar, "but my Marie, she's a good reader, went to school over there before coming to Minnesota with her folks."

Saying goodbye to Ivar, Jerrold walked out to his light buggy where the faithful little sorrel gelding stood untethered, climbed in the seat, took the reins with a click from the corner of his mouth, and began the hour and a half trip to his 240-acre farm.

After passing through a swampy lowland, then a few miles of low rolling hills of white and burr oaks, Jerrold saw ahead, with satisfaction, the stubble of a field of well-cured hay that he had put in his barn the previous day. The loft, or "mow" in the sturdy barn was amply packed with roughage for his 21 dairy cows, three heavyweight Belgian draft horses, and the small sorrel.

Jerrold was content, fulfilled, in complete harmony with his land. Where else could all the modalities of sound, sight and scent bring the surroundings directly to one's being? What could compare with the fresh aroma that every morning's dew transmutes into that mildly sweet, soft and spicy fragrance of half-grown legumes?

There were some imperfections in Jerrold's blissful world. His son Rudy was now 18 and going through that problematic and belligerent phase, coping with the energy that the young both relish and fear and that the old have sought from time immemorial to restrain and channel.

That Rudy, Jerrold mused to himself, never did like his name. *Didn't like it as Rudolph, neither. Ain't thankful for what he's got. Don't like chores, the work that has to be done.*

Jerrold shook his head ruefully. Like he had told Marie just the other day, "This boy—he's always talking 'modernizing.' He wants a milking machine, Marie, even a tractor. Now you and I both know we're gonna get them things, but all in good time. Rudy's just too impatient."

Marie in her quiet way had agreed but added a sharp warning. "Better watch out, Jerrold. Rudy's even talked of leaving farming for good. You ain't heard that talk from him? Well, you will. Sure, he thinks about the building trades, or steam-fitting or even automobile stuff, down there in Minneapolis. Yes, I'd like an electric icebox, maybe even a washing machine. I guess I'd hold off, though, if it meant fixing the farm up to keep Rudy here."

Jerrold was conciliatory. "Well, maybe we should work him in more, get him to think like a real farmer. Get his ideas how much seed to buy, fertilizer, which cow to sell."

Marie had agreed quickly. "Yes, Jerrold, I been telling you that all along. Else that boy's going to up and leave. Better start doing things fifty-fifty with him, if you ask me."

Jerrold had another worry so common in farm country: prices—that he was paid, and that he had to pay. While he had just gone through some good years, he knew well the caprices of economic times, and what farmers said about them. And what Arthur Townley said should be done about them.

Jerrold was in doubts about the NPL. His father had shaken his head in disgust at the failures of the Farmer's Alliance in the 1880s and vowed never to listen to another organizer.

Jerrold, for sheer sociability, kept in close touch with other farmers. So when the talk at the feed mill and the town hall suppers this spring swung strongly in favor of the Nonpartisan League, Jerrold decided to go to a few meetings. As a successful and literate farmer, he was immediately elected secretary of the Athena County NPL, a post he fulfilled with the same quiet efficiency he applied to his farm.

As Jerrold pulled into his wide front yard, Rudy ran to help him unhitch the branded sorrel. "Mustard is prob'ly all tuckered out from your trip to town," Rudy said. "But Sarah wants a little ride on him, so I'll unharness and saddle him."

Never thought it wise to make a plaything out of a workhorse, Jerrold mused. He'd try to discourage Rudy from that, if it weren't that his daughter Sarah liked riding so much. Dang, she's cute on that animal, knows how to handle him, too. Besides, other habits of Rudy were in more urgent need of changing. "Rudy don't feed the cattle or the horses right," Jerrold had said to Marie. "He don't see when animals is ailing. Can't seem to notice the cow that's off her feed. Never checks the horses, even Mustard, for spavins and lameness. Can't even tell when the horses need a rest."

The latter point led Jerrold to chuckle to himself. "Maybe a good thing Rudy has that lazy streak. At least when he wants a rest from plowing, the horses get one, too."

To Jerrold's mind, Rudy cut too many corners. A week or so before putting up the 15 acres of hay, Rudy and Sarah hauled in hay from a 4-acre field south of the creek before it was really dry enough. "Probably going to mold some," Jerrold said to Marie. At the worst—a terrible thought went through Jerrold—wet hay can heat in the center to the point of igniting.

"That spontaneous combustion," Jerrold said, "don't happen often but you hear of it every once in a while, 'specially among careless people."

Pulling his thoughts back to the present, Jerrold noted the clouds gathering in the western sky. Probably get a good soaker, tonight, lots of thunder and lightning. "Donnervetter," his father had called it. All the more pleasing to have all the hay in, none left out to get wet and ruined.

* * *

Crossing the front yard and entering the barn, Jerrold walked through the empty stanchion area. He quickly dropped ground feed in mangers, then walked to the west end and opened both halves of the wooden plank door into the milk house. The slake lime whitened the insides of the stone and sand mortar walls above the deepset concrete cooling tank and the cream separator. Fresh, cool water, pumped with a McCormick-Deering gasoline engine, gushed through the tank almost constantly from milking time until the butter plant truck came by in late morning to pick up the cans of rich cream. This cooling system was a source of pride to Jerrold, and he enjoyed explaining it to visitors.

Over the door, just inside the milk house, was Jerrold's collection of more than 130 arrowheads, spearheads, axe heads and grinding tools he had picked up over the years, mostly from plowing or springtoothing.

"See, that's the nice thing about horse farming," Jerrold would tell visitors. "Keeps you right there next to the ground where you can see things like that. Riding a tractor, you'd hardly ever find an arrowhead. Too much iron in front of you, and you get distracted by all the noise."

For nearly every human-trimmed stone piece he discovered, Jerrold invented a scenario about how it got there. Sarah loved this yarn:

"One day many years ago a 12-year-old boy was worried about his sick sister. His mother said food was short; there was no meat to give the little girl strength. So the boy said 'I will get her some fresh meat.' He took his bow and four arrows from the lodge and walked across these fields. He sneaked up on some grouse in the alders, aimed and shot an arrow. It missed. He shot a second one and got a grouse, which he took home for his mother to cook for his sick sister, who felt much better after the good meal. He couldn't find the arrow that missed, and it stayed where it landed for, maybe, three or four hundred years, until I found it today."

At this point, Jerrold would reach into his shirt pocket, bring out the small flint arrowhead and show it to Sarah, who would beam appreciatively, then frown and ask if the little girl really got better. And how long did she live?

The story had a few variations, some of which the children might question. If the new find was a spearhead or, far more rarely, an axe head, Jerrold modified his yarn accordingly while always keeping the touch of humans helping humans. The axe was for building lodges; the spearhead for hunting larger game. Rudy, preferring a more adventurous explanation in his earlier years, often wondered whether the arrow or spearhead mightn't have been lost in a battle between opposing braves, or maybe in an attack on white settlers.

Visitors to the Pflueger farm, young and old, rarely failed to inspect the neatly arranged rows of artifacts on the milk house wall.

One time Charles Waiting Bear from Mille Lacs visited the Pflueger farm and Jerrold told Charles the kind of yarns he had told the children. "You think it might have happened that way?" he had asked. Thoughtfully and patiently, Charles had answered, "Could be, you notice most of them are chipped?"

Jerrold had said "yes, and couldn't that be from rolling around in the fields over the years?"

"Maybe once in a while, but most good ones keep their points. More likely, Mr. Pflueger, what you have been collecting are ones the arrow craftsmen threw away, because they were broken while being chipped down. I hate to say this, but you maybe found the discards."

"The ones they threw away?"

"Quite possibly. Your field might be on a centuries-old village," Charles said. "You may have the junk pile of the arrow-makers and tool-makers, who had so much pride in their work they wouldn't make an arrow, spear or axe with a stone that didn't come out just right."

Jerrold reflected on this alternate interpretation. But rather than feeling deflated, he decided that farming the site of a centuries-old village would give new dimensions to his yarns. It eventually got around—quite erroneously but with no serious denials from Jerrold—that Charles Waiting Bear had more or less authenticated Jerrold's arrowhead stories. The fame of the collection in the Pflueger milk house was spread, and when acquaintances saw Jerrold in town they would respectfully tell their children, "This here's the arrowhead man."

* * *

The clouds in the western sky now darkened threateningly, unnerving the cattle. It was near milking time anyway, so Jerrold shouted to Rudy to let the restless animals in the barn. All Rudy had to do was open the doors; the cattle were trained to go to their own stanchions anyway, and the menacing storm impelled them in with urgency. To farm beasts generally, the barn was the haven in times of turbulence, storm or other misfortune. If hordes of biting flies or bees were bothering cattle or horses, they would stampede to the barn and its sheltered safety.

The animals now safely in the barn, the Pflueger family gathered for supper, which customarily was eaten before milking. Marie Pflueger served her family typical summer evening fare—boiled potatoes, canned roast pork, gravy, garden-fresh peas and string beans and greens. A methodical, punctual woman, Marie Nilsson Pflueger appreciated her husband and family in a taciturn way.

Marrying someone with German background was not all that unusual even for first generation Scandinavian immigrants, and, besides, Jerrold and her father Lars got on well. At one especially festive occasion, Lars had taught Jerrold some phrases from the Swedish national anthem, sung with background melody—or cacophony, depending upon the judgment of the audience—from the nyckelharpa, a box-like instrument with eight keys and a complicated set of strings that were never really in tune. Strumming this medieval musical contraption, which his father had obtained somewhere in Darnaland, Lars would repeat endlessly the words "Ja, jag vill leva, jag vill do i Norden," which meant "I will live, I will die in Scandinavia." A jovial and slightly more Americanized Jerrold had reciprocated by teaching Lars the analogous lines from "Dixie" that commit the singer to living and dying south of the Mason-Dixon line in the USA.

The usual meal-time chatter from the Pflueger children this hot summer evening was pre-empted by the thunder and lightning from a sky nearly dark at 5:30 p.m. "Well, we're getting a real soaker tonight." The words were lost in a crescendo of thundering crashes and simultaneous flashes of lightning.

It was Sarah who screamed.

"Pa, the barn."

All were on their feet at once, momentarily transfixed by the flames gushing from the hay loft door on the east end of the barn.

"Lightning." Jerrold cried. "We gotta get the cows out."

He dashed out the door, across the yard, and into the barn where he ran in front of the cows, opening stanchions as he passed. "Out, out," he shouted, the same command that daily sent the cows out into the yard after milking and feeding, a command they regularly obeyed.

But not this evening. For one thing, they hadn't been milked yet and they were conditioned to stay put until that chore was complete and they felt the relief from pressure in their udders. Even more important, smoke was rolling into the stanchion area. This was a crisis, when the barn was sanctuary not to be abandoned. So the greater the smoke and calamity amid the continuing thunder and blinding lightning crashing against the row of barn windows and reflecting violently off the whitewashed walls, the more each animal clung to its snug and protective shelter, bawling loudly, disconcerted, confused.

Jerrold was nearing panic. He thought of the rope used to lead recalcitrant calves and young bulls. *Yes, that's it, the rope. I will lead them out. But where is the rope? Ah yes, it is on the east end of the barn, near the horse stalls. But which way? Ah, it must be this way.*

In the thickening and strangling smoke, Jerrold groped along the feeding mangers seeking the gate into the horse stall area, above which hung the rope. He inched along, the pitiful bawling of cattle now a roaring in his head. He was choking; smoke burned his eyes, making breathing impossible. He heard the terrified whinny of horses—but so far away? He should be getting closer to them. Suddenly he felt the door, opened it and reached up and felt—not the rope, but the arrowhead collection. Totally disoriented in the smoke and confusion, he had gone exactly the opposite way he intended, into the milk house on the west end of the barn.

A timber fell under tons of burning hay, squarely on Jerrold. He died within seconds.

Farmers and scores of Belleville residents gathered next day to view with awe the total havoc and help the Pflueger family cope with the gruesome tragedy.

"Geez, what a smell. Nineteen cows, three calves and two horses, all roasted alive."

"Poor Jerrold. Never had a chance."

"Gawd, what a stink. Ain't nothing like that, 'cept at a rendering plant."

"Wonder where we'll find him. Probably under one of the cows? Maybe with the horses? Gotta be in there somewheres."

The grisly speculation continued.

Workers threw bucket after bucket of water on the foul smoldering debris from wood, hay, flesh, hair, and bones. They fashioned a large metal hook from a hayfork, tied it to a rope, and used it to drag animal carcasses away for burial. A hundred yards away, a team of sweating roan mares pulling a scraper dug a vast grave.

Noon passed. Some speculated—hoped aloud—that the fire was so hot that a human body would be totally consumed. Others frowned, certain that something should be left. Sheriff Alfred Mayberry assured the group that even the hottest fire wouldn't eliminate all bones. "See, you can tell that's a dead calf, now can't you? And ain't that about the size of a man?"

Others nodded in grim agreement. And then Leonard Huisby suggested they look in the milk house end, where no one had ventured. "Might's well try," Sheriff Mayberry shrugged. After more water on that part of the ruins, the hook was used on metal and hunks of masonry. What caught the attention of all in this ghastly scene were the numerous bits of stone lying on and around what was left of Jerrold Pflueger's head.

It was not a pretty sight; hardly recognizable as a human being except for the skeleton, charred viscera, and a couple scraps of metal that may have been Jerrold's pocket watch and jackknife. Around the charred head were dozens of familiar stone pieces.

"His arrowheads," someone gasped. The bits of stone so carefully crafted centuries before had been freed by the fire from the once-varnished display board to shower down on their gatherer in his fatal moment.

Everyone thought it, yet no one asked it aloud: Did Jerrold die trying to save his arrowheads? Would he give up on his cows for that sentimental collection? Silently, the workers shook their heads and, one by one, stepped slowly and gingerly out of the charred rubble of what once was the proud milk house and barn of Jerrold Pflueger.

The group became silent, as Pastor Ernest Bjornholm asked all to pause for a prayer. Then followed a period of lowered voices and murmuring, a convening of a council of leaders who produced an acceptable consensus on how Jerrold Pflueger died. He had heroically struggled to get the cattle out of the raging inferno, and retreated through the west end door into the milk house only when the stanchion room began collapsing around him. The pile of arrowheads falling about him was happenstance, perhaps divinely ordained as an epitaph to a rural man of solid character. Just how close to the truth this version was, the inventors would never know. Their silent worry—to be spoken only much later in hushed voices—was that it wasn't so, and that just possibly Jerrold Pflueger didn't have his priorities right in his moment of crisis. With a downward look and shake of the head, one would say "Maybe, just maybe, though it don't seem quite right to say it, he give up on the cows to save his goddam arrowheads."

*  *  *

Editor Ivar Lindfors was not far behind Sheriff Mayberry in reaching the Pflueger farm the morning after the tragedy. A citizen first, newspaperman second, he joined the scores of men pulling the animal remains from the smoldering morass and dragging them to the pit for burial. He worked until blackened, his printer's coveralls like the garments of all men there reeking with the stench of the holocaust.

Work-spirited as he was, the tragic scene sent tumbling through his brain bundles of words, phrases, dramatic metaphors, and compassionate aphorisms for telling the story in the *Veckomonitoren*. Such a tragedy would be written up, but in what way? And the question haunting every journalist covering a dramatic event: what would the first sentence be? Because that first sentence that big city reporters call the "lead" (rhymes with "deed") breaks the writer's block, sets the tone for the rest of the report and opens the floodgates of prose that brings the event leaping to life for the reader who would then hang on every word of the story.

Ivar recalled a disaster in Sweden before he left there, when a catastrophic fire in a textile factory left a similar scene with more human fatalities, but fewer animals killed—horses, mainly, there to haul carts laden with bolts of fabric. The townspeople had come together, so to speak, to provide food and shelter and even new livelihoods for the survivors. The incident was often cited by Social Democrats as an example of what cooperation among sincere and dedicated people can accomplish in the face of utter calamity.

The envy and animosity inherent in a group of people living and working together is set aside in shared cause.

Ivar saw the possibility of the same forces taking shape here. He had been around Athena County long enough to know that Albert Theide, Leonard Huisby, and Bjorn Nygren all probably thought well of Jerrold Pflueger, but they weren't particularly fond of each other. Theide and Huisby had once had a rancorous quarrel over where a line fence should be run; Nygren and Theide had words once at the market square over a cattle swap that, Eva Nygren said, had made her husband Bjorn look like a fool. Many persons here both in town and in the countryside had spoken ill of Ernst Hebermann and his prices at the funeral parlor. Nearly every farmer had hard words to say about J. B. Higgins, the banker who was penurious in granting needed seed and fertilizer loans to wheat growers but quick to foreclose on the farmer whose crop was ruined by hail. Or the shop owner who failed to meet mortgage payments. And so on.

Yet here were all of these men toiling and sweating together in common purpose, their petty animosities in abeyance as they struggled to help a family overwhelmed by tragedy. It was an old human story, of human bonds born of disaster disproportionately and so outrageously visited on a single household.

This, then, Ivar decided, was the story the *Veckomonitoren* would tell about the tragedy. It would be one of anguish and adversity met by heroic assistance, a compassionate community taking care of one of its own in time of misfortune. The power of human cooperation would be the underlying theme.

Along the way, the story would do two additional things, which Ivar regarded as wholly fit and proper. It would emphasize the virtue of Scandinavian customs and the specific contribution of the Nonpartisan League in helping a family make its way back from the depths of desperation. It would be topped off, as it should be, by the Pflueger family rising from destitution and meeting destiny, with young

Rudy successfully carrying on and taking over his father's work.

So Ivar, with much help from Inez and Rudy and the neighbors, gathered all the facts, anecdotes and statements needed for a series of stories on this triumph of community cooperation. The first report in the *Veckomonitoren* began as follows:

BARN FIRE KILLS POPULAR FARMER
21 cattle, 3 horses meet fiery death
Lightning is cause of conflagration that consumes
30-acre crop of fresh hay Gruesome scene
Entire community pitches in to aid
Pflueger family in their hour of need
Marie Pflueger says "they are all heroes."
Rebuilding of burnt barn is planned
Son Rudolph Pflueger to operate farm

The story spelled out in compassionate detail how the tragedy had brought the neighborhood, town and country together; Rudy Pflueger would operate the farm in partnership with his mother, a woman from a fine Swedish family; she and her late husband had most successfully instilled the virtues of Swedish and German tradition in young Rudolph; a new barn would be built by volunteers; and donated cattle and hay would rebuild the Pflueger herd.

Pastor Ernest Bjornholm, in his own column, underscored the Christian spirit displayed by the community in the wake of the tragedy.

\* \* \*

If Andressa Dahlgren had any intention of confronting Rudy Pflueger with his obligation to support her unborn child, she rejected it after the barn fire and death of Rudy's father. Bringing this up to Rudy now would be offensive to her own sense of propriety, especially since fatherhood was an uncertain toss-up between two different young men. Without doubt, the community would scorn her as a cruel trollop seeking to add new tragedy to the Pflueger family. The possibility of marriage with Rudy and joining him in farming never occurred to her.

Thus, viciously rebuffed by Bert and under a self-imposed prohibition against facing Rudy, Andressa told Inez about her situation.

"Are you certain, that you are with child?"

"Completely, Aunt Inez."

"And you did—were with—these two young men the same week?"

"Yes."

Andressa told of her brief but brutal conversation with Bert Allcott, including his threat to get football team members to claim having trysts with her.

"That may be a big bluff, Andressa," Inez pointed out.

"It's not what they would say in court," Andressa said. "It would be said up and down the streets. Bert could start the rumor easily, if he hasn't already."

Inez privately agreed with this analysis. What should she now advise this young woman, now just a few weeks shy of her 18th birthday?

She told Andressa about the Mother's Allowance law.

"Could I get money, Aunt Inez, to support this child even without being married?"

Under the 1913 law, Inez knew, that would not be possible. The law had been designed mostly for young widows, or married women with husbands physically unable to work.

"No, Andressa, you would need to be married."

Inez felt an inner compulsion to scream, to shriek, that the calamities of young love in Swedish poverty, that had so wrenched her own life before wedding chimes quieted, were now falling with a vengeance on a new victim.

*Or was she a victim? She was not destitute as Fredrika Grinnhaal had been a decade earlier. She had a good life, didn't she, in our household? Hadn't we given her a good home? Fed her well? Gotten her back in school?*

Parallels between lives are never perfect, Inez concluded. Better not to judge. But what to do? Andressa was understandably upset.

"You and the baby can live with us, Andressa," Inez said reassuringly. "You may have the luck of marrying another young man."

Andressa looked at Inez in disbelief.

"Who would marry me? In this town? Aunt Inez, I won't be able to show myself on the streets. I did it with two men, and now I'm a loose woman. I've already seen the looks at the pharmacy, at Johnston's clothing store, when I walk with Charlotte. Those people hold their mouths in thin lines and stare. You think I can't feel that? I'm going to Minneapolis. I learned to type in school; I'll get a job somewhere. If I can't support the baby, I'll put it in an orphan's home there. Maybe it will be adopted by a nice family."

"I'm sure Ivar and I would keep your child, Andressa," Inez said, not at all sure of Ivar's response but equally sure he would be in no position to object.

The matter wasn't settled immediately. Ivar did agree that he and Inez should offer to support the mother and child, or be foster parents to the child, but Andressa wouldn't talk with him about it. Two weeks later when Inez returned home with Charlotte in late afternoon, she found a note to her from Andressa.

Dear Aunt Inez:

I hope you will understand that I can't stay in Belleville a day longer.

When you read this I will be on the train, maybe in Minneapolis already. I know somebody there who will help me get a job.

Next time you see my mother, please tell her what I did. I never did tell her this. They have troubles enough.

When I get settled, I'll write to you. I love you and Uncle

Ivar and Charlotte; I will miss her greatly. Try to explain to her why I left.

With love, Andressa

* * *

The Pflueger story during the ensuing year did not play out in keeping with the idealistic narrative presented to the readers of the *Veckomonitoren*. Rudy was overwhelmed by the need to make field and livestock decisions for which he was ill prepared and ill-informed. He had to take out a mortgage to buy machinery that most people thought a waste of money. Even with the donated hay, feed, and cattle, he drove the farm deeper in debt, and banker Higgins squirmed over the magnitude of his bank's risk. It was not the time for a bank to destroy such an idyllic myth and incur the predictable wrath of an entire community, but business was business.

Meanwhile, Rudy's personal problems overcame his perplexities about managing a farm. He didn't mind Andressa's abrupt departure, but he was frustrated in his romantic pursuit of Marjorie Kiefer, who showed increasing disdain for prospects of life on a dairy farm, especially one so heavily mortgaged.

Problems on the farm mounted. Rudy and his mother argued with agonizing frequency over debts and how to run the farm.

Then on April 7, 1917, the U.S. declared war on Germany. The Minneapolis and St. Paul newspapers were splashed with headlines about patriotism and the need for loyal young men to join the army and protect Old Glory.

Rudolph Pflueger saw the war as a way out of his bewildering entanglement in the star-crossed farm and the stalled romance with Marjorie. Without a word to anyone he walked to Belleville and signed up at the U.S. Army Recruitment office. He was surprised by how exhilarating this brash act was. *What could be more patriotic than being one of the first to sign up, especially when you have a German name?* Never again would anyone, to their face or behind their backs, accuse the Pfluegers of being unAmerican sauerkraut sluppers.

Word of Rudy's enlistment moved swiftly around Athena County, and speculation began. "Had Rudy and his mother had a falling out? He didn't really have to enlist; farmers were exempt because, God knows, the country needs food now. And didn't that Dahlgren girl desert him? Well, yes, and one of Ed Kiefer's daughters, too. Aw, we all know he wasn't really cut out for farmin' anyway."

Then the talk took on a malicious undertone, voicing the thought not spoken since the fateful fire in summer of 1916. It had been known—perhaps from his own blurted admission born of grief and confused guilt after the disaster—that Rudy had put several loads of damp hay in the barn just a few days before the fire. "So mebbe Rudy caused the fire with that wet hay, and killed his own ol' man?" That such thoughts were being voiced now, about a family at its highest point of vulnerability, seemed of no inconsistency to those speaking them.

No citizen on Wells street, including banker Higgins, was more perplexed about the plight of the Pflueger farm than Ivar Lindfors. As news, the Pflueger story had run its course two months ago, and the brief spurt in readership and requests for extra copies, which the story stimulated, had dissipated. Circulation was again below 900, with no improvement in sight.

A couple of weeks later, he saw a handbill, posted on a light pole on a street corner, which announced:

> Farm Auction June 15, 1917
> Marie and Rudolph Pflueger Farm, Route 4,
> Belleville and All Possessions to Be Sold
> to the Highest Bidders

The handbill was obviously not from the Lindfors Publishing Co., a fact that hurt Ivar. He was nursing this wound when he chanced to meet Marie as she left the grocery late that afternoon, head down, fussing with things in a shopping bag.

"Marie, sorry to see you are selling out. But, I suppose there was no other way, with Rudy joining the Army."

Marie looked up slowly and said nothing.

Uncomfortably now, Ivar added, "I mean, the whole community, I'm sure is sorry to see the Pflueger farm being sold, after the—the—"

"After all, you wrote about it. Ain't that what you're trying to say, Ivar?"

"Well, after the whole town and county did so much, and there was so much good feeling and cooperation."

Marie straightened her small shoulders and gazed steadily on Ivar. "So you mean after all the town did for us, it's shoddy of us to quit?"

Slowly her eyes fell to the ground, then back and up at a sharp angle into the face of the much taller editor. Now her gaze sharpened and her words came slowly.

"Ivar, why should anyone feel sorry when we are doin' what anyone in their right mind knew we should'a done a week after Jerrold died in the fire? Ivar, you knew and the neighborhood knew and the whole county knew, that Rudy didn't have his heart in farming and never would of. We all fooled ourselves into thinkin' this would work, but it wasn't to be. I guess I was a fool as much as anyone. Fooled by my own wishes and hopes. And prayers."

She turned to continue on her way.

"You weren't a fool, Marie. The whole county was behind you, you know that, with all that help and cooperation. It was a great thing to see and a great story to write for everyone to see."

Now Marie stopped and, ever so slowly, turned back to once again fix her eyes on the editor of the *Veckomonitoren*.

"Oh, I know when I been a fool, Ivar," she said, her head

swaying slowly from side to side. "But now that you bring it up, Ivar, I think from the minute you heard about our fire, that's how you saw it. A great story. That's what it was for you, a great, big story.

"And you know something else? All that stuff about cooperation? All these folks, rich and poor, pulling together to help out a family down on its luck? Who is it gets any good from all that, Ivar? Rudy and Sarah and me who had the bad luck, or the heroes who did all those things and give us the cows and horses and hay and feed?

"Oh, Ivar, you think I ain't grateful talking this way, but I'm tellin' you what happened. You know good and well you weren't gettin' on so good with the Bank and the Wells street crowd with all that Nonpartisan League stuff, and with Ernst Hebermann who was mad as a wet hen about the letters on prices of caskets."

The slow head-shaking continued from the diminutive but now energized woman.

"All your editorials and all you say about the wonders of cooperation and what this means to the community. Ain't it possible that what's good for the community ain't no good at all for the Pflueger family? And weren't we the point of it all? Did you ever think that maybe we'd of been better off if you had just told about the fire the way you tell about any other accident?

"Don't you see, Ivar, what happens with a story like this? You get people to expect miracles from an 18-year-old kid and his Ma and sister. And the more the stories in your paper, the more people do for us and the more stuff they give us. And it snowballs, it gets as if we now owe it to them to make a miracle happen. That's what it is, Ivar—people thought we owed them a miracle. And all your stories and editorials made them think it.

"I'm taking my daughter and leaving Athena County, Ivar. I've got a sister in Fergus Falls, and she thinks I might be able to get a job in a laundry there. Our name is no good in Belleville any more."

"Your name, Marie? It is a good and noble one. And Rudy is showing his patriotism by joining the Army. I'm sure he'll be a good soldier, and make you and Belleville proud."

"I guess you ain't heard, Ivar. The army doctors looked Rudy over in Minneapolis, and said his heart ain't fit for to be a soldier. So he got rejected, and he was too ashamed to even come back to Belleville. He's in Minneapolis, cleaning streets and truckin' dead horses away."

Marie turned and, this time, walked away.

# VIII. WAR AND PATRIOTISM

Even before the Pflueger farm auction, Athena County was consumed by one overpowering theme.

War. With Germany. The Fatherland to some, the realm of the Huns, to others. And to the less ethnically committed, a mystic, creative, amusing, arrogant and often frightening European culture.

Like all wars, the prospect of this one was feared by some in Athena County while enthusiastically anticipated by others. Among the former were a very few pacificists, opposed to war of any kind and in any form, and a greater number who loathed a deadly struggle with the nation where they or their forebears were born. Among the latter were those with a variety of motivations, including those who saw the inevitable link between armed conflict and prosperity: "Prices ain't been so good lately, not like the days when Taft was President." "Naw, you ain't gonna do well in wheat, unless they's a war somewheres." "That's right; we need a war to get prices up where they should be."

Along with the concern about prices, Wells Street was caught up in patriotism and suspicions about who might not be patriotic:

"Boy oh boy, we got a lot of Sauerkraut munchers around here. Think they're gonna like fighting the Kaiser? Betchyer life they won't." "Yeah, and how about the Swedes, Norwegians, and Danes? They think like Germans, don't they? They're all Lutherans, ain't they?" "Hey, now, better watch your langwidge. They's a lot of good Lutherans around here."

"Well, let me tell you, if we git into war they better think American. Ain't no place for slackers here. No matter where your grandpa or old man was born, or you yourself for that matter, you're American now. Or if you ain't, better git on the next boat back t'where you come from."

"You know Minnesota is full of Swedes and Germans? I read somewhere that two outa three people in Minnesota came from the old country, or their Ma and Pa did. Makes you think, don't it?"

"It's a free country, you say? You mean free to be a traitor? Think you'll be free if the Kaiser and his Huns take over America? Not on your life. Comes a war, we all pull together and tar and feather those who don't. Or if that don't work, we still know how to do necktie parties."

It was also well known that war against Germany was opposed before April 1917 by some members of these ethnic groups, and by editorials in several Scandinavian-language newspapers, including the *Veckomonitoren*. There were four votes from the Minnesota Congressional delegation against the War Declaration—votes that brought charges of treason from scores of editorial pages.

Minnesota was thus considered by many in the political establishment in the years 1914-1918 to contain serious loyalty risks. This level of ethnic suspicion would not be matched anywhere in the U.S. until World War II, when the entire Japanese-American community on the west coast would be uprooted and sent to internment camps.

* * *

As a social democrat, Ivar was opposed to war in principle and to this one in particular. Furthermore, as a more or less paid publicist for the Nonpartisan League, he had considerable sympathy for the argument that a war would bring enormous profits to big business while shortchanging farmers who produced the food which would fuel a military machine.

While Scandinavians were in fact split on their views about the war, there was enough vocal opposition to the conflict to keep a steady flow of Swedish-language letters on the subject to the *Veckomonitoren*, which the editors generally published in full. Many on Wells Street, who couldn't read Swedish, heard talk about the letters. They assumed Ivar and Inez to be pro-German and, furthermore, regarded such writing in a foreign language to be subversive.

Ivar Lindfors convinced himself that cultural affinity with Germany had little to do with it. He didn't regard as credible the rumors that King Gustav V of Sweden personally favored Sweden's intervening on Germany's side and was waiting for a pretext to do so. Ivar also had little compassion for the Kaiser's yearning for military grandeur and colonial possessions.

The Lindfors newspaper did not have an "editorial" or "opinion" page. Opinions were loosely gathered, usually, on one page, all in the same type font and sprinkled in among items of news or, perhaps, fiction taken from some boilerplate service. Ivar inserted, in the usual Swedish, such items as: "It is an old thing, in German culture, to have a thirst for big armies and more land. But should we try to wash that thirst from the German mouth? You can't change what has grown in the Teutonic soul over half a millennium." This comment would be separated by a line slug from another item about, perhaps, the price of wheat and barley last week in Chicago.

In another weekly edition, Ivar would write: "Many famous statesmen oppose war with Germany. In this region, the best known and most vocal is U.S. Senator Robert M. LaFollette, Sr. of neighboring Wisconsin. 'Fightin' Bob,' as his supporters called him, is a leader in the Progressive wing of the Republican party and a former Wisconsin governor. He is well known for his attacks on railroad and industrial monopolies. He does have enemies. Yet, he is very popular because of his strength of character and political honesty. One time someone lured him to a Milwaukee hotel and tried to bribe him. Such is the treachery that some scoundrels will attempt. But Senator La Follette would have none of it, and all but threw the bribing rascal out of the hotel. Good ol' Fightin' Bob. He can't be bought, sold or traded."

In early March of 1917, a bill to allow President Wilson to arm American merchant ships passed the U.S. House of Representative, and a similar "armed neutrality" bill was debated in the Senate. It would have passed by a heavy margin, except for a filibuster by a group of 12 senators, headed by LaFollette, that defeated it. Two Minnesota members of the House, Charles Davis of St. Peter, and Charles A. Lindbergh of Little Falls, voted with La Follette against the bill, and their actions were vilified as "unAmerican, unjustified, and cowardly" by one Twin Cities newspaper. LaFollette also was branded a traitor.

Ivar Lindfors found that Davis, Lindbergh, and LaFollette expressed his own views and those of most of his readership. So the week after the Senate filibuster that killed the "armed neutrality" bill, the *Veckomonitoren* reprinted an advertisement he found in the *St. Paul Pioneer Press*, by a pacifist group called the American Union Against Militarism:

> "We cannot destroy German militarism by defeating Germany. Militarism is a condition that can be destroyed only from within by the democratic impulses of the people themselves. France tried to destroy German militarism from the outside in 1806. Under Napoleon she crushed Germany more completely than the Allies can ever hope to crush her now. That was not the end but the beginning of modern German militarism. Fight Germany to a "dictated peace" and you will only inflame the military passions of her people and strengthen the power of Prussian tyranny over them."

This editorial reignited the Wells Street outrage toward Ivar, since it fed the belief that this Swedish publisher had gone pacifist or, worse, "pro-Hun." A day after it was published, Ivar was visited by several members of the Belleville Commercial Club.

At first, they were indirect.

"Well, yes, there are different views on the war in Europe. But we are dang certain to get in, and this is no time to be shirking back. And you know, Ivar, when the war happens, folks will wonder about those who were against it. And that ain't all. When a Swedish newspaper is against the war, people get the idea that all Swedes are opposed, and that ain't so. Why, take me, the name Walster used to be Wahlstrom, so I'm a Swede mostly, but you don't hear me saying anything nice about the Kaiser or his damnable submarines. And there's a helluva lot of Swedes like me. There won't be any war slackers in this town, you can be sure of that."

Such words sent Ivar's mind buzzing. But recovering his composure, he thought he might try a debate with a few of these citizens.

"Do any of you," he asked, "really believe this war is about freedom and liberty?"

Geoffrey Blankston almost choked. "Of course it is. Those Huns want to run the world. And the ones who get in their way, they slaughter. You read a lot. So haven't you heard about the way they butchered those women and kids in Belgium?"

"Don't doubt for a moment what the Kaiser's soldiers did," Ernst Heberman added. "That's why my grandfather left that country 60 years ago. Well, one of the reasons. Anyway, don't get the idea people like me are for the Kaiser, Ivar. Come the war, you're going to find Old Glory flying from the windows of a lot of families with names like mine."

This did come as news to Ivar, since it contradicted his estimate of how Hebermann might lean. But then, considering Ernst's prominence among Wells street merchants, and the patriotism evinced by this group, his view maybe wasn't so surprising after all.

Ivar tried to play the role of the responsible American journalist.

"The *Veckomonitoren* isn't for the Kaiser. And it isn't against America. What it's against is war, especially this one that's all about world trade and which navy rules the ocean."

Walster shook his head and the three were silent for a time, all looking down. Finally Geoffrey Blankston gave Ivar the news they had come to deliver.

"Guess we just need to tell you what we've been thinking, Ivar. We're going to get the other newspaper going again, and put our advertising there. Everybody is worried about where your paper is headed with all this unAmerican stuff, and besides it doesn't get read by more than half our customers.

"So we are going to give Ollie Moller some help in starting the Athena County *Gazette* again. It hasn't been published regularly since the 'nineties, but it's time Belleville had a regular paper in English."

And," he added grimly, "one that shows some patriotism."

Ivar was startled. "Ollie—you mean Olof Moller? I thought he had left town."

Geoffrey Blankston grinned. "He did, but he came back a while ago, been working at the abstracting company. Seems to have given up the booze, and he knows how to work a press. He'll have a secretary to help clean up his grammar and spelling. And we'll be in back of him."

\* \* \*

Inez had left the shop early that day, and was outside at home, helping nine-year-old Charlotte who was sketching, with pencil and crayons, a picture of the large burr oak tree in their backyard. Once again, Charlotte, now much wiser about human reproduction and therefore saying little about the specifics to adults, asked Inez about one of the tormenting family questions: "Mama, really, why did Andressa go away so suddenly?"

A pause and deep sigh from Inez.

"You saw her note, Charlotte. She wanted to work in Minneapolis."

Turning her head to study her sketch of the tree, Charlotte thought a minute, but then blurted out.

"Mama, everyone at school talks about it. She's going to have a baby! And Rudy Pflueger is the father. They all know that. And they think I am dumb as a doorknob 'cause I didn't know it!"

Inez nodded slowly.

"Yes, that is true—I mean, that she is going to have a baby. I—I just didn't want to get into that with you."

"But Mama, I wasn't surprised. Andy and Rudy were a coupla lovebirds. I knew that. So I made the kids think I really knew it, but just wasn't letting on."

Inez sighed again. This child knows so much, she thought. *Does she know the truth about herself?*

To Inez' relief, this complicated conversation was interrupted by Ivar coming in from the street. He leaned against the heavy, coarse bark of the old tree and for a moment took in the fragrance of the summer foliage. He was depressed.

"Stand still, there, Papa. I'll make you part of the picture." The infectious good nature of this child—now as happy as Inez to change the subject—usually perked him up, but not today.

"Nice picture, Charlotte, but don't put me in it. Mama and I need to talk some business."

He took Inez inside, leaving Charlotte alone with her colorful sketching.

"Inez, the money people in town are dumping us. Even those who put money up front, like Hebermann. Know what they're going to do? They're getting Olof Moller back to start up the *Gazette* again. How can they do that? Inez, what in heck should we do? Should we sell out, take the equity we have, and go back to Minneapolis? Get another back shop printing job? Try to work for a Minneapolis or St. Paul newspaper?"

Inez, with Charlotte's upsetting question now pushed out of mind, was less ready to give up.

"Ivar, those people who have money in the *Veckomonitoren* don't really want you to go broke. Did they say where the *Gazette* will be published?"

They hadn't, Ivar realized. If it was in the same old shop next to the Walster-Blankston automobile dealership and garage, now full of motorcar parts around the ancient and unused press, it would be a very limited operation.

A little checking the next day confirmed Inez' suspicion. The *Gazette* was going to be a part-time job for Ollie Moller who would keep his clerk's job at the Athena County Abstracting Company. There were no plans for anything else—no job printing and, therefore, no competition for that side of the Lindfors business.

"You're right, Inez, they don't want us to go bankrupt," Ivar conceded. "They just want to make it tough for the paper—maybe reduce us to the printing business. That way, if the *Gazette* folds, we might get to print their pamphlets and sales signs, even if the *Veckomonitoren* is a failure, too."

They reflected on that possibility. From an income standpoint, it wasn't all that bad a prospect. Although the *Veckomonitoren* was hardly meeting costs, the printing business—stationery, greeting cards, wedding announcements, auction bills, handbills, and the Nonpartisan League contract—were doing well.

"Maybe, Inez, we could turn the flat-bed press over to job printing, to pull in more business."

Inez had still another thought.

"Ivar, how about turning the whole thing into a cooperative?"

"The newspaper? The printing business? How?" Ivar wondered. Cooperatives were well known, largely as farm marketing and service enterprises, owned entirely by the members and not as private business ventures. Publishing cooperatives, though, were rare.

"Aren't some of the NPL newspapers in North Dakota organized as cooperatives?" Inez asked.

This idea was intriguing.

Ivar drove to Leonard Huisby's place in his rattling Ford, then to Arhold Hedlund's and Bo Nygren's farm on the Willow Falls Road. Their next stop was at Albert Theide's farm, chosen because of Albert's well-known "Granary Room," a rustic corner of his grain-storage building where men often met for cajolery, aquavit drinking, smoking, or Nonpartisan League business.

Ivar stepped on the large, roughly cut stone in front of the door and, as he entered the Granary Room, his nostrils took in the musty, yet not unpleasant, aroma of wheat hulls, grain and chaff in the storage bins beyond the main wall. This aroma mixed in with the less pleasant and stale smell of pipe smoke and the spittoon in one corner. It was some distance from the farm privy, but the granary room had a back door that opened directly into a tree shelterbelt that bordered a 38-acre wheat field. This was all the latrine needed by any male.

Albert Theide, now playing host, broke the ice and cut quickly to the heart of the problem, or at least as he saw it.

"Ya, Ivar, ve hear t' people on Vells Street iss giffing you trouble? And you vould like the NPL to take ofer the paper?"

Before Ivar could answer, Bo Nygren put it in his own favorite words, consciously avoiding dialect and avoiding looking at Albert Theide.

"Ivar, I hope you told them what I said to one of the grain buyers. I said he could take a nice sweet suck of my asshole. That's what you need to tell the Wells Street bunch."

Ivar didn't—couldn't—answer that directly. He caught Leonard Huisby's frown, then said carefully: "Well, we need to make a change, and that's why I wanted to talk with you gentlemen."

All three beamed at the "gentlemen" label, which effectively squelched Bo Nygren's crude language for the rest of the meeting.

Leonard Huisby pulled the farmers' thoughts together: "See, Ivar, what we really need is a paper that's ALL for the NPL. But we also know that isn't easy to do. We know it might give you difficulty with people on Wells Street. So what would you like to do?"

"We've been thinking about turning it into a co-op newspaper," Ivar answered. "With some support from the NPL."

On Inez' earlier advice, he deliberately said "some" support, because neither of them wanted the paper to be an outright NPL organ. Besides, they correctly guessed that League didn't have enough funds to buy the paper outright, but might manage a loan.

Ivar also felt a little guilty saying "we" since the idea first came from Inez who was not at the meeting.

A plan for a cooperative newspaper quickly took shape. All three NPL men nodded agreeably, lips pursed together and eyebrows arched reflectively. Albert Theide spoke first in his elaborate—almost intentionally affected—sing-song:

"Tounds like a vunderful idea! Yoost vot ve need!"

The cooperative newspaper would be named the *Athena County Forum*. That much was agreed upon in the Granary Room, and the rest was worked out over the following weeks, with the help of a League lawyer in St. Cloud.

This plan moved ahead rapidly. Through a loan from a League-Friendly North Dakota Bank, the newly-formed Athena County Publishing Association paid off J. B. Higgins, Ernst Hebermann, and Martin Johnston—the men who had bankrolled the now defunct *Veckomonitoren*.

All profits from the new operation would be distributed among the membership, most of whom would be NPL members and owners, guaranteed a single vote apiece. Each member's annual contribution to the Co-op would purchase both a share of ownership in the organization and a regular subscription. The Co-op would provide printing services at cost, with any profits at the end of the year refunded in proportion to patronage. It reminded Ivar and Inez of consumer cooperatives in Sweden that provided low-cost groceries for their members.

One part of the arrangement was left hazy, and this was

control over editorial policy. In Ivar's mind, it would be a cooperative open to membership among any resident of Athena County with the hired editor running the paper as he or she saw fit.

To Huisby, Theide, Nygren, and Arnold Hedlund, it was now a League newspaper. No one made this an outright issue, partly because of Inez' ingenuity. She had insisted on calling the cooperative "The Athena County Independent Forum Publishing Association," with a constitution stating that editorial policy would be determined by the hired editor, not named in the charter document but assumed by all to be Ivar and Inez Lindfors. This much was accepted by all, although Leonard Huisby silently worried about putting League money into the enterprise without having total control, by the League officers, over what the paper would print.

Now, Ivar and Inez were no longer entrepreneurs, but were employees of a cooperative and would be paid salaries that would allow them to live at about the same level they had enjoyed—or endured—in the previous six years. Ivar wanted the title of Publisher and Manager, but the Board of Directors, ACIFPA, as the Association called itself, insisted they were the publishers. This crucial difference between the Lindfors couple and the League was never settled.

Ivar was Editor and Manager of Advertising and Inez was Assistant Manager of Advertising, for a salary roughly half that allotted to Ivar. Ivar was ecstatic over the wondrous opportunities the new *Forum* would provide.

A short time later, Ivar was approached by Geoffrey Blankston, who had recently been elected Chairman of the Belleville Commercial Club.

"Ivar, with all the things happening at your paper, we'd like to invite you to our Club meeting next Tuesday, where we can visit with you." Ivar drew in his breath but quickly accepted the invitation. He thought about suggesting Inez come along, but decided against it.

The Club met in the backroom of the Prairie Café, the

restaurant with the large round table in front where the town leadership regularly met for morning coffee. The backroom was large enough for no more than 35 persons, putting a limit on the number of leaders qualified to be members of the Club. No business could be represented by more than a single member, and not all businesses were represented.

It was ordinarily a dining room, with tables covered with white linen for Sunday dinner. For the Club meetings, the square tables were pushed together in a center row, and the members sat around them much as they might at a corporate board meeting. Tidy as it was, like all restaurant places the room had a heavy smell of pipe and cigar smoke. As Ivar uncomfortably noticed, several members kept on puffing when Ivar was introduced. Ordinarily, smoking would stop for a speaker. Not this time; it was a signal to Ivar that he was now a marginal member of the Club, if not excluded entirely.

"This is what a newspaper should be," Ivar said to the group, "a forum for ideas and points of view of all kinds." He explained with fervor, in his clipped accent, that the word "Forum" was the same in both languages.

"It is an old Latin word, meaning an enclosed place where people discuss and debate. Athena County, having a name that bespeaks democracy itself, is the enclosure for this forum of ideas.

"We will editorialize, casting our views upon the waters of local public opinion, which may wave and splash and crash on the shores. If we make a wave large or small, we invite countering winds that may prevail in a different direction."

Faces went blank at this point, but Ivar charged ahead, the sound of his own words reinforcing him, and went on at length about the new *Forum* being a real forum.

Ernst Hebermann, whose shares in the old paper had just been bought out, asked the first question. It was an opening shot over the new *Forum*'s bow.

"This forum idea for a paper," Ernst said, "now that's interesting and sounds like real democracy the way you say,

Ivar. But now tell me something. Can we look forward to another forum on things like casket prices, from people who don't appreciate what the retailers are doing for them?"

Ivar expected this much. "When we say a forum, Ernst, we mean a page of questions and ideas about general issues, projects and ideas that might be suggested for the town, for the state, and the country. Some of you might remember what the *Veckomonitoren* did on legislation for the Mother's Allowance law. There are other things. What about crime and punishment? Do we need a bigger jail? Care for the insane? Roads and buildings, and the condition of the state highways? Do we need a self-powered fire engine here, with better pumps? Or maybe a city swimming pool?"

Safe as each of these ideas sounded, Ivar knew each one opened the gate to a minefield for a small-town newspaper. The question of enlarging the jailhouse was a sore point that the County Board had tabled some time ago. Too many people on Wells street thought the money would be better spent on fire protection, to reduce fire insurance costs. Road maintenance? That could easily get into the shady contract that Martin Johnston's brother Maynard had worked out, providing crushed rock to the county at a price well above the market value.

The swimming pool idea was not a new one, having been brought up by a woman physical education teacher whom the Belleville City Council thought to be far too mouthy for her own good. She had left after two years at the school, to the relief of all those who thought the pool to be a harebrained idea. "What was wrong with the Great River, right on the edge of town? Isn't that where kids went to swim?"

Ernst Hebermann persisted, with a nod toward Roy Evans.

"Ivar, you aren't really answerin' my question. S'pose now someone writes a letter griping about lumber prices. You gonna publish it, or not?"

Thus forced to confront this question, Ivar retreated.

"We aren't seeking to attack responsible citizens

individually," he said slowly. "If someone raises a question about lumber prices, we are going to look carefully at whether everything that is said is correct or not. We won't print letters that don't have the facts right or slander people."

His concessions now pushing him into a near rout, Ivar tried to stiffen a bit. "What I have in mind is wholesome debate over issues. If the Belleville City Council, say, proposes an ordinance on when stores are open, or on fixing up the river bridge, we would invite letters of opinion about that."

It was Reggie Code who asked the question Ivar feared.

"Ivar, tell us, are you going to invite opinions about the war? The draft?"

Ivar tried to make his answer as deliberate and mature as possible. "We have made a decision as a nation to fight imperialism and atrocities committed by Germany. The *Forum* supports that decision; it encourages young men in Athena County to sign up for the draft; and it invites patriotic letters and patriotic statement in advertisements. Some people might raise questions about things that don't interfere with the war effort. We encourage these questions."

J. B. Higgins had been sitting quietly in the back of the room. Sensing the session coming to a head, he asked: "Ivar, there is a big Liberty Bond drive coming up this week. Is this new *Forum* newspaper, as you call it, going to support that drive?" Everyone noted the careful condescension in the wording and tone of the powerful banker. Ivar was cornered.

"Of course we will support it," he answered without hesitation. "We will also provide citizens with all the details that the organizers of the drive will provide for us."

Higgins, now paid off and with no financial hook on the Lindfors' paper, decided against confronting Ivar with the fact that the Nonpartisan League was involved in the key loan for the new *Forum*. There were those who thought Higgins and Ernst Hebermann had bollixed things up by allowing that loan to be retired, so he decided to let others raise the NPL business.

Nobody did. Not this time.

* * *

The transition to publication of the *Forum* was worked out over the next two months. In addition to being in English, the new paper had different type faces, Cheltenham for the text and Bodoni for the headlines. Under the logotype, Ivar and Inez modified the slogan, borrowed from DeTocqueville, which had appeared in Swedish in the *Veckomonitoren*: "To reach thousands of minds."

During that first month, the suspension of the *Veckomonitoren* brought plaintive written and oral protests from perhaps three dozen readers, while the rest seemed—to Ivar and Inez—strangely silent. Had the Swedish-language newspaper been that insignificant?

Pastor Ernest Bjornholm was deeply wounded. With much historical fact on his side, he regarded the erstwhile *Veckomonitoren* as his own creation. He had been a regular contributor, and considered his writing as foremost among his efforts to serve God and His flock.

As soon as he heard about the changes at the paper, the upset pastor confronted Ivar at the print shop, picking a time when he was sure Inez wouldn't be there.

"Our bright flame of Swedish Christian culture is now going out," he chided Ivar. "I would have appreciated being asked for my opinion about all of this." He was clearly humiliated.

Ivar hadn't really though about that. The pastor was overlooked not only by the Granary Room Planners, but also by the Belleville merchants in their move to renew the *Gazette*. Too late, Ivar and Inez saw their error. Abject apologies were now worse than none; the damage was done.

"What all this says," a defeated Ernest Bjornholm said, "is that the Church is losing its influence in Belleville."

This was an assessment with which Ivar and Inez silently agreed, so they said nothing. Privately, they would have added, the Pastor himself was losing influence. Nevertheless, it was a character lapse on their part to leave him in the dark, and they knew it.

The next week, the Reverend Ernest Bjornholm met with the Trustees of Trinity Lutheran Church and respectfully requested that he be transferred to a congregation in a different part of the state—or even a different state. Within two months, he moved to a parish in Minneapolis.

* * *

The first edition of the Athena County *Forum* appeared the third Thursday in April of 1917, a publication day carefully chosen after noting that the rival *Gazette* was published each Tuesday. This shrewd decision was explained in the "Editor's Message" of the first edition as (a) giving readers a chance to have more timely news, with the two papers appearing on different days and (b) giving merchants the opportunity for more frequent and timely advertising. That is, they could buy ads in both papers if they so wished. But when it became known beyond the readership and the Commercial Club that the *Forum* was a co-op paper with even stronger ties to the League, few merchants were interested in advertising in it. The exceptions were the farm machinery and feed dealers who depended on rural customers.

"We'll get them back," a worried Ivar said to Inez. "Farmers make up more than half the buying business in Belleville." It would be some time, however, before that advertising business would materialize.

In the first edition, the "Editor's Message" said:

The *Forum* will be a bulletin board for its readers, where they can learn what their friends and clubs are doing and thinking. It will be a forum for all views on all matters that inspire people. It will watch over government and business and all other institutions that affect us. Its pages will bring to you the vibrant and wholesome life of Athena County.

We want to hear from you, no matter what your views are on what subject. If it's about a new bridge over the river, let's hear it. If you think some prices are too high or others too low, let's hear it. If you have thoughts about whether America should go to war, let's hear it. If you want to agree—or disagree—with something said in this or any other newspaper, let's hear it. If your card-playing club or your lodge has something to report, let's hear it. This is a newspaper of the people, and the newspaper columns are there to serve you.

The invitation to agree or disagree with "any other newspaper" was a signal that the *Forum* and the *Gazette* would no doubt be knocking heads on some questions. This would not be exactly new. Older Belleville residents recalled times since the Civil War when a new, and usually short-lived, newspaper would challenge an older, established one, often in strong and rabid invective. Ex-editor Moller, before the arrival of Ivar and Inez Lindfors, had editorially rebuked a now-defunct paper called the *Citizen*, that is, when he was sober enough to do so. In one famous stream of vitriol, Moller had suggested that "a good horse-whipping might persuade that editor to live up to his paper's name."

Launching the *Forum* had two rather different consequences for Belleville merchants. For one, it solved for the Bank and the affiliated investors the sticky problem of pulling out support of a newspaper in which they had money invested. They had privately figured on driving the Lindfors operation to bankruptcy, an event which had been expertly analyzed by banker Higgins as allowing the creditors to recover most if not all of their investment. While a forced closing hadn't happened, they had their money back.

The other consequence was foreboding. The emergence of the Nonpartisan League reignited the old rancor between farmers and Wells street merchants, leading some farm families to direct their patronage increasingly to the Athena County Cooperative Supply Association, which was stocking more and more groceries, hardware and farm utility items. Especially irritated by this development was hardware store owner Reggie Code, who saw fewer of his regular farmer customers buying nails, chicken brooders, wire fencing, and all the other paraphernalia needed on home and farm. Both gregarious and suspicious by nature, Reggie let his displeasure be known up and down Wells Street. He spoke to grocer Jeb Merriweather who had similar fears, because the *Forum* was advertising the grocery store at the Cooperative, in direct competition with him.

Thus, the new cooperative *Forum*, which was far more than an English-language version of the old *Veckomonitoren*, seemed certain to drive more deeply the wedge between farm and town. It was ultimately agreed among the merchants that "this new paper won't last a year." And they tacitly agreed to ensure the accuracy of this prophecy.

* * *

Declaration of war against Germany opened the way for new ventures for Belleville banker J. B. Higgins. He noted with approval the announcement in the *Minneapolis Morning Tribune* of the legislature's creation, 10 days after the Declaration of War, of the Minnesota Public Safety Commission. This would be an agency to help prosecute the war. The legislative statute of April 1917 that created the Commission said it:

> "shall have power to do all acts and things non-inconsistent with the constitution or laws of the state of Minnesota or of the United States, which are necessary or proper for the protection of life and public property or private property of a character as in the judgment of the commission requires protection, and shall do and perform all acts and things necessary or proper so that the military, civil and industrial resources of the state may be most efficiently applied toward

the successful prosecution of such war."

This remarkably broad language was widely taken to mean that this body could do nearly anything it saw fit in the interest of maintaining patriotism among Minnesota citizens. The Commission could acquire property for its own uses, seize or condemn property, require any citizen or governmental agent to testify under oath, and investigate and remove elected public officials.

While J. B. Higgins anticipated some outcry against granting such sweeping powers to one agency, he foresaw accurately that a main target of the Commission would be the doubtful loyalty of the Nonpartisan League. J.B. quietly but effectively recommended a membership slate for the Athena County chapter of the Public Safety Committee. He couldn't be chairman himself or even on the committee; as a banker, he should stay officially in the background. Nevertheless, he would still wield a heavy hand over the Committee. The logical choice for the Directorship was Roscoe E. Thurstone, the county attorney, whose nickname "Pudgy" misleadingly suggested an affable public official. Affable he was not.

Pudgy Thurstone, a former attorney for a major railroad company, had accumulated impressive property and investment wealth after settling in Belleville in his 52nd year. He was a tough prosecutor who brooked no nonsense from anyone thought to be a threat to public order. He had been known to say, for example, that "hanging is too good" for agitators like those in the I.W.W—the "radical union" organizing mine and timber workers.

Such devotion to public tranquility had earned Pudgy election twice to his position—the second time without opposition. He argued that being kicked out of the U.S. Senate was the kindest treatment that ought to be accorded Senator Robert M. LaFollette from neighboring Wisconsin, who had opposed war with Germany. Court martial would be better.

As trusted Safety Committee members to serve with Thurstone, Higgins arranged for appointment of Manfred Walster and Geoffrey Blankston, the automobile dealers, and Ernst Hebermann—who now spelled his first name "Ernest" and dropped the second "n" from his family name. He also arranged for appointment of a prominent farmer with a Scandinavian name, Tony Alquist, noted in equal measure for his success in hog production and his antipathy toward the NPL, who to Alquist's mind were dupes of the Bolsheviks. Alquist, who had shed the name "Anton" given him by his immigrant mother, had been an officer in Adams township, a one-term Athena County Commissioner, and a land speculator.

All of these committeemen had been suspicious of the *Veckomonitoren* and cheered the appointment of Judge John F. McGee to the State Commission of Public Safety, the governing body. McGee was to become the best known of the State Commission officials, absolutely unbending in his views of how patriotism and support for the war should be maintained. To Judge McGee, regular display of the flag and regular expression of absolute loyalty should be expected and demanded of every last citizen

The Athena County Committeemen agreed. With a state law and the powerful bank behind them, Thurstone's Committee could act as investigator, judge, and jury in dealing with any person or group in Athena County deemed in any way to be obstructing the war effort.

So what about the local newspapers? Initially, Thurstone ignored Ivar and Inez Lindfors and the new Athena County *Forum*, since Thurstone and Higgins now had a more than reliable editor in Ollie Moller at the rejuvenated *Gazette*. In announcing the establishment of the Athena County Public Safety Committee, the *Gazette* said:

> "Responding to the outpouring of patriotism of Athena County residents, the Minnesota Commission on Public Safety has authorized a local Committee to aid in prosecuting the

war effort. The zeal with which local patriots will enlist in the military services and do their part to defeat the barbarous Huns of Germany will not be dampened by the traitorous but raucous few who mingle in our midst. Citizens of this area may be assured that the noble war effort, which is requiring so many of our boys to risk their lives in the trenches of Europe, will not be threatened by the acts of any slackers or persons with questionable motives."

The rest of the article, in addition to naming all the members, left little doubt about who might be categorized as having "questionable motives." The next paragraph stated that:

"Chairman Roscoe Thurstone tells us that the Committee would watch closely the acts of groups that have expressed pro-German, socialist, or 'pacifist' sentiments in the past, such as the I.W.W. and the Nonpartisan League."

Editor Moller was even more specific about how responsible citizens might conduct themselves should they find themselves in gatherings or meetings where such sentiments might be expressed. His account concluded:

"Now, Athena County citizens may be assured of full backing for their righteous indignation when they hear treasonous utterances. If the ilk of A. C. Townley or Eugene Debs should come to Belleville, they must be forewarned that the loyal citizenry might greet them with a lively showering of overripe tomatoes, hard cucumbers or perhaps even more convincing missiles such as the smooth but firm rocks from Athena County's rich fields. Or perhaps a smart whack on the buttocks with a barrel stave would serve to remind such troublemakers of the sentiments of upright locals. As Chairman Thurstone has said, the stave treatment is what these bums and sluggards might well wish for, since many public-spirited leaders have mentioned more drastic correctives such as tar-and-feathering and even necktie parties.

* * *

The war was not the only hot issue in Belleville—another was liquor. A temperance union chapter had earlier persuaded the Athena County Board to pass ordinances that, in the interests of throttling Demon Rum, limited the hours of the three local saloons. These establishments were required to close at 11 p.m. on weekdays, at noon on Saturdays and all day on Sundays.

In the past, such leading figures as Pudgy Thurstone, J.B. Higgins, and Ernest Heberman had accepted the saloons as marginal local businesses, attracting people who might not be in Belleville otherwise. Whether they would have any shopping dollars left after a few hours in a saloon was sometimes debated. The usual consensus was that women would shop with money kept in their purses, while the men drank.

The saloons had been scenes of carousing, some fights, one near-murder, and other unsavory activities that centered around a few young women from Minneapolis who had been hired by the Imperial Palace Saloon two blocks down from Wells street, on Chapman avenue, ostensibly as bar maids. It was widely assumed that the occupational responsibilities of these persons went well beyond serving liquor.

* * *

In their first meeting in early May, Roscoe Thurstone's committee members lost no time in getting to their foremost concern: The Nonpartisan League. Reggie Code suggested bluntly that the Committee simply run out of the county any organizer or speaker the League might truck in. Ethan Kendall advocated confiscating their literature, along with "all the trash from the I.W.W.," which was, in fact, rare in a nonlumbering and nonmining town such as Belleville. Roy Evans and Al Allcott nodded concurrence.

Roscoe Thurstone privately agreed with all sentiments,

but he showed why he, and not one of the others, was chosen as chairman. "What we need," he pointed out, "is a popular action that both jolts the community and gets most people here to back us up—one that gets headlines in the Minneapolis and St. Paul papers. If we go after the League first off, there would be too much of an uproar. So we get everyone on our side at the beginning with a different move. Something that even much of the League bunch would agree with. Especially the League women."

"And what would that be?" Ernest Heberman asked.

A tolerant smile crossed Roscoe's face. "The Imperial Palace is a den of lust and immorality, and a widely recognized threat to public safety. So we give them some firm rules to clean up their businesses, in the public interest." The rest of the Committee marveled at this sage suggestion. The saloons had brought no end of complaints from the responsible citizens and here was a chance to respond favorably to those complaints and look good in the process. Roscoe was quite aware that his Athena County Public Safety Committee contained nobody with any direct investment in, or relatives associated with, any of the liquor establishments. In membership, the Committee was more or less the Belleville Commercial Club, with a few politicians like Pudgy Thurstone added.

The issue decided, the committee went straight to work on a notice to be given to the three saloons:

1. Close Friday evening and all day Saturday, as well as Sunday.
2. Remove all employees and patrons of "questionable character."
3. Make certain no customer is seen inebriated on Belleville streets.
4. Be responsible for any "seditious, treasonous or unpatriotic talk" that might occur in "or be encouraged by the atmosphere created by" their establishments.

After reading it through, Geoffrey Blankston wondered

aloud whether those requirements weren't really impossible for any of the saloons to meet. Again, Roscoe Thurstone smiled patiently. Finally Tony Alquist grunted, "Isn't that the idea, Jeff?"

Acting as the agent for the State Commission, the Committee issued the order to take effect the following week in May, and delivered it to the Imperial Palace and the other two saloons on Wednesday. That timing allowed the *Gazette* to be the first of the two newspapers in Belleville to announce the order.

The owner of the Imperial Palace asked for a meeting with the Committee, to no avail. His barmaids left late Friday for Chicago and, without any weekend business now possible, he closed the saloon. The other two saloons simply ignored the directive until Sheriff Mayberry arrived Saturday afternoon with two heavily-armed deputies to order the patrons out and padlock the doors. These closures occurred on a Saturday afternoon, when Belleville streets were crowded with hundreds of shoppers who observed the events first-hand.

The following Tuesday, the *Gazette* announced the improved protection of the public safety. It quoted Committee chairman Thurstone as saying that the closing came only after extensive, but, unfortunately, futile efforts were made to persuade the saloon keepers to mend their ways. In his editorial, editor Moller said:

> Respectable citizens of Athena County have long tolerated these seamy, immoral and unwholesome places where liquor and loose talk flow freely. Where opposition to the Draft and the Great Cause flourishes. Where our young people are enticed to sins of the worse kind.
>
> Good to be rid of these dens of iniquity. Let all citizens rejoice that our state legislators had the courage to empower a Public Safety Commission to act so decisively. None of this folderol and fiddlefaddle of requesting injunctions and interminable court procedure. Something needed to be done, and by gum, we got it done.

This appeared on Tuesday, giving Ivar and Inez a day to ponder whether and how to respond. It wasn't easy, because while neither was exactly a teetotaler, they were more or less sympathetic to the Prohibition Movement. Inez couldn't let pass the obvious irony of the Moller editorial.

"Do you suppose Ollie was sober when he scribbled all those words about seamy, immoral and unwholesome places?"

Ivar could only nod and grimace.

In their editorial in the *Forum* on Thursday, Ivar and Inez wrote:

> Let's not be too quick to cheer the closing of the Belleville saloons. Yes, it may be wise to rid Belleville of liquor sales and all that goes with it, but why not do it in the American, democratic way? Our Constitution says we shouldn't lose our lives, liberty, or property without due process of law.
>
> We do not believe the end justifies the means. To condone this way of getting rid of the saloons is to adopt the very ways that we despise when they are done by the German government.

For the next month, each newspaper berated the other for its most recent misguided views on the saloon closing. At first, the attacks were more or less on substance; ultimately, the barbs became personal and vindictive:

> *Gazette*: It must come as a rude shock to the patriotic citizens of Belleville to learn that they have in their midst a newspaper that so brazenly opposes the efforts of our Public Safety Committee to get rid of vice and anti-American talk. Well, at least we know where the sentiments of those editors are.
>
> *Forum*: It is a matter of sheer wonder that a newspaper should assign to itself the lofty job of judge of who is or is not American, and act as if that newspaper is the conscience of the whole county.
>
> *Gazette*: We find it rather curious that the opposition

newspaper in this town should be so skittish about proclaiming itself to be on the American side. Even a Stockholm newspaper said that sympathy for Germany as well as food for Swedes went down with a ship torpedoed by the Huns. Too bad the *Forum*'s editor doesn't read the papers from his own country.

*Forum*: The other newspaper in this town will stop at nothing to be insult the entire farming community and those leaders within it who stand for cooperatives and other ways of providing better equity for the ones who produce food.

*Gazette*: Think of it. The Nonpartisan League, which the "other" newspaper touts so pompously, would have the state own public utilities, banks, railroads, grain elevators, mills, and the Lord only knows what else. Bolshevism, that's what it is. Except Townley and the other NPL big guns are filling their pockets by fleecing their members of $16 apiece.

*Forum*: If the other newspaper editor would considerate elementary economics, this gentleman would understand that, but perhaps this is asking too much. Also, if they would say one ting that fits with our great Constitution, we might considerate them as American.

*Gazette*: It would help if the *Forum* editor, with all his fine education, knew how to write and spell in good English. It seems to us they don't really want America to win this fight, even though anyone with a lick of common sense knows it's a fight to end all wars.

*Forum*: Common sense is what editor Moller of the *Gazette* calls for. It occurs to us that if he really wished to apply this thing he calls common sense, he would understand that the flourmills we have now are not giving farmers a fair price.

*Gazette*: If the esteemed editor of the *Forum* had at least the mental capacity to grasp his posterior with both hands....

Ivar bemoaned the occasional lapses in his writing and spelling that even Inez hadn't caught, but were jumped on by Moller with editorial glee. The "be insult" was a result of slovenly oversight; he noted too late that "considerate" is not a verb like "proliferate." Misspelling "thing" as "ting" led to much amusement at the expense of people speaking

Scandinavian-American dialect. Publishing the Swedish-language paper hadn't helped Ivar and Inez master English as completely as they wished.

Not lost on either newspaper, though, was the fact that this running exchange of barbed and ad hominem assaults was producing heavy readership of both. Shoppers would buy whichever paper was most recent, often on their way to the grocery. In more than a few cases they complained to the grocer that they couldn't find his listings in one paper or the other. After all, the saloon closing was a feverish topic, and animosity between editors added some color and excitement to the fray. As a result, grocer Jeb Merriweather divided his advertising in the summer of 1917 between the rival newspapers. A few other merchants followed suit.

Yet the fiery excitement that these editorial exchanges ignited couldn't last. It was like overhearing bickering neighbors: entertaining at first but irritating as it drags on. Furthermore, however much loathing there was among the significant citizens of Belleville, they would not tolerate a newspaper feud if it threatened their business or community positions.

The *Forum* received and printed one letter supporting its editorials on the saloon issue. It was from a retired postal worker, a querulous old crank who publicly opposed city officials on nearly everything and was, therefore, influential on nothing. This fellow wrote that "if they can close saloons and get away with it, they can close churches and get away with that, too." This point of logic was widely dismissed as preposterous.

In fact, this editorial page wrangle wouldn't have occurred at all if the Nonpartisan League hadn't, by this time, become a formidable force in Athena County. More than half the farmers had paid at least one year's dues, and another fourth were probably in sympathy with the League, at least in their antipathy toward the commercial people who either sold them goods or bought their produce.

Pudgy Thurstone and his mentor J. B. Higgins pondered

whether they should simply shut the *Forum* down as a threat to Public Safety. For the time being, they chose to let the paper go, since, in their minds, it was doing little more than taking the bait dangled every week by Ollie Moller and the *Gazette*. In time, these two figured, the *Forum* would do itself in. "Give those Scandihoovian editors enough rope to hang themselves," Pudgy counseled. "Then we shut them down after others start screaming for their throats."

There was another reason for allowing the *Forum* to continue. It had wide circulation and the Wells street merchants other than grocer Merriweather found that the *Gazette* failed to give them a real alternative for advertising. The *Gazette* had only modest circulation, owing to its boycott by two-thirds of the rural population. Nobody wanted to risk putting enough money into that newspaper, knowing it would never carry food and clothing and hardware ads to more than a third of the county population. Ollie Moller and his part-time helper were no match for Inez Lindfors when it came to setting up attractive ads that brought in customers.

J. B. Higgins would be the last to risk more loan money on an operation like the one Moller was running, regardless of how patriotic Ollie's editorials were. Nobody in Belleville was more acutely aware of the problems of the *Gazette* than Ivar and Inez Lindfors, especially its failure to deliver local advertising from the merchants who supported it to the wider population of Athena County.

"Ivar, we can get that advertising back for the *Forum*," Inez said one day when the press stopped for a cleaning. "Irma Johnston came by today and bought a big ad—three columns wide and 18 inches deep—to announce a big clothing sale."

"Wonderful. Can we get any others?"

"Just watch. Isn't that Roy Evans coming down the street? Bet you he stops here."

Inez quickly remembered that when the Pflueger barn was rebuilt, the boards and timbers came from Roy Evans' Lumber Yard, and the old *Veckomonitoren* had made much of this fact in print. She mulled this over as Evans, sober-faced, opened the door slowly, stepping inside and up to the high counter where people paid their subscriptions or bought this week's edition.

Evans, a short, stocky man about Ivar's age, was sullen until Inez smiled and greeted him. He first wondered whether he should discuss his problem with "the man in charge," but then, remembering the tense encounter at the Commercial Club's meeting, thought she might be easier to deal with than Ivar.

In his hand was a wrinkled copy of an advertisement, ripped from a trade magazine, for barn materials. He handed it to Inez. Without any preliminaries he asked: "Suppose you folks could run this? I need to get the word out that we've got good lumber for barns. And I think many farmers would buy it if they thought about it."

Inez read the copy—that is, the wording—of the advertisement. It said:

Are You Thinking of Building a New Barn?
We Have Just the Right Lumber and Parts for You
at _____ Lumber Yard.

Roy Evans had penciled his own name in the blank.

Inez looked at the words and chewed the inside of her left cheek. "Oh, we certainly can run it. But I have a question about these words.

"Suppose a farmer reading the paper just says 'No' to the question. What then? Maybe we can say it in a way that makes the farmer believe he *should* be thinking about it."

Roy shrugged. "Well, how could we do that?"

"Give me a few minutes. I think about it." In her excitement, Inez again dropped a word.

"Okay, take your time. I'm not selling enough lumber to keep me busy anyhow. Let me know when you come up with some better words." With that, he walked around the counter and had a perfunctory chat with Ivar, next to the now clanking printing press.

With a black crayon, Inez scribbled this on a sheet of blank printing paper:

> Your Old Barn Isn't Just What You Want, Is It? You Really Need It, So Why Not Build a Much Better One? At Evans Lumber Yard, We Have All the Boards, Timbers, Windows and Stanchions for a Barn That Will Keep Your Animals Happy and Make You Proud!

In a box of old engravings, Inez found an attractive barn with a gambrel roof and a cupola on top. With an inkpad, she blotted the engraving on a clean sheet and then wrote the words around the picture, using the same lettering skill that had impressed her future husband back in Graskoping. She showed it to Roy Evans, with an added thought: "See, the idea is to ask a question that gets a person thinking. Every barn—like every house—has some things the owners would like to change. So most people will say 'yes' to the question and maybe then mull it over. That's what we want: Keep a person thinking about it."

Roy Evans was impressed.

"Just might do the trick, Mrs. Lindfors. Let's run it for the next month. Send me the bill." With a glance back toward Ivar, he added. "No hard feelings, Ivar. I'll sell to any farmer, League member or not."

Ivar nodded. "So long, Roy," he said, as the lumber dealer left the print shop and headed back to his place of business. Ivar had heard talk about the League starting a cooperative lumber business. He quietly hoped they would decide against that.

During the next month, three farmers bought large orders of lumber from Evans, two for new barns and one for remodeling to make an old barn bigger and better. All three mentioned seeing the Evans advertisement in the *Forum*.

Roy Evans watched with satisfaction on a warm day of June 1917 as his truck—one of the largest in town—rumbled out of his sprawling yards with timbers, boards, and shingles for the first of the three buyers. His sheds stretched some 100 feet across his back lot and alongside the railroad spur where both white pine from northern Minnesota and fir from farther west had been piled up without a sale—until this month, that is, after three weeks of the advertisement put together by that clever woman at the *Forum*.

Roy Evans would have to defend running that advertisement when he next sat down with Commercial Club men. Sure, he hated the League, too, but "business is business, isn't it?" He wouldn't mention that the purchasers took loans from a League bank in North Dakota. Of course, J. B. Higgins would know that, eventually.

\* \* \*

Probably no other grade-school child read as much of the *Forum* as did Charlotte, largely because she spent much time at the print shop with her parents. One day, sitting on one of the high stools near the press, her blue eyes bugged at a freshly–printed headline saying:

### WAR AIRPLANE NOW FLIES 140 MILES AN HOUR

"Gee, it would be fun to go that fast. Mama, can we fly in an airplane some day? See the world like birds do? Papa, do airplanes flap their wings like robins?"

"No, Charlotte, their wings are stiff and solid."

"Not always. Miss Everson said someone tried to make a plane like a bird. It's called an ornithopter."

"Where did you hear that word?" It was new to Ivar, and it sounded disturbingly off-color.

"Mrs. Everson wrote it on the blackboard. It means a machine that flaps its wings like a bird." Ivar made a mental note to look up the word.

Charlotte skipped another headline saying 13 ocean vessels had been sunk by German submarines. One war question a day was enough.

She saw an advertisement, far more interesting:

### GIRLS! GIRLS! TRY IT! BEAUTIFY YOUR HAIR!

Under these words was a box two columns wide and 10 inches deep, describing a patented rinse available by mail order.

"Mama, what does 'Beautify' mean?"

Inez hadn't written this advertisement; it came from boilerplate sent by the company selling the product.

"I guess it means to make your hair pretty. Maybe a different color."

"Oh, I want to try it! I'm tired of blond hair!"

"Oh, really. What color would you like"

"Red. Like Kathleen Hannigan."

"She's Irish. Her hair is naturally red."

Charlotte frowned, then brightened. "Then why don't we change my name to something Irish?" Charlotte quickly put her hand over her mouth, fearing she had said something forbidden.

It was forbidden, but it startled Inez who was reminded again, in a peculiar way, that Charlotte was not her child and seemed, somehow, to sense it. "Now don't be silly, Charlotte. Come, it's time to go home."

# IX. THE SPEECH AT THE RALLY

As many as a third of the attendees arrived in Fords, either the two-seaters with tops down, or the so-called touring car versions that looked like cheap surreys with odd little engine boxes instead of horses at the front. Some Fords displayed added contraptions, bought from the Sears-Roebuck catalog that allowed modification for pumping water or even plowing, but doing neither one adequately or reliably. Albert Theide drove an imposing Hudson six, a vehicle that cost three or four times as much as a $500 Ford. Bo Nygren proudly drove his 1915 Ford town car, a second-hand but shiny, rare and stately machine that Doctor Blake had traded for a new one at the Walster-Blankston Garage.

By these conveyances, some 385 farm families from Athena County—totaling well over a thousand people—came to the Nonpartisan League picnic on Leonard Huisby's expansive farm the last Sunday of July 1917.

As they gathered, many of these folks couldn't help wonder why this big picnic came at the height of the wheat harvesting season. They talked and murmured about it and came to a consensus about politics and cohesion:

> "Makes you wonder, don't it, if we shouldn't be out cutting and shocking the wheat."
> "Ya, but dey got ol' A. C. Townley himself to talk and it had to be now."
> "Why now?"
> "Vell, ve aren't getting enough people into de En Pee Ell."
> "That's right, you know Arnie Hedlund? He's in charge

of getting new folks, and he ain't getting enuf signing up and paying dues."

"Ya, and den dere's politics. Dem elections ain't much more than a year away."

"So Townley, he's going to fire us all up for the1918 election?"

"Ya, dat's about it."

"Well, there's more to it, now. Al Theide and Bjorn Nygren, they ain't been getting along, and they're s'posed to be officers. Maybe with this big get-together, they can bury the hatchet, you think?"

"Ya, dey still takin' it hard ofer dat silly deal vit the calfs. Efen vorse, you know, Eva, Bjorn's vife, she von't let it drop. My Ingrid says Eva told the whole Lut'ran supper club how dumb her man was."

"Well, let's hope they shake hands today. We need ever'body pullin' in the same direction. Townley's talk should help."

But not all the talk was about the organization. Farmers talked about farming:

"Think this weather will hold for threshing? Been awful good, but we can't be sure. Ah, smell that red clover. Ain't that a good smell?"

"Ya, but that wheat stubble, smells musty, prob'ly got some smut in it."

"Well, there's another smell here, too. Seems we're down wind from some pig farm."

"What if it rains or hails hard next few days? Say, any of you got cows with grubs in their hide? How do you get 'em out?"

"Easy, take yer thumbs and jus' pop 'em out."

"Dang, those grasshoppers are bad."

"Well, it's the dry weather, you see."

"I need a new horse, my ol' King got the heaves bad and I got to sell him to the mink farm. Anyone know one for sale?"

"What? Get a tractor? Ah, ain't got time for those new-fangled things. Cost too much and always stuck. Takes a forty to turn one around on."

While the men clustered in their groups, the women gathered around the long tables where all manner of beef, chicken, pork, potatoes, peas, and bread and gravy would be spread out by each family. And the women talked and laughed about different things:

"Sure is a nice day, isn't it?"

"Oh, yes, it's hot, but ain't that a lovely breeze? The Lord has been good to us, we should all be thankful."

"How's Melanie Moen's man Delbert after that nasty fall in the silo?"

"He just broke his wrist, now there's something to be thankful for."

"Gertie, didn't I hear you made blackberry jam?"

"Yes, after canning all those tomatoes."

"Say, I wondered, do you cook them tomatoes in open kettles, or cover them?"

"Oh, cover them, not that it makes much difference"

"Oh, look at that strawberry sauce. How long do you cook it, Maryann? How much water did you add?

"Oh, none, really. Just put on sugar and that brings out the juice."

"Oh, really, Melissa is leaving Elmer? Why, for land's sake. They say she's in the family way, too."

"Oh, Marie, what's that bouquet you have there?'

"Vell, chust a bunch of marsh marigolds, some vild wiolets and lilies I picked along the road."

"My, they're lovely, and smell so good, too."

Dozens of topics were covered by people of various ages and gender. Gossip, horseshoes, and politics at the same gathering made sense, because each was a cherished element of diversion from the dreary tedium of rural life.

Leonard Huisby thoughtfully marked off one area of a field for a baseball game and another for horseshoes, organized games and dances for the smaller children, leaving the orchard and oak grove area for the picnic. The hay from these areas had recently been mowed—too early, really, for second-crop harvesting, but it was a needed concession for the big event. Better than putting the picnic on a pasture, where visitors would hazard the sordid leavings of flatulent cattle gorging daily on fresh grass.

A hay wagon was pulled to the south side of the picnic area, where the speaker of the day would regale and inspire the crowd with political exhortation. Just who that speaker would be was not known for certain until the day of the picnic. Speculation ran between N. S. Randall, a well-known League organizer, and A. C. Townley himself. Rumors that Townley would show up had circulated throughout Athena County, helped by Leonard Huisby's own allowances that such might occur.

Those rumors eventually reached the advisory council of the Athena County Public Safety Committee, and this august body concluded quickly that any speech by an NPL agitator was a threat to the public order and should, therefore, be prohibited. Roscoe Thurstone summoned Sheriff Alfred Mayberry and directed him to prevent the speech "if one of the known disloyal agitators like Randall or Townley" showed up.

Alfred Mayberry was not exactly enthralled by this directive. He had run for the Sheriff's office and won twice, first on his experience as a captain in the Spanish-American war and, for his second term, on his ability to hit it off with farmers. He had even been given some credit for helping quiet such outbursts as the bitter Theide-Nygren feud over the quirky calf sale.

The Sheriff had been uneasy about shutting down the liquor establishments in Belleville and was glad it was over; it had not turned out to be difficult, with only three owners involved. However, confronting an organization that spoke for some 2,000 farm people was a different matter. Antagonizing this formidable organization by shutting down a speech at a picnic on a popular farmer's property would spell his doom in a future election. So he said to Thurstone: "Roscoe, if I'm to keep a Nonpartisan League speaker off the platform, I need a warrant. You gonna get me one?"

Pudgy wet his cigar and, with the aid of two stubby fingers in a V, curled the stogie between the thick lips that contributed to his moniker. "You don't need one, Alfred," the County Attorney responded, "not with that order from the Public Safety Commission."

"What order? They didn't give me nothing. Didn't have time to get one, even if we tried."

Pudgy settled back in his swivel chair and chewed some more on the cigar, now gone cold.

"Well, I'm giving you one now, verbally. Don't forget, our local committee acts in the name of the state Commission. Simple case of preventing public disorder, Sheriff. These are slackers, right? People known to be disloyal. They've been talking against the draft. They don't buy Liberty Bonds. Way I hear it, loyal citizens are so mad they might go after 'em with sticks or baseball bats while they are speaking. Now it's your job to keep the peace, right? Prevent turmoil. So, to keep the peace, you keep these buggers from talking."

Sheriff Mayberry chewed the side of his mouth in thought. "I s'pose you know where this speech will be, Pudgy—at a big picnic at Huisby's place. He's a good man. Everybody speaks well of him. One of the finest rural citizens of the county, right? Then, too, you and I both know folks at the picnic will treat the speaker as a god or something. So how do we figger that speech will cause turmoil?"

The Sheriff, not well trained in legal theory but comfortable with everyday principles of law and order, wondered to Pudgy Thurstone about "this First Amendment business"—that seemed to protect speech and peaceful gatherings.

Pudgy shook his head. "That First Amendment talk is fine in peacetime, but Sheriff, this is war. You don't talk that junk when you're fighting Huns. Did you yell First

Amendment to your troops when you tried to make them fight Spaniards in the Philippines? Of course not.

"Disloyalty, treason, those things aren't covered by the First Amendment. You can't go up and down the street yelling your love for the Kaiser any more than you can yell that someone is sleeping with someone else's wife. That is, not without opening yourself up to a libel charge."

The cold, wet cigar was out of Pudgy's mouth now, cradled again between the index and middle fingers of his left hand. "If you can talk them into canceling the speech, fine. But if it takes an arrest, go ahead and do it, under authority of the Safety Commission." Then, his smile baring teeth that again clamped down on a cigar growing steadily colder and wetter, Pudgy added: "Always remember, you'll be serving your country well."

Then he threw in the clincher: "What judge, Alfred, would go against you when the country is at war?" His thick lips wrapped tightly around his moist but diminishing cigar, then loosened as he continued.

"You must be reading, Alfred, about what's going on down at New Ulm? The mayor, the city attorney, and the county auditor spoke at a dumb meeting, said some things against the draft system. You know what I bet happens? The State Commission of Public Safety—the agency we answer to—will kick them all out of office."

Sheriff Mayberry had indeed read about the New Ulm fracas, but he stuck to his argument. "Pudgy, the judges don't elect sheriffs, or county attorneys, neither." Pudgy Thurstone simply shrugged. His stature and position was such that no attorney in the area—and there were few—would be likely to run against him when he was up for re-election.

Alfred Mayberry left his County Attorney's office still not entirely sure what he would do at the Leonard Huisby farm Sunday, or even whether he would take deputies. He got along with farmers better than any of his three deputies did, and retaliation from farmers at the next election was something to be avoided.

The sheriff drove his county-owned Studebaker that Sunday to the Huisby farm, alone. He arrived as League workers were setting up a crude podium on the hay wagon platform. He had never seen A. C. Townley in person, and he was a bit nonplussed when the tall man with the large nose and soft brown eyes eagerly took his hand.

"Why, I am most pleased to meet you Sheriff. Nice you could join us in this festive gathering," the Great Organizer said. "Give you a chance to hear what I have to say and find out that I'm not the fire-breathing disloyal traitor that the Big Biz people have painted me to be."

"Look at this gathering," Townley continued, sweeping a long, dark-coated arm toward the gathered crowd, most of them sitting, standing or squatting around picnic baskets, the clang of horseshoes in their ears from matches not quite completed. "These, Sheriff, are the most loyal and vital Americans you'll find anywhere today."

"There's a great war on, Sheriff," Townley said in a somber tone that held out the possibility of benign ignorance in the listener, "and fighting men in a war, not to mention the civilian victims, need food in quantities never before imagined. These are the loyal American farmers who will produce that food, and all they ask is that they get just compensation for their patriotic efforts."

"Well," the Sheriff answered, "if that's what you're saying, there should be no problem. Just don't get into the business of whether we should be in this war—or worse, whether young men should report for the draft. If the papers don't report any treasonous statements, nobody will mind this meeting."

With a smile, Townley shook the Sheriff's hand again and with lumbering steps climbed up on the wagon and faced the crowd. After a brief introduction by Leonard Huisby, Arthur Townley spoke.

"My friends, I have been eager for months to come back to Minnesota and to encourage you who have the most blessed occupation in the world. As I rode the train down from Fargo, through my home town of Alexandria and to Belleville, I could only marvel at the bounteous fields of corn, newly harvested oats and wheat, ripe clover—and the magnificent cattle you are raising to produce the milk to feed a state and a nation at war.

"Yes, you farmers are doing American Freedom and Democracy a great service here. And what thanks are you getting for it? From the government? From the big business people? From the railroads? Any rewards at all? My friends, those tycoons are getting their share while you get dribbling pennies, have no mistake about it."

Sheriff Mayberry, standing near Bo Nygren about 30 feet to the front of the wagon-podium, shifted uncomfortably and caught the speaker's eye.

"For those of you who haven't already seen him," Townley continued, "let me recognize your well-known and highly respected Sheriff Alfred Mayberry. I understand he has been directed to come out here and check on this gathering to be sure nothing said or done is disloyal. Oh, he's only doing his job, or that is, his job as the Minnesota Public Safety Commission sees it. There he stands, over there by the good, courageous editor you all know, Ivar Lindfors and his wife Inez and their charming daughter. Wave your hand Sheriff, to all your friends and constituents. It's so good of you to be with us and to allow all of us in the League to assure you of what loyal Americans we are."

"We farmers and former farmers"—Townley added with a mischievous and mildly self-deprecatory tone that gave way immediately to a serious one—"we are the heart of loyalty in America. It is our loyalty to food production, our loyalty to feeding people, our loyalty to raising crops in good weather and bad, in good times and bad times, that keeps this great country on its feet."

He paused, and then, with a magnificent gesture, Townley thundered: "We would like to see equal loyalty on the part of all other parties and all other persons in this country, in this state, and in this county."

"I—ask—you," he said, delivering each of these three words as a separate intonation preceded by a 45-degree turn of his head, "is it loyal for anyone to make triple the profits from a business because there is a war on? Is it loyal for those profit triplers to question the loyalty of those whose pockets are empty? Is it loyal to interfere with an organization that is giving new strength and life to farm families who are the mainspring of the country?"

Townley paused deliberately between the questions, giving the crowd an opportunity to shout their agreement with a loud and prolonged "No-o-o."

Sheriff Mayberry scowled and thought to himself, oh shit, here comes that stuff the Commission thinks is disloyal.

As if he read the Sheriff's mind, Townley shifted his ground a bit.

"Yes, there are counties in Minnesota and I dare say one or two even in North Dakota where farm people and town people don't see things from the same side of the fence. But as I'm sure Sheriff Mayberry would agree, Athena County is a place where the merchants and farmers know how to put aside their differences to work together in a great cause.

"I challenge the farmers here and the merchants in Belleville to continue to work together to set fair prices for buying and selling and to cooperate in what needs to be done to get this war won and behind us and bring our boys home safely from over there."

He's a smart cuss, Sheriff Mayberry thought. *He's turning the loyalty business around, and he's doing exactly what he denies: attacking business people without claiming to or naming them. Sure, everyone knows who and what he means: the Grain Terminals and the Wells Street Merchants.*

Sheriff Mayberry was content now. He could go back to the Public Safety Committee and tell them Townley preached cooperation between farm and town. This was technically true. Whether what he had heard was genuine, the Sheriff had his doubts, but he figured he was off the hook now for neither banning this speech nor arresting the speaker.

Which was exactly what the speaker had intended for the Sheriff to conclude. The crowd roared its approval of Townley's speech. He waved his arms and the roar erupted again, this time punctuated by whistles and "yew tell 'em, A.C..", stamping of feet and a few other remonstrances normally unheard and unseen in this reserved culture. The picnic was over, but it was nearly an hour before the last family had left.

* * *

Reactions to Townley's speech among the departing crowd were mostly enthusiastic, although not entirely uniform.

"Feisty cuss, ain't he?"

"By golly, he'll show those scalawags down in Washington what farmers can do when they stick together."

"Real stem-winder, wa'n't it?"

"Yah, more life in him 'dan we git from the minister."

"Yep, wait'll those shop people in town hear about this."

"Bet this gets 'em riled up. Talks with fire, don't he?"

"He could have talked against getting into this consarned European war."

"Well, now, that would get him in trouble with this big Safety Committee. He was smart to stay away from that. You saw the Sheriff here, din't you?"

"Hey, Charlie, you ain't said much. What did you t'ink of it?"

"I dunno, Wally. An inch of rain would've done a helluva lot more good."

* * *

Sheriff Alfred Mayberry was not the first to tell the Public Safety Committee about the Townley speech. Pudgy Thurstone already had reports from a half dozen farmers who had attended the picnic either as uncommitted persons, or, in a few cases, simply as spies.

Ollie Moller's *Gazette* was the first to give a report in its Tuesday edition:

### NPL HEAD ATTACKS AMERICAN BUSINESS LEADERS

---

TOWNLEY SPEECH SAID TO CONTAIN FAMILIAR

---

ANTI-AMERICAN SLOGANS AND INNUENDO
SHERIFF ALLOWS SPEECH AFTER TOWNLEY
PROMISE TO AVOID DISLOYALTY

---

BROKEN PROMISE, AUDIENCE MEMBER SAYS

In a typical demagogic speech from the rabble-rousing head of the Nonpartisan League, we are told, A. C. Townley continued his inflammatory use of disloyal innuendo to attack American business and governmental leadership during a Nonpartisan League gathering Sunday in Athena County.

This speech was clearly disloyal and treasonous, according to several in the audience who heard the speech and could hardly believe their ears. It is said that demagogue Townley libeled business leaders in the entire nation, accusing them of earning TRIPLE profits from their dealings with the government

Even more appalling is the fact that the Sheriff of Athena County was so intimidated by the speaker and certain agitators that he was unable to fulfill his obligation to drive the rascal Townley off the podium and out of the county.

On Thursday, the *Forum* displayed its version of the speech, complete with a response to the *Gazette*:

### NPL SPEAKER UNDERSCORES
### LOYALTY OF NONPARTISAN LEAGUE

---

Townley's dramatic speech challenges

other Americans to match League in
serving a country at war

_____

In patriotic spirit, Townley   calls for
farm-town cooperation in Athena County

It has unfortunately become the rule, rather than the
exception, for the other newspaper published in Belleville to
give its readers a second-hand account of a major event
without the writer of that account even being there.

Had the esteemed editor of the *Gazette* made the effort
to attend the gigantic rally on the Huisby farm last Sunday,
he would have heard a stirring call to farmers to support the
national effort and to join forces with town people in doing so.

But no. That newspaper has no compunctions about
sowing discord in this county and spreading lies about the
Nonpartisan League and what a famous and loyal American
said to thunderous applause at a country picnic. A paper of
that ilk will stop at no mischief to fan the flames of distrust
between local citizens.

Lest anyone fear the *Forum* is feeding distrust, let us
take this opportunity to offer the county a chance to heal. The
*Forum* proposes that a FORUM ON AMERICANISM be held
in Belleville, and that noted speakers of every political
persuasion be invited to give their views on what loyal
Americanism means in prosecuting this Great War.

We even have a suggestion for at least two speakers for
this *Forum*, which should be held September 8 in Belleville.
We propose Judge John F. McGee of St. Paul, the noted
member of the Minnesota Commission of Public Safety who
has voiced most concern about disloyalty and Senator Robert
M. LaFollette from Wisconsin, who is already scheduled to
speak the following day in St. Paul.

Ivar was pleased with and grateful to Clara Ferguson
for supplying him with terms like "ilk" and "compunctions"
that gave his writing a rather contemporary tone. Ivar had
originally written that the *Gazette* was worthy only of sale at
second-hand stores that dealt in junk of all kinds. Inez and

Clara had counseled against that, as an unwise slap at a couple of marginal but wholesome retailers of used goods in Belleville who had shown no particular hostility to the *Forum* or the League. Many a cash-strapped NPL farmer had bought used items at these stores, at very low cost.

\* \* \*

Throughout her first 10 years of acting as mother to Charlotte, Inez silently and privately trod a vexing and endless trail of self-interrogation, replete with dark and distressing side passages, none of which promised a way out of her dilemma. She could hardly find her way through a week without that inner, convulsive wrenching nurtured by dubious posing as a real mother.

She was sure her quandary never hindered her motherliness toward Charlotte; the child was as attached to her as any child could be to a parent. People seemed to think of Inez as nothing less than the ideal mother. At worst, they would say, "too bad she don't have more kids, so she don't spoil this one so bad." So it was rather easy to leave the whole thing unmentioned. But unmentioned forever? Especially to Charlotte?

Befuddled by this tangle of circumstances, Inez mentally rehearsed, in recurring cycles, alternative scenarios about how all these things had happened, and what if anything she would do about them. Her first version was one founded on pure trust and conviction of duty. Her husband had unfortunately and unknowingly, but through no especially damning misbehavior, begotten a child who suddenly and catastrophically lost her mother.

She would then negate this account at every crucial point. Ivar was an irresponsible rake, he probably had fathered several children, he feigned innocence and perhaps even drove Charlotte's mother to suicide.

Such a black tale being too much to tolerate, Inez would erase it in part. Then on her mind's messy palimpsest she would concoct a muddled variant, usually one that left Ivar innocent of lying while convicted of the gentler wrongs of naiveté, stupidity, insensitivity or some combination.

Ivar had never agreed to reveal to Charlotte who her true mother was. "Why not leave it all as it is?" he would ask.

"Well, suppose Charlotte wants to return to Sweden to visit her birthplace? Mightn't she learn then and come to hate her parents as a result?"

His answer would be quick: "Oh, but this war makes it unlikely that any of us will ever see Europe again."

Then there was Inez' own inability to conceive a child. She was now nearing her mid-thirties and had conceived once—shortly after being married—aboard a pitching steamship, and that brief pregnancy had ended in a miscarriage. While she enjoyed the freedom to work with Ivar at the newspaper, she simply wanted a baby of her own. Carrying a fetus and giving birth would not dilute her affection toward Charlotte, she assured herself. To the contrary, her love for that child would be enriched by the presence of a younger one.

Andressa was gone now. Charlotte would soon be ten years of age, old enough to see a new baby as a wonder of family creation and not as a competing sibling. She would soon be able to share in the tasks of looking after a small child. Such responsibility would certainly further Charlotte's attachment to the infant, Inez assured herself.

A doctor she saw in Minneapolis, during her first year in America, had told Inez flatly that she was unable to conceive. Dr. Irving Blake had, during her one physical examination in his office since she came to Belleville, reached much the same conclusion.

Nevertheless, she continued to wonder about it. She had read somewhere that, according to leading medical authority, infertility could be traced to the male roughly as often as to the female. This was totally contrary to popular view, and it gave her some encouragement.

She thought, often, of what seemed the logical

possibility that Ivar was insufficiently aroused. Accordingly, she regularly approached the love act with as much enthusiasm as she could muster: Her warm hands in late evening would tousle his hair, caress his neck, rub his chest and help him disrobe. She had no doubt that this total, energized commitment to connubial enjoyment added, visibly, to his response and arousal. So the ultimate union was so complete, pleasurable, and fulfilling that she was sure conception would follow.

Yet she did not conceive.

Her confidante Clara Ferguson knew of a hospital in Minneapolis that regularly had in its clinic visiting doctors and interns from around the country, as well as some from Europe. Clara suggested that Inez pay a visit to that clinic because, who knows, they might have some new ideas.

Clara and Inez made occasional shopping trips to Minneapolis, usually taking a morning train, and returning late in the evening. Occasionally, they would make it an overnight trip, staying at a modest hotel a polite distance from the notorious "Bridge District" of the City.

"We nice girls—we dassn't get too close to those bridges," Clara warned, with a bit of mischievous, homespun mimicry. "Just this side of the Jim Hill Bridge, the one with the beautiful stone arches, we'd be running into nasty drunk men, crooked gamblers, panhandlers, purse-snatchers and shady women all over the place. Why, they would think we were there doing business!"

Then, more seriously, Clara added, "Those cheap hotels, those saloons and gambling dens, those brothels—they just prey on poor people and you know what? They've been paying off the police and the city government for years."

"Yes, Ivar once told me about that. What was the name? Like a president—Lincoln?—Stevens—no, Steffens. He wrote about this, didn't he? And how shameful it was?"

"Yes! It was Lincoln Steffens," Clara answered, impressed that a recent immigrant, even one as well-informed as Inez Lindfors, would know that much about what had been written about the Shame of Minneapolis more than a decade earlier.

In late summer of 1917, Clara and Inez spent a "shopping day" in Minneapolis that was, more truthfully, the first of several trips to a hospital where a Russian doctor was in residency. French-trained, the doctor had found her way to Paris for medical training in a specialty rare for the time, problems of human fertility and conception. She had completed her studies and was in America for a year's leave to continue her research.

Inez found Dr. Olga Ravinovich in a small and crowded medical office in a Minneapolis hospital. Sitting behind a desk piled high with an assortment of medical journals and records, the short, heavy woman wore her dark hair straight back and tied, leaving without further shadow dark eyes that glowed directly but easily through steel-rimmed eyeglasses toward the visitor. Her English was nearly perfect; her accent noticeable but muted.

She interviewed Inez, covering all details of the reproductive history of Inez and her husband. She then conducted an extensive physical examination of Inez and told her what Inez both hoped and feared: that she could see no reason, at least clinically, why Inez should not be capable of bearing children.

"It would be most helpful," the doctor said, "if we could examine your husband and do an analysis of his sperm. Might that be possible?"

Inez blanched at the thought. Ivar, convinced of his own virility, would in all probability not understand why she was questioning it, and would be highly upset over her getting such counsel from medical people without his knowledge. Having ventured this far down the path of private inquiry, she decided not to deviate now. So reluctant was Inez to raise the question of his fertility with Ivar that she had even considered the possibility of a clandestine affair with a willing male that would leave her pregnant and Ivar none the wiser. If she went that route, his naiveté might even be a blessing.

Inez had rejected such a course of action. She would never forgive herself even if Ivar was forever ignorant of the fact. The possibility that it might also be an enjoyable diversion didn't help a bit in her moral assessment.

"I'm sorry," she said finally to Dr. Ravinovich. "As you may well understand, I am looking into this behind my husband's back. I would not find it possible to even bring the subject up with him. He is most progressive on some things. He was a public champion of laws to give money to widowed mothers with small children. At the same time, he is—"

"Vain like most men where his own maleness is concerned?" the doctor asked helpfully.

"Yes—yes. I suppose that is the way to put it," a grateful Inez answered. "So I am hoping there are things I can do, by myself. Are there ways to—"

"Improve your chances of having a child?" Dr. Ravinovich was experienced in completing her client's questions. "Yes, there are certain things you can do. Today, the possibility of aiding couples with such problems through artificial means is a matter of considerable study and experimentation. I am familiar with a procedure known as artificial fertilization, and I am capable of performing it as one of my experiments if you are interested. There is no certainty that it will be successful, but you might consider it worth a try."

Inez sat speechless but alert, while the doctor continued.

"We would need you in the clinic, of course, at the right time, which we can determine quite easily. We then gather sperm from several male medical students, all of whom are chosen because they have features more or less similar to that of your husband. This will cost you nothing, since it is experimental work for which I have some funding from my medical school in Paris. There is little medical risk to you, except whatever guilt you may experience from, shall we say, keeping your husband uninformed.

"All the males contributing sperm, of course, would be

totally unknown to you, and you would be unknown to them. This way, with several contributors, none would be sure whether he had been a father. You, of course, could be secure in having had no liaison with any male and can truthfully tell your husband you have slept with no one else."

Inez wondered: "If most doctors here hate this kind of thing, how can you get away with it?"

Dr. Ravinovich smiled. "I was brought here for a one-year visit as a specialist to apply new knowledge about problems of human fertility. Then I shall return to Paris, perhaps even to Russia, and the local doctors need not take responsibility for what I have done while here."

Thus did Inez Lindfors become one of the first 20th century American women to participate in an experiment in artificial conception. It took three "shopping trips" to Minneapolis, each one more or less a month after the previous one, for Dr. Ravinovich to be satisfied that Inez would probably have a successful conception.

After the first of these "shopping" trips, Inez wondered how her experience would affect her relations with Charlotte, now nine, and her husband. Would Inez betray herself with obvious displays of guilt? With a little thought, she handled the matter with her usual adroitness.

First, she asked Charlotte to guess what she had brought in the paper sack from a Minneapolis department store. Charlotte squealed with delight at the colorful new frock, just right for her first day of school. "Oh, Mama, I can't wait to show this to Ethel and Lizzie!"

After a happy Charlotte fell asleep that evening in her cozy trundle bed, Inez sat with Ivar and told him in detail about how Minneapolis had changed since they had lived there—the new stores, the street cars, the exciting new automobiles, the things you see on the streets. She then slipped easily onto his lap, curled her warm hand around his head, caressed the nape of his neck, and kissed him until he was thoroughly aroused.

Inez then took Ivar to the marital bedroom with her

familiar passion. There was, of course, nothing unusual about her fervor, except that she was more aggressive than usual. She cooed, repeatedly—but with conviction—that being away from him for even a single night was unbearable. Ivar accepted all of this at face value, without suspicion of any kind. It had never occurred to him that Inez would be capable of anything unusual where their private life was concerned.

About eight weeks after the third visit to Minneapolis, in December of 1917, Inez paid a visit to Dr. Irving Blake. That evening, a radiant Inez told Ivar that she was expecting, and Charlotte learned that next summer she would have a baby brother or sister.

"Oh, Mama, I hope it's a boy, and I hope he looks like Papa."

Inez smiled warmly, hugged Charlotte and said that would be nice.

"But we will love the child, boy or girl, right?"

Ivar Lindfors reported proudly, although with due seemliness and only to his close friends and associates, that he was to be a father again. Lumber yard owner Roy Evans, now on friendly terms with the *Forum* editor and his creative spouse, said what many thought. "That's wonderful, Ivar. Nice to know you're as good a man as ever."

# X. THE PARADE

In late August 1917, the Minnesota Commission on Public Safety demonstrated, in no unmistakable terms, its crushing political power. It recommended to Governor Burnquist that he suspend three elected officials in New Ulm for expressing "antidraft sentiments" at a public meeting. On the final day of that month, the Governor took this recommended action, which the *Forum* reported in full, quoting the Governor's words: "Any public official who makes anti-American speeches or statements is subject to the same action that has been taken with regard to the New Ulm Officials."

Inez rummaged through the pile of newspapers in the print shop, and found the New Ulm newspaper that reported those "antidraft sentiments."

"Ivar," she said, handing the page to him. "Those speakers didn't exactly talk against the draft. They just didn't want drafted men sent to Europe."

Ivar shrugged. "Nobody has any sympathy for these speakers, Inez. Look at the other papers. See what they call women who marry young men now, to keep them out of the draft? 'Slacker war brides,' that's what they call them, in the headlines."

\* \* \*

Athena County and the entire Minnesota prairie anticipated, with either excitement or dread, the upcoming "national" meeting of the Nonpartisan League. It was set for late September 1917, in St. Paul, and the controversial Wisconsin Senator Robert M. LaFollette was to speak there on the 20th. Whether he could be enticed to come a day early for a speech in Athena County a few hours train ride northwest of St. Paul was not known, but the NPL leaders figured it was worth a try.

Also, the idea of putting Judge McGee and Senator LaFollette on the same platform struck most of the NPL officers as perfectly reasonable, if not inspired. Senator LaFollette retained his popularity from his earlier Chatauqua performances. A debate with the controversial Judge McGee seemed certain to draw a huge crowd. Reasoning this way, Arnold Hedlund, as League secretary, sent an invitation to the famous Judge.

But some disagreed about the wisdom of doing this. The older and shrewder Leonard Huisby knew the idea might backfire, because it could be dismissed quite easily as cynical. He doubted McGee would show up. Yet, Huisby found it difficult to object, because the idea fit the theme of wholesome debate about Americanism that the League was advocating. Given the ruckus about the elected officials in New Ulm, the League wished to appear properly patriotic yet favorable to its supportive politicians. So, Leonard Huisby decided not to object to Arnold Hedlund's invitation.

His hunch about Judge McGee's reaction was correct. Barely a week after sending the formal invitation to McGee, Arnold Hedlund received a reply that the *Forum* printed:

SAFETY COMMITTEE OFFICIAL ADVOCATES
FIRING SQUAD FOR PERSONS DEEMED "DISLOYAL"

———————

Judge John F. Mcgee Said to Be Wishing
"Kaiser Tactics" on    Anyone Who
Disagrees with Committee

———————

Says Senator Lafollette Should Be Arrested

# If He Appears on a Speaker's Podium in County

## Local Agricultural Leaders Aghast at
## Intemperate Statement of Safety Committee Official

A well-known member of the Minnesota Commission of Public Safety has insulted the farmers of Athena County and the state and has taken the most inflammatory position yet on how he would deal with persons who disagree with the Commission.

A week ago, Mr. Arnold Hedlund, secretary of the Athena County Chapter of the Nonpartisan League, invited Judge McGee to debate Senator LaFollette in Athena County. We print here the Commission member's response.

August 10, 1917
Mr. Hedlund:

My first reaction to your letter was to toss it in the trash or, better yet, the incinerator or a spittoon. However loathsome as it is to attempt a serious response to a disloyal group such as yours, there may be some value in sending a message that makes it clear to all good citizens of Athena County and the rest of Minnesota what I think of your league.

First, as anyone with a clear mind would suppose, I refuse to have any truck with a traitorous bunch such as yours by appearing at one of its plot hatching sessions, which is what your "*Forum*" would of course be.

If you want more specific reasons, I will list a few:

1. The so-called Nonpartisan league is a contradiction in terms, since it is the most fractious and partisan political concoction in the land.
2. Your NPL opposed our entry into the European conflict and you now engage in an 11th-hour attempt to claim pure loyalty. Once you have sullied the American flag with your greasy ways, our resolute disapproval will prevent you from shinnying up the liberty pole quite so easily.
3. Your NPL is nothing more than a party of

discontent—its agitators spreading contemptible falsehoods and encouraging disrespect for honest and patriotic men in public life.

4. Your NPL is a rabble of failing farmers and henchmen of socialist and I.W.W. connections and sympathies.

5. In this time of war, there are but two kinds of people: the loyal and the disloyal.

6. It is outright treason to call this a "rich man's war," since casualty lists already from this war include names of patriots from all levels of wealth and fortune, without favor to one over the other.

7. Given your detestable history of condemning all patriotic men, your invitation to me obviously lacks any sincerity of purpose whatsoever and is intended merely to confer undeserved decency and respectability on your unseemly riffraff.

To put all of this in a nutshell, an NPL lecturer—that is, one who deigns to speak at one of your perfidious assemblies—is a traitor every time. No matter what he says or does, a League worker is a traitor.

We need a firing squad to take care of this rampant disloyalty in our midst. There is no call for allowing treacherous scum to stab our doughboys in the back. We all know where this disloyal element is. It is largely among the German and Swedish people.

(signed)
Judge John F. McGee, Member
Minnesota Commission of Public Safety

Seeing the McGee response, Leonard Huisby concluded that it had all been a tragic mistake—that the county NPL chapter had given the venomous judge a weapon to mortally wound them. He went immediately to the *Forum* office, and found Hedlund, Theide, Nygren, and nearly a dozen other chapter members there, some standing in front of the counter near the door, some behind it, others leaning on the printing presses without worrying about ink or grease stains on their overalls.

Ivar stood near his desk, the top rolled down as if to protect something unknown from premature public exposure; Inez sat in the creaky swivel chair usually occupied by her husband. Ivar spoke first, as if the question was not the Judge's act, but how well the *Forum* had reported it.

None of those present was thinking about journalistic technique. It was a question of strategy and whether any reporting should have occurred at all.

Nearly all agreed with Huisby that, in hindsight, inviting McGee was an error and that printing it in the *Forum* was even worse. "We shouldn't have given that goddamned tyrant a chance to slap us with our own newspaper," was the way Bo Nygren put it.

"Yah, I vould haf to agree," Albert Theide nodded in perhaps his first public agreement with Bo Nygren in four years.

Once such admissions were made by the top NPL people, second guessing from others came in a flood.

"Y' know, we mighta known this would backfire. It was one thing for the Gov'nor to say what he did and have it all over the Minneapolis paper, which hates us anyway. But in our own paper."

"Mebbe we should talk these things over before we go off half-cocked like this. We're going to be the laughing stock of the business bunch, after this."

Arnold Hedlund, who had brought the letter to the *Forum*, saw it differently.

"Look," he offered, "this Judge McGee is the one way out on a limb. He's talking of shooting anyone who disagrees. He wrapped himself in patriotism, but it ain't gonna happen that Governor Burnquist down in St. Paul can go along with this firing squad stuff. He's insulted everyone with Swedish or German blood."

"See?" Arnold persisted with vehemence, clenching a fist. "We've smoked him out. The *Forum* shows him for what he is. We gave him enough rope to hang himself, and that's just what he did, by gum."

Leonard Huisby turned with wry and quizzical scrutiny toward Arnold Hedlund. "Now you say this whole thing here was set up, that we never expected him to come? And we got him to talk firing squads? Ever occur to anyone that we might get blamed for pulling this crazy idea outa this crazy judge? Maybe that's what we did, too. Tell me—anyone here really think he'd come and talk to us, the kind of joker he is?"

Inez stood up, folded her arms and mouth in a straight line, faced the weathered farmers and took what Ivar considered the only position possible. Ivar wished only that he had formulated this view himself.

"We publish a newspaper," she said, "We report all news. Including what we don't agree with. By printing that letter we let this Judge McGee speak for himself. Without any fancy words we think up. We take it that anyone brings us things, they expect us to publish any part or all of it. We do what we see fit as editors. Then people who read can think or say about these things anything they wish."

In an ordinary newspaper, this would have been a perfectly reasonable statement of how things work. The catch here was that the *Forum* was no ordinary newspaper. It was a cooperative organization with a board of managers that could remove the editor if it so chose. Inez knew that, but calculated correctly that under the existing circumstances getting a new editor was not exactly what the board would want to do.

There was a long silence, with at least half the group members looking down. Lips of several pushed out as if to deliver a horse command often used by some immigrant farmers. This was produced by pressing the teeth against the inside of the stressed lips and inhaling, producing a sound that cannot be spelled out in consonants and vowels. It was sarcastically called "kissing the horses," especially by farmers from old Yankee stock who preferred the traditional "Giddyup" and "Whoa."

Albert Theide looked straight through those in front of

him and puffed thoughtfully on his well-used, smelly pipe.

"Dey vorry about pa-a-triotism," he singsonged, "vell, ve are ass American ass all uf dem. Ve came here becauss ve tought dis to be a better country. Ve stay, becauss ve say America is good."

Ivar noted that if one took away the affected dialect in pronunciation, Theide was speaking in perfectly acceptable English. He wondered how many in public life maintained their popularity and character by persisting in, or affecting, an old-country accent. He shrugged to himself, thinking populism takes many forms.

Then Albert added, "So vy don't ve haf an 'America' parade or sumting like dat ourselfs?"

His suggestion gave birth, in short order, to a plan for an NPL Patriotism Parade in Belleville. It would accomplish two things: Show the undying loyalty of the NPL and, with that accomplished, attract some new members. It would take place on a Saturday when the most people would be in town.

It was to be on Labor Day, shortly before and leading up to the big national NPL convention September 19 and 30 in St. Paul. The keynote speaker then would be "Fighting Bob" LaFollette, the controversial senator from Wisconsin who opposed the war. "Yah, some say he's a traitor for that. Big newspapers say so."

A. C. Townley and N. S. Randall also would speak after a parade in which cars and wagons would meander down Wells Street, each adorned with a small American flag and a flier glued or tied to a bumper or buggy fender saying, "Join the Nonpartisan League—the Farmer's Voice." Maybe a thousand farmers, carrying various NPL signs, would march in something approximating military precision. Signs would say: "NPL Farmers Feed the Boys Over There," and "Food for Victory, the NPL way."

A huge crowd along the streets was assured. Marshals with NPL armbands would cooperate with Sheriff Mayberry and Police Chief Ezra Morse in keeping order. The heavy hand of the Athena County Public Safety Committee was inserted immediately in the planning. Roscoe (Pudgy) Thurstone, with J. B. Higgin's approval, chose Geoffrey Blankston and Tony Alquist to pass the word to both the Sheriff and the League members about how the parade would be run.

Things moved so rapidly that on the day of the parade, with more than 900 farmers bringing their automobiles, trucks, and horse-drawn rigs for the parade, banning it did not seem practicable. A wholesale riot might well result. While a riot could turn to the advantage of the Safety Committee, there was the possibility that people might think the Committee itself had directly provoked the melee. Tony Alquist, with full authority of this Committee and the Sheriff as his diffident servant, would do most of the official talking.

A crowd of mostly young men gathered on the far side of Wells Street, away from the assembling NPL group, flying small flags and hoisting a sign saying "NPL=NonPatriotic League." It was not, however, the classic encounter of the silent screens, in which a grim-faced Douglas Fairbanks stared straight at his evil adversary, with his back-up group equally grim, impassive, and imperturbable. The two groups were edgy, with much shuffling about, some heads pointed down and some up, as if scanning the heavens for divine inspiration or, failing that, a sign of rain that might mercifully deluge the town and end it all.

Not all participants fidgeted. Leonard Huisby strode calmly on the one side near the NPL people, while Tony Alquist straightened his thick shoulders and walked with his feet a bit wider on the other as the anti-NPL group stood in rather menacing postures. This ominous aggregation was spoiling for a fight.

Alquist spoke first. "This parade will not be allowed the way you have it planned. Mr. Townley and Mr. Randall aren't to speak in this town. So why not tell your people to go home, on the advice of the Athena County Public Safety Committee?"

This was answered from the NPL group by some

grumbles: "Whut'n the divil for? Well, now, ain't that goin' a little far? What will Townley and Randall say about this? Oh, ain't you heard? They figgered there'd be a ruckus and they said they couldn't make it here? That so? Sure is. Well, now, ain't that a fine kettle of fish? Kind of takes the steam out of this parade, don't it? What the Sam Hill are we goin' to do now?"

Alquist noticed the sagging enthusiasm from the would-be parade group, and he raised his voice. "This so-called Nonpartisan League is known to have disloyal and treasonous yellow-bellies in its membership. Now we know there are some good men among you. We all have nothing but respect for people like Leonard Huisby there, and a good young farmer like Arnold Hedlund." As he ended that sentence, Alquist deliberately looked past and ignored Bjorn Nygren.

Sheriff Alfred Mayberry was now walking slowly toward the front and near Tony Alquist, his eyes sweeping both groups but watching carefully the young toughs from town. Equally alarming was a comparable group of young farm workers behind the NPL officers, also rolling up their sleeves and pulling their grimy flat caps down to more determined angles.

Sheriff Mayberry was dumfounded by what happened next. Bo Nygren stepped in, eye to eye before Tony Alquist and, face red as a sun washed barn, said, "Why don't we settle this, just the two of us Tony, like men? With our fists. I win, we parade. You win we all go home. If," he snarled, "you can still walk."

Jesus, the Sheriff thought, Nygren has lost his head, trying to settle this like a Saturday night dance hall brawl. Bust each other's noses or asses and everyone else goes away satisfied. That sometimes worked in lumber and mining camps, where they picked champions to fight it out. It would be diversion from a drab life as much as for working out their group enmities.

What was brewing here, though, was no ritual brawl

between a pair of loudmouth drunken gladiators. All the animosities begotten of the mix of cultures, of political beliefs, traditional hatreds, and class antagonisms in Athena County were roiling in one composite convulsion. At the first swing of a violent fist, the two groups of toughs, farm and town, would be mixing it up and there would be a full-scale riot and mayhem.

Sheriff Alfred Mayberry moved to intervene. "Cool down, now, Bo. Ain't gonna be no rough stuff here. We got some disagreements here, but we're gonna solve them in a quiet way."

Privately, Tony Alquist felt the excitement of the challenge and had a wild itch to accept it. He was, however, too shrewd to be dragged into a brawl that would reduce him to Bo Nygren's level. He muttered just audibly enough for those nearby to hear. "Sheriff has good sense. Mr. Nygren just shows what a hot-tempered bunch of sonsabitches this NPL can be."

"And you, Mr. Alquist," Bo snorted, "can just go stick it in a big oak tree."

At this point, Inez Lindfors strode into the midst of the group, as if she hadn't heard the vulgar exchange. "You all sound like small children. What is wrong with a parade where the flag is fly?" she shouted, with excitement of the moment getting ahead of her English. "This is a patriotism parade, what is wrong wit' that? Whether it's good or bad, let's fight it out. But wit' vords between the *Gazette* and the *Forum.*"

Tony Alquist answered this female intervention in his heavy baritone voice. "What is wrong, Mrs. Lindfors, is that this is a treasonous group, trying to wrap themselves in the flag. You got some traitorous vipers here, misguiding some honest farmers," he added, borrowing the condemnatory words from the Commission of Public Safety. "Vipers," he added with analogy as vicious as it was biologically fallacious, "too slimy to hang onto the flag pole."

With loud protest now from the NPL side, the Sheriff

made another move. "Mrs. Lindfors is right. Ain't gonna be no fighting here. It's s'posed to be a patriotic march, so let's talk about how to make sure that's what it is."

Cheers went up from the NPL side, groans from the town leaders and the toughs behind them. A committee of men from both sides withdrew to work out rules for the parade. They fell immediately into bickering, about how the flag would be displayed, and whether it should be alongside Old Glory, or whether both flags should even be on the same wagon, buggy, or car.

Deep principle was argued:

"What happened to free speech, anyway? You look at the First Amendment to the American Constitution, they got it right there in the district school, it says—"

"Now, don't go giving us any of that free speech stuff. This is war. Look at what happened down in New Ulm. You either come out for Uncle Sam or you go against him. Which you gonna do? Be a backer or a slacker?"

"But we want to tell folks the League is patriotic."

"That's out, 'cause everyone knows it ain't. You can tell folks how patriotic you are as men, but not as a league. And even that's handin' you a lot, because loyal folks are startin' to have doubts about each of you, standin' right here."

Once the men got these recriminations off their chests, they worked out a complicated scheme, in infinitesimal detail. There would be exactly 184 vehicles, moving in four sections with four groups of walkers, one in between each section of wheeled vehicles. Only 46 vehicles would display emblems of any kind, 23 with flags or other suitable patriotic symbols and 23 with NPL banners or slogans. All slogans were to be approved by the Safety Committee, to ensure the absence of any treasonous phrases such as "rich man's war." Two walking groups could carry Old Glory and two could carry only NPL banners, thereby avoiding juxtaposition of the two flags.

Technical points remained. How would a slogan saying "Farmers united to win the war" be classified? As a League saying or as a patriotic slogan? Most from both camps considered this loyalist enough, but Geoffrey Blankston demurred. To him, it was obvious that not all farmers in Athena County supported the NPL, It was quite likely, in his view, that a majority didn't, though he wouldn't make a big point of that. Therefore, he concluded, that word "united" was off base.

Finally, the parade began.

It did not get far. Among the growling, restive group of young town men moving ceaselessly back and forth alongside the street was Bert Allcott, listed days ago in the *Gazette* as a volunteer for enlistment in the U. S. Army. He was a worthy scrapper, both on and off the football field. He was known, when tackled in a displeasing way, to roll over on his back, withdraw a cleated foot and deliver a vicious strike directly to the face of the offending tackler.

Bert's peers had more than once called him, in muffled tones, a rich man's bully son. That was somewhat misleading, since Bert had a certain egalitarian streak. He chose his comrades not by family wealth or rank, but according to their demonstrable toughness and their willingness to accept his domination, whether in a brawl or in competition for females.

In Bert's following this day were a number of young, poorly-paid workers from the quarry, wagon shops, pickle factory and foundry—all spoiling for a tussle with the NPL. Someone asked Bert once "why would underpaid workers in town join a group dedicated to harassing a group of underpaid farmers?" Bert Allcott simply replied: "These yellow-bellied farmers want higher prices for their wheat and corn and milk and pickles and hogs. Now isn't that just nice? They want their pay to go up when there's a war on, and you and I get told our wages are frozen."

It might have been ludicrous to suggest that Bert, as only son in a well-to-do merchant family, was ever without pocket money. But few if any raised this point of logic. Bert had almost mythic stature—a 20th century Roland leading his peasant brigades against the Saracens at Roncesvalles, with men of power allowing him his way if not urging him on.

Now, Bert led three comrades, each toting a bucket of yellow paint, directly in front of a Ford pulling a wagon carrying some 14 or 15 older farmers waving Nonpartisan League signs.

"Here's your true color," Bert shouted, throwing a gallon of the yellow paint over the windshield of the Ford, some of it splashing across the shoulder and face of the driver who was unable to raise a protective arm soon enough. Indignant shouts arose from the farmers. Several rushed toward the splash-painted Ford and its attackers, only to meet more paint flying from the other two cans. "Yeah, yur belly has the right color now, yuh greedy, slackin' sonsabitches." one of the paint throwers yelled.

This scuffle gave Tony Alquist and Sheriff Alfred Mayberry a pretext to stop the parade. They arrested the farmers covered with paint but somehow opted not to arrest Bert or the other paint-throwers. Their novel legal reasoning was explained in the headlines of the Athena *Gazette* the next week:

NPL PARADE STOPPED AFTER
DEGENERATING INTO A BRAWL

———————

Disloyal "League" cited by
Safety Committee and Sheriff
as threat to public order.

———————

Inciting to riot is a serious offense.

———————

"Traitors provoke patriots into
well-meant and determined reaction,"
Safety Committee Head Thurstone says.

———————

Parade halt seen as protecting

both the public and the NPL
members themselves.

>Athena citizens last week could see for themselves what
>happens when a bunch of slackers try to wrap themselves in
>the flag and flaunt their traitorous ways right here in our own
>streets. This ragtag "farm organization," as they called
>themselves, began their parade while loyalists who represent
>the vast majority of the county population looked on in pure
>disgust.
>
>One group of citizens found it so difficult to contain their
>righteous anger at this sorry scene that they yielded to
>expressing their revulsion in a way carefully designed to harm
>no one physically but make their point most effectively. They
>applied paint to some of the "marchers" and one of their
>rattletrap machines.
>
>While this display of righteous indignation may seem
>most understandable, the Public Safety officials courageously
>forbade this and any other "parades" by the NPL or any other
>disloyal group until the war is victoriously concluded.

To this account in the *Gazette*, editors Ivar and Inez
needed a potent riposte the following week. That Saturday,
they welcomed a timely call at the *Forum* shop from Amos
Ferguson.

Ivar asked him: "Doesn't the Bill of Rights allow all of us
to have parades, to say and print what we think? Is that why
so many millions came here? Didn't this all get settled in the
other wars? The Mexican Wars? The Civil War? The Spanish-
American War?"

Amos shook his head slowly. "No, Ivar and Inez, it isn't
settled. People think the right of free speech, or right to print,
means anything goes any time. But no one would agree with
that. Suppose you find out the American army plans to send
50,000 doughboys to France, and print that, naming the ships
and when they leave New York, knowing you might be telling
German spies who would get the word to their submarines.
Now would that be the right use of free speech?"

Ivar and Inez both shook their heads. "No, Amos, the League isn't telling spies anything," Ivar said. "All they want to do is say they are patriots. They would like to say that to fight the war, money should be drafted like people. Can the Public Safety Committee keep us from saying that?"

"Oh, they could do it. And the courts might even back them up. Fact is, hardly anyone has gotten the higher courts to listen to complaints from editors or people who have been silenced in war time, or any other time. Not up to now, anyway. A lot of people, you know, are talking about censorship laws. That would mean somebody in the post office reading everything you write, let us say, before you can mail it."

"Has anyone tried to pass a law like that in this country?" Inez asked.

"Maybe they have. I'm not sure," Amos acknowledged. "I teach American history, but there's a lot that goes on in different states I wouldn't really know about. Look, this country gets much of its system of laws from the old English courts. What they call Common Law. Now under Common Law, there would be no censorship at all, or what they sometimes call 'previous restraint' on printers and editors."

"Well, then the First Amendment is no better than old Common Law," Ivar observed.

"Oh, don't give too much credit to Common Law," Amos answered. "Those old courts said you could print anything you wanted, but then you took the consequences. You might get sued for libel or slander, and not just for hurting someone's business or reputation. If you criticized the king, you might get hanged or drawn and quartered. Or both."

"So under that reasoning," Amos continued, "you had freedom to stick your neck out but without knowing whether it would then get chopped off. The idea of the First Amendment is that Congress can't pass any laws that violate freedom of speech. That's to keep them from making it a crime to criticize government, among other things. So we hope to get protection for what we said or printed in the past."

"Well, do we?" Inez asked.

"It's going to depend," Amos replied, "on what kind of government survives in this country. In the medieval days and before, the kings and barons were considered superior to everyone, and the people were their servants. The Magna Carta and the French Revolution and the American Revolution were supposed to turn that around. Now we say in civics books that our government serves the people—"

"And that means," Inez interceded, "that our newspaper serves the people, too, when they write letters complaining about government?"

"We say that, too," Amos acknowledged, "but most people don't believe that. They talk about 'responsible' citizenship, and that washes away the notion of rights."

Ivar remembered a recent editorial in a St. Paul newspaper. "The only patriotism acceptable in these trying days," the editorial had said, "is the through and through, true-blue kind; half-hearted, johnny-come-lately, bleats of faintly-professed loyalty won't do; they will earn nothing more than the overripe tomatoes and rotten eggs they deserve."

At this point, the back door to the print shop creaked open, announcing the uninvited arrival of Pudgy Thurstone and Tony Alquist. Ivar could not hide his alarm.

There was Safety Committee work to be done here, and Pudgy Thurstone had decided, with J. B. Higgin's urging, to head it up himself, with Tony Alquist as a potent backup.

Pudgy was blunt and direct. "We are here to put you on notice, Ivar, in the name of the Minnesota Commission on Public Safety," he said. "The County Safety Committee is going to watch everything you write about that miserable parade this week. You print one word that's disloyal or that doesn't show red-blooded support for America, and we shut the *Forum* down, at least until the war is over."

Tony Alquist added, "We've given you a lot of rope, Ivar. You've been cozy with the NPL and you've never come down hard on the I.W.W.—bunch of rats like that. So write this up the patriotic way, or we treat you like the saloons. You ain't forgot that now, have you?"

Amos Ferguson leaned his left elbow on the heavy cast iron frame of the paper cutter, his hand cupped downward not quite in a fist and supporting his slightly inclined head just below the ear. Eyes soft, belying his inner contempt, he quietly and patiently awaited the course of conversational events.

As often happened in tense circumstances, Ivar hesitated and Inez answered first. "So it has come to this, has it? Here in America, a newspaper can be closed up because of what we say, because we might tell what people think?"

"You durn right, Mrs. Lindfors," Pudgy Thurstone said, now addressing her directly and with some condescension. "Y'know, we hate to say this to a lady, but your husband, and mebbe you, too, gotta think what you're doing and, well, whether you really want to be part of this country or not."

Ivar's mind began reeling under this avalanche of wartime authority. He wondered whether to respond on principle, following Inez' lead, or simply ask whether anything the *Forum* said would make any difference, anyway. He chose Inez' tack, partly because letting her hang alone would infuriate her and partly because he wanted Amos on his side.

He walked to the wall behind the Brantjen-Kluge job press and pointed to the somewhat faded but still legible poster he had tacked up there his first week in Belleville in 1912. It stated, in 42-point hand-set type, in both English and Swedish, the First Amendment to the U. S. Constitution.

"Gentlemen," he said as slowly, somberly and respectfully as he could, "how can you talk about closing our newspaper when we have this, the first of the Bill of Rights—the one that has probably brought more loyal people to America than any other part of the Constitution? Look what it says: People are free to speak, free to run a press, free to get together, free to tell the government what they think is wrong. Isn't that just what we are fighting to protect?"

Roscoe Thurstone, from his years as lawyer and county attorney, answered with easy, arrogant confidence. "Aw, read the whole thing, Ivar. It's about Congress, isn't it? It just says we can't have certain federal laws about speech and press and religion and that assembly stuff. You see anything there about a state law? Our Public Safety Committee was formed by the State Legislature, in case you forgot that."

Ivar hadn't thought through that point about what Congress can do and what States can do. Now, a formidable local politician and legal heavyweight had him in a box.

Seeing Ivar's weakening, Alquist closed in for the kill.

"When are you League-lovers and lovers of peace at all costs going to get it through your heads that this is a war to save Democracy? To save America, and our whole way of life? You know damn well what happened to those dumb politicians in New Ulm. The Governor canned them, thanks to the Safety Commission's recommendation. Who says a traitorous newspaper can't be next?"

Amos Ferguson now entered this dialogue. "Pudgy," he began, to Roscoe E. Thurstone who turned suddenly and glared viciously, betraying malicious hatred toward such assumed familiarity by the young teacher. "If this is a war to save Democracy and America, why do we use the methods of the very militaristic nation we are fighting?"

"MISter Fer-r-rguson," the county attorney said slowly, his words dripping contempt wrapped in menacing timbre. "I can't believe a teacher from our own High School right here in Belleville would say such a thing. What are you? Not German, or are you? Your wife is a Kaiser-loving Swede, is she? Or d'you belong to one of these socialist peace unions?"

Amos Ferguson wasn't intimidated. "Could you answer the question, sir? Do we fight the Kaiser by using the Kaiser's ways?"

Tony Alquist blurted, "Maybe, Mr. Ferguson, if you did know something about Germany, you'd know the things those Huns do to women and kids. Man, you got your nerve comparin' us to the Kaiser."

Pudgy Thurstone had time to formulate his next measured response. "Amos, when you are in a fight with rattlesnakes you sometimes damned well—excuse me, Mrs. Lindfors—do need to use their own poison. It takes fire to fight fire. Before you go off on this Democracy thing, let me remind you we speak for the majority. Now if I remember my American civics and history, the majority rules here.

"And now, let me tell you, the majority is fed up. Remember when the sheriff stopped the parade the other day? We did that to save the lives of those farmers. Maybe those young men like Bert Allcott went too far in their outrage, and, again, maybe they didn't. At least Bert and most of the others volunteered for the Army, something damned few young farm men do."

"You should have heard the cheers in town," Pudgy continued, "when word got around about how they took care of that sleazy parade. Frankly, it was a mistake to let it go in the first place. Now, take Lincoln. You think he didn't keep newspapers from opposing him during the Civil War?"

Amos looked almost amused. "Oh, there were times in the Civil War when people were kept from meeting, talking and printing. And yes, General Burnside did shut down the *Chicago Times*. And a federal marshal jailed an editor down at Dubuque. But you know what? President Lincoln took a lot of heat for that. After a very short time, he told Burnside to let the *Chicago Times* publish. And a few months after they imprisoned him, they released the Dubuque editor.

"Remember Pudgy, this was in Civil war, when General Burnside thought he had good reason to declare martial law. Do we have martial law now? Or is that what the Public Safety Committee is all about? I read the Minnesota law creating it, and martial law isn't mentioned at all."

With heavy sarcasm, the county attorney answered slowly: "Most interesting, you mentioning martial law, because that's exactly what we need. Let your yellow-bellied skunks get tried by military officers who know how to hand out justice. Judge McGee is damned right about that."

Thurstone then stiffened. "You're on notice, Ivar. You, too, Amos Ferguson. People wonder what you teach our boys and girls. I haven't paid much attention, but I will now."

Amos Ferguson reddened. "Won't you admit, Pudgy, that this has nothing to do with patriotism and loyalty at all? That's it all about Minnesota politics? That business people in town don't want the Nonpartisan League to take over their party or elect a Governor other than Burnquist? That you're just wrapping yourselves in the flag while trying to keep your own party in charge?"

"No, Mr. Ferguson," Pudgy responded. "This isn't good ol' politics at all. It's a question of treason. You say on your front page, Ivar, that your job is to reach a thousand minds. Well, let me tell you, one word of treason in your newspaper is treason a thousand times. Don't forget that. Enough said. Let's go, Tony."

With that, Roscoe E. "Pudgy" Thurstone, Athena County attorney, and Tony Alquist, aspiring politician and former county commissioner, went out the same back door of the print shop they had entered nearly an hour earlier.

# XI. A Teacher Is Fired

The next week, Inez noticed something odd. There were no copies of the rival *Gazette* for sale at Merriweather's or the pharmacy. A few inquiries turned up the fact that the paper had been quietly suspended. Ollie Moller was once more out of the publishing business and back to living off his part-time work at the abstracting company.

Inez had a thought while she was marking up an old car advertisement, changing it the way the Geoffrey Blankston wanted it to read. She looked up and asked: "Ivar, why don't we hire Ollie?"

A pause, and a stifled guffaw from Ivar. "Inez, are you being serious?"

"Of course I'm serious. Don't you see? He writes editorials the way Wells Street likes. So we have two kinds of editorials. One kind the *Gazette* used to have when it was alive, and the other kind that we have. That way, we are true to what we say we are, a forum. He can be a columnist. And you or I or both of us can be the other columnist. We can give both sides of things."

Ivar thought, yes, and that way we have the strongly pro-America view on everything. Maybe a chancy thing to do, but a great idea, maybe worth the risk. It might save the *Forum*.

\* \* \*

Once inside his cramped office in the Belleville High School building that morning, Amos Ferguson pushed back a pile of books, atop of which was *Debs, His Life, Writings and Speeches*. He grunted to himself, knowing that the name of Eugene Debs, perennial Socialist candidate for President, was hated on Wells street as a synonym of pure radicalism and anarchy.

Amos' job was to instruct future elementary teachers in the history of U. S. government. Today's class didn't go well, since it went through the lunch hour, a concession students had to make to do the "Normal" program along with other high school subjects. The students, mostly young women, were hungry and fidgety—not ill-mannered, just ill at ease. It was the beginning of the fall term, and the class wasn't off to a promising start.

On his desk, Amos found a note obviously placed there by the dour office secretary.

September10th, 1917
Mr. Ferguson:

The School Board of the Belleville City School District
wishes to have you present at their meeting this
afternoon, Friday, Dec. 10, 1917, at 2 p.m.

Yours, Gerald Robertson,
Superintendent of Belleville Schools

A puzzled and anxious Amos Ferguson went to the meeting to face three members of the School Board along the far side of the table, with Gerald Robertson at the left end and the secretary with her steno pad at the other. Chairman Reggie Code began immediately. "How long you been teaching here, Amos?"

"A little more than six years. But first I—"

"Came from Illinois, didn't you?"

"Look, could you please tell me what this meeting is about?"

"Well, Amos," Code said, wiping his chin, "you been saying things against America wagin' war on Germany?"

"As a matter of fact, I haven't, though I've been wondering, if I may say so, about why people who have their doubts can't express them. But you haven't answered my question. Am I charged with something, or what?"

"Naw, there's no charges here, Amos. We just want to visit with you. Now you got some books about socialism, haven't you? And you've got some Nonpartisan League printed stuff?"

"Of course, several," Amos said, exasperated. "I'm a teacher of American history, and socialism is part of that—"

"Does bein' a history teacher give you leave to propagate anti-American stuff?"

"American history is a mixture of different ideas. A teacher reads, students read these thoughts and ideas, without necessarily endorsing any one. We need to look at different political ideas down through history the way, in a science class, you look at tree leaves or types of animals."

"Well, bein' in or out of this war isn't like picking a kind of leaf or furry animal. Why don't you just say how righteous this war is?"

"Am I being accused of being anti-American? Against the war?"

"Not accused, Amos. People are wonderin', though, and seems to be for good reason, way you're talkin' here."

"All I've said to anyone is that this is a democracy, and that a democracy is based on free speech and free association, and that we don't fight countries opposed to democracy by becoming antidemocratic ourselves..."

"I said, Amos, we wanted to talk to you about things people around Belleville are asking, and you aren't—"

"Reggie, is it 'people around Belleville,' or is it just Pudgy Thurstone and Tony Alquist? Are they sore about a chat we had in the *Forum* print shop a while back?"

"Well, now, that's gettin' pretty pers'nal, if you ask me. 'Specially when you bring up the names of two of the finest, most upstanding folks in this town—men doin' everything they can to help with the war effort. And now you keep goin' 'round the bean pole, here, 'stead of answering our questions straight."

"Okay. Just what would you like to know?"

"Well, to put it simple, we just want to know if you're teaching red-blooded American ideas, and how you're doing it. For one thing, how many Liberty Bonds have you bought? None, I'll bet. Nah, I guess we're not really getting anywhere, here. Anyone else on the Board got anything to say, or ask?"

The room was a study of deathly quiet and human immobility, as a realist painter freezes action, thought, and objects in time. After this ominous moment, Reggie Code said, "Well, guess that's all for now, Amos. You can go back to your office, and if we want to ask you more, we'll send for you."

At 14 minutes to five that afternoon, the office secretary appeared at Amos' office. With a piercing gaze, she handed him an envelope, turned, and left.

On a single sheet inside the envelope was typed:

WHEREAS, it is the purpose of the Belleville School District to teach unswerving dedication to American ideas and patriotism, especially when the nation is threatened by the most menacing European military might in history, and

WHEREAS, it has come to the attention of the Belleville School District Board that one of its employed teachers, Mr. Amos B. Ferguson, has been known to oppose American entry into the Great War, even while teaching in the Normal program for aspiring grade school teachers, and

WHEREAS, said Mr. Ferguson in lengthy and extended discussion with said Board has failed to show unswerving dedication to the aforementioned purpose of education in Belleville Schools,

NOW, THEREFORE, BE IT RESOLVED that, effective immediately, all employment relationships between the Belleville School District and Mr. Amos B. Ferguson are terminated, and said District will move immediately to seek a different teacher of American History.

The document was signed by all three School Board

members and by Superintendent Robertson.

"That asshole Robertson," Amos thought. "He not only didn't object, he probably wrote this resolution for them, to make it look legal."

For all his knowledge of history and politics, Amos Ferguson was dumfounded. He knew he had nettled Thurstone and Alquist a while back, but why this?

٨ ⚹ ⚹

In telling a distraught Clara about his firing, Amos shouted at the top of his lungs. "Why, Clara? Why? Are we no better than the inquisitors? You speak your mind in America and they fire you? Or should I be happy they didn't put me in a tower to be drawn and quartered. With my head on one spike and my guts on another."

Emotionally drained, Clara murmured, "Well, I wasn't here for that ruckus you had with Pudgy Thurstone and Tony Alquist, but your problem was that you stood up to two of the big powers that be around here. You, with the most vulnerable job in town."

A dispirited Amos agreed. "Yes, it does make sense, in an insane way. Shutting down a newspaper might bring howls from the NPL and from a few editors who actually understand the First Amendment. Easier to fire a poor sonofabitch of a teacher."

Inez and Ivar next day had an idea. They would hire Amos at the same time as hiring Ollie Moller, thereby bringing to the *Forum* a view the Public Safety Committee would accept.

"Interesting idea," Amos said. "Let's all think it over. Now, I've got to see a lawyer."

Ambrose Cathcart, Attorney at Law on Wells St., was little help. He wanted to know how much money Amos had, knowing that "teachers don't get paid all that much." Amos ignored that and asked what chance he might have in court.

"Hard to say," Ambrose answered. "There's pretty strong

feeling around here about the League and Liberty Bond sales and registration for the draft, and—"

"Wouldn't a judge go according to the law?"

"Well, you know, judges feel the political winds like everyone else. Besides, you know who would represent the School District? It would probably be the County Attorney, Pudgy Thurstone, and he's head of the County Public Safety Committee."

"I'll do my best," Ambrose said, "but it won't be for free." He added, with a trace of a grin, "It wouldn't be free with any other lawyer, either. Unless you get one of those Jew lawyers out of Chicago who go around defending Socialists."

So if Amos retained Ambrose Cathcart, he would have bigotry in his own camp. He shrugged. Most people he knew were capable of saying the same thing. The fee was crushing. Amos and Clara gave Ambrose a mortgage on their personal property—a piano, Clara's violin and cello, some jewelry bequeathed her by a wealthy grandmother.

\* \* \*

Amos Ferguson declined to work for the *Forum*, insisting that taking the school board to court was work enough. Ollie Moller accepted Ivar's job offer without hesitation. Once again, he had a job that might return some of his self-respect, since printing was his first love and he detested abstracting.

He was immediately expansive in sharing his views of Belleville with Inez and Ivar. "This business crowd in Belleville? Take any of 'em one at a time, they ain't a bad bunch. I mean, half of 'em might give you the shirt off their backs if they thought you needed it. But get 'em riled up or scared and they're the meanest buggers you ever saw."

Inez smiled. "Ollie, you wrote some nasty things about the Nonpartisan League. And you probably will next week, in our paper. Now tell us, what do you think of the League?"

"Aw, that NPL is a humdinger of an outfit. I'd a never

admitted it outside this room, but it's fun once in a while to see them scare the pants off our merchant crowd here. But watch out. The scarier this NPL gets, the tighter these business guys'll bunch together to wipe it out. To them, NPL means socialism and that gets them right in the gut."

"Ollie," Ivar said, "if you think this way about the business group, how could you take their side the way you did at the *Gazette*? Which is what you'll be doing with us?"

Ollie Moller chuckled a bit. "Well, folks, fact is, I think they're right on most things. I'm not all that hot on the Socialists and I think the Bolsheviks are crazy. Watch Russia; see if I'm not right.

"I'll tell you something else, so you know where I stand. Clara Ferguson is a fine writer, good gal. She minds her own Ps and Qs. But Amos, I don't frankly think he's worth a fart in a whirlwind. Seems he got Pudgy Thurstone and Tony Alquist pretty mad at him and from what I know about it, maybe serves him right.

"Then, too, Ivar, you may not remember it, but you once told me about a famous ancestor who sometimes sailed with whatever ship had the biggest purse. I do that, too. So when they paid me to do the *Gazette*, I wrote what they wanted. Course it helps I believe some of it."

"Ollie," Ivar asked, "would you have editorialized in support of firing squads if they had asked you to?"

Ollie paused, then swung his head slowly and abjectly. "You got me there, Ivar. But I s'pose I would have if they insisted. Sure as hell wouldn't have liked doing it. If you remember, I didn't say anything about that mean letter you printed from Judge McGee, on the Safety Commission."

Ollie shook his head again. "This McGee, he's tougher than boiled owl piss." Inez went to the other end of the office and pretended not to hear the vulgar and fractured country simile. Ollie continued: "Now this idea about a forum in the *Forum*, well, it might work, but don't hold your breath. You might all be out on your fannies anyway."

Then Ollie Moller's eyes twinkled. "You know, they

might be after my hide, too, just for hanging around with the likes of you people."

* * *

Although Amos Ferguson declined to work for the paper, he had some thoughts about the "forum" idea. "Ever since the Civil War, lots of small-town editors have been cussing at each other, the way you people and Ollie did when he ran the *Gazette*. Now, your idea of having writers at loggerheads on the same paper, that's different. Probably unheard of in most newspapers, especially in small towns. Remember, these Wells Street merchants are going to see through this, as a way to keep the Safety Committee off your backs."

Ivar and Inez agreed but thought it was worth a try. They decided that the new editorial page would be called FORUM OF OPINIONS. In the next edition, the front page of the newspaper told its readers:

> With this edition, the *Forum* editorial page will have columns written from at least two different points of view, or two sides of the fence, so to speak. We will call this the "Forum of Opinions."
>
> We have been joined at the *Forum* by Olof Moller, whom many readers will remember as the straight-spoken editor of the *Gazette* that was published here until recent weeks. His views may often be exactly opposite ours, and we believe this regular exchange will help stir up some lively thinking and discussion.
>
> So write us. Say what YOU think.

When this edition was distributed on Wells street, J. B. Higgins showed it to Pudgy Thurstone, who said: "Well, I'll be goddamned."

When Leonard Huisby showed Albert Theide the new editorial page, Albert said: "Vell, I'll be gotdamned."

* * *

The editorial page contained one column titled Our View printed in large type and 1 1/2 times the ordinary column width. Alongside, same width and type size and roughly the same length, was a column titled Moller's View. The topic in this first FORUM OF OPINIONS was the speech by Robert M. LaFollette on the 20th of September in St. Paul.

This speech had been preceded by several newspaper reports and editorials, castigating in advance the well-known Senator who was one of the best-known political orators and gifted Chatauqua speakers in the nation. A former Progressive Republican governor of Wisconsin, he had crusaded vociferously for years for regulatory reform of railroads, warehouses and trusts generally. He had been long opposed to involvement in the European conflict and had spoken at length against the Declaration of War resolution in the U.S. Senate.

Already widely denounced, LaFollette's scheduled appearance before the Nonpartisan League national convention in September of 1917 in St. Paul was predicted in advance by several papers to be treasonous and seditious. That convention was originally designed to portray the League as loyal and patriotic. The leadership, including A. C. Townley, had indicated publicly that LaFollette would not discuss his views on the war.

LaFollette's speech began innocuously enough, but after scattered heckling in an otherwise sympathetic and packed meeting hall, the Senator ad libbed about the war anyway. What he actually said would be debated for years. A stenographer's text of his spoken words was published the following day in a St. Paul newspaper. An Associated Press story about the speech included one crucial word, "no," that was absent in the verbatim text.

The national daily newspaper furor over the LaFollette speech had already broken when, the following week, the *Forum* carried its two-sided commentary:

On the right hand side of the page was Our View.

Senator Robert M. LaFollette is being unfairly lambasted for his talk at the Nonpartisan League convention in St. Paul. The most awful words are being used to describe this honorable and courageous Progressive political leader.

Let us tell you exactly what the Senator said, according to a professional stenographer who transcribed every single utterance during the speech:

"We are in the midst of war. I wasn't in favor of beginning the war. We had grievances. The German government had interfered with our rights to travel the high seas—as passengers on the munitions ships of Great Britain."

Now the Senator was referring to the sinking of the Lusitania, two years before we declared war. But note the important sentence. The Senator said "WE HAD GRIEVANCES." But those of you who read the Associated Press report in New York newspapers saw the Senator quoted as saying "We had NO grievances."

Think of it. The Associated Press deliberately and falsely stuck in that word "NO." Now, they refuse to correct it. These are the lengths some will go to in besmirching the character of great political leaders like the former governor and now great senator from Wisconsin.

We would like to point out that a week later, even the U. S. District Attorney told the Minnesota Commission of Public Safety that nothing said by the Senator gives any cause for concern or investigation. That official is right, so let's put the LaFollette speech behind us.

On the opposite side of the page was Moller's View.

Whether the disloyal Senator from Wisconsin said "we had grievances" or "we had no grievances" is not the real problem with that speech in St. Paul before the sniveling Nonpartisan League.

Ask anyone who heard that speech and how the words came out. They'll tell you what really happened. If you purse your lips and say sarcastically "We had grievances," it's like a snippy third grader saying "Oh, Johnny is SO big and tough" and meaning exactly the opposite.

That's what we had with the LaFollette speech. He mentioned grievances in that sarcastic, curled-mouth way of his. Then, if you read the rest of that speech in the St. Paul paper, you see that he made light of all those grievances and seemed to think the Germans had a right to sink the Lusitania.

It's time the whole country got wise to this cowardly slacker from Wisconsin who is always so cozy with all the Kaiser-lovers in Milwaukee and the rest of that state. In fact, guess who has already gotten wise? No less than the NPL itself, because their own puff sheet out of St. Paul last week allowed that La Follette "said things he should not have said." What better evidence is there that this was treason? Let us hope the Senate expels that Judas forthwith.

Six letters were written to the *Forum* from local citizens with comments on the "Forum of Opinions" page a week after it first appeared. Two were cautiously favorable. The chairwoman of the Belleville Library association said this new page would "stir up the juices of civic-mindedness among local readers." Irma Johnston judiciously called it a "noble experiment in wholesome public education that I am sure will in each edition lead to the conclusion that this nation must prevail in the greatest war of all history."

A letter from Pudgy Thurstone was ominously neutral, saying that "patriotic citizens will watch this page closely, assuming it will support our leadership in fighting this holy war. What Ollie Moller had to say was fine, but after what you said, people still aren't sure." Another two letters expressed outright hostility, such as the unsigned scribbled note that accused Ivar Lindfors of being a "yellow belly" who might see his "miserble printing plant put to the torche" if the paper said anything more that would give "aide and cumfort to the ennemy."

The sixth letter, from a chronic and cynical letter-writer, berated the *Forum* with a parable of skepticism:

> Once I went to a wrestling match at a carnival. They had a big, burly wrestler with a hairy chest who said he would take on anyone with guts enough to get in the ring with him.

Well, one tough guy in the audience raised his hand and said he'd wrestle that big hairy sonofagun. He did, but the hairy fellow won.

Then after the fight, you know what I found out? This tough guy from the audience turned out to be working for the big hairy wrestler. A phony.

The way I see it, Ollie Moller is like the man in the audience at the wrestling match. Your "two sides of the fence" page is a putup job. There is a difference, though. The phony wrestler was just trying to make money. You folks are trying to make money and hide behind a drunk patriot at the same time.

"Damn," Ollie Moller thought when he read the letter. "I could have written that one myself. This chap may be a crackpot but he hit the nail right on the head."

The editors published none of these letters, but they forged ahead with the "Forum of Opinions" page. The next one debated a curious occurrence on Wells Street in late October of 1917.

Our View

An incident last week showed how patriotic citizens are often wrongly accused of disloyalty in these trying times. This citizen, Mr. Bjorn Nygren, was driving his team and hay wagon into town to pick up a load of lime.

As his beautiful Roan mares stepped smartly off Grant Avenue and turned down Wells Street, the high front standard of the wagon unfortunately caught a line which a local committee had draped across the street to hold the bunting for Friday's Liberty Bond parade.

The damage was minor and easily repaired, as Mr. Nygren attempted to point out. Yet, someone unfortunately thought the police should be brought into this matter and this fine, upstanding rural citizen and leader was required to submit to questioning at the local station before wise and cool judgment prevailed and Mr. Nygren was allowed to go about his business.

We should add that Mr. Nygren patriotically offered to

replace the bunting line and any emblems that may have been soiled, through no fault of his own. Unfortunately, this loyal and civic-minded offer was declined.

## Moller's View

The Nonpartisan League is never going to convince patriotic citizens of its loyalty if leaders like its man Bjorn Nygren continue to insult Old Glory the way he did in the mess that "Our View" passes off as merely "unfortunate."

We'll tell you here what really happened, according to several responsible witnesses. This "patriotic" NPL officer Nygren deliberately steered his prancing horses (known for running away when they have the least chance) directly toward the bunting line that held several banners and draped The Flag itself in the center of the street.

Citizens working on the flag display immediately informed Mr. Nygren that his hayrack had damaged the line holding the buntings and Old Glory. They heard him say, "Well, keep your ... flag out of the way next time." His blasphemous exact words we shall not repeat here except to note that they invited divine execration on Old Glory.

No wonder Mr. Nygren was taken to the police station, after a treasonous utterance like that. Only through the intervention of other citizens such as Leonard Huisby, who assured the complainants they would be responsible for Mr. Nygren's actions in the future, was this individual released WITHOUT FACING ANY CHARGES.

Bo Nygren was furious over one more embarrassing public incident, and saw no help in Our View's portrayal of the whole thing as an innocent mishap. He thundered in to the *Forum* office when several townspeople were there, swore venomously at Moller and told Inez: "A lot of goddamned good this filthy paper is doing the League and its leaders after that bunch of garbage."

News of Bo's outburst in the *Forum* office spread quickly. It had a curious, albeit temporary, dampening effect on those who were considering closing the paper.

After hearing of this incident, Pudgy Thurstone thought "Now isn't this interesting? Been wondering whether to shut that damned paper down, but not now. They've got the slackers in that goddamned League at each other's throats, so let them go to it."

No close friend of Bo Nygren, Albert Theide nonetheless expressed concerns to Leonard Huisby and Arnold Hedlund about the damage wrought on the League through the hay wagon incident and its being "dragged t'rough t'at noospaper. Maybe ve shoult cancel our loan to them, for giving that Moller space and reason to shoot us up."

The three men considered their options.

"Forcing a shutdown of the paper wouldn't look good, now, would it?" Huisby said.

"Vell, but it vill look vorse ven dey get Moller writin' who knows vot next veek" Theide said.

"Yes," Hedlund added, "but we're gettin' meeting announcements and membership ads and other news of ours in that paper, don't forget that."

"Vell, yah, but don't people wonder ven a paper vit League money in it prints all t'at crazy stuff from Moller?"

"They sure might," Huisby said, "but it shows we aren't afraid of criticism, doesn't it? Maybe we just need to give Ivar some good arguments that'll make us look better next time.

"Well, now, that's a thought," Hedlund said. "It just might work."

"Yah, maybe, but t'at's gettin' to be a t'ick-headed crazy bunch at t'at paper. So, okay, ve von't do anyt'ing rash right now, yoost talk to Ivar some."

Thus, the "Forum of Opinions" left the antagonists in Athena County in a curious stalemate. The fuss over Nygren's hay wagon fiasco got so much attention, often guardedly jocular, that the firing of Amos Ferguson by the Belleville School Board was being forgotten. For the moment, Amos found that to be a relief.

For Bjorn Nygren, there was no relief in sight. One more humiliation, and now his wife Eva was following through on her long-standing threat to leave him. "You've made a fool of yourself one too many times, Bo. I'm going on up to Fargo to live with my folks for a while."

His humiliation all but overcome by rage toward his detractors, Bo didn't argue with her leaving. Without her thorny verbal jabs, he could concentrate now on a line of retaliatory action he had privately figured out. He sat down and struggled through the writing of a letter, in a nearly forgotten language, to Gothenburg, a coastal city in southwestern Sweden. That done, he eased back in his old bentwood chair and thought about how printing presses work, compared with, say, McCormick-Deering mowers or wheat threshing machines.

*  *  *

For the next few weeks, the "Forum of Opinions" page dealt with tiresome questions before the state legislature and whether Congress should put more funds into the National Parks. These weary topics roused little reaction, an outcome Ivar and Inez were happy to accept.

In January of 1918, Ivar had an unannounced visit from J. B. Higgins and Pudgy Thurstone.

"Ivar," J.B. said, going directly to his point, "we're expecting the *Forum* to give us some  big promotion for the next Liberty Bond Drive. The county's going to go right over the top of its quota this time, believe you me. Did you know Minnesota was two million dollars short on the first drive? Well, nobody's going to call this a state of slackers again, and especially not in Athena County.

"We're expecting a couple of things from your newspaper, Ivar. You're going to run a big advertisement and a story promoting this Drive, and you're not going to have any two sides of comment about it."

Pudgy Thurstone pulled his ever-present cigar from his mouth with his two fingers in the usual vee and added: "Where buying Liberty Bonds is concerned, there is only one side, Ivar. We back up our boys. That's the loyal side. We told you long ago that you were on borrowed time, and now your time's up. Can't tell you how many people are demanding we close you down. Some want to run you out of town on a rail. Even talk of tar and feathers, if you can imagine that.

"So you can thank the Athena County Public Safety Commission, and leaders like J. B. Higgins here, for the fact you're still in business." Pudgy chomped hard on the cigar, under menacing eyes, as a point of exclamation.

"Now back to the way this works," Higgins resumed in a softer and more tolerant tone. The bank, Higgins said, in cooperation with the Athena County Public Safety Committee, was preparing to send letters to all households in Athena County, stating how much each one was expected to buy in Liberty Bonds.

An ability-to-pay-principle was put to work: the more the income and net worth, the more the expected Bond purchase. For J. B. Higgins, learning a citizen's net worth was workaday routine. Savings and checking accounts he had at his fingertips. If further evidence was needed, it was easy to check property values and tax assessments at the courthouse.

Ordinarily, few if any objected to this benign tradition.

In the case of Liberty Bonds, there might be some question but few raised any, because the assessment was imposed from above by leaders who insisted on its absolute necessity for salvation of nation and world. The fact that it also further entrenched their positions of political puissance in the community was of course something they did not mention.

Ivar asked, "I take it this is a persuasive letter you are sending? These are suggested amounts to contribute, like people get from their churches?"

Higgins' restrained Pudgy Thurstone, who glared diminishing patience at this half-hearted editor.

"Ivar," Higgins said softly but distinctly, "these are not 'suggested' amounts. These are 'expected' Liberty Loan purchases that upright citizens will regard as obligations, just like property tax bills. They are figured according to what we know they can afford."

"So what about people who simply refuse to pay," Ivar persisted.

"You can say in the *Forum* that the few slackers who don't buy their requested amounts briskly will get a visit from representatives of the Athena County Public Safety Committee who will want to know why. If they continue to hold out, they'll find themselves in court, won't they, Pudgy?"

"Damned right," came from behind the re-lit cigar.

Even after the closing of the saloons, the shut-down of the parade, the temporary detention of Bjorn Nygren and the firing of Amos Ferguson, Ivar was still unsure exactly how much of this was mere bravado. "How about people who, very honestly, don't have the money? They've had a fire, they're waiting for the money from selling their heifers and pigs next spring—"

"We know what people can afford," Higgins said evenly. "Now if someone's short on cash right now, the bank loans them money to buy bonds, and they pay us when their money comes in. Simple as that, no questions asked, no delay or anything."

Pudgy Thurstone cast an appreciative look at the banker. "Damned fine of the bank to help out that way, I'd say. People around Athena County are going to thank you for that, J. B."

"Pudgy, here, and Tony Alquist'll be bringing you the ads for the Liberty Loan drive. You'll get paid your usual rate for those, of course, from the county Public Safety Committee. Don't forget, though, we expect a good strong pitch for this drive on your front page."

# XII. Supporting the War Effort

Inez quietly studied the wording of the Liberty Loan promotional advertisements in the *Forum*.

SUPPORT THE BOYS AT THE FRONT

---

Buy Liberty Bonds

---

Fly the Flag Every Day
Fight the Huns in Every Way
Keep Old Glory Fully Unfurled
As Doughboys Go to Save the World.

---

Second Liberty Bond Goal:
75 Dollars for Every Man, Woman and Child

---

"Whatever I'm expected to contribute,
I'll double it": Words of Local Patriot

---

"I'll TRIPLE my purchase:" Words of Zeal
from Another Loyal Citizen.

That was for the first week. The one for the next week spoke even more directly to what was meant by patriotism. This promotional ad would say:

PATRIOTISM MEANS:

* Buying more Liberty Bonds
* Displaying the Flag Every Day
* Kissing the Flag in all Parades
* Reporting pacifists to authorities
* Reporting pro-Germans
* Reporting slackers

Patriotism means supporting America in this holy war with every word and breath. Don't be misled by anyone who whines about "free speech." If some blockhead talks against the draft, we should toss him in the jail.

Inez asked Ivar how such things could be said in a newspaper devoted to Democracy.

"But that IS democracy, Inez," he protested. "Remember, when the Nonpartisan League first came to us, we took ads we didn't necessarily believe in. We advertise many things we wouldn't buy ourselves. People can say what they like in paid space."

"So if the League brings us an advertisement opposing jailing people, we will print it?"

Ivar exhaled in defeat. "I'm not sure," he said, hardly audible. "It would be hard to refuse, though, since they have the most money in this paper."

The promotional advertisements paid for by the Athena County Public Safety Committee were printed in successive weeks, along with front-page articles about the progress of the Second Liberty Loan Drive. These articles praised the patriotic civic leaders who organized this drive and told how the bank would loan money to cash-short patriots to buy Bonds in a timely way.

One of the articles explained the consequences of too little zeal for such purchases:

There are, of course, a few slackers, and authorities are dealing with them swiftly. One person of more than adequate means declined to respond to the letter of obligation. Another had the gall to pay a mere half of the designated amount. Both recalcitrants were admonished by subpoenas to appear in County Court to show cause why they should not be fined under law. Both citizens, with this prodding, dug into their pockets and contributed their share.

This front-page article and others like it were written by the *Forum* editors.

\* \* \*

Writing the Liberty Loan pieces finally twisted Ivar's insides. His freedom as an editor was quashed; he was powerless and humiliated. In his despair, he sat in the Bungalow sitting room early one evening with a copy of the *Atlantic Monthly*, must-reading for a small-town editor. He read a headline and the first three paragraphs three or four times and realized he hadn't remembered a word. Such was his depressed state, when 10-year-old Charlotte ran in carrying her violin.

"Papa, this broke." She held up a loose string, curling up and backward toward the short neck of the child-size instrument. Ivar's heart leapt. He had never learned to chat easily with his daughter, much as he tried. Fixing her toys and gadgets and musical instruments, though, was something he could do. And now it was just the right escape from his journalistic turmoil.

"Hm-mm-mm," he murmured as he took the instrument gently, ran his thumb over the fingerboard, and felt the base of the bridge. He held the violin at an angle and squinted through the left F-hole. "Well, Charlotte, seems both the bridge and sound post are out of kilter."

He took the violin, with Charlotte in tow, to his crude workshop in the summer kitchen at the back of the bungalow and proceeded to reposition the sound post and bridge as he had been taught by a veteran repairman whom he had watched redo his sister Gretchen's violin in Graskoping 20 years earlier. Somewhere, he had acquired the right tool for reaching through the F-hole and moving the sound post to its critical position.

This repair and all the regluing took several days, most of it with Charlotte watching intently and chattering all the while. When he finished it, he asked her to play "Twinkle, Twinkle, Little Star."

She drew the bow and did a few strains of the old Twinkle song. "Doesn't sound out of kilter now," she pronounced. "Thanks, Papa."

Then instead of saying "You're welcome," her beaming Papa patted her head and thanked her, leaving the child puzzled. He later told Inez that come December, they should take Charlotte on the train to a ballet concert in Minneapolis. He thought she would enjoy the "Nutcracker," or Leopold Mozart's "Toy Christmas."

Ivar was in good spirits again.

* * *

On a side alley just off Wells Street, the Belleville Livery Stable for nearly a decade had been yielding gradually to the relentless assault of the automobile. Now, this onslaught was temporarily delayed, owing to fuel shortages brought on by the war emergency. In early 1918, the stable owner added two more carriage horses for a total of eight, still far short of the 20 or more he kept in years before horseless carriages, but enough to meet current demand.

Except for the professional groomsman who expertly tended the horses' exercise and veterinary needs, working in the livery stable was debasing. It was a constant, humiliating, ritual of pitching in hay and shoveling out dung. It was filthy work, but always there as a last resort for the down and out.

Thus did Rudolph Pflueger return to Belleville to be the cleanout man in February, 1918. Shoveling horse manure was hardly an advance over the street cleanup job he had in Minneapolis, and a long step down from running the family farm during those months after the barn fire that killed his father.

When people asked him why he came back, Rudy never answered in a way convincing to himself or the questioner. His words would be "Aw, Minneapolis, you know what kind of a place that is. Don't pay you nothin'—just living takes all you got. Unions want everything you make. Ain't a good place for ennybuddy." And the listener would continue to wonder why he would return to the county of his disgrace in farming and romance.

*   *   *

It was the first day of March 1918, a Friday, when Bo Nygren, now alone at his farmhouse after the departure of his wife Eva, found two letters in his mailbox. One was from the Bank and the other looked like a response to the letter he had written in painful Swedish the previous October and sent to Gothenburg. It came in a heavy, brown and now badly soiled and wrinkled envelope covered with several smeared postmarks in blue, black, and red ink, some in Swedish and some in English, the edges and corners of the envelope showing numerous small tears.

Bo took from his pocket the long, narrow and slightly s-shaped jackknife with the mottled brown and white bone handles that he used for cutting twine and rope, scraping rust from tools mistakenly left out in the weather, peeling apples picked ripe from the McIntosh tree on the hill behind his house, or cleaning the mud and animal feces from the bottom of his boots before going into the house. The knife had two blades, one long and curved in the overall shape of its body, the other short and stubby and kept razor sharp. The first was for aforementioned general utility; the second reserved for jobs that required maximum sharpness on materials that wouldn't dull the edge, like cutting rope or castrating young male pigs.

Bo opened the long utility blade, carefully inserted the

point under the partially torn top fold of the envelope, slit it open and pulled out a two-page letter, penciled in Swedish on dull, coarse paper. Reading and comprehending it was less laborious than scripting his own note three months earlier.

Bo read and re-read this letter from Gothenburg until he had the contents virtually memorized. He nodded to himself in satisfaction. This letter gave him what he needed, a weapon of retaliation against an editor who had added to his embarrassment.

Then after studying the letter from the bank, Bo was once again irritated. That letter said:

Dear Mr. Nygren:

It has come to the attention of the executive council of the Athena County Public Safety Committee that you have not yet purchased any Liberty Bonds, as part of either the first or second Liberty Bond Drives. We know that you are financially able to purchase at least $200 worth of Bonds.

Unless these purchases are made within the next week, we shall take measures that are fully compatible with the responsibilities given us by the Minnesota Legislature in furthering the cause of the United States of America in the Great War against German aggression. Firstly, we shall publish your name, along with any other individuals failing to make purchases, under the heading:

DELINQUENTS IN LIBERTY BOND DRIVE

Should you persist in failing to fulfill this civic responsibility, we shall take still further measures to enforce compliance.

Liberty Bonds may be purchased here at the Belleville Independent Bank. If you do not have funds available for your assigned amount, this bank will immediately grant you a short-term loan WITHOUT ANY FURTHER INVESTIGATION OF YOUR CREDIT STANDING.

It has been gratifying to note that more than 90 per cent of Athena County residents, including many with resources far inferior to yours, have already and gladly made their purchases, many going well over their quotas.

Expecting your immediate reply,
J. B. Higgins, Pres., Belleville Independent Bank
Roscoe E. Thurstone, Chrmn., Athena County Public
Safety Committee

Bo Nygren felt his blood boil. Leonard Huisby would be no help, since Leonard had been one of the first to buy Liberty Bonds for the Second Drive. "Can't give them reason to say Nonpartisan League members are disloyal," Leonard had said.

Bo Nygren went to the bank and told the cashier he would stand good for the $200 in Liberty Bonds, but that he would be short on cash until he marketed his fattening hogs three months later. Fine, the cashier said, and immediately wrote out a $200 loan for six months.

Bo, always wary of fine print, noticed the interest rate of 7 percent per annum, which meant that the $200 loan would cost him $7 in interest. The interest paid on the Liberty Bonds, however, was 4 per cent, or 3 points under what the bank was charging. That was a loss of $3 that he would not get back when the Liberty Bonds matured.

Bo returned home and wrote another letter that he would take to the editor of the Athena County *Forum*, hoping it would have the same influence as the one he had written about grain grading, three years earlier. Make people wake up to what this crooked bank is doing.

His penciled draft of this letter about the bank said:

Dear Editor,

All the patriotic people in Athena County should know that their willingness to support the war is lining the pockets of our local bank. You know how that works? Well, it's their loan to people who don't have ready cash. You see, the Liberty Bonds pay 4 percent, and that's after they mature. But you know what the bank charges for a loan, so you can buy a bond? 7 percent, that's what. And you have to pay them back both the principal and interest in just six months.

Maybe you think that doesn't amount to much? Well, get your pencil and do some figuring. We've had more than 1,100 people here buy bonds, and they've laid out money for $116,234 worth, last total they gave. They won't tell us, but let's say almost half of that is from people who don't have the money in cash or their checking accounts. For easy figuring, let's say the bank makes 7 percent loans on $50,000. You know what that comes to, over six months? That's one thousand, seven hundred and fifty dollars in interest, that's what it is. That is $750 more than the Bond buyers will ever get back from the government for the same money.

Well, now we know why bankers can buy new cars that cost $700 or more every year. They get that money by taking it out of the hides of all of us, and they say they're doing it to be patriotic. Sure, it's only a few dollars from someone who buys $100 or $200 worth of bonds, but see how it counts up.

Arthur C. Townley was right when he said this country should draft wealth the same way it drafts people. And I'll tell you, we got plenty of moneybags in Belleville that ought to be drafted.

Bjorn Nygren

Bo re-read his letter, satisfied that it was what he wanted to say. If Ivar Lindfors refused to publish it, well, Bo would tell him about the Gothenburg letter and hold it as blackmail over Ivar's head. And if that didn't work, he would threaten to wreck the goddamned printing press—yes he would. A lot like other machinery; some sand in the gears would ruin it, for sure. In his twisted solitude, with no Eva to hear his schemes and furnish counterpoint, Bo had himself thoroughly convinced of both his own moral rectitude and the efficacy of his plan.

He knew Ivar Lindfors had a habit of working late at the print shop, and he figured it best to catch him alone if at all possible, since the discussion might get touchy. He did his feeding and milking chores early and, about dark, he tossed the two letters—the one from Gothenburg and the letter exposing the corrupt bank—onto the back seat of his Ford Town Car, cranked it up, and headed down the Willow Falls road for Belleville.

* * *

Less than two blocks away from the livery stable and in a small building on Wells Street, another Belleville resident was grappling with a frustrating job change. Amos Ferguson, fired history teacher, now worked for the Athena County Abstracting Co., replacing Ollie Moller who was now working full-time at the *Forum* as a printer and once-a-week columnist.

Amos would have left town, had he not been determined to seek legal vindication for being fired from his teaching job. There was also Clara's job at the *Forum*, although it didn't pay much—$2.25 per day. That was slightly less than Amos got paid for the tedium of looking up deeds and transfers and encumbrances for a document solemnly termed an Abstract of Title.

Ivar had offered Amos a jack-of-all-trades job at the *Forum*, where he would have been rubbing elbows with that fool Moller. Try as he did to appreciate the merit of philosophical differences on a single newspaper, Amos just didn't cotton to that fellow. He had no doubt that Moller was keeping counsel on the side with J. B. Higgins and Pudgy Thurstone. As Amos saw it, Moller probably figured that if the merchant group decided to push Ivar and Inez out—or if the NPL undercut its financing—Moller might again become Belleville's foremost editor.

So lost was he in these reflections on this Friday afternoon in early March of 1918 that Amos almost disregarded the commotion across the street. Squinting through the long shadows inclining away from the low sun of a late winter day, he saw the familiar Bert Allcott in his sheepskin coat, standing on the back of a dilapidated Reo truck—one originally owned by Roy Evans at his lumber yard. Bert was either haranguing or goading or entertaining the young toughs surrounding him.

Something was up.

Whenever these roughnecks got together, Bert would take charge. Amos couldn't hear the words, but he caught Bert's intense timbre of exhortation, answered by whoops and cheers from the small throng. The figures moved about and, as the angled sun illuminated a half dozen faces, Bert recognized one with a start.

It was Rudy Pflueger, who, Amos thought, had left Belleville forever.

Why, he wondered, would this rejected Army volunteer, a failure in farming and in courtship, return to Belleville? Why would Rudy pay obeisance to the very ruffian who had vanquished him in competition for Marjorie Kiefer, a heartbreak that had quickened his decision to leave town and join the Army?

Amos shrugged as he watched the gathering grow into a seething mass of waving fists and stamping feet. It wouldn't be the first time a victim of superior prowess in battle or love returned to grovel before his conqueror. Amos had heard of some psychoanalysts in Europe who had a term for this kind of thing, but he couldn't recall what it was. Something about prisoners who fawn before their browbeating guards.

Amos felt a twinge of sadness as he watched the excitement grow. As a teacher for five years in Belleville, he had known nearly all these young people, at least briefly. Young men who were staying in town, while the young women left. The consequent shortage of females no doubt contributed to turmoil like that taking shape before him.

Now Amos saw an American flag rising on a long pole above the upraised and doubled fists. So, this was another "surge of patriotism," as the Twin Cities newspapers called it. Then he saw something more, licks of flame from under some object on the ground. With alarm, Amos saw a bucket of tar cooking over a fire partially contained in a half-size oil drum.

Pulling his weathered alpaca coat about his shoulders, Amos edged closer to the milling group. He then noticed a small cluster of older men just outside the ring of active men. This cluster included many of the same men visible at the ill-fated parade. Among them was Einart Dahlgren, saying little, but watching intently.

Amos could now pick up the dialogue. First some scattered words, then statements and declarations fused imperfectly and floating his way through the quieting air of the early dusk:

"Buncha yellow bellies, they are. Yellow bellies with no guts and red brains. Say—yellow bellies and red brains, now that's a good one. Ha, ha. They're so gutless if you shot at their goddamn bellies, yuh wou'n't hit nothing. Ha. Ha. That's another good one. Who's the yellowest of all? Krauts or the NPL'ers? Why, the yellowest is one that's both."

"Well, now, all Germans ain't bad. Look at Pflueger here, he's got a Kraut name and he hates the NPL, don't yuh, Rudy? Hey, Rudy, you wuz a farmer, you know how to tie rope? Make a good noose? Not that kinda noose, you say? Well, betcha could learn. Anyway, we got a man here's good at the hangman's noose. Hey, Walt, show us how you did that again."

"Well, see, you get a rope at least three-quarter's inch thick, like good block and tackle rope, take this much of it, loop it back and then start to turn it back here, and keep turning it, exactly 13 times. Then pull the end through here, tug at the lower end and you got the knot and the loop below it. Yep, that's a hangman's knot, all right. Dang right it is. Now count those turns, again. Somebody made a scientific study of this, know what they found out? A knot breaks a neck best when it's got exactly thirteen turns."

"Huh, whaddya know. That's somethin'—what a hay rope'll do to a neck."

"Hey, we gonna hang some slacker tonight?"

"Well, can't say for sure. See what Bert and the others think."

Bert Allcott was standing with his booted feet spread wide on the flat bed of the lumber truck, both fists in front pumping up and down as he led a crude chant:

We are the Knights of Loyalty,
Backing up the Boys who fight to be free,
All you scum in the N-P-L,
Traitors like you can go to hell.

Lusty cheers erupted after the intoning of this and similar cudgel verse, followed by yells to get the "shit-assed slackers."

"Who's the slacker we're after? Ain't sure. Maybe we get that guy Stegenheimer out on the edge of town. He's got that Iron Cross on his mail box post, Jeezus. Hangin's too good for a bastard like that. Oughta hang 'im by his heels, cut off his balls. Ha. Ha. Just like a pig. Give Rudy Pflueger the knife; he'd know how that's done, wouldn't yuh, Rudy. Ha. Ha."

"Nah, fergit ol' Stegenheimer. He's just a crazy old coot—oughta be in the nuthouse. Get someone who's been trying to talk us out of enlistin'. Hey, someone try to do that to you?"

"Naw, not to me, they'd know I'd knock 'em down. But they're doing it to other boys, yuh hear it alla time. Oh, sure, it's those goddam Nonpartisan League nuts."

"Yeah? Which ones?"

"They's this one guy thinks he's a bigshot farmer. Leonard Huisby?"

"Nah, not him, he's too close to the bank bigwigs. He don't talk that way. Smart old codger, that one. No, it ain't the guy with all that Scandihoovian talk, neither."

"Aw, you mean that Bo—Bo Nygren?"

"Yep, that's the one. Another big shot? Huh. Big goddamn mouth, you ask me. Alwiz shootin' it off. You're right, though. He thinks he's big—drives that funny lookin' car. Looks like a ritzy buggy, but it's just a dolled up Ford. Got it second hand, he did, from the dentist."

"He's a hot shot in the NPL, ain't he?"

"Yeah, he's the one who ran his wagon through the American Flag. Remember?"

"We really gonna put the noose on him?"

"Naw, we ain't gonna kill nobody, just warm 'im up with some good old tar. And then put some feathers on it, so he stays warm. Ha. Ha."

Amid this mumble, someone mentioned the Willow Falls road, a rather remote route Bo Nygren ordinarily took into town. This was Friday night when businesses were ordinarily open, so there was a chance Nygren might be traveling that route at the moment. Voices lowered from blustery bravado to genuine but cautious conspiracy. This would be some night.

Amos, standing in the shadow of a blacksmith shop, caught the ominous words—hangman's noose—get someone—Nonpartisan nuts—Scandihoovian—pour some tar—Willow Falls road. He looked around, saw a few onlookers like himself, but no police or sheriff or deputies. Well, the Willow Falls road came in from the northeast, meaning it would be out of town, in a rural township. This would be a job for Sheriff Alfred Mayberry.

The Athena County Sheriff knew all about Amos Ferguson's abrupt dismissal from the High School and didn't particularly mind. No skin off my behind, the Sheriff figured. If he is a troublemaker, get him out of the schools, fine. Fine, that is, so long as the Sheriff doesn't get involved, since there was talk that Amos was somehow sympathetic toward the Nonpartisan League and a Sheriff with the next election in mind didn't need another run-in with that group.

He hoped the League people would remember that he hadn't interfered with Townley's speech at Huisby's farm and that, at the parade, he was just doing his job. Problem was, the NPL men probably figured that "doing his job" meant being a lackey for Higgins and Thurstone, and Alfred Mayberry couldn't stomach that idea getting around among the farmers.

The Sheriff fully expected someone to tell him about Bert's ruckus today, but he wasn't prepared to get it from the recently fired teacher. Furthermore, "hot tar" was something he had hoped to never see or smell in Athena County. The business about a hangman's noose was even worse, *but maybe that was all bluff. If they were actually cooking tar, that's probably all they planned to use. But, Christ. When these hotheads go that far, hard telling where they'll stop.*

"You go home and stay there," the Sheriff told Amos. "I'll take some deputies and amble out toward the Willow Falls road. Maybe nothing'll come of this, but I'll have a looky see."

* * *

Bo Nygren was always leery about driving his automobile to town in winter. The dirt-and-gravel Willow Falls road was through the more rolling part of the county. It wound over low hills, down through tight curves over narrow bridges and, after a heavy snow, would be completely unusable until graded, usually by Bo and his neighbors. Where there were heavy drifts, it would take a crew of strong men with scoop shovels, shiny clean from a thousand thrusts into piles of wheat, to manually clear the road.

There hadn't been much snow for several weeks and the road was still reasonably clear from the last grading, although it was packed with snow and ice and a sudden warm spell could turn the surface to slush and mud. As a precaution, Bo Nygren put chains on the rear tires.

He was about five miles from town when he saw the battered Reo truck standing kitty-cornered across the road, one back wheel down in the ditch. A young man he couldn't recognize was peering at that wheel. Looks like a dumb driver who doesn't know these old roads, Bo concluded, as he carefully pulled his Ford up to the tilted front end of the truck.

He was hardly out of his car when he heard the roar of husky voices in hoarse unison and saw himself surrounded by the young ruffians of the Belleville Knights of Loyalty. Before him was Bert Allcott—hands on hips, his leer outlined by eerie facial shadows created by two lanterns held high on either side. A hot musk of creosote hung in the air.

Bo Nygren heard in the excruciating next few minutes all the braggadocio and bravura rehearsed less than an hour earlier in Belleville. Menacing jaws and clenched fists lunged toward him, then backed off, yielding to others. The hot tar was lugged from the woods clump beside the road by two of the young toughs, their blazing eyes threatening under lantern shadows darkened further by the bent and soiled visors of cotton work caps. Their hot breath gave off the smell of cheap whiskey.

Bo's head went abuzz with the confusion. He thought absurdly of somehow racing to safety inside his elegant Ford. As if reading his mind, someone yelled, "Hey, let's fix the yellow bastard's goddamn car. Paint it yellow, like him."

A bucket of yellow paint splashed across the side of the vehicle, through the open front door and onto the mouse-colored, velvet-textured and ribbed front seat cushion. Throwing the paint was a committing and facilitating act, like cutting off the ear of a victim about to be drawn and quartered. With that much done, the gorier next steps are now both logical and obligatory.

"Hey, let's paint the car's belly the same color. Everyone on this side, get hold of 'er."

About 18 of these strong hands were all it took to lift one side of the shiny black car with its fresh yellow defacing up and over on the narrow dirt road. Pitching on its side, the car kept rolling until it was nearly upside down, its handsome top disappearing in the snow-covered elder and berry brush that lined the ditch alongside the roadbed.

The sight of the tumbling car and its wheels pointing skyward brought a lusty roar from the seething mob. A second bucket of paint went flying over the car's underside. "There you are, a yellow belly with a yellow bellied car."

Grotesque laughter again.

"Now pour the tar on the goddamn bastard," was the

next cry. Five pairs of hands and arms around his shoulders, neck, waist, and ankles wrested Bjorn Nygren into bent helplessness. Think of something, he thought. In his panic, he went for the most rational solution his life experience and outlook could produce.

"You've got the wrong man," he shouted in a bellow as deep as he could muster.

"Wrong, hell. Yuh're Bo Nygren, ain't you? And that's your fancy goddamn Ford ain't it? Or wuz."

The last two words brought another ugly howl.

One particular fellow, familiar with Bo's personal ordeals, shouted in a high pitch: "Hey, Nygren, yuh cheap draft slacker. Whatsa matter? Your wife so fed up with you not respectin' the flag, she's left yuh? Well, write 'er a letter not to come back. You won't do 'er no good after we cook your crotch in hot tar."

Still more laughter, now louder and ever more obscene.

"I said you got the wrong man," Bo Nygren repeated. "I ain't done nothing to let the country down."

"Bullshit you ain't. 'Member what you said that time your goddam wagon ran into the flag? Jesus, can't no one print what you said then."

Bo persisted in his defense strategy. "Say, now, that was an accident. I didn't use any bad words about the flag. They made me run into that line. If you want to tar somebody, get a real socialist, like that teacher at the school. He's so bad they fired him, did you know that?"

There was a momentary pause, and Bo Nygren silently praised himself for grasping a stratagem that just might work. They were bent on doing something, so it wasn't a matter of stopping them. Just directing them to a different target. He felt a surge of adrenalin that gave him hope and a measure of confidence.

"I'll tell you something else," Bo continued, his jaw thrust out, lower teeth bared. "That teacher—you know his name, Ferguson. He's going to court, trying to get his job back. Now whaddya think of that? A traitor like that teaching kids." Mumbles of affirmation now from the small mob, most of whom recognized the name and many of whom had felt more kindly than not toward the feisty history teacher.

The pause didn't last long.

Strong, calloused and dirty fingers tore the coat from Nygren's back, then the shirt and woolen underwear, exposing bare skin. A pail was dipped into the larger bucket of tar, partially cooled from its bubbling state less than a half hour earlier in town. The whole pailful of tar went sloshing down Bo Nygren's back, covering his neck and back and oozing under his waistband. He cursed heavily.

A new voice, as mature as Nygren's but even deeper, bellowed from the gloom a few yards down the road.

"Now just hold it right there, boys."

Sheriff Alfred Mayberry and two deputies strode into the suddenly quiet circle of the Knights of Loyalty and their unhappy quarry. The Sheriff looked slowly around and saw Rudy Pflueger near the back of the crowd, holding a second bucket of tar.

"Hey Rudy, wrong time of year to be paving the road, now isn't it?" the sheriff boomed. "Besides, I don't recall the County Board listing this partic'lar road as one to get tar, anyways.

"And look here, Bert," Mayberry continued, "You fellows got so eager trying to repair the road you went and accidentally spilled some road tar on a good citizen.

"Now just put that tar away, boys, and get back to town, unless some of you want to help get Mr. Nygren's car tipped back up. Guess this road needs fixing after all, the way it made that nice car of his tip over."

The Sheriff had rehearsed this ridiculously transparent subterfuge all the way out from town. He was not at all sure it would pan out, but it was worth a try. These punks had screwed their courage up a long way to go after a prominent—though controversial—farmer. Tangling with three law officers, though, was outside their experience. A few of them had been known to forcibly resist arrest at dancehalls or saloons. But resisting arrest and assaulting the Sheriff himself were very different things.

Much mumbling ensued.

"We're just helping you and the Safety Committee do your job, Sheriff," Allcott said. "You knew damned well this cuss should have been fined after he tore that flag down that day. We're just trying to make him more patriotic. Ain't we, fellas?"

An affirmative roar arose and subsided.

"Well, Mr. Nygren's patriotic enough, you can be sure of that. Why just yesterday, he told me he was going to buy another $200 worth of Liberty Bonds," Alfred Mayberry lied. "Didn't you, Bo?"

"Sure did." Nygren, no longer held by the mob, was using the remains of his torn coat trying, unsuccessfully, to wipe the black, sticky tar off his head and neck.

A handful of the Knights of Loyalty had now moved back out of sight of the Sheriff. One standing near Allcott grumbled something about getting the lumber truck out of the ditch.

The Sheriff said little more. The Knights easily pushed the truck out of the shallow roadside ditch and got it headed back to town. After more indecisive mumbling in low tones, someone looked back toward the overturned Ford and muttered, "Might's well." Several of the group strode to the upside-down, yellow-splashed vehicle.

The men tried to no avail to bring the car upright. It was an uphill push, without decent footing in the ditch and against gravity and resistance of snow, shrubs, and brush. Besides, the hearts of the lifters were not in this task.

"Gonna need a log chain or somethin' to pull that car back over," Sheriff Mayberry suggested. "You boys got something in that truck?"

From under a battered wooden toolbox, the vehicle's driver found a dirty coil of heavy rope. They looped one end around both the left wheels, and tied the other end to the truck. Just as Nygren was shouting, "Easy now, don't bang 'er down too hard," the Ford came over on its side with a jarring crash, shattering the two windows that hit the ground.

"Holy Jeezus," Bo Nygren screamed, as the Sheriff held out a hand to suppress further complaint.

Next the rope was looped over the box-like top of the car and another tug from the truck brought the Ford to a badly tilted but technically upright position on the edge of the narrow road. A dozen or so Knights pushed the now dirty, dented and yellow-splotched car back to the road center, oil and gasoline and radiator water oozing freely onto the frosty and rutted ground.

A strong smell of wood alcohol from the emptied radiator hung in the air, mixing richly with the aroma of tar.

As the Knights of Loyalty climbed on the flatbed truck, one asked, "Hey, Sheriff, who sent you out here, anyways?"

"Nobody sent me. I just happened along as you fellas were going to fix the wrong road."

Half-covered with tar while seeing his treasured car upside down alongside the road, Bo Nygren was now safe from the mob, but cursing vehemently.

The lumber truck, loaded to overflowing with the 20-odd disheartened young men, had hardly left the scene of the near-tarring-and-feathering when Rudy Pflueger remembered something that brought the spirits of all surging back.

"Hey, boys, know what? I saw somebody watching us back there in town, when we were cooking the tar."

"Hell, wasn't nobody else there, was they?"

"Damned sure was. I seen Mr—I mean, I seen Amos Ferguson standing there, right next to the blacksmith shop, watching us. Didn't think much of it, then. Betchyur life it was him sicked the Sheriff on us. Betchyoo anything."

Someone else provided additional confirming evidence to Rudy's story. "Yeah, it was a man, too, and, come to think of it, someone short, like ol' Ferguson."

"Never did like history. Neither did I. Didn't seem like Ferguson really ever told us quite right about how America won all its wars, did he? No, but he did like to talk about those Russian and German Bolsheviks, didn't he? Well, I never thought too much about him, but the School Board sure figgered him a socialist. And not patriotic at all. And now he went and give us away."

# XIII. TARRED AND FEATHERED

Bert Allcott heard this theory of Ferguson disloyalty developing and decided to spur it along. Wouldn't be too good to have everyone go home now, all let down, he thought. It would be next to impossible to get them worked up again for a long time.

"Hey, Rudy," he shouted to the back of the truck, "you sure you saw Ferguson there?"

"Damned sure," Rudolph Pflueger said with confidence and authority.

Thus did this clique swiftly change Amos Ferguson from a once respected history teacher to a confirmed socialist, Bolshevik, traitor, slacker, and informer. Within an hour, Amos answered a knock on his door. Before he could close it, husky young men dragged him to the lumber truck while a terrified Clara screamed in horror. They hauled him to a remote forested area northwest of town and covered him with freshly cooked tar, dusted with feathers. They tied him to a rail, carried him a hundred yards down a snowy woodland trail, and dumped him into the snow. One of the Knights of Loyalty cut the twine tying Amos' hands and feet before they all rode away, leaving him stranded in this condition seven miles from Belleville on a Friday night during the first week of March.

\* \* \*

After the tarring and feathering of Amos Ferguson, Bert Allcott returned, not to his house, but to a vacant apartment upstairs from his father's pharmacy. He often slept there on a cot after his late outings. This way, he would explain to his family, he would keep from waking them at home.

As he threw himself on the cot, Bert's thoughts went to Marjorie Kiefer in a strangely satisfying way. The tarring and feathering of the shamed history teacher had aroused the young male crowd to an apex of electrifying exhilaration that left all except the victim in a euphoria of gratification and fulfillment. *Yes, giving that history teacher what he deserved was just as good as a sleep with Marjorie Kiefer.*

* * *

One member of the Knights of Loyalty did not join the ride out to the woods in the northwest township. Rudy Pflueger had a change of heart immediately after three others yanked Amos from his doorway and hauled him to the back of the truck.

"Where we takin' him?" Rudy had asked.

"Hell and gone out in the woods," someone had answered.

"And haul him back full of tar and feathers?"

The other laughed rudely. "Hell, Rudy, we just might let him find his own way back. With all those feathers on him, maybe he'll be able to fly. Ha. Ha. Ain't that another good one."

Rudy found himself losing stomach for this business. *Would Amos Ferguson perhaps be killed? Would Bo Nygren have been killed if the Sheriff hadn't come along?*

Others also saw things getting out of hand; the older men, such as Einart Dahlgren, had not gone along on the Willow Falls road escapade and none was around for the abduction of Amos Ferguson. Rudy drifted slowly to the back of the group and let the truck leave without him. He wasn't missed, immediately.

As he returned a short time later to his cot in the back corner of the livery stable, Rudy Pflueger's thoughts were also about Marjorie Kiefer. In his torment, he remembered her flowing dark hair, nubile figure, and thighs that felt so warm the one time he had held her close to him. He ached for another whiff of her perfumed neck; he fantasized complete union with her, an intimacy he had never come close to achieving.

Now, alarmed at having forsaken Amos and depressed anew over his failed romantic life, Rudy Pflueger was unable to sleep. He heard the distant and mournful whistle of the midnight train heading toward Fargo. There would be another at 3 a.m., this time going to Minneapolis. Rudy got up, dressed, and made his plans. When that train pulled into the Belleville depot on its way east, Rudy boarded it. His return to Belleville had gone awfully sour.

\* \* \*

Later that morning the body of Amos Ferguson was found by a trucker heading out on his rounds, picking up cream for the butter factory. Amos had made it almost to the Belleville City limits before collapsing alongside the road. He fell within 20 rods of the first house he might have reached along this deserted trail that branched off Athena County highway 277 and wound into the oak forests scattered on low hills arising from marshy prairie.

\* \* \*

A frantic Clara Ferguson ran first to the Lindfors house after the abduction of Amos that Friday night. She had recognized only one of the young men at the abductor scene—Rudy Pflueger. Ivar found one policeman at the station and later spotted Sheriff Alfred Mayberry as he parked his Studebaker behind the Courthouse. Mayberry listened worriedly to Ivar, but said nothing about the incident with Bjorn Nygren on the Willow Falls road earlier in the evening.

The sheriff and the policeman conferred, mostly about jurisdiction. The policeman called Chief Ezra Morse, and all three searched the streets and alleys of Belleville, ostensibly for some sign of Amos Ferguson. No law officer in Belleville during that night questioned members of the Knights of Loyalty or their leader Bert Allcott. At 3:15 a.m. Morse checked the livery stable and found Rudy Pflueger's cot empty.

"Well, looks like that trouble-making teacher went and got himself in more trouble," Morse observed. "Wonder what he did to make someone so mad?"

After the trucker brought Amos' body to the Sheriff's office, Mayberry and Police Chief Ezra Morse had another jurisdictional conference.

Mayberry said, "Well, this here abduction was in town, so looks like it's really one for your police in Belleville to investigate, huh?"

"Now wait, he was found outside the city limits and there's no sign he died in town, so now that makes it one you and the sheriff's deputies should take care of, doesn't it?"

"Maybe and maybe not. Why don't we go talk to Pudgy Thurstone about this, or maybe Judge Branson?"

"Well, now that's a pretty darned good idea. These things sure get complicated, don't they?"

\* \* \*

After the incident on the Willow Falls road, Sheriff Mayberry had taken an angry Bo Nygren back to his farm home. The sheriff and his deputies waited while Bo found some kerosene to wipe off the remaining tar, change his shirt and jacket, and find some liquid for the Ford's radiator and oil for its crankcase. These materials in hand, the group returned to the site of the incident where the abused Ford waited in its crumpled state. They finally got it started and turned around so that Nygren could return home. He had no interest in continuing his trip to Belleville that evening.

This time with Nygren was useful for the Sheriff, since it gave him a chance to calm this potentially influential but mercurial and now wildly irate NPL officer. Bo shouted repeatedly "the whole goddamned bunch should be in jail." The sheriff answered that jailing a mob never works and, besides, making a fuss would have everyone talking about Bo Nygren almost getting tarred and feathered and did he want that? No, Bo didn't, and he sulked into an infuriated silence. The sheriff was satisfied that given the man's vain character, Bo probably wouldn't say much about the incident. At least, nothing that would harm the sheriff's chances for re-election.

By the time the sheriff and his deputies left Bo Nygren, more than two hours had passed since the incident on the Willow Falls road. The law officers returned to Belleville only after the Knights of Loyalty had abducted, tarred, feathered, and abandoned Amos Ferguson in a stand of oak trees on the edge of a swamp in a remote corner of Athena County.

\* \* \*

Standing inside the small police station across Wells Street from the Post Office, Ivar Lindfors overheard the gist of the jurisdictional debate in the Chief's private little office. As the two law officers emerged from the office cubicle, Ivar asked if they were going to pick up Rudy Pflueger.

"His bed's empty," Chief Morse said. "Probably left town."

"So are you putting out a wire on him? To towns up and down the rail line?" Ivar asked.

"Yeah, we'll do that," Morse said, "after we get through with the coroner stuff. That's the important thing right now."

Ivar persisted. "You going to question other people in town?"

"Don't have any leads yet, Ivar," the Chief responded, now showing some irritation. "Rudy's a farm kid, used to anyways, so who the others were, we don't know. Could be country men, maybe could be from town—"

"Now Ezra, you know this bunch that calls itself the Knights of Loyalty, they've been making loud noises up and down the streets and in the square for a month. Aren't you going to talk to them?"

Sheriff Mayberry said nothing.

"Say, Ivar, you tend to your newspaper and I'll tend to policing," the Chief said. "The Sheriff and I will take care of this. You gotta remember, this guy was a big slacker, even anti-American. Why, the school board didn't see fit to keep him teaching. Maybe all this is tough on Mrs. Ferguson, but a lot of people hated his guts. There's no sign anyone killed him, he just—"

Ivar shouted, "He was left out in the woods at night in winter. Covered with tar and feathers. If that isn't murder, what is?"

The Chief held up a hand. "Don't go telling me how to do my job, Ivar, or I'll have to write you up for interfering with police work."

* * *

A perplexed, agitated Ivar Lindfors started for the *Forum* building after he left the police station that Saturday morning—then remembered that Ollie Moller had a habit of coming on Saturdays. Ivar needed to talk with Inez, alone.

He went straight home, only to find Inez and Charlotte gone. A note from Inez said she was going with Clara Ferguson to Heberman's mortuary, then to the Trinity Lutheran Church. Charlotte was at the Shurstad's house, playing with friend Abigail; her violin was broken again, so she couldn't practice.

Ivar's first stop was at the small mortuary at the back of the furniture store. He met Ernest Heberman, who was wearing a gray smock that served as a coroner's gown. He had just stepped out of what passed as a cadaver receiving room.

"Oh, Ernest. I was looking for Inez, said she was coming

here."

"She came with Clara Ferguson to look at the body, Ivar. They left here about ten minutes ago."

Ivar turned to leave.

"Ivar, are you going to write this thing up for your paper?"

"That's exactly what I'm trying to do, Ernest," Ivar said, as evenly as he could manage. "This is one story that needs to be told in every detail that I can figure out."

Heberman paused.

"You know, don't you, Ivar, that this man was in trouble in town? That he was known for his disloyalty to the American cause? Even talked disloyalty to young women studying to be teachers? That it had become dangerous for him to stay here?"

Ivar considered shouting: *Look at who is saying these things. Someone who is trying to beat age-old suspicion of his own nationality.* Instead, he said, "I have heard these things, but right now the question is what we know about how he died and who did it, Ernest. I'm going to find that out if it's the last thing I do."

He heard his own words echo bravado more than courage, conviction or likelihood. But he looked steadily at Ernest Heberman.

Heberman breathed deeply, two or three times, then sat down heavily in a cheap stuffed chair, its tag hanging from the shipping paper still covering the back. He gazed idly at four caskets stacked against the opposite wall, lying there as nettlesome reminders of his earlier infuriation with this bullheaded editor.

"I've got to admit—I've got two minds about you, Ivar," he began. "You know I was so damned mad at you about those casket letters in your Swedish newspaper, I could have stopped advertising, tightened up on that loan, and made it so tough you'd have to quit. I didn't do that though, mad as I was, and to tell the truth, I don't know exactly why not. I wasn't sure whether you had guts or were just thick-headed."

He smirked without humor, more of a grimace than a grin. "I did you a favor by not making it harder on you, both back then and again when you got into that stuff about the war and free speech and all. I'm on the Athena County Public Safety Committee, and they all wanted to shut you down six months ago, 'case you didn't know. You maybe won't believe it, but I did as much as I could to let you go on publishing. I told them getting Ollie Moller to writing for you would help.

"You know, saying all that to the Safety Committee wasn't easy for me, because I've got this German name and there's always a chance someone in town will get leery. Lucky for me, I've got a son in the Navy—yes, that's right, Hermie is a sailor, a gunner on the Utah—so that takes some of the heat off me, that way.

"What I'm saying is, I don't know what the hell you are going to write about this Ferguson thing. After I get done here, I'll give you an official coroner's report—that's all I'll do, no more, no less. Frankly, I think you'd be better off letting this whole thing go, and let the Minneapolis or St. Paul papers write it up. That could be a good excuse for you to not cover it, wouldn't it?"

Ivar answered with only a steady, fixed stare. This was his best response, since he always seemed inept at sharp retort. Furthermore, he had little inclination to lash out at Ernest Heberman, alias Ernst Hebermann, who differed from the fanatical likes of Pudgy Thurstone.

"Well, just one thing, Ivar," Heberman continued. "This is friendly advice, take it man to man. Don't make this thing into a Shame of Belleville, the way that magazine writer did with Minneapolis that time, maybe ten years ago. You won't get even with the Athena County Safety Committee. They'll get even with you, though, if you try."

Ivar left the Heberman furniture store and mortuary and coroner's office and went to the church. He found Inez and led her to a pew in the empty sanctuary.

Together, they reexamined the beliefs and events that brought them to this point: Ivar's early enthusiasm about newspapering and destitute children; their efforts to play up the idea of people working together to change things; stories that backfired. It was an emotional purgation. Ivar could now manipulate the English language well enough to vent more adequately his views of himself and the situation.

"Naive idealism is what we have had, Inez. Absolutely naive. Foolish, like children."

Inez sat in the pew studying him intently, her feet drawn up, her chin on her arms wrapped around her knees.

"Inez, I admired Amos and I've come to despise Ollie Moller, but both were right. Remember? Ollie Moller told us that the Belleville merchants are going to run things, no matter what. Hate each other's guts, but they'll stay in charge. They're not going to let the League get the upper hand. Their fear of the League overpowers their hatred for each other.

"What's more, we fool ourselves by thinking the League wants us to print both sides of things. We fooled ourselves by trying to put ideas from Alexis DeTocqueville and Thomas Jefferson to work in Belleville. It was nice of Jefferson to say a press without government is better than the other way around, but not a soul here except for you and me believes that. We fool ourselves even more when we think we can write things up like an Upton Sinclair, or a Lincoln Steffens, or an Ida Tarbell, or any other muckraker.

"You know, don't you Inez, what 'muckraker' means? It means digging into the muck. And muck, excuse me Inez, we never talk this way to each other, but muck means, well, what in Sweden we called skit, or lort. Or dynga, which isn't quite so vulgar. Remember how Amos told us that Teddy Roosevelt called those reporters muckrakers back in 1907, before we got here? That name stuck, but not quite the way he intended. He degraded those reporters and magazines who wrote about the corruption and waste and greed and exploitation by saying they were raking through the muck of the country.

"Ollie Moller was right when he said we don't 'rake' the

muck in Athena County. We just shovel out the stuff that sloughs off from everything else that happens—that people just want to get out of the way, cleaned out, to make way for more. A new shop opens, this street is closed, that one paved, this block gets telephone wires, that lodge announces its new members, this sporting club tells who won the turkey shoot and the raffle and so on. Oh, it's important to the people who want it reported, but it's just the stuff that sloughs off from our humdrum lives. That's the residue, and it's just so much dynga.

"Then there's all that boiler plate, from the medicine companies, the Encyclopedia publishers, the Temperance League and Lord knows where else. By tossing in that stuff we convince ourselves that we really do print what we like.

"You remember the series we did in the *Veckomonitoren* about the Mother's Allowance law?" Ivar asked. "It was something burning at me from years back, you know that. I really thought we were on—a mission, a crusade. Something that held real promise for changing the way the country takes care of its children from families that are down on their luck."

Inez listened quietly to this catharsis. Ivar had never really quit struggling with his residual guilt from the horse-barn trysts with Fredrika Grinnhaal. Each rendezvous and the eventual progeny remained as vexing counterpoint to his convictions about obligations of the male, and especially the father of misbegotten children. As usual, Inez let him continue.

"You got Irma Johnston to run that meeting about orphanages and Mother's Allowances, Inez. All those important speakers came, everybody felt good about it.

"Then when the legislature passed that law, I really and truly thought we had some part in getting it through. That we had helped bring about a piece of real change in how this country does things—how it looks after its people. It was how the Social Democrats in Sweden felt when they passed all those laws about orphan children and poor families.

"When I look back on it now, I'd say we fooled ourselves into believing we had changed some minds in this town and county. Fact is, we didn't do anything of the kind. They all just tolerated what we wrote, in a sort of kindly way, because the law didn't really amount to much at all. It was a small change, something they had all expected for some time and they were just taking it with a shrug. Those people who gave us high marks weren't praising us for our courage at all. At most, they were thanking us for not pushing something radical. The Mother's Allowance law was fine, because it upset nothing the town leaders ordinarily do. It was no skin off their backsides.

"Maybe we fooled ourselves with the town's help, kind of the same way Marie Pflueger fooled herself with our help," Ivar continued. Inez blanched.

"Marie Pflueger? She fooled herself? Ivar, what are you talking about?"

Ivar had never told Inez about the severe admonishment from Marie after the loss of her farm. In its searing moral insight, Marie's reproach had haunted him more than any of the blisterings he'd taken from town leaders, over complaints about funeral costs or wheat grading or the Nonpartisan League or Liberty Bond drives.

For the first time, he related that encounter to Inez, as accurately as he could.

"She really told me off, she did. She said all we wrote about community cooperation, after the fire that killed Jerrold, didn't help the Pfluegers at all. She told me we did it to please the merchants and the NPL at the same time, to make the newspaper look good. She said we got people to expect a miracle to happen, because only a miracle could have made Rudy an able farmer. When I tried to tell her how patriotic Rudy looked to people when he enlisted, she let me know Rudy had a bad heart and was turned down by Army doctors. And then she turned her back and I never saw her again," Ivar concluded.

Silence for some time.

"Ivar, we should have talked that one over. We might have done something good."

"Such as?"

"We could have apologized to her and Rudy in print. We could have said that maybe the whole town and the whole county made a mistake. That would include us."

To have apologized to Marie Pflueger in the newspaper seemed incredible to Ivar. He believed that such repentance would have betrayed the wholesome community spirit of cooperation and help to a family bathed in tragedy. But hearing Inez say this, he squirmed, because he was fully aware of why it had been so easy to avoid a public apology. It was the obvious inability of a Marie Pflueger to bring political or business pressure to bear on the Lindfors family enterprise.

Now totally depressed, Ivar searched for a change of subject. "This freedom of speech is qualified, as Amos said. It's qualified by the Hebermans and Higginses and Thurstones who have their hands on the money and the government. It's qualified by the Nonpartisan League, too, when it doesn't really want a forum newspaper. It's qualified by our own notions of what is and isn't good for the eyes of the town."

"Ivar, we just had a murder. What are the sheriff and police doing about it?"

Ivar looked up at her slowly. "Inez, you should have seen these champions of law and order just an hour ago down at Morse's office. Each one is trying to get the other to take jurisdiction. They don't give a damn about Amos Ferguson.

"They're both scared of Pudgy Thurstone and the Safety Committee. The sheriff was all tight-lipped, but I think he knows a lot about it—about who dragged Amos off and tarred and feathered him, I mean. And left him to die."

Another pause.

"So, Ivar, what do we do now?"

"First, I guess, we admit to ourselves how weak we are, Inez. That Amos was right when he called free speech a complicated thing, that it doesn't mean we can print anything we like.

"But, weak as we are, we figure out how to print all that we can, which may be different from what we should. What we can do is get to the bottom of the story about Amos Ferguson. It's Saturday and that leaves us about four days to find things out.

"That sheriff and police chief know Amos got fired by order of Pudgy Thurstone and J. B. Higgins, and they don't want to make much of his getting killed. They'll keep hiding the real facts, so it won't look bad for the County Safety Committee and the Belleville business crowd."

Inez regarded her husband with the same beaming admiration that she had accorded him a dozen years earlier in Klas Lindfors' printing enterprise in a small city in southeastern Sweden. She offered encouragement tinged with practical caution. And she felt a sudden impulse to pour out to him the story she was withholding, that what she carried in her womb was not a result of his seed, but a miracle wrought by an enlightened medical researcher from Paris.

No, not now, maybe never, she told herself. Ivar is upset enough as it is right now. Better not distract him with another thunderbolt.

"Ivar," she said, "this would be the first time we ever tried to report on a crime without the help of the sheriff or the chief of police or a judge."

She smiled and said, teasing, "So now you are going to be your own detective? Just think. Ivar Lindfors, Pinkerton Investigator. Who knows? Maybe then you can run against Alfred Mayberry for sheriff, in the next election."

It was a bad joke but a needed break in tension for Ivar.

"Yes," he answered, "from editor to sheriff, what a switch that would be. Right now, I do need to think like a sheriff, and figure out how and where to find Rudy Pflueger. Any ideas?"

"Grab the next train to Minneapolis, Ivar. It's a big city,

but that's where he went, I'll bet."

* * *

After the sheriff and the deputies returned toward Belleville on the Willow Falls road, Bo Nygren nursed his once sumptuous but now battered Ford Town Sedan back toward his farm and house. In his fury, he hadn't thought about either the letter from Gothenburg or the one he had written about the crooked interest rates the bank was charging people needing money for Liberty Bonds. He had tucked both of them in an old envelope and then tossed it on the back seat of the Ford Town Car. Where was it now? The car had been overturned and two windows broken. With a lighted lantern, he searched the insides of the car, and under the rear seat, which had fallen loose when the car was flipped over. Nothing there.

The following morning, Saturday, Bo Nygren returned to the locale of the previous evening's terrifying incident. After a half hour of searching, he found the envelope in the snow; at some point it had apparently fallen out a broken window. The two letters, though encased in cold snow and badly smudged, were still there.

* * *

The Livery stable owner remembered a postcard that a disconsolate Rudy Pflueger had written from Minneapolis, asking about a job. The owner had written a reply and remembered the name of a flophouse on First Avenue, in the Bridge Square district. There, Ivar found Rudy, and quickly learned the troubled young man's version of the abduction of Amos Ferguson. Rudy freely named all those he knew on the grim foray up the Willow Falls Road. This information led Ivar to various individuals and officials in Belleville and other parts of Athena County.

First on Ivar's list was Bo Nygren, whose displeasure

over the incident was not improved the next morning by hearing Ivar Lindfors' jalopy clatter up his driveway, the rattle of the rear wheels only partly muffled by mud from the first thaw that went only an inch deep, leaving frozen ground below that surface ooze, just enough for wheel traction.

Not wanting Ivar Lindfors in his cluttered house, Bo met him, with a grunt, in the soggy driveway of his front yard.

Ivar was direct. "Bo! Tell me everything that happened Friday night. I must get the whole story."

Bo Nygren, ever seeking advantage, tried for a bargain that might achieve all his ends. Without a word, he walked back to the house without inviting Ivar in, found the soiled envelope recovered from where his Ford Town Car had been turned over, and pulled out only his handwritten letter to the bank. He walked slowly back to the muddy yard where Ivar waited beside his Ford jalopy, deciding not to mention the Gothenburg letter right now. The familiar odor of exhaust, a warm radiator, and hot oil hung over the Ford in the quiet morning air.

"Tell you what, Ivar. I'll fill you in on everything if you'll agree to publish this letter here about the bank's goddamned crookedness."

"The bank's crookedness?"

Bo then produced his badly smudged letter about the bank's charging 7 percent interest to lend money for purchase of Liberty Bonds paying 4 percent.

"We'll make a deal, Ivar. I'll tell you all if you'll run this here letter on the front page."

Ivar recalled the fable about a contemptible calf deal Bo Nygren had tried to cut with Al Theide a few years ago. Everybody, including Bo's wife Eva, questioned Bo's judgment because of that deal, and Ivar questioned it now.

He wondered briefly, but quickly realized, what Inez would say: *The truthful reporting of the story is a matter of honor, not to be besmirched by a devil's bargain.*

"Bo, I don't know about that. I see the point of the letter, but we don't make deals of that sort. Just mail the letter in next week, and we'll think of it separately from the story about Amos Ferguson's death. For one thing, we would want a lawyer to check it for libel."

"Come on, Ivar," Bo Nygren growled. "You make deals all the time, with both the NPL and with the Commercial Club in Belleville. You know well's I do. This ain't nothin' unusual."

"Bo, I can't do that, not where the Ferguson thing is concerned. He died because of craziness, and I'm not going to defile him by making deals to get the facts."

"Then you can go suck my hind end like all the rest, goddamn it," Nygren said and strode without another word back to his empty house. Ivar restarted his weathered Ford and drove away. He had many more people to see and he was sure several would talk, if only to boast. He would promise only to use no names, except for the victim and the law officers. That was one deal he would make.

After three days of talking and listening, Ivar wrote a piece that used up the entire front page of the Athena County *Forum*. In writing it up, he and Inez made a momentous decision. This time, they agreed, *we will report more than what we can. We will write what we should.*

REPORT OF A LYNCHING

The report of the tragedy appeared under an eight-column banner headline on the front page, followed by a two-column deck in the upper left corner:

MOB JUSTICE LEADS TO TRAGIC DEATH
OF A CONSCIENTIOUS TEACHER

———————————

UNSPEAKABLE ATROCITY

———————————

Amos Ferguson Tarred, Left to Die.

———————————

Local Law Officials Seem Disinterested.

Has War Hysteria Overtaken Athena County?

By now, through rumors and gossip and hearsay, Belleville and all of Athena County have become abuzz with events of Friday and Saturday, March 1st and 2nd, 1918. What everyone knows is that Mr. Amos Ferguson, who taught history until recently in Belleville High School's Normal program, was found dead on a road north of Belleville Saturday morning, his partially clothed body covered with tar and feathers.

We would like our readers to know that preparing this report would have been far easier had the experienced law enforcement agencies in the county been as cooperative as they always have been in the past. As a result, it was necessary for us to go about investigating this tragedy in ways that are ordinarily left to papers in Minneapolis, St. Paul, and New York, who enjoy large staffs of seasoned reporters who devote weeks, if necessary, to getting the inside stuff.

We have been warned by various parties around Athena County not to print this report. By now, we are used to such warning and we know full well that some may make good on their threats. We simply believe that people must be informed. They must know what facts can be trusted, and which ones are in doubt. We are giving you the truth as we can best determine it.

Late Friday afternoon, there gathered in the back streets of Belleville some thirty, possibly forty, men who are often seen together in public, flying the American flag and shouting menacing words about persons suspected of disloyalty. Leaders of this gathering called themselves "Knights of Loyalty."

Many things were said and done at this gathering. It is widely agreed that a can of tar was heated to the bubbling point over a fire, around which the gathering took place. Names of various recipients of this tar were suggested, and it seems the group settled on one particular individual connected with the Athena County chapter of the Nonpartisan League.

As night fell, about two dozen members of this group took a truck to a place where the intended victim might be encountered, and blocked the road. This person, a prominent citizen, sought to help the driver of a truck that, he thought, had unfortunately slipped one rear wheel into a ditch.

As the citizen left his car, he was immediately surrounded by members of this Knights of Loyalty group who emerged from the woods, shouting the most obscene and insulting phrases and accusing him of the most dastardly acts of disloyalty, none of them accurate. His automobile was doused with yellow paint and turned upside down in an act of pure, brazen and shameless vandalism.

Notwithstanding the plaintive appeals for mercy from this citizen, some tar was poured on him. Fortunately for his sake, the tar had cooled somewhat in the air of a wintry evening. Much was said in this fracas, and the name of Amos Ferguson was mentioned as more seriously disloyal than the citizen here.

At about the time the tar was poured, three members of a law enforcement agency appeared on the scene, all of who are to be praised for their courage in seeking to take charge in such a mob scene. Through various entreaties and calls for calm, these law officers achieved remarkable success in saving this citizen from further abuse. They even convinced members of the Knights of Loyalty to return the citizen's automobile to an upright position.

As we have said, these law officers are to be commended for the courageous and resourceful means they employed in dispersing the Knights of Loyalty mob. Yes, we say "Knights of Loyalty mob," because that is exactly what it would be called by any rational person.

We pause here in our narrative to relate to our readers how this particular event was recorded in the Athena County Sheriff's department's report for Friday, March 1st, 1918. The reader will note how that report, entered as an official account of what happened, varies from what we learned from actual participants in the incident. The report says:

"On Friday evening, March 1, 1918, officers ... were traveling on the Willow Falls road and encountered an unusual scene. It seems that a number of public-spirited

Athena County citizens were taking it upon themselves to make some road repairs and had parked their vehicle carrying the repair materials in such a way that it blocked the road. Coming from the opposite direction, a prominent rural citizen was unable to get past the truck and, unfortunately, his automobile slid off the road and overturned. The law officers happened on this scene shortly after the vehicle had overturned, and while at least one of the wheels pointing upwards was still spinning. After some discussion, which included points of view about various matters of public interest, the talk turned to ways to correct the unfortunate damage done to the automobile of the citizen and to his clothing which had been partially soiled by the material with which the first party was attempting to make road repairs. In a spirit of mutual aid, the road repair group up righted the automobile and extracted it from the ditch, leaving it in such condition that with the replacement of vital engine fluids it could easily be started and driven away. Because of the accidental nature of the events, growing out of conscientious and well-meaning efforts on the part of all concerned, no citations were issued."

Some citizens might condone this way of toning down the outrageous events that Friday evening, were it not for what followed. Parties we have heard from agree that after the arrival of the law enforcement officials, the name of Mr. Amos Ferguson was mentioned frequently as an informer, who told the law officers that a tarring and feathering was about to take place.

The Knights of Loyalty group returned to Belleville and proceeded directly to the home occupied by Mr. and Mrs. Ferguson. They knocked on the door and grabbed Mr. Ferguson as he answered, then dragged him to the truck, and hauled him to another remote rural area. This time, they built a fire and reheated the pail of tar. They next removed Mr. Ferguson's coat and shirt and poured hot tar on Mr. Ferguson's BARE SKIN. This not being enough, they covered him with feathers and, his hands tied behind him, forced him to ride on a rail carried by mob members shouting the most obscene insults to this good teacher.

Ultimately, Mr. Ferguson fell off the rail. One member

of the mob cut the bonds from his hands and feet so that he could walk. Instead of going further to correct their most callous, cruel and sadistic mistreatment of this good human being, the mob members abruptly abandoned him along a timber trail in the woods, went back to their truck and left.

The body of Mr. Ferguson was found the next morning a short way out of town by a milk and cream delivery truck driver. It appeared that in spite of the barbaric and savage treatment he had endured, this man had mustered enough human energy to walk more than five miles before collapsing, unclothed as he was, in the snow alongside the road.

The official report of this death in the Athena County Sheriff's office is as follows:

"At about 8:10 a.m. Saturday, March 2, 1918, the body of a dead male was found on the County Road 277 north of Belleville. It appeared that death had occurred some hours earlier, since the body was frozen. The county coroner's report indicates that death was due to the combined effects of burning brought on by spilling of road tar on the skin and exposure. Whether this spilling was accidental or intentional or self-inflicted could not immediately be determined. The body was eventually identified as that of a Mr. Amos Ferguson, a former history teacher in the Belleville School District. Whether this accident is linked to the attempted road repair job of the previous evening on a different road is unknown, since no one recalls having seen Mr. Ferguson at that particular scene. Investigation is continuing."

This, we would like our readers to know, is all the Sheriff's report says about the tragic death of Mr. Amos Ferguson. This, in spite of the fact that we at the *Forum* had no difficulty finding a half dozen individuals eager to tell us what happened. While there are many more embellished accounts floating around the county, we are giving readers the pure, unvarnished facts as we can best determine them.

Up to this point, we have reported the facts that we have uncovered in our interviews with numerous persons around the county. Each fact given here is agreed to by at least three persons interviewed separately.

Now, having reported these facts in what we believe to be the best tradition of American newspapering, we would like to add some points of view about all these sorry events. We believe that "lynching" is the correct word for the way in which Amos Ferguson died. Most people think of "lynching" as unjust death by hanging, but the dictionary says the word correctly refers to any killing by a mob through other than official and legal procedures.

Amos Ferguson was lynched. He was lynched because of what he had said about freedom of speech and of the press, which we believe many people incorrectly interpreted as disloyalty to the American cause in the Great War. Was Amos Ferguson a patriot? Yes, he was, because he was most vociferous in calling for following the U.S. Constitution. Did he oppose the draft? Never to the knowledge of anyone. We know of one thing that he did do, because it was in our office and directly before our eyes and ears. He challenged some of the leading citizens of this community on questions of freedom of speech and whether the Athena County Public Safety Committee was destroying Democracy while claiming to protect it. He was subsequently fired after a brief meeting with the Belleville District School Board, a meeting to which he was summoned without any indication of what it would be about. He was pursuing legal redress for having been fired from his teaching job when he was so wantonly murdered by a lynch mob.

It is our opinion at the *Forum* that the tragic death of one of the best minds in Athena County may be laid at the doorstep of zealotry, under the guise of patriotism, and of failure of our foremost leadership. It is one thing to espouse patriotism and to respect the flag, especially in time of war. We now use accusations of disloyalty, true or not, to brand or wantonly murder individuals whose only crime is engaging in lawful speech. Is this the way we fight to save the world for Democracy?

* * *

When we talk about failure of leadership, we are

intentionally painting with a very wide brush. It touches on the leadership of government, of business groups in Belleville, and of farm organizations in Athena County who have of late been at odds with the business groups. It touches on leadership at the state level, up to the legislature that created an agency called the Minnesota Commission of Public Safety that has turned out to be a contradiction in terms. It touches on Governor Burnquist who has put some of the most tyrannical persons on this commission and allowed them to overrule elected governments and even the courts. It touches on the failure of President Wilson's administration, that has admitted the Nonpartisan League is a loyal group but does nothing to put a rein on this dictatorial agency in Minnesota.

Yes, the Commission of Public Safety has done some good things, such as fighting forest fires in Northern Minnesota, conserving supplies of kerosene fuel in wartime, encouraging young men to sign up for the draft, and keeping the railroads in good order. The problem is that this Commission has, in the name of patriotism, done other things to destroy the sense of democracy that makes this country great. Think of what it can do. It can remove elected public officials from office if they say or do anything this Commission thinks unpatriotic. It can and does prevent meetings of people who are planning nothing illegal. It can and does feed a mob mentality, as events of the past week in Belleville give witness.

\* \* \*

The March 7, 1918, edition of the Athena County *Forum* quickly became the talk of Belleville. Calls went to other citizens who hadn't seen it yet; at least two long-distance calls were made to reporters in Minneapolis and St. Paul about the tragedy, which somehow had not yet made wire news.

Bert Allcott had made himself reasonably scarce since that fateful night of March 1, finding work to do in the back room of his father's pharmacy store on Wells Street. Bert spent his nights in a small bedroom in the second story above the store and thus avoided daytime walks on the streets. He wasn't especially worried about the sheriff or chief of police, but since Amos Ferguson had died he figured there might be an investigation from the outside.

From the back room late that Thursday after the *Forum* was distributed, Bert kept an ear out for what was said in the store. What he heard, he found, was reasonably assuring.

"By Gawd, Al. This thing in the county paper about that teacher, ain't that awful?"

"Sure is, Reggie, when a paper thinks it's Jesus Christ or something better'n the Sheriff and police. Listen, they ain't a lick of evidence the Sheriff could get."

"Cripes, Martin, imagine an editor getting away with that kind of stuff."

"Oh, I tell you, he won't get away with it, you can be sure of that. I'm not sayin' what should be done, mind you, but I would say that printing shop ain't a safe place to be right now."

"Yuh think so? Jeez, someone heard Pudgy Thurstone saying the same thing. He's good and mad about this damned high and mighty editor writing that stuff, screwing things up. If they was something to investigate, the police and the county attorney would have a helluva time making a case."

"Well, that editor will get a taste of his own medicine, one way or another. Like I say, I don't want any thing rash, nothing to hurt him, I'm just saying people here aren't going to stand for this. That editor's always been a socialist, never got it through his head he's in America now, damn him. He and that teacher, Ferguson, they was in cahoots, you know, figuring out ways to talk against the draft, that's what people say. There were those, you know, who figured Ferguson was a candidate for a firing squad, like Judge McGee and others say we should have. Not that I would go that far, but it makes you think, doesn't it?"

After hearing such talk, a young man potentially open to a charge of felonious incitement to civil disorder and contributory negligence leading to a wrongful death—if not to manslaughter or even first-degree murder—concluded easily that the activities he had led were proper and justifiable if not downright honorable. It wasn't that the leadership told him directly what to do. It was the absence of any strong moral strictures from them that gave him the message he needed.

* * *

On his way to Huisby's farm, Arnold Hedlund picked up Albert Theide and two other chapter members. He drove out the Willow Falls road to Bjorn Nygren's home, but the mercurial chapter officer was not home. The mangled Ford with the broken windows and yellow splotched seats was there; whether one of Nygren's horses was missing, Arnold wasn't sure.

This leadership group was far from being of a single mind about the damning and accusatory report about Amos Ferguson's death they had all read in the *Forum*:

"Vell, we haf quite a mess here now. A teacher is killed dead, dis gang of hootlums is getting avay vit murder, I mean it yust t'at vay."

"Well, yeah, that was quite a piece of writing. Ivar really hit the nail on the head, from what I've heard."

"Well, you heard anything for sure?"

"Oh, ve all know who did it, it's dose gang boys who call t'emselves so loyal. Vy don't t'e sheriff round t'em all up?"

"Say, anyone talk to Bo Nygren about that?"

"Well, yah, I saw him over to the feed mill the other day, Tuesday it was. He wouldn't talk about it, seemed all grumpy about it."

"Vell, yust vat did t'ey do to him anyway?"

"Nobody knows just for sure, 'cept what Ivar said in the paper. Whether that's right, I dunno. The Sheriff says they was fixin the road—Aw, gawd, no one believes that, he was just coolin' down some hot heads. How was he to know they'd go and tar and feather that teacher?"

"Say, don't you think it's time our chapter wrote another strong letter to Governor Burnquist? Things are out of hand here, way Ivar says. That governor has finally got to put the clamps on that Public Safety Commission. Ivar, he should get a good hand for what he wrote."

"Now, don't be too sure. 'Member, we ain't a bunch of socialists, the way that teacher was. He wasn't no farmer, no member of the League."

"Aw, say, now, wasn't he on our side?"

"Well, don't be too sure. You remember, those socialists in North Dakota sort of kicked Townley out way back in 1914; they had different ideas."

"So geez, you're saying we shouldn't get riled up about that poor guy dying after being tarred and feathered?"

"Well, now, I didn't say that. Killin' ain't right, everyone knows that. But that sheriff has been on our side, 'member? He came out to this place for that speech by Townley, didn't cause no trouble. Now, if we write to the governor, we cause trouble for that sheriff, he might get sore, and with Thurstone backing him up, he just might keep us from ever having meetings."

"Well, shit, we can't meet in Belleville now."

"Now that's maybe so, but ain't nobody keeping us from meeting out here in the country. But get that sheriff sore by writing the governor and who knows what'll happen to us then?"

"Yah, maybe writing to t'e gufernor isn't such a good idea after all. I'll talk to the boys at the legislature, den ve can talk about it again, you t'ink, Leonard?"

"Well, that might be the best."

\* \* \*

A nervous Einart Dahlgren knocked softly and rapidly on the door of the apartment over the Allcott Pharmacy store Friday evening. It was a full week after the death of Amos Ferguson. Without waiting for a response Einart entered quickly, carrying a gunnysack heavy with deadly contents. Bert Allcott sat on an aged cot, rolling a cigarette, licking the paper, and tying the ends to keep the Velvet tobacco from falling out.

"By god, Einart, you old farthead, you made it. Got to

hand it to you. I didn't think you had guts enough to show up here."

"Dennis Amery found me this morning, showed me what the paper wrote and said you were looking for dynamite. I didn't let on to him I knew where to find any. But I also want you to know I didn't say a damned thing to that editor, cuss his hide. Did he talk to you?"

"Tried to. I told him to go jump in the river. Seems he got other guys to talk, though."

"Oh, that sonofabitch. Took my daughter from me, he did, worked her to death and didn't pay me a cent," Einart said, shaking his head. "Even thought I should buy a subscription to that damned Swede paper he used to print.

"She's a good-looking one, that girl of mine," he added with a grin toward Bert. "Bet you'd like to get to know her good, huh?"

Bert chose not to answer. *This dumbhead doesn't have the faintest idea what his good-looking daughter and I did already*, he thought.

"You bring the dynamite?" he asked.

"Yep. Knew just where to find it."

"So where did you get it? Or shouldn't I know?"

"They had this bundle in the back of the livery stable—left there by a guy from the slaughterhouse. I helped him one weekend, he rented a team of horses to go blast some stumps, then drag them out, on a dinky little place he's got out in the country.

"That's where I saw how to use the stuff. Had more than he needed, so he left seven sticks in the livery barn. Told me where he put it, one day when we was guttin' hogs."

Einart added, with a twisted but proud grin, "Won't no one suspect me, this way. I snuck into the livery barn a half-hour ago, back of where that Pflueger kid used to sleep. There the dynamite was, just like the guy said. Say, what happened to that Pflueger, anyhow? Seems he was raring to go earlier that night."

*This idiot keeps getting off the track,* Bert thought.

"You ready to blow up that goddamned newspaper shop, Einart?"

"Christ, no, Bert, I'm a family man. I can't get mixed up in that, much as I hate that damn paper. I just done what you wanted, got you the dynamite, and the fuse and the caps."

"Ah, you're chicken shit, Einart. Wouldn't go out on the job, all this crap about your family. Well, guess the real work always falls to me. How do you make this work?"

Einart explained the wrapping of the dynamite sticks, the placement of the cap, the fuse.

"They ain't but a few feet of fuse there, Bert, but it's plenty to light it and get the hell out. Burns about a foot a minute, the fuse does. You should have four minutes or so. Just make sure you don't disconnect that fuse from the caps. Light it right there with a match, make sure it's sparking, then get the hell out of there."

About 11 p.m. that evening, Bert Allcott went down the back stairway, carrying the dynamite bundle with the cap and fuse attached. He followed the alley down to the back end of the Lindfors printing shop on Oak Street, just a half block from the intersection with Wells.

He pried open the back door of the building, then pushed the door aside and edged his way into the darkened building. The door was hooked to a tight spring that slammed the door shut just as Bert made it inside. Had anyone heard the noise? Unlikely, since the area out on the street, on the other end of the printing shop, was active with sounds of a noisy automobile and at least one clattering buggy.

Bert inched forward toward the printing press, visible in the shadows to his left, then felt a tugging. The dynamite fuse, extended behind him, had caught in the door. He eased the door open and carefully ran two fingers along the fuse, to see where it had been pinched. The slamming door had partially cut the fuse and some of the black powder had flowed out at that point. He could feel the grainy substance and caught its acrid odor, familiar to an experienced hunter like himself.

He felt along the fuse from the cut to the outer end, finding he would lose about a foot and a half. He pulled a jackknife from his pocket and carefully, in the dark, cut off that part of the fuse, leaving less than two feet. Well, that will burn for nearly two minutes, according to what Einart had told him, plenty of time to get out that back door and back to his apartment. The back alley was totally deserted; he could sprint up the back steps and be back at his room when the whole thing blew. Then, he could also be among the first on the scene, helping in a heroic search for the cause of the blast and any victims.

His eyes now adjusted somewhat to the dark and shadowy light, Bert placed the dynamite bundle directly under the platen of the Babcock press. He wedged it in cautiously, as well as he could in the dim light trickling in from the lamp post on Oak Street. Cupping his hands, he lit a wooden match. It went out immediately.

Damn, must have got it wet somehow. His hands were moist with sweat. Two more tries and a match caught fire, emitting a long tail of flame that illuminated the entire dynamite bundle under the press platen, and the fuse. He held the flame up to the woven fuse end and waited for it to light. After a few seconds, sparks from deep inside the fuse began spurting out as a small Roman candle. Damn. The fuse lost even more powder than I thought, he said to himself. It probably had hardly a foot to travel before it would ignite the cap and the whole shebang.

Bert started toward the back door, saw it open just as he took his first step. A dark figure moved inside quickly, crashing into Bert. Both persons went tumbling over a paper bale, falling headfirst toward the sputtering fuse.

# XIV. TRUTH AS WE KNOW IT

Earlier that same Friday, Bo Nygren took his copy of the *Forum* from his mailbox and read through the piece on the Ferguson tragedy. Goddamn, he thought. Everybody knows now exactly who was mixed up with the bunch of hoodlums on the Willow Falls road, and nobody believes it had anything to do with road repair. Well, if that editor wouldn't make a deal to learn what Bo knew about the events of a week earlier, he'd think differently when he saw that letter from Gothenburg. He would set in motion his original plan—the one that had run afoul of the Knights of Loyalty on the Willow Falls road. He banked again on finding Ivar at the newspaper shop late in the evening. He knew he was physically superior to Ivar. He would tell Ivar he had two choices: print his letter about the bank's crooked interest rates on Liberty Loans or let the story about his kid get spread around town. And if that wasn't enough, he'd get his goddam printing press ruined.

Bo didn't want to show his face around Belleville just now, especially in his half-wrecked Ford. The humiliation would be too much. He thought of hitching a horse to a sleigh he once bought for Eva, but rejected the idea as too complicated. He took a dusty saddle from the granary and put it on the one horse he used occasionally for riding. This way, he could take some back roads and woods trails into Belleville and maybe avoid being seen at all.

New snow in the past two days had made some of those back trails treacherous and slow. It was well past 10:30 p.m., when Bo on his horse reached the outskirts of Belleville.

Since horse riders were still common enough, he didn't attract any particular attention. He cut through a number of back alleys and entered one that led directly to the back of the *Forum* shop.

He dismounted quietly, tied the horse to a post in a fence that outlined the shop's property, and pulled from a bag on the saddle a soiled handful of paper that contained the envelope with the Gothenburg letter and the yet-unprinted letter to the editor about the bank's Liberty Loan methods. By god, this time he'd get that damned editor to print it, or else.

Bo looked toward the shop to see whether Ivar might be there. The place was dark, yet he was sure he heard, above the clatter of traffic on Oak and Wells streets, some movement inside. Through a small window he saw a flickering light of some kind, maybe from a candle, he wasn't sure. It was probably Ivar just getting ready to leave, Bo surmised. He found the back door unlocked and slipped quickly inside. He was barely past the spring-held door when he saw a small shower of sparks about 15 feet ahead. He sensed a rush of movement just before he collided hard with somebody, both of them tumbling over a paper bale and toward the spark shower.

Bert Allcott and Bo Nygren both saw stars, then a flash, and then blackness. Bert hit his head on the base of the newspaper press just as the dynamite went off with a boom that rattled every window within a mile and was heard throughout Belleville and much of Athena County.

The blast and ensuing fire destroyed the building and most of the printing equipment. It was all the Belleville Volunteer Fire Department could do, with its horse-drawn steam-pump wagon, to prevent the fire from consuming adjacent buildings.

* * *

Police Chief Ezra Morse and Sheriff Alfred Mayberry

talked briefly with Ivar and Inez Lindfors that evening. When had the editors last been in the shop? Six p.m.? Any explosive materials left in the shop? Ink solvents? Could they blow up?

A question these lawmen didn't ask was whether the paper had received any threats. The answer, in fact, would have been no, not lately. The most recent threat, the editors said, was back in early autumn, delivered by the County Attorney Pudgy Thurstone and Tony Alquist on a day when Amos Ferguson happened to be in the newspaper shop. This information the lawmen dismissed without comment.

With daylight on the following day, men from the Fire Department and Police and Sheriff's Departments and a crowd of gawkers converged again on the remains of the *Forum* building. The rubble was cool enough now for some inspection, which led shortly to discovery of the bodies of the two men.

One of the onlookers let her gaze veer away from the rubble and discovery of human remains. Inez Lindfors walked alone around the back of the destroyed building to where she saw a dangling piece of leather strap tied to a fence post, as if the end had been freshly torn away. Others would surmise that the blast had so startled Bjorn Nygren's horse that it jerked against its bridle hard, enough to break the aging reins.

Looking down to the heavily-trampled snow, now filthy from ashes and debris of the blast and fire, Inez saw the corner of a dirty envelope. While others had their eyes fixed on the grisly business of body recovery inside the destroyed building, Inez reached down, picked up the envelope, and shook out the contents—two soiled and badly smudged letters. One was in excellent Swedish handwriting, as good as her own had ever been, the other in a less stylish but readable English scrawl.

Inez read first, rather quickly, the letter in English carrying Bo Nygren's signature. It was, she supposed accurately, a letter to the editor, complaining about the

Belleville Independent Bank's short-term loans for Liberty Bond purchases. Inez shrugged and put the wrinkled letter back in the soiled envelope.

She then read the Swedish-language letter from Gothenburg and addressed to Bo Nygren. In good Swedish, this letter said:

My esteemed Bjorn:

It was most enjoyable hearing again from a relative we know only by reputation as a most successful farmer who carries on the traditions of all the Nygrens who were so close to Agrarian pursuits. We knew your father well, of course, and are so gratified to have regular communication with his son whom we know to be carrying on our great customs in the new land.

We shared your letter with our family and friends. All send you blessings and wish you to enjoy continued good fortune.

As you requested, I was discreet with the additional page you enclosed, in which you asked about the family background of Ivar Lindfors from a printing company family in Graskoping. As a matter of happenstance, my wife Alva had heard a talk at a local meeting of the Social Democratic Party, during which a speaker named Gretchen Sallstedt referred to a brother who was publishing a newspaper in a place in Minnesota, America, called Belleville.

Alva forgot the details but, since you inquired in your most recent letter, she had occasion to see Gretchen again at a more recent meeting of this political party. Gretchen's family name was Lindfors, and the story she had related, and about which we had told you because of her mention of Belleville, was part of a lecture she had delivered concerning progress in public programs for destitute mothers and children in Sweden. Many of these programs had been advanced by the famous politician Hjalmar Branting.

Mrs. Sallstedt verified the fact that she had mentioned her brother Ivar Lindfors of Graskoping as a model of family responsibility. While he had fathered a child borne by a woman he did not marry, this Ivar had stood ready to provide for the support of both the woman and the child. Upon the sudden death of the mother, Ivar had taken the next most responsible step. Ivar and his bride adopted the child, a blessed infant named Charlotte, and soon sailed for America. Mrs. Sallstedt presumed that her brother and her sister-in-law, I believe her name is Inez, have by now told this child of her adoptive status.

There is an additional fact Mrs. Sallstedt mentioned which we pass along only on the understanding that you will treat it with the utmost confidence. After this Ivar and his family sailed for America, a worker with the Poor Relief programme found a diary left by the deceased mother of the child. This diary, it turned out, indicates that the mother was quite certain that Ivar Lindfors was not the father of her child. She had reached this conclusion after consulting with a knowledgeable nurse about times of intimate contacts with various males, of which there were apparently several, and phases in her own cycle of which she alone had specific knowledge.

I trust that you will regard this information with discretion and that it will be helpful as a laudatory instance of moral responsibility being shouldered by one of our countrymen. I trust further that none of this information will be used in any way to embarrass or disgrace the family of Mr. Ivar Lindfors.

We share your sadness in having been unable to bring children into this world, but may the Lord bless you with the wondrous gift of parenthood in the near future. May we even suggest that you consider the example of fellow countryman Ivar Lindfors, and keep in mind the possibility of adopting a loving child who is otherwise without parents or wholesome home.

We hope that Providence will continue to bestow success upon you and your modern farm, and that you and your wife Eva have a happy life.

Your cousin, Lars Nygren.


While the buzz of activity continued around the smoldering and stinking ruins of the printing shop, Inez stood transfixed by the revelations in the Gothenburg letter.

She read and re-read the phrase that burned into her comprehension: "... the mother was quite certain that Ivar Lindfors was not the father of her child."

Inez' mental world swirled and buzzed in consternation confounded. It had never occurred to her that any events or fresh tales would bring new light on her ambiguous position as wife and mother. Yes, she had simultaneously entertained various scenarios, including a most sordid one of Ivar as an irresponsible rake who recklessly fathered Charlotte and who knows how many other children—without a word later on to his betrothed.

Inez thought she had rejected this view of wanton male irresponsibility. Now, she realized she had acted in terms of it by consulting the Russian doctor from Paris and getting into the experimental fertility experiment that led to her pregnancy. No question about it, her doubts about her husband's honesty had given her justification for her Minneapolis adventure.

Now, that self-justification crumbled. Perhaps Ivar had been quite careful, even to the point of asking biological questions of Fredrika before their intimacies. But if so, why had he never professed as much? Then again, maybe he has more character than she had allowed; he had accepted being mistaken and made no lame excuses or protests of assumed innocence. He hadn't told her about Fredrika's possible pregnancy because, she now concluded, he had no good reason to suspect it.

In her self-righteous retaliation, she had compounded her own deviousness by climbing into bed so passionately with Ivar within hours after each "experiment." This might fool Ivar, but in all likelihood it was the artificial insemination that produced her fetus.

Furthermore, it was inconceivable that she could keep her adventure secret from Ivar very much longer.

Her vision dimmed, Inez thought she might faint for the first time in her life. She looked for a place to sit down, found a rusted and empty ink barrel that, having been put out in back of the shop earlier, had escaped the conflagration. She turned it on its side and sat on it, and this move caught the attention of Ivar who turned his gaze from the smoldering mess to see where she had gone.

She was waving something at him. *Curious—not like her to sit down, especially on a dirty old barrel that might soil her serge coat.* He walked toward her, seeing the crumpled envelope balled in her right hand that rested on the barrel as if to hold her up. Her face was ashen.

"Ivar," she whispered, "you need to read this."

"And then," she added hoarsely, "we've got to talk."

But after Ivar finished reading the letter, Inez' only response was a passionate hug of her husband, right there next to the murmuring group of workers and onlookers at the print shop tragedy.

"Yah," someone said, "those two, they've been through a lot these few days." So this sudden but brief public display of affection was acceptable, as it might be at a funeral where a loved one is laid to rest.

Inez couldn't bring herself to tell Ivar anything more.

* * *

Destruction from the explosion and fire was total. Everything in the newspaper shop, including the printing presses, engine, linotype, and printing supplies was burned or demolished beyond repair. Later, a couple of pulleys from the line shaft disappeared. There were signs someone rummaged through the debris a few nights later.

Athena County would be alive for years with speculation about why Bert Allcott and Bjorn Nygren, thought initially to be mortal enemies, were together inside the building when the dynamite went off. No specific answer was advanced by either the police or the sheriff's department. Speculation narrowed quickly to three versions of what happened.

One version, favored by the NPL membership and its sympathizers, had Bert Allcott discovered in the act of lighting the dynamite by a "heroic" Bo Nygren, who fought Bert in a vain but valiant effort to yank the fuse.

A second version, favored in downtown Belleville, reversed these roles, with "good-and-patriotic citizen" Bert seeking to protect a Belleville business from the wanton acts of an NPL madman who never really trusted the newspaper that his own rural nincompoops were backing.

A third version had two crazed men joining forces in a devil's pact to silence a newspaper they both hated, but botching the job and getting blown to bits. This version was advanced mostly by farmers who were equally unimpressed with the NPL and the business crowd, wishing a pox on both houses.

\* \* \*

Things did not look promising for the Athena County Independent Forum Publishing Association that had issued the *Forum* under Ivar's and Inez' editorship. The North Dakota bank that provided the initial loan for the cooperative venture was not disposed to extend still more credit for rebuilding, since the shop and its equipment had been only partially insured.

Leonard Huisby, Alfred Theide, and Arnold Hedlund came to the Lindfors home to express sympathy for the disaster and sorrow over the tragic death of Bjorn Nygren. About Allcott's death, they said little. They did make it clear that they accepted Version One of what happened. Bo would be remembered as a hero, and Leonard was saying as much in his letter to Bjorn's estranged widow, Eva, now living in Fargo. Heads of all three NPL leaders shook slowly up and down when Leonard said she couldn't really be blamed, "but you had to wonder, if all this would have happened if maybe she had stayed—"

Inez softly but directly interrupted this speculation by asking whether the NPL chapter had any intention of getting the newspaper started again. Holding his gaze to the floor,

Leonard Huisby spoke for the organization.

"Well, you see, after this explosion and these killings and all, well, to be good and honest, a lot of people are wondering whether backing a newspaper here again is all that good an idea. Now, don't get me wrong, there's a lot of good things said, around the county and even in other places, about all the things you people did. Course, then, they's others never could figure out why a League paper had stuff by this Moller—"

"Leonard," Ivar interrupted, "you know as well as I, this was never a 'League' paper like the one in St. Paul, or in a few towns in North Dakota. It was not intended to be that. This was an independent cooperative paper, with editors who ran the paper—"

"Aw, we know all that, but don't you see, all our members had it set in their minds they owned this paper. We keep gettin' heat from lots of them. I don't mind saying and I think you know, about how things were going. Anyway, we've decided to have our own chapter letter printed up in St. Paul—the state office will do that—to keep each other informed from now on. So we came to thank you folks for all your hard work, and best 'o luck from here on out." The other two mumbled in agreement and the visit was over.

That was it. The *Forum* was dead.

* * *

Within less than two weeks after the explosion and fire at the *Forum*, the Belleville Commercial Club revived the Athena County *Gazette*. The newspaper was again established as an independent corporation, but the financing, much as before, was in the hands of the bank and various members of the Club. Much to Ollie Moller's dismay, the corporation ignored him, hiring instead a printer from Illinois. The new editor was a man in his mid-40s named Harold Allan, a former reporter and promotional writer.

Ollie Moller, seeing his dreams of another editorship in

Belleville evaporating, went on a monumental drinking binge, mostly on wine he had picked up in St. Paul but left unopened for nearly a year. After he sobered up, he left Belleville for good.

\* \* \*

The first two editions of the reincarnated *Gazette* gave extensive front-page coverage to the Liberty Bond Drive, complete with figures about the total dollars subscribed, how much from the city of Belleville and how much from each rural township. The statement was made that not a single Athena County resident had failed to subscribe his allotted amount. It was also said that the no-questions-asked short-term loan program of the Belleville Independent Bank was a matter of no small moment in this 100 percent success. Citizens of the county would be forever grateful toward such an unselfish financial institution for "backing up our boys over there."

Also in the *Gazette* during the next two months were items about:

● Citizen Groups protesting against the Nonpartisan League, including the statement that, in North Dakota, "Flicker Tail farmers are now aware that having handed over control of the legislature to a little band of despots, it is all going to the benefit of the Socialist Party."

● A minister's interpretation of Matthew xxvi: 52, where it is written "All they that take to the sword shall perish with the sword." The clergyman noted that Peter carried a sword in Jesus' company, so this scripture means that anyone who attacks with an offensive weapon will fall by the defensive one. Thus, America is not only justified, but is under divine obligation, to impale the Huns on the blessed sword of defense.

● Protests in Stockholm during the past year by masses of people seeking better life conditions and more food, which would be forthcoming were it not for the Swedish government's unwise softness toward Imperial Germany.

● Judge J. F. McGee of the Minnesota Commission of Public Safety calling for establishment of a firing squad in his meeting with the U.S. Senate Committee on Military Affairs in Washington, D.C. The Judge was quoted as saying "the disloyal element in Minnesota is largely among the German-Swedish people," that "the nation blundered at the start of the war in not dealing severely with these vipers," and that "we should now get busy and have that firing squad working overtime."

● Nonpartisan League official Joseph Gilbert was under arrest on a charge of obstructing Army enlistments in Martin county in southern Minnesota.

● In Wisconsin, a traitorous editor named William Evjue was attempting to prevent that state's legislature from condemning the notorious, pro-German senator Robert M. LaFollette.

● A disloyal U.S. senator named Borah (no first name or state given) had the effrontery to oppose the Chamberlain bill in Congress, a bill that would have established court martials and swift penalties for sedition and treason.

Nothing was said in the revived *Gazette* about the deaths of Bert Allcott and Bjorn Nygren. Many in Athena County read a brief account of the fatal explosion in a Minneapolis newspaper. This account included the statement that:

> "...found in the rubble of the destroyed building occupied by the Nonpartisan League newspaper were the bodies of two local men. One was Bert Allcott, a young man soon to join the army and known as a fervent loyalist who had organized numerous patriotic meetings for support of fighting troops at the front. The other was Bjorn Nygren, an Athena County farmer about 40 years old, who was an official of the Nonpartisan League itself and who had been investigated for possibly disrespectful treatment of the U.S. flag last fall.
>
> Police Chief Morse says a coroner's report intimates that both men were killed by the blast, but that in spite of laborious and painful investigations, it is not possible to determine which one, if either, may have set off the explosion.

Although Mr. Nygren was known to be displeased with the performance of the newspaper, amid considerable dissension within the Nonpartisan League itself, the Chief says the investigation is continuing."

* * *

Ivar Lindfors found a temporary job with the Athena County Abstracting Company, the same low-paying work Amos Ferguson had been doing before his death. The job provided barely enough income to feed Ivar's small family until they made up their minds what to do next.

One might have expected Ivar to be totally despondent after the disastrous dynamiting of the *Forum* building. Such, however, was not exactly the case. He felt a sense of relief, that he would no longer need to confront the contentious problem of publishing words that would stir violent emotions and embroil his own conscience.

* * *

On a Saturday in early April of 1918, Ivar nursed a cold cup of coffee in the kitchen of the Lindfors bungalow. It was the same place rented in 1912 and since purchased on a mortgage contract, payments which could hardly be met now on an abstract worker's salary.

A visibly pregnant Inez walked in with a small bag of groceries—all she thought they could afford this week—which she had carried from the Merriweather grocery several blocks away. "Ivar, guess what I just heard. Andressa has a baby boy and she's marrying Rudy Pflueger. Now how about that?"

Ivar hesitated. When he had found Rudy in Minneapolis, to ask him about the last night of Amos Ferguson's life, Andressa's name had never come up.

"How did that happen?" was all he could ask.

"Seems they had both been found by Pastor Ernest

Bjornholm, somehow, in Minneapolis. He got them together. Said the baby needed a father. Think that marriage will work?"

Ivar said he didn't know. He hardly thought about it; he had something else on his mind. "Inez, if we had it to do over, would we have run that piece about the lynching, or not?"

With a deep sigh, Inez said "yes, of course. We owed it to Amos, if not to our own belief about what was right. We get to a place, Ivar, where there is no turning back. Our self-respect wouldn't let us do anything else. If we hadn't done it, we would have quit the newspaper anyway. But that would have been quitting in shame. Now we quit in pride."

Smiling without amusement, Ivar added, "In pride and in poverty."

"Poverty in money, but maybe wealth in self-respect. Ivar, we have always said our newspapers were to tell people the truth. Truth in bits and pieces, dropped at the same time in a thousand minds, we said. All we have done is tell the truth in print."

"Not quite, Inez," Ivar answered heavily. "What is the real truth? What really happened out on Willow Falls road? Rudy told me very little, except for giving me names. Nygren told me nothing. I got a bit here and a bit there from two or three other Knights of Loyalty, all of them bragging more than explaining.

"How exactly did Amos Ferguson die? Who exactly did what to him, and who decided they should go off and leave him? Wasn't there a single decent man there to try persuading others to at least bring him, tar and feathers and all, back to town?

"We don't tell the truth—only the truth as we know it."

"But we do that, don't we Ivar? We give all the truth as we know it, at least at that time. Or do we?"

A pause.

"Truth, Inez—speaking of truth brings up the subject of truth to Charlotte, doesn't it? We have a truth we haven't told her. Truth held back is as good as a lie, isn't it?"

"Yes—I suppose so—no, that is right."

Ivar threw his head up with a start. Inez was not a person to stammer.

"Ivar," she said slowly, "there is an awful lot I need to tell you about."

But Ivar ignored that for the moment and continued talking. "Remember the barn fire that killed Jerrold Pflueger? It seemed to everyone that lightning caused it, didn't it? Then there was that speculation about wet hay, and spontaneous combustion. Should we have mentioned that speculation? We mentioned the speculation to say it did not fit the facts, but Marie felt that by mentioning it, we made it seem to be the truth."

"We have not told Charlotte anything," Ivar said as if saying it for the first time, "about her real mother. Should we now?"

Ivar, now ready to question any truth, remembered once more his esteemed and heroic progenitor from the 17th century wars, Anders Lindfors. And it occurred to Ivar that, quite possibly, Anders found a way to quit the war polemics in the midst of a political inferno that his own broadsheets had fanned. When Swedish politics started to unravel over whether to continue or abandon the war in the 1630s, Anders retreated from the publishing battlefield. And now, perhaps in ancient and dubious family tradition, Ivar was seeking an escape from a political battlefield strewn with total destruction of credible journalism.

"Just a minute ago, Inez, you said something about a lot of things here in Minnesota, that I didn't know. Now what would that be?"

Inez got up and crossed their kitchen to a high cupboard. She dragged a chair to the base, stood on the chair and took from the wainscoted cupboard a half-empty bottle of brandy. She stepped down lightly and deliberately, plunked the bottle on the table, got two glasses and said she needed a drink. This was only the second or third time in her married life she had made that particular statement.

"Ivar," she said, "we have one more truth to share."

The brandy bottle stood unopened, as a warped symbol of loquacity, if not confession, as Inez related her own tale to Ivar. She told him of her clandestine visits to medical people, first to Dr. Blake then to the visiting Dr. Olga Ravinovich from Paris. In a telling punctuated by pause and hesitation and struggles with pronunciation, she recounted the story of the experiment on "fecondation artificielle" in which she took part and became pregnant. She told about the procedure used by the doctor, including collecting sperm from a half dozen medical students, none of whom she ever saw.

Ivar was speechless for some time. Yes, he had erred in his lifetime. Yes, this errancy, though not apparently as serious as originally thought, had led to a problem resolved only by unloading it on an unsuspecting bride. And, yes, he thought of himself as one of the new generation of enlightened young Swedes. But artificial insemination? Arranged in secret by Inez? The innocent young woman from the windmill operator's family on the island of Oland?

Inez waited for Ivar to absorb this new information, this new truth. Finally, he asked, "Have you decided, Inez, just when we tell Charlotte all of these things?"

"Yes, Ivar, as soon as possible. Today. There is no question in my mind that we will tell her, and tell her completely. There is nothing else we can do."

"You see, Ivar," she added softly, "we are true newspaper people. We tell each other the truth as we best know it."

"So why wait at all?" Ivar asked.

Inez nodded in agreement, then rose and called, "Charlotte, please come inside. We have something to say to you."

The back door rattled and Charlotte bounced breezily into the room. "First, I got something," she announced. "My violin bridge broke again."

Hesitation permeated the room. Inez and Ivar stared at each other.

Ivar then reacted in his customary way.

"I know how to fix that cussed bridge on your violin so it'll stay fixed, Charlotte. Let's go do it."